Rocks in the Stream

LEWIS WHELCHEL

Meryton Press

Oysterville, WA

ROCKS IN THE STREAM

ISBN: 978-1-936009-06-0

Graphic design by Ellen Pickels

Chapter 1

"I do not know what is to become of us all; indeed, I do not!" cried Mrs. Bennet.

"Oh, Mama!" Jane crossed the room to stand by her mother who was looking out of a window fronting the house. She lightly touched her shoulder. "You can see that we are all well. Please do not make yourself uneasy."

A passing feeling of resentment washed over Mrs. Bennet. "I do not know why your father left the estate to you. I am sure there was some mistake on someone's part."

Mrs. Bennet returned to her chair to resume her work. It had been three years since Mr. Bennet died, and in his will, he had specifically left all of his property, including Longbourn, to his eldest daughter, Jane. It had not been left to his wife, not even for use during her lifetime. Mr. Bennet's instructions to Jane were that his widow should always have a home at Longbourn.

"I would have sold the estate and got dowry money for you girls so that you could marry rich gentlemen. Just think, we could have taken a house in London, attended all the balls and parties, and in no time, I would have seen you girls well settled in marriage," said Mrs. Bennet mournfully. This was her continual lament when the topic of Mr. Bennet's will was brought forward. "Now we are just as poor as before. Worse, since you are forcing us to save money, though I know not what for."

Jane was always sad to be reminded that her mother seemed to grieve more over the married status of her daughters than the passing of her husband.

IT WAS TIME FOR HER morning walk, and Elizabeth was ready to escape the house. In her hasty descent of the stairs, she nearly stumbled into Jane.

"It is beautiful today, my dear sister. Will you not join me for a walk?"

Rambling through the countryside was one of Elizabeth's dearest pleasures, which could only be improved on by sharing it with Jane.

"You know I would like to join you, but I must see to all the accounts today. You will have to go without me."

"You are too busy. I do not understand why you do not employ a steward. A young woman of your age has better things to do than manage an estate."

"Lizzy! You sound just like Mama!" A burst of laughter filled the hall. "Where will your walk take you today?"

"Oh, I have not decided. Perhaps I will know when I step outside and smell the fresh air. Are you sure you cannot come?"

Jane smiled and shook her head.

"Very well. Goodbye, Jane." And fetching her bonnet, Elizabeth ran out the door.

THE MISTRESS OF LONGBOURN WAS sitting quietly at her father's old desk reviewing the account books when she was interrupted by her mother.

"Jane, I would like to go into Meryton to see my sister Philips and then to visit Lady Lucas on the way home. Would you please call for the carriage?"

"We agreed that Mondays would be the only day the horses left the farm. It is a lovely day for a walk, and I am sure Kitty and Lydia would be happy to join you."

"You are as difficult and troublesome as was your father!" Mrs. Bennet stamped her foot and called for the housekeeper as she hurried up to her room. "Hill, Hill!"

"NOW, THERE, MRS. BENNET," SAID Mrs. Hill, as she tried to calm the woman's nerves. "Remember, there will be an assembly next week, and perhaps the new tenants of Netherfield Park will attend. They should be moved in by then, you know. I have it from the housekeeper herself."

"Do you really suppose they will come?"

"Of course, they will."

"Well, I do hope so. Oh, Hill, Jane is so stubborn about the horses. She will not let me take the carriage into Meryton today."

"Miss Jane has managed the estate well since the passing of your dear husband, and I know I am grateful for her kindness and generosity. She is a sharp one, that girl; nothing gets past her." What Mrs. Hill thought — but did not say — was that the daughter was doing a much better job of it than the father ever did.

Elizabeth was happiest when outside on one of her walks in the country. The summer air and the solitude revived her from the trials that had to be endured in a household of six females.

Today she found herself walking towards Netherfield, where, since the place had been vacant, she frequently went to enjoy the pleasure gardens. This would be her last visit, for the new tenants were to take possession any day.

Of course, she was curious about whom their new neighbors would be, but she was not burning with speculation as were her mother and younger sisters. She had no fantasies of a rich young man seeking a wife from among the neighborhood daughters, and even if he were, he certainly would not choose her. Jane was five times as pretty as any young woman in the country. He would choose Jane.

Elizabeth was walking on the edge of a horse trail, almost within sight of Netherfield, when her attention was caught by a rabbit hopping along the other side of the path. In her momentary distraction, she did not notice a tree root protruding from the ground in front of her. With a cry, she tripped and fell, striking her head on a rock.

"It is a relief for me finally to get a place of my own outside of Town," Charles Bingley declared triumphantly.

"You are always welcome at Pemberley," replied his companion, Fitzwilliam Darcy.

Bingley had recently purchased a lease on Netherfield Park and this was to be his first night in the house. Staying with him at Netherfield were his sister, Caroline, who had gone directly to the house. Bingley and Darcy were taking a more scenic route in order to see some of the surrounding countryside.

"I know, and I thank you for it," said Bingley, "but it seems as though there is something different in having a place that one can call his own. Netherfield is nothing to Pemberley, I know, but the neighborhood is pleasant, and I believe I shall enjoy living here very much.

"Do you not find country manners to be a bit savage?"

"Country manners? They are delightful."

"Well, then, I suppose you will be happy here," said Darcy with a laugh.

As they rounded a corner, Darcy saw a purple bonnet lying across the trail. As he drew nearer, he was horrified to find a young woman lying on the ground next to it. Darcy instantly reined in his horse and dismounted.

"Bingley!" Darcy shouted as he ran over to the fallen figure. Her foot was twisted in a root, and there was blood on the side of her forehead.

"Is she dead?" asked Bingley in frightened curiosity as he came up beside Darcy.

Kneeling down and bending over her, Darcy felt her warm breath on his cheek. "No, she breathes. Come, we must get her to Netherfield."

"Very well, Darcy, I will stay with her and you can —"

"No!" interrupted Darcy, "I will stay with her." Then he said more calmly, "Bring back the carriage and send for a physician to meet us at Netherfield."

"Yes, at once!" Bingley jumped on his horse and rode off at a gallop.

DARCY DID NOT KNOW WHAT to do. The young woman was breathing, and the bleeding had stopped, but her skin was cold. He had no idea how long she might have been there. He took off his coat and wrapped it around her, cradling her in his arms.

BINGLEY BURST THROUGH THE FRONT door of Netherfield.

"Fosset, have Rossiter bring the coach round at once, then send to Town for Mr. Manning!"

"What is the matter?" asked Miss Bingley, who was already bored of being in the country.

"Darcy and I found a young woman lying unconscious on the side of the trail we were following. She appears to have fallen and hit her head on a large stone."

"Who could be so clumsy as to do something like that?" laughed Miss Bingley. Her thoughts centered on the insipid nature of country folk. She would never forgive her brother for bringing her here.

"I am sure it was an accident, Caroline. Will you come with me in the carriage to go to her?"

"Oh, very well," said Miss Bingley with some exasperation.

DARCY FOCUSED ON THE BLOOD that had trickled onto the young lady's cheek. A memory from his childhood came unbidden to his mind at the sight of it.

"Ready, Fitzwilliam?"

"Yes, Richard. Are you?"

"Yes! Go!"

Fitzwilliam took off running down the sloping hill on the side of the house towards the stand of Spanish chestnuts. This was their daily challenge. The loser would have to water the horses. His cousin, Richard, almost always won, but today he was determined that he would be the victor. He focused all his strength in his legs, so much so that he even closed his eyes. Suddenly, a dog barked, and he turned his head towards the sound. At that moment, his long legs became twisted up, and he fell.

When he stood and examined himself, his pant legs were torn, and he had a trail of blood running down his sleeve from a cut on his elbow. Even though he lost that day, Richard was kind enough to water the horses anyway.

Darcy recollected himself, realizing that he had been staring at the young woman. What would she think if she were to wake up suddenly and find herself being held by him? Regardless of convention, he would not leave her on the ground.

TIME HAD PASSED SLOWLY FOR Darcy, but at last, he could hear the carriage. In moments, Bingley and his sister were out of the coach and at his side.

"We came as fast as we could, Darcy," said Bingley. "Did she wake up? Has she said anything?"

Though he had accompanied Miss Bingley in the carriage, Bingley sounded out of breath, as if he had run the entire distance from Netherfield.

"No, nothing. She is just as she was. She must have been here quite a while, for she is very cold. I am extremely worried about her." Darcy pressed her closer to his body.

"Really, Mr. Darcy, one might think that this creature had enchanted you the way you are holding her," sneered Miss Bingley.

Darcy did not respond but looked down at the young woman and realized he was cradling her against his chest, her head in the crook of his elbow. Who was she, and why did he feel such a need to protect her?

He lifted her into the carriage and laid her gently on the seat opposite Miss Bingley. After hovering over her just a moment to arrange his coat around her, he stepped out and made room for Bingley to enter the carriage.

"Drive on, Rossiter. Carefully!" ordered Bingley.

"Yes, sir."

Darcy walked back to the place where the young woman had fallen. Retrieving her bonnet, he noticed that a piece of light purple ribbon had become detached from it. He placed it in his pocket before mounting his horse and galloping back to Netherfield.

MRS. BENNET AND THREE OF her daughters were in the drawing room, sitting around a table cluttered with books, pins and cloth. Jane had finished the accounts and was standing by a window nearest the paddock, staring across the front lawn.

"Mama, Lizzy has been gone far too long. This is not like her at all."

"You worry too much, Jane. You know how she likes to wander. She will be back soon."

"But, Mother —" Jane stepped away from the window towards Mrs. Bennet.

"You already have too much to worry about, Jane. Do not worry about Lizzy," scolded her mother.

Jane was not convinced. Lizzy never stayed away for more than a couple of hours at a time, and it was now afternoon. She should have been back. Elizabeth would never do anything to cause worry about her, and Jane was worried. Very worried.

"Perhaps I should ask some of the tenants to look for her."

"You will do no such thing. Elizabeth is just fine and certainly does not need our help. You will only embarrass us with your false alarm. She will turn up soon enough, and then you may have words with her," said Mrs. Bennet as she left the room.

Jane did not believe it. She knew in her heart that something must be wrong.

DARCY GALLOPED PAST THE CARRIAGE and was waiting impatiently at the front entrance to Netherfield by the time the coach arrived. Never had horse and carriage seemed to move so slowly.

Bingley had given directions to the housekeeper to ready a bedchamber for an injured young woman, so preparations were well underway for her arrival.

When the carriage finally stopped, Darcy himself lowered the step and opened the door. He handed Miss Bingley out, Bingley followed, and then he entered the carriage. He paused to look at the woman. Nothing seemed to be different, and he was relieved that she appeared no worse. He picked her up and began to carry her into the house.

"Mr. Darcy, surely you can let a servant take care of that," Miss Bingley snidely remarked.

"No, I cannot."

"Come upstairs with me, sir," said Mrs. Thomas, the current housekeeper and former housemaid at Bingley's townhouse.

Darcy followed Mrs. Thomas to one of the bedchambers where a maid was waiting and set the young woman down carefully on the bed.

"Thank you, Mr. Darcy. Anne will stay with her. Please send up Mr. Manning as soon as he arrives."

"Yes, of course. Please let me know at once of any change in her condition."

"Yes, certainly, sir. I will send you word immediately."

Mrs. Thomas wondered at the depth of his worry. She had known Mr. Darcy for quite some time and realized he was not one to reveal his emotions; with that expression of concern, he had illuminated his whole soul.

UNABLE TO FIND ELIZABETH, MRS. Hill sought out Jane. "Ma'am, Mrs. Bennet has asked me to send for Miss Elizabeth. Do you know if she has come back yet?"

"No, Hill," answered Jane anxiously, "she has not yet returned."

Jane walked slowly up to her mother's room, feelings of dread disrupting her peace of mind. She found Mrs. Bennet arranging the pillows on her bed, obviously bored and unconcerned.

"Mama, Lizzy has not yet returned from her walk!" Jane said heatedly. "Oh, Mama, I am sorry, it is just that I am so worried about her."

"What do you mean she has not returned? Of course, she has returned."

"No, she is not here. Mama, we must begin a search for her. I fear that she has been injured ... or worse." Unable to mask her worry, Jane began to pace the floor in front of her mother.

Mrs. Bennet was immediately alarmed upon hearing Jane's concern. Though Elizabeth was not her favorite child, her maternal feelings were roused at the possibility that her second daughter might be suffering.

"But it is so late now," whined Mrs. Bennet. "What can be done?"

"Mother, I am not going to sit by and do nothing while Lizzy may be lost or hurt!" With that, Jane hurried from the room.

JANE WENT INTO THE LIBRARY to pen a note to their nearest neighbor.

Sir William Lucas,

I am begging your assistance. My sister, Elizabeth, has been missing since this morning. She went for a walk and did not tell me in which direction she would be going. Would you please send servants to search around the area of Lucas Lodge for her and alert Colonel Forster that she is missing? I fear that some type of mischance has befallen her.

Thank you.
Jane Bennet

Jane also sent word to her Aunt Philips, begging her to spread the alarm.

"HILL, WILL YOU PLEASE SEND for David?" Jane would ask him to deliver her letters.

"Certainly, ma'am."

Jane felt helpless. There had not been a night in her life that she did not spend at least a portion of it with Elizabeth, talking about the events of the day or sharing their hopes and dreams for the future. Of all her family, Elizabeth was the one for whom she felt the most affection, and while she loved all the others, she believed that only Elizabeth returned her love equally.

It was a surprise to everyone who knew how devoted Mr. Bennet was to his second daughter when the estate was left to Jane. She wanted to share it with Elizabeth, but Elizabeth steadfastly refused to take away from Jane's inheritance.

Jane depended on Elizabeth for her courage. When Elizabeth knew that she was right, she was firm and steady, and Jane relied on her strength while she learned to deal with all the people she had to encounter as a landowner. It had been a slow and difficult process for her.

The news that Elizabeth was missing had spread quickly through the servants' quarters, and when David was asked to go to his mistress, he was already armed with sympathy and understanding. Miss Elizabeth was a favorite with him as she was with all the servants. She always greeted him with a kind word and a smile.

"Did you send for me, ma'am?"

"Yes, David. I need your help. Miss Elizabeth is missing, and we must find her before nightfall. Please gather the servants and have them search all the paths as far as Meryton while you deliver these two letters. My sister is missing," she repeated with a broken voice, "and I cannot bear the thought of her spending a night out alone."

"How long has she been gone?" he asked gently.

"She left on her walk this morning." Jane went to a window and stared at the rose garden. Elizabeth so much enjoyed flowers. Elizabeth so much... Jane's eyes began to burn. "She invited me to come with her, but I told her I was too busy." Jane wiped a tear from her eye. "She should have been back hours ago."

David averted his eyes from Miss Bennet when he saw her tears. "You do not really believe she is on a path between here and Meryton, do you?"

Jane stared at him. It was difficult to admit what she had begun to fear. "No, I do not, but I do not know what else to do."

UPON HIS ARRIVAL AT NETHERFIELD, Mr. Manning, the Bingleys' physician from Town, was taken upstairs to see his patient. Later, he joined the party in the drawing room.

"I have completed my examination of the young woman. She appears to be in good health except for a slight injury to her ankle and a bump on the side of her head. She has suffered a concussion, which explains why she is unconscious. I expect that she will wake up any minute. Please do not let her remain alone under any circumstances, for she will not know where she is and probably will not remember falling. The shock of finding herself alone in a strange place will be very distressing to her. I have seen many such cases," Mr. Manning reassured, "and there is every reason to expect a satisfactory outcome."

"And what if she does not wake up right away?" asked Miss Bingley. Having this person in her home was quite an inconvenience.

"She may become a little dehydrated, but there is no immediate danger." In all his years attending the Bingley family, Mr. Manning had grown to dislike Miss Bingley very much and to distrust her motives.

Darcy looked at the floor and shook his head as he slid his hand into his pocket and fingered the purple ribbon.

"I have taken a room at the inn and will return again tomorrow to examine her." Mr. Manning had gathered up his belongings and was heading to the door when Darcy detained him.

"May I visit the young lady?"

"Mr. Darcy, really!" scolded Miss Bingley.

"I see no reason why not. Please speak softly around her," cautioned Mr. Manning. "She will have quite a headache when she wakes up."

DARCY KNOCKED ON HER DOOR and waited anxiously. Was she awake, and if not, when would she awaken? What was her name? From where had she come? Darcy knew he would not be able to rest until these questions were answered.

He was relieved to hear footsteps approaching and then finally a hand on the doorknob. The door opened slowly as the maid was being most cautious not to disturb the sleeping patient.

"May I help…sir?" Anne whispered. She had thought that perhaps Mrs. Thomas had returned and was completely unprepared to meet a gentleman.

"I am Mr. Darcy, a guest of Mr. Bingley. I assisted in bringing the young lady here today. Mr. Manning said I may visit her."

Although hesitant about allowing a gentleman to enter the young lady's bedchamber, she was asleep, and as Anne would remain with them, there was really no harm to it.

"Please come in, Mr. Darcy. My name is Anne, and I will attend the young lady while she remains at Netherfield."

"Thank you, Anne."

Darcy slowly approached the slight figure in the bed. Her hair had been let down around her face and shoulders. It was dark, curly and luxuriant, magnifying the brilliancy of her fair skin. Anne must have cared for her for she looked remarkably well. Mr. Manning had bandaged the wound on her head, and that was the only evidence that she had been injured. As Darcy looked at her, he recognized an air of intelligence about her even while asleep and the faintest hint of a smile graced her lips.

"Who are you?" he asked the sleeping figure. "I am sorry this happened. Bingley and I are grateful that we came upon you when we did. I shudder to think what might have happened had we not." Anne looked up as Darcy walked around to the other side of her bed.

"Do you know who she is, Mr. Darcy?" asked Anne in a surprised voice. He was talking to her in a familiar manner.

"I . . . no, I have never seen her before."

Anne returned to her work, and Darcy returned his attention to the young woman.

"Mr. Manning, Bingley's physician, has told us that you have suffered a concussion but expects that you will be well and should wake up soon." He stood over her, unable to take his eyes off her. "I am so sorry," he whispered. All the horror of what might have been flashed through his mind, forcing him to turn away from her.

He moved to the foot of the bed and looked at her once again. "I will come back in the morning. Good night."

The same need to protect her flooded once again through his body. Finally able to tear his eyes away from her, he turned to Anne.

"Please send me word, no matter the hour, if her condition changes or if she should wake up." Although he spoke gently, Anne knew she had just received a command.

"Yes, Mr. Darcy."

JANE WAS SITTING BEHIND HER father's desk in the library, trying to busy herself with anything to keep her mind off Elizabeth, when she was accosted by her mother who came bustling into the room.

"Oh, Jane, why did you not tell me that Lizzy was missing?" complained Mrs. Bennet, who had just begun to realize that Elizabeth might not be coming back.

"Mama, I —"

"Now it is dark, and no one has found her, and I am sure she is dead!"

"Mama! Please do not say such things. We must hope for the best."

Jane moved around the desk to where her mother stood and held her in her arms, taking no delight in witnessing her mother's tears.

In as soothing a voice as she could muster, Jane said, "Lizzy is a strong girl. At first light, they will go in search of her again. Colonel Forster has promised the support of the regiment. I am sure she will be found unharmed."

Unable to speak further, Mrs. Bennet slipped out of the library and up to her room. This time there were no cries for Hill to attend her. Mrs. Bennet was in pain for the loss of her daughter.

Jane wished she felt as certain as she had sounded. Weakened from constant worry and upset, a sudden feeling of despair overtook her, and she collapsed into a chair in front of the desk. Giving vent to her feelings, she dropped her head on folded arms and wept. She would never forgive herself for not going out with Lizzy that morning.

Jane and Lizzy looked at *each other and smiled as they ambled together across the lawn past the swing to the edge of a very small rise in the ground. They each took three steps then dropped to their knees and rolled the rest of the way down the little hill, landing on top of each other in a pile of blonde and brown curls, bonnets, and flying skirts. Their laughter filled the air.*

Little Mary, who had been watching them with a puzzled look, came over and asked, "Lizzy, what are you doing?"

"We are falling," she answered with a grin. "Do you want to fall, too?"

"No, I think I will sit inside."

Jane and Lizzy watched Mary walk toward the house. They held each other's hands as they climbed to the top of the hill.

"Ready, Jane?" asked Lizzy. Jane nodded, and away they went down the hill again.

As Jane awakened, her face felt warm, a welcome change as she had been so cold. When she opened her eyes, she was blinded by a shaft of sunlight burning through the window. This was odd, she thought, because her room was on the west side of the house. As her blurry eyes adjusted to the light, she slowly began to recognize her surroundings and realized she had fallen asleep at her father's desk.

Falling.

She had dreamt about one of the many times she and Lizzy had rolled down the hill behind the house. Had Lizzy fallen? Where was she? Was there someone to take care of her, or was she all alone?

Jane's eyes burned, so she went up to her room to seek the relief of cool water and a soft cloth. While there, she would take a moment to pray for Lizzy.

SHORTLY AFTER BREAKFAST, COLONEL FORSTER and Sir William Lucas called at Longbourn. Mrs. Hill showed them into the drawing room and then went to the library to let Jane know she had visitors.

The gentlemen stood when Jane entered the room.

"Miss Bennet, I have come to let you know that training exercises for the regiment have been cancelled for the day and that all the men and officers will be searching the area around Meryton for your sister," Colonel Forster informed her. "I am deeply grieved. This must have been a horrible night for you. Please be assured that we are doing everything in our power to find her."

"Thank you, Colonel. Your concern and assistance on Elizabeth's behalf means so much to us all." Jane would not cry! She would not!

"Have you any idea at all where she might have gone, which paths she might have taken on her walk, or how far she would go?" asked the Colonel.

"Elizabeth loves being out of doors, and it was such a beautiful day yesterday. She had invited me to go with her." Jane paused. "Do you not see that this is my fault?" she cried in frustration. "I should never have let her go alone!" Jane's eyes filled with tears.

"Miss Bennet," Sir William soothed, "it is well known that Miss Elizabeth is an independent young woman who loves to explore the countryside. This unfortunate event is not your fault. You could not have foreseen it. And if you had been able to, of course you would have done something to prevent it."

"Thank you, Sir William," sniffed Jane. "You are right. My crying does no good." She went to a chair and sat down.

"Lizzy's favorite walk is to Oakham Mount, and she would also go to Netherfield Park to visit with the gardener, but I am certain she would not have gone there because the new tenants were to move in yesterday. I believe she knew that. She enjoyed solitary, secluded places."

"I have the farmers searching all the main pathways between their farms and Longbourn village, and the area around Meryton is being searched by the regiment," said Sir William. "I will send you word throughout the day."

"Thank you, gentlemen."

"We will do all in our power. I wish I could offer you better news," said the Colonel. "Good day, Miss Bennet."

Chapter 2

The morning of the next day found Bingley and his friend downstairs early for breakfast. As they were standing together at the sideboard filling their plates, Darcy decided to ask one of the nagging questions that had been weighing heavily on his mind.

"Who do you think she is, Bingley?"

"I cannot imagine. She seems finely dressed. Perhaps she is some gentleman's daughter out on an errand," said Bingley thoughtfully, "but it is odd that she should be out alone."

"Yes, it is." This misfortune further confirmed to him that young ladies should not be out unaccompanied. It did not occur to him to examine whether young men were less likely to suffer from accidents than young women were.

Darcy pulled the purple ribbon from his pocket and held it up to the light, thinking about its owner. His reflections, while mostly pleasant, were tinged with apprehension. While it was truly unfortunate that she had been injured, he was grateful that she was safe at Netherfield. He hoped that she would soon wake up and that he could become acquainted with her.

"What do you have there, Mr. Darcy?" asked Miss Bingley as she entered the room.

Darcy colored and quickly placed the ribbon in his pocket. "Something I found, that is all." He rapidly changed the topic of conversation. "And how are you this morning, Miss Bingley?"

"I survived my first night in this lonely house. Charles, why did you have to bring us all the way out here?"

"You are welcome to return to London anytime you wish. I like it here." He took his plate to the table and began to eat.

"Any news of the little creature you found, Mr. Darcy?" asked Miss Bingley. She was standing close to Darcy at the sideboard pouring tea. "It is such an inconvenience to be troubled by sick people."

"I have not seen her yet this morning."

"Yet? Do you mean you intend to see her?" Miss Bingley was jealous of the attention this mysterious nobody was receiving from Mr. Darcy, attention that she felt rightfully belonged to her.

"Yes, I will look in on her throughout the day to ensure that she is receiving careful attention."

"Is not that Mr. Manning's purpose in being here this morning?"

"The young lady is injured, and I intend to do all in my power to assist in her recovery," he said firmly. Miss Bingley had made no effort to hide her feelings, and Darcy's patience with his friend's sister was becoming strained.

"You are too kind, I am sure," replied Miss Bingley coolly.

"What shall we do about her, Darcy?" Bingley felt responsible for her health and safety as she was under his roof. Not knowing who she was or from whence she came was unnerving. He wished he had Darcy's ability to remain calm.

"What do you mean?"

"Well, she must have a family who is worried about her."

"I have no idea from which direction she came..."

Darcy was interrupted by the appearance of Mr. Manning, just down from examining his patient.

"How is she, Mr. Manning?" asked Darcy. Miss Bingley looked at Darcy with a frown.

"The injury to her head is healing, but she has developed a slight fever, a result of the concussion. If it increases in severity, she will need to be kept cool with compresses. Right now, though, she seems to be resting quietly. Anne is taking very good care of her. I have given her instructions, and she seems quite capable."

DARCY KNEW THAT MR. MANNING was the Bingleys' physician, and therefore had no doubt that the young woman was receiving the best care possible, but he wanted to be absolutely certain that the good doctor's opinion was correct. At least, that is what he told himself.

The truth was that he just wanted to see her again. He left the breakfast room, and when he was out of sight of the others, he hastened down the hall to the staircase, took the stairs two at a time to the next floor, and hurried to her room. He paused outside the door to catch his breath. Being a strong and healthy man, he knew that his run up the stairs was not the reason for his shortness of breath. Inhaling deeply, he knocked on the door, which the maid presently opened.

"Good morning, Mr. Darcy. Would you like to see our patient, sir?"

"Yes, if I may."

"Please, come in."

Showing less enthusiasm than he felt, Darcy walked silently into the room and stood between the young lady and the window so he could see her clearly in the light. She was really quite pretty. Anne must have brushed and arranged her hair. It had an attractive, healthy luster to it, and it had been styled to flow to one side of her face. Her hands were folded at her waist outside the blankets. Her fingers were very delicate and smooth, unused to hard, physical labor. Bingley was right: This was a gentleman's daughter. But what kind of gentleman would allow his daughter to walk about the countryside unattended?

Strangely, that thought was appealing to him — a young woman willing to defy convention, who enjoyed being outside and did not need or want a constant attendant, a woman who enjoyed solitude and quiet. What a tragedy it would be if she did not wake up.

"Good morning," said Darcy to the sleeping young woman. "We have all been worried about you. Even Miss Bingley asked about you." He chuckled. "I wish you could tell me your name so I could send word to your family. They must be very anxious about you. I am also quite concerned about you, and I do not even know who you are."

Mrs. Hill knew where to find Miss Bennet and so immediately went to the library. Jane had been making a note in her pocketbook.

"Yes, Hill?"

"David is waiting in the breakfast room and would like to see you. He says he has a message from Colonel Forster. Shall I bring him to you?"

"No, thank you. Tell him I will join him there."

Mrs. Hill curtsied and left.

Jane slowly rose and followed Hill. It was late in the morning, and Elizabeth should have been back by now if she had been lost in the dark.

Lost.

Elizabeth had been wandering around the countryside from almost the moment she could walk. She never became lost.

Jane felt Mary's eyes rest heavily on her as she entered the breakfast room, but all her attention was focused on David and his news, be it good or bad. Everything might depend on what he had to say.

"Jane…" began Mary as soon as Jane entered the room.

Jane closed her eyes and summoned all her patience. "Please, Mary, I must speak with David."

"But —"

"Please!" Jane turned to David, looking at him expectantly.

"Miss Bennet, Sir William Lucas and Colonel Forster asked me to tell you that there is nothing new to report in the search for Miss Elizabeth. I am very sorry."

This was a message he had not wanted to carry, but it was his responsibility, and he would fulfill his duty. The Bennets had been very good to him and his family, and he would do all he could to return the favor of their kindness, even if it meant being the messenger of ill tidings.

Jane felt herself close to tears. "Thank you." David made a slight bow and left the room.

Then Jane turned to Mary. "Please forgive me, Mary. What can I do for you?"

"I just wanted to know if you knew where Lizzy was."

"I do not know where she is, but she will be fine; she must be fine. Have faith."

Mary felt the pain in her heart increase. "I do not think I treated Lizzy as well as I ought to have done. I used to ignore her when she would speak to me about my playing or suggest I change my hair. I always felt that I knew best and that I was better than she. Lizzy is always so happy all the time, and I can never understand it. Nothing ever makes her angry, and look at me; I am either impatient with her or I ignore her." Mary started to cry.

Jane gave her a hug. "Mary, dear, we are all different. Because you do not like the things Lizzy likes does not mean you do not love her, or she you. Do not distress yourself."

Mary spoke through her tears. "I am horrified at how Kitty and Lydia seem unaffected. They have not pronounced a word of concern for Lizzy. All they talk about is going into Meryton tomorrow when the officers are back at their camp. How can they say they love her and behave like that?"

"They are young, and perhaps this is their way of hiding the pain." Jane confessed to similar feelings regarding Kitty and Lydia's thoughtlessness.

"They have never cared for Lizzy. They are heartless."

Jane used her handkerchief to wipe away Mary's tears.

"I know that you love Lizzy very much, and I know that you are worried about her. What they say or do is not important. What matters is the relationship you have with her. I think it is easy for us to take each other for granted. When Lizzy gets back, you can tell her how much you love her."

DURING HIS VISIT WITH THE young woman, Darcy resolved that something must be done, and hoping that someone in the country would know of a missing girl, he determined that he would go out on horseback in search of her friends and relations.

Darcy rejoined Bingley and his sister in the breakfast room and made known to them his intentions.

"Darcy, however will you do that? We have lived in the neighborhood but one day. We have visited no one, and no one has been to see us. We do not even know where the principal houses in the district are located. I have been to Meryton once, and you, never. Where do you intend to go?" Bingley was incredulous.

"This is reckless, man!" cried Bingley, not letting him answer. "You are as likely to become lost yourself as find anyone connected with the young woman. Certainly you cannot be serious!"

"Mr. Darcy, you must not go. Please, do not think of entertaining such a risk," seconded Miss Bingley.

"Bingley," Darcy replied patiently, ignoring Miss Bingley, "I believe that if she is from Meryton, someone would have come inquiring after her by this time, so I am going to assume she is from a place in the opposite direction. I shall ride out and begin inquiries at any cottage I come upon or with anyone I meet. She is all alone, and her family must be afraid for her. I must do something to help."

Darcy had been acting strangely, thought Bingley. He had attributed this behavior to his becoming accustomed to a new neighborhood and a new house, but as he reflected upon it, he realized that Darcy had always shown quite an interest in their unfortunate visitor. Bingley was aware of Darcy visiting her room at least twice since they brought her to Netherfield.

"Why do you care so much, Mr. Darcy?" asked Miss Bingley.

"I...I just care."

Bingley looked at him thoughtfully. "You are determined to go?"

"I am."

"Well, then I shall accompany you."

MRS. BENNET HAD NOT LEFT her room all day, and as usual, Jane was both disappointed and relieved — disappointed that her mother could not think of

20

anyone beyond herself in a time of crisis and relieved that, if she must behave poorly, she did so closeted in her own room.

Jane was restless, and indeed, how could she rest when her sister had been missing for a full four and twenty hours? At any minute, she was expecting to hear the worst.

Lizzy must have been abducted, injured, or worse, for her not to return home. Jane dared not speculate further. Lizzy had spent her whole childhood wandering the neighborhood for miles in each direction. Many of those miles they had walked together, but usually Lizzy ventured out on her own. No, Lizzy was not lost. Something had happened to her.

Jane moved from the drawing room out of doors to the lawn, somehow feeling she would be closer to Lizzy if she were outside. The air was fresh and filled with the fragrance of the countryside. It was just the sort of weather Lizzy loved. She could not be contained within doors when the air was as pleasant as it was today, and that was what drew her outside yesterday. Instead of being beautiful, the day filled Jane only with pain, as everything reminded her of her missing sister.

In the late afternoon, David appeared before Jane once again.

"Yes, David?" Jane looked at him hopefully but was immediately downcast when she saw no look of encouragement on his face.

"Colonel Forster has sent me to report that nothing new is known of Miss Elizabeth's whereabouts." David could not look Jane in the eyes. "I am sorry, Miss Bennet."

"Have they looked everywhere?" Jane felt immediately ashamed. "No, I am sorry. Of course, they have. Thank you for telling me."

David hesitated for a moment then turned without a word, and Jane watched him walk slowly back down the road towards Meryton.

Darcy and Bingley rode silently back to Netherfield. It had not been a successful search. The young woman could not have come from the area in which they had looked, for there was nothing but farms and cottages on that side of Netherfield. Darcy had asked some farmers if they knew of a girl who was missing, but no one had heard a thing. It was as if she had dropped in from nowhere.

The Netherfield party was sitting quietly in the drawing room that evening after dinner. Darcy was trying to distract himself with a book, Bingley was similarly employed, but his sister was bored and eager for conversation.

"Mr. Darcy, you have been very quiet tonight." Miss Bingley's tone was frustrated. Her efforts to engage Mr. Darcy's attention had thus far been futile.

"Pardon?" Darcy looked up from his book with a startled expression on his face. "What did you say, Miss Bingley?"

"I said that you have been very quiet tonight, sir. You hardly spoke a word at dinner. What could you be thinking of all this time, I wonder?"

"I was thinking about what is expected of me."

"And just what is expected of you?" She was pleased at having drawn him into conversation.

Darcy laughed to himself. "To increase the importance and value of the Pemberley estate, to marry a woman of wealth and status, and to seek a good match for my sister. Of course, I must attend plays and balls during the season in London and enjoy the country as a gentleman should." His words were laced with sarcasm.

Darcy closed his book and walked over to stir the fire, astonished at having made such an admission of what he thought to be a weakness.

"You do not sound happy with those prospects."

"I should be. Is that not what society expects of me? Is that not what a gentleman of wealth and property is supposed to do?" Darcy returned to his seat. "But little does society care about what my wishes might be or what it is that I want."

This was a surprising revelation from a man Bingley always considered as knowing his own mind and determining his own future. "Darcy, just what is it that you want?"

Darcy grew pensive and was silent for a moment. Then with an air of gravity, he began to explain. "I want to hire a manager to run Pemberley, allowing me more time to spend with my future wife and our children, to allow Georgiana to marry whomsoever she will by settling her fortune on her now so that she can make that choice without my interference, to remain at Pemberley and avoid London altogether, and to live quietly and in retirement with my family and amongst my friends."

Darcy was unaware that the others in the room were listening. He watched the coals burn in the center of the fire, felt a stirring in his heart, and struggled against the impulse to join the young woman upstairs the way a dying leaf struggles against the wind on an autumn day.

IT WAS NOW DARK OUTSIDE. It would be Lizzy's second night out alone. At any minute, Jane was expecting David to return with more news. Instead, it was Colonel Forster who was shown into the drawing room.

She arose at his entrance, searching his face for any sign of hope. She found none.

"Miss Bennet, I am sorry," began Colonel Forster, confirming what she had already gathered from the expression on his face. "We have searched all the roads and paths around Meryton, Longbourn and Oakham Mount, and your sister is nowhere to be found. I do not know what more we can do. It is growing dark. I have sent the men back to their quarters and have asked Sir William to do the same with his servants." He spoke as gently as he could. There was much sympathy in his voice.

"Unfortunately," he continued, "General Delford is coming tomorrow to inspect the regiment, so we will be unable to continue the search."

"Thank you for your help, Colonel," she said tearfully as she fell back into her seat. All of her hope had been pinned on the efforts of the regiment. If they could not find Elizabeth, who could?

"I wish we could have done more." He met her gaze with moist eyes, and then looked away, unable to endure the agony chiseled onto her features.

"I will find my way out. Good evening, Miss Bennet."

Jane was stunned — absolutely shocked! The full realization of what Colonel Forster had said began to dawn on her. The hunt for Elizabeth was over. She would not be discovered, and she would be forever missing.

She could not stop the tears that were pouring from her eyes. As weak and as overwhelmed as she felt, she knew she had to be the strong one. She had to be the one upon whom her family could depend. It was certain now that Lizzy would not be coming back. Neither would they ever know what had happened to her.

It was her fault that Lizzy was not coming home. It was her fault because she had not gone with Lizzy on her walk. She had not been there to prevent whatever tragedy had befallen her sister. Now it was too late, and there was nothing she could do.

TO ESCAPE THE CONFINEMENT OF the drawing room, and perhaps to relieve the slight embarrassment he felt because of his confession to Miss Bingley, Darcy decided to retire early. As he ascended the staircase, however, his progress slowed. By the time he reached the top, he had not the energy to take himself anywhere but to her room. He knocked on the door.

"Come in, Mr. Darcy."

He smiled at the playful display of impertinence and opened the door.

"Hello, Anne. How did you know it was me?"

"We have been anticipating your visit for some time now," said Anne with a knowing smile.

"We?"

"Well…I have been expecting you. Our young lady has not yet awakened, though she has begun to stir a little in her sleep."

"I am very glad to hear it."

Darcy walked over to her bedside. She looked so fragile surrounded by all the pillows and blankets. Color had returned to her cheeks, though, which made her look healthy and vibrant. In his mind, she had gone from merely pretty to breathtakingly beautiful.

He knew it was foolish to think himself in danger of falling in love with someone who had neither looked at nor spoken to him. He could only imagine what her voice sounded like, but he felt himself succumbing. She radiated liveliness and playfulness, and he felt his spirit refreshed just by being around her.

"Good evening," Darcy said to her. "Bingley and I rode out today looking for your family, but we met with no success, I am sorry to say. I will try again tomorrow."

Darcy wanted to hold her hand. He did not know if it were she who needed the comfort, or if he did. He knew that if he were ever allowed to touch her, it would be a day he would never forget.

"You look well today. Anne is taking very good care of you."

"Thank you, sir," said Anne. She had carefully dressed the young woman's hair, knowing that Mr. Darcy's visits were becoming quite regular.

Darcy bent down closer to her face, tempted by her lips.

"Please," he whispered to her, "if you can hear me, please know that I am doing everything in my power to take care of you. Please trust me." He gazed at her face, willing her eyes to open. "Please, come back."

JANE DISMISSED THE SERVANTS, WHO quietly left the room. Sleep was out of the question. She had to resign herself to the fact that Lizzy was not coming home. If she had been hurt, this was her second night outside exposed to the elements. If she had been taken by someone…well, Jane did not even want to think of that.

Her tears would not stop. Mary had sat with her for a while, but Jane had sent her to bed. She felt the responsibility for all her family on her shoulders. She felt guilty for Lizzy's loss and knew she could not face any of it while in her bedchamber. For the second night, there would be no Lizzy to come and visit her there.

In what seemed like only a moment or two, Jane woke with a start. She had fallen asleep sitting up on the sofa. It was pitch black. Her candle had gone out, and there was no moon.

"Oh, Lizzy!" she cried as she sank back down on the couch.

MRS. THOMAS DECIDED TO GO to the butcher's in Meryton herself rather than send a servant. Wanting to acquaint herself with the town, she left her carriage at the end of the street and walked to the shop.

"Good day! I am Mrs. Thomas, the housekeeper at Netherfield," she said to the butcher as she walked into his shop.

"Hello, ma'am, my name is Evan. What can I do for you today?"

"It is nice to meet you, Evan. This is my first visit to Meryton. You have a lovely town."

"Not too lovely of late, ma'am."

"Why not?"

"One of the popular young ladies of the country has gone missing these past three days. Everyone has been searching for her, but it is as if she vanished."

"Oh, that is awful. What is her name?" she asked, quietly rejoicing at this news.

"Miss Elizabeth Bennet, of Longbourn."

For an instant, she wanted to tell him, to tell everyone, that she knew where Miss Bennet was, but thought better of it. There would no doubt be a chaotic rush to Netherfield to claim her, and no telling how her family would take the news of their missing daughter being in the home of strangers. No, she would quickly return to Netherfield to tell the gentlemen and allow them to restore Miss Bennet to her loved ones.

"And nobody knows where she is?"

"No, ma'am. The regiment was out searching for her yesterday and all the farmers looked on their land. Everybody has kept their eyes open for her, but she has disappeared."

"That must be terrible for her family."

"Her elder sister, Miss Jane Bennet, who is the head of the family, is struggling to keep up the appearance of composure, but there is no doubt that everyone is suffering greatly. Such goings-on as these just do not happen around here. We are not accustomed to tragedy and loss."

"Evan, I have just remembered something I must be about. I will send a servant by later for some venison. Goodbye." So saying, Mrs. Thomas quickly left the store.

Mrs. Thomas's heart was gladdened by what she had heard. This was the first news they had received of the young woman. Mr. Darcy would be very pleased to know something of her.

Jane was in Lizzy's room curled up on her bed when she heard her mother calling for her. Lizzy's scent was everywhere, and while consoling in some ways, it was agony in others. She was wrapped up in her sister's quilts, remembering one of their many conversations in that room, on that bed, wrapped up together under that same cover. Without warning, she was once again struck with the overwhelming conviction that she would never see Lizzy again, and she started to cry.

Her mother called out to her once more. Making an effort to compose herself, Jane answered Mrs. Bennet's summons. Her mother began to speak to her as soon as she entered the room.

"Oh, Jane, I do not think the regiment searched as well as they ought. I think there was some gross mismanagement on their part that caused them to overlook where Lizzy was to be found, and now she is dead."

"Mama, the men made every effort to find Lizzy. We may never know…" The spoken truth was more awful.

"What do you mean 'never know?'" cried Mrs. Bennet, panic filling her voice.

"Oh, Mama, I do not believe we shall see Lizzy ever again."

"Jane!" screamed Mrs. Bennet. "I cannot endure this! Please…I am growing faint!…Oh, Lizzy, what have you done?"

She could not comfort her mother, for Jane's feelings ran in the same vein, and she had not the strength to support the spirits of anyone else.

Mrs. Hill had been above stairs when she heard Mrs. Bennet's cry, and she shook her head in agreement. She had been part of the household since the year before Miss Elizabeth was born, and she felt her loss exceedingly. The nature of her position at Longbourn, however, prevented the display of emotion that relieved the grief of the sufferer.

She was descending the stairs when there was a knock at the door and she frowned at the inconvenience of callers when the family was in such a state of mourning. Nevertheless, propriety and good manners called upon her to open the door.

Before her were two gentlemen whom she had never before seen. The young man standing closest to her, and who seemed about to speak, was of medium height, with light hair and pleasant blue eyes. Of the other man, the only word that would describe his looks and his air was dark. She invited them into the hall.

"May I help you, sir?" Mrs. Hill addressed herself to the first gentleman.

"We need to speak with a member of the family. We have news concerning Miss Elizabeth Bennet." He spoke with a sense of urgency.

Hill paled. Forgetting herself, she cried, "Oh!" and then hurried upstairs, leaving the gentlemen standing in the entryway. She entered Mrs. Bennet's bedchamber in haste, neglecting to knock.

"Miss Jane, there are two gentleman to see you. They say they have news of Miss Elizabeth. They are —"

Jane ran down the stairs and into the hall, leaving Hill with Mrs. Bennet, who was calling for her salts.

As Jane was making her way to the drawing room, she saw two men standing in the entryway.

She ran up to them and breathlessly said, "Gentlemen, I am Jane Bennet. Do you have news about Elizabeth? Do you know where my sister is?"

The fairer man spoke. "Yes. She is safe at Netherfield Park."

The color drained from Jane's face, and she raised one hand to her head and stretched the other out in front of her. The gentleman saw her knees begin to give way, rushed to her, and held her in his arms.

Jane had been unable to choke down a sob, and with the knowledge that Elizabeth was alive, all the stress and tension of the past three days fled from her body, leaving her weak and unable to support herself. Suddenly, she was being cradled in strong arms, her head leaning on a firm shoulder. Endeavoring to recover herself, she returned the embrace as her legs regained their strength. Never had she felt so sheltered. Never had she felt such protection. Whoever it was who had just saved her from falling was endeared to her forever. Allowing herself to relax for just an instant in his arms, she slowly pushed away from him.

"Miss Bennet," said the fair-haired man, "allow me to help you."

Her color returned with the heat of confusion as he placed his arm around her waist and nearly carried her to a sofa.

"There," he declared, as he sat her down.

"I shall call for some water," said the other man.

As her vision cleared, she turned her eyes to the first voice and beheld the most handsome face she had ever seen.

"I... thank you... sir."

The dark-haired man returned with a glass of water, but before she could reach for it, the other man took it from him and handed it to her.

"Please allow me to introduce myself. My name is Charles Bingley, lately of Netherfield Park, and this is my good friend, Fitzwilliam Darcy."

Chapter 3

Bingley continued. "You must forgive us for not coming sooner, but we had no idea who the lady in our care was so that we could inform her family of her whereabouts and condition."

Jane's heart skipped a beat at the sound of his voice. She looked directly into his clear blue eyes and felt an immediate connection to him. She barely knew his name, yet she sensed his kindness.

The other man was tall with dark hair and penetrating eyes that seemed to look right through her. He moved very deliberately and seemed nervous in her presence.

"Please, tell me everything," she begged Mr. Bingley, who looked hesitantly at his friend. He answered with the briefest nod, and Mr. Bingley then began to speak.

"Three days ago, Darcy and I were riding towards Netherfield when we found a young woman lying on the side of the horse trail we were following. Her foot was tangled in a root, and it appeared to us that she had fallen and struck her head on a rock. She was unconscious, but alive."

Jane raised her hands to her horror-stricken face.

"Darcy stayed with her while I went for a carriage to carry her to Netherfield where we installed her in a bedchamber. We summoned Mr. Manning, our family doctor from London, not knowing whom else to call. He told us that she was well and had no significant injury other than a blow to the head. Mr. Manning said she suffered from a concussion and was certain that she would wake up, but could not say when."

"Thank you!" cried Jane. "Thank you for finding Elizabeth and caring for her. You cannot understand the... We had thought the worst. We had assumed she had… Please, wait here while I share the news with all my family." She rose and quickly left the room.

Darcy had expected to see someone similar in appearance to Miss Elizabeth Bennet, but Jane did not resemble her sister at all. She had light blonde hair, blue eyes and was taller. During his and Bingley's investigation in Meryton, he learned that Jane was the eldest of five daughters and was in possession of the Longbourn estate after the death of her father.

Bingley never in his life had beheld such beauty as had been present before him in the form of Miss Jane Bennet. Her movements were graceful and pleasing. Besides her outward beauty, Bingley could sense an inner strength. It was apparent that the nightmare of her missing sister had weighed heavily upon her and that it was likely she bore the burden of her whole family. If her father had left the estate to her, he must have acknowledged her — not her mother — as the source of strength in her family. Miss Bennet was confident and was not afraid to look him in the eye. The set of her chin told him that she received him into her home as an equal. She obviously cared for her sister very much. It grieved him that their acquaintance had to be made under such awful circumstances, and he hoped it would not ruin his chances of getting to know her. She was an irresistible combination of beauty and virtue. Before he knew it, Bingley was in love. Miss Bennet had captured his heart.

As there was no doubt in his mind that Miss Bennet would wish to see her sister immediately, Darcy took the liberty of ordering her carriage.

Darcy's memory returned to that awful moment when he discovered Miss Elizabeth on the trail. He remembered holding her, trying to comfort and warm her. Had he known her name then, he would have gently repeated it to her, hoping that she would recognize the sound and wake up. Now, at last, he had her name.

"Elizabeth," he murmured.

After Mrs. Thomas had brought the news to the gentlemen at Netherfield, Darcy had immediately gone to Miss Elizabeth's room to tell both her and Anne that Miss Elizabeth's family had been discovered. Anne had been delighted. Miss Elizabeth was still unconscious, but he had spoken to her anyway, assuring her that he would bring them to her that very day.

Darcy did not understand his feelings for Miss Elizabeth. He felt a great need to protect and cherish her. It was inconceivable that he was falling in love with someone he did not know, who could not possibly return his love, and who might not be his equal in social standing or temperament, but somehow none of that mattered. Her beauty and perceived innocence had touched his heart. Perhaps, when her family came to Netherfield, she would recognize their voices and wake up. His heart leapt at the prospect.

JANE'S CARRIAGE ARRIVED AT NETHERFIELD with Bingley and Darcy, who came on horseback. Mr. Bingley handed her out of the carriage and escorted her into the house where Mrs. Thomas awaited them.

"Miss Bennet, this is my housekeeper, Mrs. Thomas.

"I am pleased to meet you, Miss Bennet, and am so grateful that you could come to visit your sister. Please call on me for anything you might need. I have directed a footman to wait outside your sister's room. Should you need anything, please dispatch him with your request."

"Thank you, Mrs. Thomas. You are very kind."

"This way, Miss Bennet." Bingley ushered her down the hall and to the staircase. Darcy followed them up the stairs.

Bingley knocked on Elizabeth's door; Anne opened it and stepped back to allow them room to enter. Jane's eyes filled with tears as she ran to the bed where Elizabeth lay. She knelt on the floor next to her, holding Elizabeth's hands against her cheek, and quietly cried.

"Lizzy, it is Jane. Thank goodness you are alive and safe. Oh, Lizzy, I thought I had lost you forever!" Jane could not stifle a sob and wept for joy and relief.

"Please, Lizzy, it is time for you to wake up, dearest." Jane wiped her tears away. "I have been so worried. We have all been so worried. I imagined the worst — that I would never see you again — and here you are! You look so well. Oh, please, wake up and tell me that you are all right!"

Bingley and Darcy left the room to allow the sisters some privacy, retiring to the library for brandy and conversation.

"SO, WHAT DO YOU THINK of her?" Bingley asked as he pulled the stopper from a bottle and poured out the liquid.

Darcy took the glass he offered. "She is beautiful. I wish she would wake up. I am very concerned about her. I only hope that hearing her sister's voice will make a difference."

Bingley laughed. "I was talking about Miss Jane Bennet."

It never occurred to Darcy that Bingley would be speaking of anyone other than Miss Elizabeth.

"Oh! Yes, well," said Darcy, confused at his mistake, "she is very pretty, too.

She seems to be under enormous stress right now." To hide his embarrassment, he quickly added, "Still, I was a little surprised at her display of emotion."

"Well, I forgive her for it. I like her very much. I feel close to her already, and I am looking forward to getting to know her better."

"Be on your guard, Bingley," counseled Darcy. "These are not the best of circumstances for developing an attachment."

"I suppose I could give you the same warning," smiled Bingley. "Be on your guard."

JANE SPENT THE AFTERNOON WITH Elizabeth, speaking quietly to her, holding her hand, weeping over her, praying over her, and begging her to wake up.

From time to time, Bingley came to the room to see if he could be of any assistance to Miss Bennet. In every instance, he was taken by her beauty and grace. Each movement of her hand or turn of her head when she looked at him endeared her to him. He marveled at the wisps of hair that trailed against the nape of her neck and the curls that framed her face. He strained to hear the sound of her voice as she spoke soft words to Miss Elizabeth. Bingley knew he was in danger of falling in love with her, but it was a danger he welcomed.

On one of these visits, Bingley announced himself with a light tap on the door.

"Miss Bennet, I have come to offer you some refreshment. Would you care for tea?" If she accepted, Bingley would be able to sit with her for a few minutes.

"Thank you, sir. I would be grateful."

Bingley went to the door and spoke to the footman, and then took a seat across the room from the two sisters and spoke with Anne while trying not to stare at Miss Bennet.

In a short time, a maid entered with the tea service. Bingley took it from her and set it on a small table. Jane walked over to pour the tea, but Bingley was there before her. She watched him fill a cup for her.

"Miss Bennet," he said gently, handing it to her.

"Thank you."

Jane sipped the cup and looked up at him, returning his smile. He was an attractive man and very attentive. He made her feel comfortable and welcome, not like an intruder. Jane knew Mr. Bingley was looking at her, perhaps longer than propriety allowed, but she was pleased by his attention. She remembered the strength of his arms when he held her for that brief moment at Longbourn. She knew she could trust him. Elizabeth was in safe hands.

Jane set her tea down and returned to her sister. "Oh, Elizabeth, please wake up. I have so much to tell you," she whispered. Elizabeth was the one person in whom she could confide all the feelings of her heart.

Jane had now been alone with Elizabeth for some time, for Mr. Bingley had withdrawn shortly after tea, claiming to have estate business.

"It is growing late," commented Jane to Anne. "I must return home. I am sure we will meet again soon." Jane combed Elizabeth's hair back with her fingers. "Anne, thank you so much for looking after Elizabeth. The care you have taken in making my sister both comfortable and beautiful is very much appreciated."

"Thank you, Miss Bennet. I am doing my best for her."

Jane left the room, and the footman escorted her down the stairs and to the drawing room where the gentlemen were sitting. They rose at her entrance.

"Miss Bennet, I hope you are satisfied with your sister's treatment," said Mr. Bingley, pleased that she had sought him out before leaving Netherfield.

"Thank you very much for caring for her, sir. You cannot know how much it means to my family and me. We despaired for her life, but you have saved her. You cannot imagine the relief I feel. I love her so much. I could not have lived without her. I could not..." Jane turned away with tears in her eyes.

"Miss Bennet," he said softly, "it is our pleasure to help your sister." Then looking away, he made her an offer that he hoped she would accept.

"I would like to invite you to stay at Netherfield with us until your sister is well."

Jane paused for a moment to reflect on his invitation. She would like nothing better, but she knew her mother would make accepting such an offer impossible.

"Thank you. You are very kind, but I must decline. I must return to Longbourn. My mother must be informed of Elizabeth's condition. She is beside herself with worry."

"Then please come to Netherfield as often as you like. Will we see you tomorrow?"

"Yes, I would like that very much."

With that, Bingley escorted Jane to her waiting carriage, handed her in, closed the door and watched the coach until it was out of sight. With a sigh, he returned to the house.

Bingley walked into the drawing room where he found Darcy at a window, seemingly lost in thought. During that brief moment when Darcy was unaware of his presence, Bingley summoned up his courage to make a confession he had been longing to make.

"Darcy, I like her," he blurted out. This drew Darcy's attention away from the window and towards his friend. Bingley continued, "I like her very much."

"Miss Bennet, you mean?" Darcy knew full well whom he meant.

Bingley sat in the chair opposite Darcy, wondering if it were truly possible that he could be so dense as to not know of whom he was speaking. With a shake of his head, he enlightened his friend.

"Miss Jane Bennet, of course! Is she not the most beautiful creature you ever beheld?"

Bingley rose and began to pace back and forth in front of Darcy, unable to contain the happiness he felt whenever he thought or spoke of her.

"She is very pretty, I grant you."

Bingley stopped pacing and stared at Darcy with an expression of incredulity.

"Pretty? You grant me? Come, man! You have never seen a woman more attractive than she."

Darcy chuckled as he returned his attention to the window. Although the prospect was pleasing, his eyes would not focus on it, for his mind was concerned not with scenery but with a certain lady. He absentmindedly pulled out the purple ribbon from his pocket and wrapped it around his fingers.

Bingley was watching Darcy with no small amount of curiosity. Staring out of windows with a far-away expression on his face and playing with ribbon was not typical behavior for his friend.

"What is that?" Bingley inquired with great interest as he moved closer to obtain a better view of what Darcy was holding.

Darcy's face reddened. "It is nothing — just a piece of ribbon I found."

Bingley decided to pursue the matter.

"And where did you find it?"

Darcy hesitated. Not wishing to own the truth but not knowing how to evade the question without resorting to a falsehood, he was forced to make a confession.

"It belongs to Miss Elizabeth Bennet. I believe it came off her bonnet at the time we found her on the trail."

The room was silent as Bingley reflected on this piece of information. He had already noted Darcy's strange behavior ever since he had encountered Miss Elizabeth, behavior that might be explained if Darcy felt himself attracted to her. Bingley wondered at the power Miss Elizabeth might have over his friend when she finally awakened if she had this much influence while still asleep.

"Hmm... Perhaps you *have* seen someone more attractive than Miss Bennet."

JANE JUMPED FROM THE CARRIAGE as soon as the door was open and ran upstairs to her mother's room.

"Mama, I have seen Elizabeth!"

"How is she? Is she awake? What did she say?"

"She appears to be fine. She is unconscious, but she has good color, and they are taking very good care of her. I am going to return to her again tomorrow."

"Did you see Mr. Bingley or Mr. Darcy? They are fine-looking gentlemen." Mrs. Bennet's motherly concern for the well-being of her second daughter waned. She had watched the gentlemen mount their horses and ride away from the house when Jane left in the carriage. It would do very well to have Elizabeth engaged before she came away from Netherfield. Either gentleman would suit that purpose. Perhaps the other would prefer Jane.

"I saw them both, Mama, and I thanked them with all my heart for their assistance. Both are so kind and well mannered. Indeed, everyone in Mr. Bingley's household is a pleasure to be around. He has given Lizzy a maid who attends to her night and day."

"Netherfield Park is such a beautiful old home. I am sure, with the proper attention, it could be fixed up nicely. I would like very much to see you or Lizzy settled there."

"Mama! Please do not say such things! Both gentlemen are very kind and have been very good to Lizzy, but we hardly know anything of them. Besides, there is every reason to believe that they are not looking to form an attachment, or if they were, they certainly could make much more advantageous matches. We know them just as new acquaintances, so please do not consider the matter any further. You will only embarrass us."

"My daughters are good enough for anybody!"

Mrs. Bennet, once again frustrated with Jane, sent her away and called for Mrs. Hill so she could complain about the ill-treatment she suffered at the hands of her eldest daughter, who first refused her the horses and now refused to marry either of the Netherfield gentlemen.

DARCY RETIRED EARLY THAT NIGHT, his head full of enchanting images of Miss Elizabeth Bennet. After an interminable period of tossing and turning, he finally slept. He was roused an hour later by a pounding on the door.

"Mr. Darcy! Mr. Darcy! Please wake up, sir!"

"What? Who is there?"

For a moment, all he could see was a shadow as his eyes focused on a candle.

The light fell across the intruder's face; Darcy recognized Anne, Miss Elizabeth's maid, and he immediately became alarmed.

"I am sorry to have entered your room and to have disturbed you, sir. I have been knocking for quite some time, but you did not answer. It is Miss Elizabeth," she cried. "She is very hot and feverish. I have tried all I know to bring down the fever, but it is no use. I do not know what else to do for her."

As Darcy rallied his wits, all his faculties became engaged to one cause — Elizabeth's welfare.

"I will come immediately. Go to her," he commanded. Anne exited the room, and he jumped from his bed, dressing quickly. He ran to Elizabeth's room, entered without knocking, and rushed to her side to feel her forehead and cheeks with the back of his hand. She was indeed very hot, appeared quite uncomfortable, and was making unintelligible noises. It was an unsettling sight to witness.

"Mr. Darcy, what shall we do?"

Darcy clenched his eyes shut as the answer to her question presented itself in the form of a dreaded memory.

"When my mother was ill, before she…she… We need to cool Miss Elizabeth and bring the fever down. I will fetch some ice from the icehouse. We will break it up, wrap it in cloth, and lay it around her head and shoulders. I will return immediately. Stay with her."

He ran down the stairs and through the door at the rear of the house. Crossing the lawn, he came to a door set in a small rise in the ground next to a large tree. Opening it, he went down a few steps and then passed through two more doors and into a chamber lined in brick and straw. Sheets of ice were stacked on shelves lining the walls. He used a hammer to break off chunks and slivers of ice, which he placed in a bag and carried back to the house.

Once again at Elizabeth's bedside, he took out ice chips, wrapped them in damp cloths, and placed them around her neck, on her shoulders, and across her forehead. Contrary to their hopes, the ice was not immediately effective. Elizabeth continued to moan and began to thrash about.

When he had done all he could do, he took her hand and spoke to her gently, encouraging her with soft words and urging her to rest and be still.

"Miss Bennet," he said, pouring out his heart, "Elizabeth, shh…you will be fine. We are caring for you and all will be well. Please do not be afraid. I will not leave you alone. Please, Elizabeth, shh…"

Repeating his entreaties, he began to caress her hand. Despite the assurances he gave her, he was afraid for her. He knew his mother had been treated with ice when she was feverish before she had died, and that in her case, it had been to no avail. He knew he had to be strong for Elizabeth, so making every effort to bury his own fear, he continued his ministrations to her.

He alternately refreshed the ice and wiped her skin dry, never ceasing to speak softly to her in a manner he hoped was soothing and calming. His mother had spoken to him in this way when he had been ill as a boy, and he hoped for the same efficacy with Elizabeth.

Darcy did not notice the passing of time. All his thoughts were focused on comforting Elizabeth and cooling her with the ice. Very gradually, it appeared that his efforts began to make a difference. She became quiet, she stopped moving about, and a look of peace overspread her face.

Exhausted, Darcy sat back in his chair, still holding her hand, still speaking softly to her. He would not leave her. The emergency passed, his eyes slowly closed, and he drifted off to sleep.

ANNE HAD FALLEN ASLEEP IN her seat by the table, but she awakened when her scissors fell off her lap onto the floor. The light of dawn began to show through the window, and as Anne was certain that Mr. Darcy would not wish it to be known that he had passed the night in Miss Elizabeth's bedchamber, she walked over to his chair and touched his shoulder. His eyes flickered opened. "Mr. Darcy, she is sleeping peacefully."

He observed Elizabeth narrowly for a moment. "Yes, she seems to be."

"I will continue to watch over her. Dawn is approaching, and you should return to your room. You have saved her, sir. The emergency has passed."

He was still holding Elizabeth's hand, which he placed beside her on the sheet, for they had taken the blanket off her long ago.

"Do you think she is cold now?"

Anne touched Miss Elizabeth's cheek. "She seems to be comfortable now. I will watch her closely, and I will send you word if her condition changes."

"Please do that." He was feeling the effects of being up most of the night but did not regret his decision to nurse Elizabeth.

"Thank you for your help, sir. I did not know what to do. Thank you again and again."

WHEN THE OTHERS HAD ARISEN for the day and gathered in the breakfast room, Miss Bingley could not help commenting on Darcy's appearance. "Mr.

Darcy, did you not sleep well? Is there anything I may do for you?"

"No, I thank you."

"You seem so tired and distracted. Are you unwell?"

"I am quite well, thank you." He would not admit to his weariness nor confess to anyone how he had spent the night.

"May I pour you some tea? Would you like another muffin? May I get you anything?"

All he wished was for her to refrain from speaking to him. His head ached, and the muscles in his neck and arms felt stiff.

"No, nothing! Please do not concern yourself." Darcy responded more heatedly than he intended. He stood and went to the sideboard for more tea. Miss Bingley did not press him further.

It was becoming unbearable. The wait for Elizabeth to wake up was trying Darcy's patience. How much longer would she remain asleep? He had to see her. Earlier than appropriate, but no later than he could tolerate, he was off to Elizabeth's bedchamber. He knocked on the door, waiting expectantly for Anne to open it.

A new voice — one that he had never heard before — beckoned to him.

"Please come in."

He was astonished at the feelings of gratitude that coursed through him when he considered that it was in all likelihood Elizabeth answering his request. He forced himself to open the door slowly and entered the room with some show of restraint.

He was greeted by the warmest smile he had ever received, one which he could not help returning.

"Please come in, sir," Elizabeth repeated cheerfully.

Her voice touched his soul. He felt soothed, invigorated, and refreshed just from the sound of it.

He walked over to the foot of the bed. "Please allow me to introduce myself. My name is Fitzwilliam Darcy," he said, bowing slightly. "I am a friend of Charles Bingley, whose residence this is. I did not expect you to be awake. Please forgive me for intruding on your privacy." He tried to turn to leave, feeling most uncomfortable in this situation, but he could not tear himself away from her. As he looked into her luminous eyes for the first time, their beauty quite overcame him. He had never seen anything so remarkable as her eyes. When she smiled at him, she positively glowed.

"Please, do not leave, sir, and please do not feel ill at ease. Allow me to express my gratitude." Elizabeth paused. When she saw that he no longer intended to leave, she continued. "I am Elizabeth Bennet, and I believe I have you to thank for rescuing me and bringing me here. Thank you for your kindness."

"It was not kindness, I assure you. I —"

With a blush, she interrupted him. "And I also thank you for nursing me last night. Anne tells me that you very likely saved my life."

Not wishing to discomfit Elizabeth and feeling quite uncomfortable himself, he did not comment on her last remark. "Bingley and I came upon you as we were traveling to Netherfield. It has been our pleasure to care for you." His heart went out to her, and it was painful to take his eyes away from her.

"I must thank Mr. Bingley as well, it seems, sir."

"Your elder sister came yesterday."

"Jane? Jane was here?"

"She was very upset at first. You see, we did not know who you were for three days, and did not know to whom we should send word of your condition and whereabouts."

"I was asleep for three days?"

"You were, and we all feared for you exceedingly," he said painfully. "I am — we are all grateful that you are awake now."

There was no mistaking the tone of his voice, she thought. He had been quite concerned about her.

"I am surprised at how weak I feel for having slept so long. Anne told me she was to inform you immediately when I woke up. I begged her not to so that I could be more recovered when you might come to visit me as she said you would." Elizabeth colored and looked at her hands.

Darcy glanced at Anne and chuckled. "Yes, I have come regularly since you arrived. Perhaps I might be allowed to come and visit you again later when you have had the opportunity to regain your strength?"

"I would like that very much, Mr. Darcy. Thank you." Elizabeth's voice wrapped itself around Darcy's heart, and he felt himself weakening. Her beauty threatened to overwhelm him. How he longed to take her in his arms.

"Until later, Miss Bennet."

"Very well, Mr. Darcy."

Chapter 4

Darcy shut the door of Elizabeth's room behind him, feeling heady with excitement that she was awake and that she had asked him to stay and talk with her. The musical sound of her voice filled his body. Her eyes were beautiful. Their dark color matched her hair and gave symmetry to her face.

The thought that he had imagined himself in grave danger from a woman that he did not know made him laugh. Nonetheless, he was experiencing an immediate kinship with her. He felt bound to her as if somehow they were connected. He knew she would be gentle but not passive. She would be confident but not arrogant. He knew she would be witty and intelligent but not conceited. She was beautiful, but she would not know it herself.

Unfortunately, he also knew by now that the younger Miss Bennets had no dowry, no estate to inherit, and no position in fashionable society. As he reflected on his new relationship with Elizabeth, he realized that this had been apparent to him when he found her on the trail. Women of consequence would not deem it appropriate to dare the solitude of the country, let alone go out of doors unaccompanied.

ELIZABETH FELT THAT MR. DARCY held her at quite an advantage. He knew much more of her than she did of him. Consequently, after he had gone away, she began to seek more information about him from Anne. "Please tell me what you know about Mr. Darcy."

"I really do not know him. Indeed, we all moved to Netherfield the day he found you and carried you here. He is a kind gentleman, and I told you that he is always coming to see you."

Always coming to see me, she repeated to herself.

40

"He is very handsome, and the sound of his voice pleases me." Elizabeth rolled onto her side to look at Anne. It seemed to her as though she recognized his voice. He must have spoken to her a great deal during his visits.

"I brought Mr. Darcy here last night when your fever was at its worst. I was very frightened. He held your hand and spoke very softly to you the whole night. It was his idea to cool you with ice."

Elizabeth was a little surprised at the intimacy he assumed with her. "What did he say to me?"

"I did not hear the words, but I remember that the sound was calming and comforting." Anne looked back at her work.

"That I can believe. I feel very safe with him."

Elizabeth settled back into the bed, burrowing deeper under the blankets, content for the moment with what she had learned. He was a handsome, strongly built man who carried a determined look in his eye. She felt he was a quiet man, though possessed of great feeling.

Elizabeth tried to understand Mr. Darcy. From what little she knew of him, he appeared to be very gentlemanly, though not unwilling to defy convention when it suited him. Indeed, his constant attendance on her while she was sleeping could be deemed most improper, and when he administered the iced and damp cloths, he had gone beyond the bounds of propriety. She had no quarrel with him and was quite grateful. She knew she should be on her guard, but how could she resist such a man?

EARLY THE NEXT MORNING, JANE was pleased to receive a note from Netherfield written in a strong, masculine hand. The news was the very thing for which she had been hoping and praying.

Netherfield

Miss Bennet,

Please excuse the liberty I am taking in writing to you, but I know you will forgive me when I tell you that Miss Elizabeth awoke this morning and is in good spirits.

I know that she would appreciate a visit from her family, and Mr. Bingley has asked that I extend an invitation to you to come to your sister just as soon as may be.

I do not wish to alarm you, but Miss Elizabeth was very feverish last night.

*However, in the early morning hours, we got the better of it, and she slept
peacefully for the remainder of the night. She is resting now, or I am certain she
would have undertaken the task of writing to you herself.*

    I will look forward to seeing you and your family.

*Sincerely,
Fitzwilliam Darcy*

On reading the missive, feelings of relief and gratitude swelled in Jane's
breast as she realized that all her wishes for her sister had been answered. She
was alarmed at the news of the difficult night Elizabeth had passed, but apparently, she had been carefully attended. In Jane's mind, the person responsible
for that care could only have been Mr. Darcy himself, otherwise, how could
he have known of her condition in the "early morning hours?" The service he
had rendered to her sister was invaluable. His compassion exceeded any limits
she had ever established as reasonable and generous. While Jane was grateful to
Mr. Darcy, she wished that she had been the one to care for Elizabeth. Surely,
it was her place.

"IT IS A FAIR PROSPECT, is it not, girls?" said Mrs. Bennet to Jane and Mary,
who were accompanying her in the carriage.

On reading Mr. Darcy's note, Mrs. Bennet had been mildly alarmed, but
as that same note brought reassurances that Elizabeth was recovering apace,
her thoughts turned once again to more pleasing subjects.

Her comment on the prospect of Netherfield was more a statement of fact to
herself than an inquiry that she cared to have answered. Mrs. Bennet wanted
to thank Mr. Bingley and his sister for their kindness towards her daughter
and do all in her power to forward some kind of a match. She considered Lizzy
and Jane, and Mr. Bingley and Mr. Darcy. Somewhere in that combination
an attachment could be formed, and she would see one of her daughters well
married.

"Everything about Netherfield is beautiful, Mama," Jane remarked. "What
do you think, Mary?"

Mary had not bothered to look out the window to see the house. She had
seen it before. "I think that the beauty of a home is not determined by its
outward appearances, but by the quality of the relationships of those that live
within. A modest home may be a mansion, while a great estate may be a prison."

Mary was proud of her opinion. She thought it showed an uncommon degree of intelligence.

"Oh, Mary, hush girl! It is a beautiful house," scolded Mrs. Bennet as she leaned towards the window to admire the place.

A footman came out to meet the ladies and handed them out of the carriage. They ascended the stairs to the door where they were met by a servant.

"We are here to see Mr. Bingley," said Jane with a smile for the servant.

"Yes, ma'am. This way, please. Mr. Bingley is in the drawing room."

The ladies followed the servant, who announced their arrival. Mr. Darcy, Mr. Bingley, and Miss Bingley stood to greet them, and the men and women exchanged bows and curtsies. Jane found herself immediately under the scrutiny of Miss Bingley.

"Mrs. Bennet, you have a charming little family," said Miss Bingley with mocking civility. "I am sure that Miss Bennet takes a prodigious good deal of care of you all."

"Not such a little family. I have two more daughters at home, and Jane does take very good care of us. She inherited Longbourn after her father passed away some years ago, and manages the affairs of the estate to the advantage of all her family."

Miss Bingley was astonished. "Miss Bennet, you are in possession of an estate?"

"Yes. By law it is mine, I suppose, but I view it as my family's home."

"Of course, you do," said Miss Bingley dryly.

"Mr. Bingley, you have a fine looking room here. Netherfield Park is such a delightful place. I hope you will never wish to leave it." Mrs. Bennet surveyed the room, looking for an indication as to the wealth of the two gentlemen.

"For now, I consider myself quite fixed here, I assure you."

"Do you not wish to go into Town for the season?" asked Darcy. The Bingleys and Mr. Darcy spent part of each year in London. Bingley's intention to remain in the country took Darcy by surprise.

Bingley looked directly at Jane. "No, I am quite content to remain just where I am."

Darcy followed Bingley's line of sight until his eyes rested on Miss Bennet. Darcy could not tell whether Bingley was serious or this was just another one of the passing love interests he seemed to stumble into each time he went somewhere new.

"I am sorry, Mrs. Bennet," said Mr. Bingley. "I am certain you did not come to talk to us but to see your daughter. Please, allow me to show you to her room." The ladies followed Bingley from the room.

When they were alone, Miss Bingley had some private words for Darcy. "I fear that my brother is going to make a fool of himself with Jane Bennet. You saw, I am sure, the way he was staring at her."

"She is an attractive woman. I cannot blame him."

"But you know how quickly he falls 'in love,' as he calls it, every time he meets a pretty face. With his charm and good looks, he is very capable of making any woman love him."

"Your brother is a handsome, amiable man. I know of no one who feels anything but the highest respect for him. It should not surprise you that women are attracted to him."

"Yes, but Jane Bennet…" She paused to calm herself. It would not do for Mr. Darcy to see her discomfited by the likes of Miss Bennet.

"Pray, continue."

"Jane Bennet will be no different from the others, and you know there have been many others, and —"

"Harmless flirtations, Miss Bingley. That is all."

Pressing her point, she spoke quickly. "She is just another fortune hunter seeking an easy conquest, and my brother will fall under her power if we do not prevent it."

Miss Bingley's frustration was growing. She was counting on her brother making an excellent marriage in order to increase her own importance so that Mr. Darcy would consider her a worthy match.

"Fortune hunter, Miss Bingley? She has an estate of her own. She is independent." Darcy smiled at her. "Perhaps you are jealous of that?"

"I am told that Longbourn is worth no more than two thousand a year, and the daughters have no dowries. Their father could give them nothing. All they have is the estate. Yes, Miss Bennet is a fortune hunter, and we must protect my brother."

"Although Miss Bennet has not shown any undue attention to your brother, it is true that she is just the sort of woman with whom he would declare himself to be in love." Her point was well taken. As much as he disliked agreeing with her, she was right. If Bingley decided he was in love with Jane Bennet, he would insist that they marry, and with his generous heart, he would seek to improve the fortunes of all her family.

"Please, sir! You will help me, will you not?"

"I always look after my friends, Miss Bingley." Darcy furrowed his brow, undecided as to any course of action.

MRS. BENNET ENTERED ELIZABETH'S BEDCHAMBER, approached the bed-side, and took her daughter's hand, quickly noting her condition. With a slight nod of her head, she satisfied herself that Elizabeth was indeed well. She was then free to deliver the message that occasioned the true reason for her visit.

"I am pleased to see you looking so well. Lizzy, you are doing a very good thing by remaining here at Netherfield. I hope you are being kind to Mr. Bingley and Mr. Darcy." Mrs. Bennet dropped her daughter's hand and gazed about the room. It was beautifully appointed, and the furnishings appeared quite expensive. "Oh, and I hope you are feeling better."

"Mama, it is a comfort to see you again, too," laughed Elizabeth. She had not been ill long enough to forget what her mother's reaction would be to two single men of fortune living in the neighborhood and she herself now under their roof.

"Mama, Lizzy has been asleep these three days," cried Jane, rushing to Elizabeth's side. "You must not talk that way; you must not." She was hurt by her mother's apparent lack of concern for Elizabeth, though not surprised by it.

"Never mind that. Lizzy, you must remain here as long as possible."

"Mr. Manning says I must not be moved for two weeks. I can assure you that I will not be going anywhere for quite some time."

"Mr. Bingley comes very often to visit you, does he not?" asked Mrs. Bennet with an eager look on her face. Mr. Bingley's constant attention to her daughter would be just the thing.

"Actually, Mr. Bingley has never come to see me. I do not know him at all."

"Lizzy," asked Mary, "are they treating you well?"

"I have only been awake since this morning. Anne has been very kind to me, and I have wanted for nothing."

"But are you not often alone?" asked Mary. "Would you not prefer to come home with us? I am sure the ride would not be too difficult for you. I will walk so that you may have a whole bench in the coach." Mary felt all the shock of having nearly lost Elizabeth and wished to mend their strained relationship, and she could not do that if Elizabeth remained at Netherfield.

"Mary, come and sit by me." Elizabeth motioned her sister to the bed. "The physician has requested that I remain here to avoid further injury, but I am certain that Mr. Bingley would welcome you at anytime so that you may visit me, and I know I would be glad of your company."

"I was afraid of what might have happened to you — of what I was certain had happened to you. I was —"

"You do not need to worry any longer. I will be well soon enough," Elizabeth reassured her. "I will grow stronger every day."

"Lizzy, you look very well today," said Jane. "Almost happy, I would say." There was a brilliance to her eyes and a playfulness of expression that spoke of delight. Jane wondered how much of her apparent happiness could be attributed to Mr. Darcy's society.

"I am happy, and I am grateful to be getting well again."

"Are you certain that you cannot return with us?" Mary asked again.

"Thank you for your concern, but I must remain here."

Mrs. Bennet wanted to turn the conversation back to matters of the most importance to her. "Has Mr. Darcy been to see you, Lizzy?"

Elizabeth had been looking at Mary, but quickly turned her head so she could eye her mother. Jane, who saw it all, realized that this was a precarious subject and acknowledged the anxiety that Elizabeth would feel if their mother should learn of Mr. Darcy's attention to her.

"Mama, come and look at the view from this window. It is quite remarkable." She took her mother's arm and tried to lead her away from Elizabeth.

Mrs. Bennet was not at all interested in the view. "Oh, I am sure it is beautiful," she said, freeing herself from Jane's grasp. "Everything about Netherfield is beautiful. I would certainly wish one of you to be well settled here."

Elizabeth knew that if she were to be settled anywhere, it would not be at Netherfield, for Mr. Darcy's residence was... She could not stifle a blush at the thought. "Jane, how are you? How is Longbourn?"

"I am fine." Jane sighed. "But to be honest, I have not spent much time on estate matters since the day when..." Jane's voice broke "...when you did not come back." Jane's spirits had recovered because Elizabeth was recovering, but the horror of that day would never be forgotten.

"I am truly sorry to have caused you such worry."

"Well, girls, I think we should not overstay our welcome. Goodbye, Lizzy," said her mother brusquely as she collected Mary and left the room. Jane did not immediately leave, but moved to the edge of the bed next to Elizabeth and took her hand.

"Goodbye, Lizzy. I will come again tomorrow." She brushed a curl from Elizabeth's face. "Please remember that I love you."

"How could I ever forget?"

As soon as Mrs. Bennet and her daughters had departed, Darcy climbed the stairs to Elizabeth's room. He pulled out the ribbon, laced it through his fingers, and recalled his admission to the Bingleys of desiring the unexpected in his life. Certainly, Miss Elizabeth did not meet the expectations required of the mistress of Pemberley in terms of wealth and status. She would not receive the approval of either his family or society. He dismissed the thought.

Darcy had never considered himself to be in love before, but he knew what it was to feel attraction. With Elizabeth, it was more. He was completely enchanted.

"Come in," Elizabeth responded to a familiar knock.

Before entering the room, Darcy looked over at Anne, who favored him with a smile as he entered.

"Good afternoon, Miss Bennet, did you enjoy your visit with your family?" Darcy walked to the foot of her bed.

"Yes, I did. I feel as if it has been so long since I have seen them, though I know it has been only a few days."

"May I ask if all is well at home?"

"I am a little worried about my sister, Mary. She seems upset and is acting strangely around me."

"Well, I am certain she was afraid of losing you, as we all were. Even though she knows you are out of danger, perhaps she is still gaining confidence in these new feelings."

"Perhaps she is. Perhaps *I* am."

"Were you afraid, Miss Elizabeth? Do you remember falling?"

"I do not recall anything about it. I am certain I dreamt while I was asleep, for I usually do. There is one thing that I do remember." Their eyes locked. "I remember your voice. You must have always been speaking to me."

"I was afraid for you. Every moment that you were asleep, my apprehension grew that perhaps you would not wake up, and I could not bear the thought of losing…of anything happening to you."

Elizabeth felt her pulse quicken at this admission of concern. He cared for her much more than as an acquaintance, and she rejoiced in the thought.

"Mr. Darcy, have you ever lost someone?"

Darcy turned away from her and glanced at Anne, who sat quietly in the corner.

"Yes, both my parents. My mother died when my sister, Georgiana, was born, and my father passed away five years ago."

"I am sorry, Mr. Darcy. Please, forgive me. I should not have spoken."

"No, no. I was ten when my mother died. I had been under the impression that she was a strong woman, but such is the impression of a child. I have learned since that she was actually ill rather often, though with what seemed like trifling colds. Her lungs were affected, however, and she died shortly after Georgiana was born, her body weakened by the exertion. Georgiana never knew her."

Darcy glanced back at Elizabeth and saw her smile at him in a reassuring way. Her hands were clenched together in fists on her blanket. She rolled one hand over towards him and opened her fingers, as if she were inviting him to come near her.

"She was in bed much of the time before Georgiana was born. I would ask my father if I could see her, but he would say that she was too ill. I wondered if I had done something to anger her. I used to slide down the staircase on a blanket, and she would become so angry. Sometimes I would make a great deal of noise about the house, and perhaps, because of that, she could not rest and get well. I thought I had caused her illness."

Darcy pulled a chair up next to Elizabeth's bed. "I was very glad when Georgiana was born, so my mother would not be ill anymore, and we could return to the way we were, but she did not come out of her room. The nurse let me hold Georgiana." He smiled to himself when he remembered holding his little sister's tiny hands. "I was allowed to go to my mother only once after the birth. She asked me to climb up on the bed with her and lie down beside her, and then she took me in her arms and cried. She brushed my hair with her fingers, touched my face, and held my hands. I have never felt so much love. I woke up the next morning in my own bed. My father told me that, during the night, she had grown feverish, and even though they tried everything to break the fever, it was to no avail. She had died."

He paused, and then spoke unconsciously, "Elizabeth...I..."

She started at his use of her Christian name. He realized his mistake. "Forgive me." He lowered his eyes. "I thought... I was so afraid... I thought when you became feverish that you were going to..." He could not continue.

She was quite affected by his reaction. "I understand, Mr. Darcy."

With a deep exhalation, he went on with his tale. "Somehow, I knew she was dying. I think a child almost always knows. After she died, I became very sullen and quiet and would spend hours with Georgiana, holding her hands and talking to her. At first, my father wanted to send Georgiana to be raised by my Aunt Catherine, but he knew I would never allow myself to be separated from her, and he was unwilling to let me go."

Darcy felt all of the pain of that time come back to him. "Instead, my father left. He would be gone for weeks at a time. I would ask our housekeeper, Mrs. Reynolds, when he would return, and she would just shake her head and ask me if I wanted something to eat. I was convinced I had hurt my mother and had now driven my father away. I never used that staircase again. I would go through the whole house and come down by the back stairs. It seemed that if I were to use that staircase, it would be an insult to my mother."

"My father was not at Pemberley when Georgiana began to walk or to talk, and when he was home, he would sit in his study for hours. Mrs. Reynolds kept us in the nursery and schoolroom. The house was so silent and forlorn. It was as if my mother had died all over again. On occasion, when I was home from school on holiday, my father would ask for me, and I would be brought by one of the servants to the drawing room."

"'Come here, Fitzwilliam,' he would say. I would walk to him, he would have me sit beside him on the sofa, and then we would silently stare into the fire. Sometimes, I would fall asleep there. That is one of my few recollections of spending time with my father. I think Mrs. Reynolds was angry with him for neglecting me."

"Many years later, I was with my uncle, my mother's brother, when I received an express from my father's steward telling me that he had died. I returned home immediately. I spoke with everyone who had been in the house the day he died, and I learned that he had passed away in his sleep. He had suffered no pain."

Darcy became silent for a time, and when he looked at Elizabeth, he realized that he was holding her hand. How had that happened? He made a weak effort to withdraw his hand, but she would not release it. "Please go on."

Why had he told her all of this? He scarcely spoke of his parents' deaths, and he had not spoken of it with Georgiana in years. He felt as if a weight had been lifted from his shoulders. Did the relief come in speaking of it after all this time or in speaking of it to her?

A wave of sorrow flooded through him. "I so much regret having done anything to have hurt my parents."

Elizabeth took his hand in both of hers. "As a woman, I am very sensitive to the perils of childbirth, but I cannot imagine the courage your mother must have had, for she must have known that she would not live. It must have been horrible for your father to watch her die, knowing he was powerless to help her. She loved you very much. I know this from your own words. You must take comfort in knowing that your father loved your mother, so much so, that a part of him was overwhelmed when she died."

"But, Miss Elizabeth, why did he shun me? Why did he stay away?" This was the question that haunted him.

She had a tear in her eye when she answered him, a tear for his sake and hers. "His heart was broken by her loss, and you suffered for it." Elizabeth paused for a moment. "Were you ever close to him?"

"No. He sent me off to school, and during the summers, he toured alone. Georgiana stayed at home." Darcy paused to feel the warmth of her hand in his. Her skin was so soft. Had he touched her first or had she touched him? Right now, he knew it did not matter. Their hands were joined. His heart, first dulled by the memory of his parents, now rejoiced in Elizabeth.

"You have lost a loved one, have you not, Miss Bennet?"

"Yes, my father died three years ago."

"Please tell me about him."

She felt her eyes burn. She was willing to take his pain upon herself but felt awkward sharing her own. "There is little to say … "

"Please." His smile reassured her.

"I was always my father's favorite. When I was younger, I would sit with him in a big chair in his library. I felt dwarfed by its size. I would ramble on to him about my childish affairs, and he would read to me from the books that were his constant companions. I loved the attention, and he learned to treat me as a friend. As I became older, my habits never varied, except he would talk with me instead of read to me, or we would read together."

Elizabeth felt his fingertips caress her hand. His touch was so delicate.

"My father had not been ill at all. The family was in the drawing room one evening, and he was sitting next to Jane. Suddenly, he leaned to the side and fell into her lap. We were all horrified. Mama screamed for the servants, and she was immediately taken ill. Jane was crying and shaking his shoulders. I knelt next to him and listened for his breath. Thankfully, he was still alive, and a servant was sent for the apothecary."

Darcy saw tears escape her eyes as she spoke. He gripped her hand more tightly, sympathizing with her, understanding her, and knowing what was eventually to come.

"He was a pitiful sight. He could not move his left arm. He could not walk. He could not even stand. He could barely speak. I stayed with him that night and all the next day. Mama demanded that I leave him, but I would not. Mr. Jones came often, but would not say whether my father would live or die. One evening, I fell asleep in the chair next to his bed, and he must have recovered somewhat during the night, because I heard his voice. 'Lizzy,' he said to me, 'I am sorry that I did not take better care of you.' I told him that he had taken good care of me, that I knew that he loved me, and that his being my father was all that I wanted. I told him I would give my life for him. 'Lizzy, you must keep your life, but thank you for your love.'" Elizabeth choked on a sob. "And then he was gone."

Elizabeth withdrew her hand from his to wipe her eyes. Darcy immediately felt the loss of its warmth.

"My father loved me very much. I miss him terribly, and like you," she said looking at him hopefully, "I have never felt such love and affection since. Jane is a great comfort to me, but I often feel so alone. At first, I was angry with my father, wondering why he left me, but I soon realized that he would never leave me of his own accord and that he was taken from me."

He offered her his hand, she placed hers in his, and he brought it to his lips and kissed her fingers. Without releasing her hand, he stood, and looked intently into her eyes. She met his gaze with such a look of longing that he could not but be touched. Never, not since the last night his mother was alive, had he wanted to love and be loved as he did now, as he wanted to be by Elizabeth.

Darcy released her hand.

"Thank you for allowing me to talk to you of my parents. I rarely speak of them." He smiled down on her. She looked both beautiful and vulnerable. He grieved for the hurt that she felt regarding the passing of her father.

"I have never spoken to anyone about my father's death. I am both pained and pleased by the experience. I thank you for your kind attention." She hesitated for a moment, "...and for comforting me."

"I...I think I should return to the others.

As Darcy turned to leave, Elizabeth spoke. "I hope you will visit me again soon. I know your parents now, but I feel I know so little about you."

She seemed to be pleading with him. How could he refuse anything she wanted? "I would like that very much. Goodbye."

Elizabeth slid down in the bed and held her hands to her lips. "Goodbye, Mr. Darcy."

Chapter 5

There was nothing pleasant about the carriage ride back to Longbourn as far as Jane was concerned, for she was forced to listen to her mother's schemes for her.

"Jane, I am so excited for you. The assembly is Friday night, and Mr. Bingley and Mr. Darcy will be there," said Mrs. Bennet with great pleasure. She had great hopes for the gentlemen of Netherfield.

"Mama, I am not going to the assembly."

"Yes, you are!"

"Mama, no! I am going to spend the evening with Lizzy." Jane steeled herself for the dispute that must follow such a declaration.

"Nonsense, you will go the assembly and dance with the gentlemen and make them fall in love with you. You cannot be so pretty for nothing." Mrs. Bennet's voice took on a commanding tone. "And I will not have you waste the opportunity on Lizzy. She is just fine where she is."

"It is not right that Lizzy should be alone and especially on an evening when everyone will be enjoying themselves at the ball. Mr. Manning says she cannot be moved, and so I must go to her." She was sitting on the same bench as her mother and unconsciously moved away from her.

"You will go to the assembly. Send Mary to be with Lizzy. She never dances, you know, and it will be no loss to her to miss it."

Mrs. Bennet was resolved. She could not understand why Jane was being so stubborn. How else could she secure Mr. Bingley or Mr. Darcy unless she was dancing with them at the assembly?

"I will stay with Lizzy. She need not spend the evening alone." Mary never enjoyed the assemblies. She felt plain compared to her sisters and was rarely asked to dance.

The balance of the ride to Longbourn passed in silence. Mrs. Bennet's frustration with Jane was growing, Mary's gratitude was increasing as she realized she was free of the assembly, and Jane's embarrassment warmed her cheeks as she reflected on the way her mother was throwing her daughters at the gentlemen of Netherfield.

NETHERFIELD, IN HERTFORDSHIRE NEAR MERYTON

Dear Georgiana,

I write to inform you as to the goings-on here at Netherfield. Bingley and his sister are well settled and quite comfortable. It is a handsome home that I know you would like very much. The countryside is beautiful, and I find occasion for riding and walking out. There is a pleasant stream not too far from the house that is ideal for fishing.

I have met a young woman named Miss Elizabeth Bennet, and she is like no lady I have ever known. She is staying with us at Netherfield recovering from an injury that involved a very worrying bump on the head that she acquired when she fell on a path near Netherfield. Bingley and I brought her here, unconscious and you can imagine the anxiety we have suffered on her behalf. She is awake now, and she and I have become good friends. She is to remain here for another week until she makes a full recovery. I confess I wish that time could be extended.

She is everything that is kind, compassionate, and lovely. I know you would like her very much, and I am certain that she would like you. We share many interests, and I find no greater happiness than being with her.

We have exchanged many confidences and have spoken of our parents' deaths. I feel such great relief in having had a chance to talk to her about a matter that has grieved me for so long a time, and I want to apologize to you for not allowing you the same opportunity. I have found that though the pain may be buried, it never goes away. She makes me want to be a better person, and I am committed to becoming a more caring and loving brother to you.

Please let me hear from you soon. I hope you are well.

Affectionately, your brother,
Fitzwilliam

THE NIGHT OF THE ASSEMBLY finally arrived. Jane had dressed with care knowing that she would certainly encounter Mr. Bingley. She anticipated with pleasure talking and dancing with him, though that pleasure was allayed somewhat by the absence of her dearest sister. She took comfort in knowing that Mary was with Elizabeth, and she resolved to enjoy herself as much as possible.

As Jane entered the assembly room, her pulse quickened when she saw Mr. Bingley approach her from the far side of the hall. He was a very handsome man who walked with purpose and confidence. His blue eyes sparkled with good humor. This was the moment for which she had been waiting.

"Miss Bennet, I am so happy to see you again." His voice caused ripples of happiness to course through her body, and she moved to stand a little closer to him.

"The pleasure is mine, sir."

"It is so agreeable to be settled in Hertfordshire. Everyone is so kind and friendly. I would not wish to be anywhere else." Bingley was enchanted. Jane was the loveliest woman he had beheld. He marveled at his good fortune in choosing Netherfield as his home. If he were allowed to hope, he would choose it as her home as well.

"We…I…am glad you are here, sir," Jane stammered. "I hope that means you will be spending a good deal of time with us."

"Do you often hold these assemblies?"

"Yes, about every four weeks, depending on the season. It is a pleasure to gather with one's friends to dance and talk. This is the only occasion I have for seeing some of them, as I am not a great walker like Lizzy."

"I hope that you will count me as one of your friends."

The expression on his face as he spoke gave her reason to hope. His every word and every phrase spoke of a heart that was giving itself to her. A smile lit up her face. Here was an unexpected opportunity to tell him a little of what she felt.

"How could I not? Indeed sir," she said shyly, "although we have only known each other for a short time, I count you as my best friend."

Bingley's heart leapt for joy. Her plainly expressed statement was to him an open avowal of her affection for him. Though he had suspected that he was growing in her esteem, she had never said anything to confirm this hope. Now she had.

Jane looked up at him, met his eyes, and smiled. Mr. Bingley was a handsome man, but what meant more to her than his physical attributes was the impression he had made on her heart. He was open and honest. He made no effort to hide his feelings from her, and in turn, she did not hide hers from him.

Miss Bennet was acquainted with many of the young men who lived in the neighborhood surrounding Meryton, but she had never felt attracted to any of them. She had thoroughly canvassed the subject of love with Elizabeth during their late night talks, but it had always been from an abstract perspective. This was real. She could feel Mr. Bingley's words in her heart, could sense his affection when his eyes rested on her, and positively knew that giving her heart to him was what she desired above anything.

"You cannot imagine how happy it makes me to know that I am your friend, Miss Bennet. I want you to know that there is no one I would rather be with than you. You mean so much to me. I... I wish I could say all I feel."

She looked around her at the others in the assembly room but could not see anyone who appeared as happy as she. Mr. Bingley loved her, and her joy was full.

Bingley was fascinated by her and mildly embarrassed when she caught him staring at her. He had lost himself in her eyes. In them, he saw love, happiness, and every good thing that he desired for his future and hers. It was humbling to be admired by such a woman as Miss Bennet.

"How is Miss Elizabeth feeling?" asked Mr. Bingley gently, unwilling to break the spell of tenderness between them. "I am sorry that she could not be here."

"I am disappointed as well, for she loves to dance. She is growing stronger each day, though, and anticipates with pleasure returning to her normal activities."

"When we found her on the path, Darcy insisted that he remain with her. He carried her to her bedchamber when we arrived back at Netherfield, and he is most solicitous of her comfort. He spends a great deal of time with her each day."

Bingley did not know if he was betraying a confidence, for he and Darcy seldom spoke of Miss Elizabeth, but he had observed his friend's behavior since she had come to Netherfield. He had grown kinder and more personable. He must be falling in love with her, for there could be no other explanation.

"I am glad to hear it. I dread the thought of her spending so much time alone."

"She is not alone very often. Darcy is with her every moment when he is not out riding, shooting, or in company with my sister, Caroline."

Jane was struck by a disturbing thought. She had forgotten about Miss Bingley, the rich and beautiful Miss Bingley, who had made it plain that the Bennets were unwanted at Netherfield. It appeared to Jane that Miss Bingley and Mr. Darcy were a natural match. Her beauty and fortune would grace his distinguished family. What was Elizabeth if not a poor, country girl? What was Mr. Darcy about? Surely, he would not toy with Elizabeth's affection, would he? Jane recollected herself though the chill that this thought inspired did not leave her.

"I would be with Elizabeth more often, but I am uncomfortable being away from Longbourn for extended periods. I do not have a steward. There is no one on whom I can rely."

"You have my admiration and respect. I could never manage an estate alone."

Jane smiled at his compliment. "I am trying to set aside money so that my sisters will have at least small dowries. As of now, all the income is tied up in the estate. I feel responsible for them, and sometimes I fear for their future." She lowered her eyes.

"But you have Longbourn."

"Mama would like me to sell it, but it was my dear father's wish that it be kept. It is our home." She would never be persuaded to give up Longbourn, and that was why her father had left it to her. Her mother would have sold it, the money would have been spent, and poverty would have followed.

"Of course. If I had an estate of my own, I would never wish to sell it. I hold a lease on Netherfield. Darcy persuaded me that I must live there a full year before I purchase it in the event that something does not quite agree with me. My father waited his entire life; I can wait a year."

"Mr. Darcy's advice sounds very wise. Has he been your friend long?" She was curious as to the nature of the relationship between the two gentlemen. Darcy appeared to be older than Bingley, and they had such differing personalities.

"I have known him since I was at school. We were introduced by chance at Cambridge. I happened to be walking between buildings when I came upon Darcy and his father walking in the common area. We were introduced, and soon after, Darcy and I became close friends and have remained so over the years. We spend part of each year together, and he is now assisting me in getting settled at Netherfield."

"I have always thought that being sent off to school would be a lonely proposition and have always had my sisters with me. I am pleased you were able to find a friend."

"And I am pleased to have found a new friend in you." He hoped he had not said too much, but he wanted there to be no misunderstanding as to his regard for her.

She made no reply, but was pleased with the thought.

"Miss Bennet, would you do me the honor of dancing with me?"

"I would be delighted, sir." He took her hand, and they walked off together to join the set that was just forming.

MARY WAS SITTING IN WHAT Elizabeth considered to be Mr. Darcy's chair, reading notes to her from a recent book. Elizabeth attempted to be patient and attentive. After a particularly trying speech, Mary began to express an opinion that Elizabeth did not share.

"Lizzy, I much prefer being here with you than at that dreadful assembly."

"I would prefer to be with you at the assembly," laughed Elizabeth. In a more serious tone, she added, "But Mary, why do you not like them?"

Mary set aside her book and smoothed her dress. "I am never asked to dance."

Elizabeth was thoughtful for a moment, only then understanding the pain Mary might feel at being ignored for an entire evening.

"Perhaps if you were to converse more and not bring a book with you, young men would not be afraid to approach you." Elizabeth knew that Mary attended the assemblies only out of obligation to their mother.

"Young men are afraid of me?"

"I think that gentlemen are sometimes nervous when they approach a young woman who sits alone in the corner. They need help. Smiling and talking with other young women causes you to appear more amiable."

"I have difficulty in speaking to strangers. I stutter and feel awkward. I am not attractive like you and Jane. Why would anyone want to talk to me?" It was a painful confession of the inadequacy that she felt, but it was honest and true.

"Oh, Mary! I suppose that just like the pianoforte, as you practice speaking, you will become more comfortable with it. And you are not awkward. You are intelligent and good-natured."

"That is easy for you to say, being beautiful yourself. Do you think that someday there will be a young man who will love me?"

"I do." Elizabeth smiled. "I know there will."

DESPITE JANE'S PLEASING AND ACCOMMODATING disposition and desire to see the good in everything and everyone, she was a woman of strength who took her role as the head of her family very seriously. It was in that capacity that she found herself uncomfortable with the unprecedented access Mr. Darcy had to Elizabeth.

Perhaps she read more into his comments than they deserved, but Jane could not help but think that Mr. Bingley would not have mentioned the circumstances surrounding Mr. Darcy's rescue of Elizabeth unless there was more to Mr. Darcy's attentions than he had suggested.

Mr. Darcy was a very fine man with a large estate who had lived and traveled much in the world. He had no need of a country girl like Elizabeth, and Jane was persuaded that should Elizabeth form an attachment to him, it would only lead to heartache and pain for her. She felt it incumbent upon herself to let Mr. Darcy know that Elizabeth was neither friendless nor unprotected.

Circling the room in search of Mr. Darcy, she came upon him standing alone watching the dance.

"Good evening, Mr. Darcy," she said as she walked up to him.

He bowed to her. "Good evening, Miss Bennet. You look lovely tonight."

"Thank you. Are you enjoying yourself?"

"Yes, I am. And you?"

"I am happy to be here."

Darcy was quiet as he looked at her. If he were to be honest in his observations, he would have to confess that Miss Bennet was a prettier woman than her sister was, but as he was quite partial to Miss Elizabeth, it was a concession he did not feel obliged to make.

Jane eyed him closely. "Mr. Bingley has told me of your attentions to my sister. It is a relief to me to know that she is in a place where she is being watched over by people who care for her."

Darcy paused for a moment and then looked away as if embarrassed. "I do care for her." From the expression on Miss Bennet's face, he could tell that she was not pleased to hear this, and he wished his comment unsaid the moment he voiced it. "That she is increasing in health each day brings me great pleasure, though being selfish, I must admit that I am grateful to have her at Netherfield where I can enjoy her company."

"Of what do you speak when you are with her, if I may ask?" Jane knew that the answer to this question might reveal the extent of Elizabeth's feelings for him.

"Most recently, we have spoken of our families. My parents have passed away, as has your father. We shared our experiences." He began to realize that this was no longer a conversation, but an interrogation.

"Elizabeth rarely speaks of my father's passing, even to me. I hope the conversation was not too painful for either of you." She found it remarkable that Elizabeth would have shared her feelings about their father's death with him, a man she barely knew. He must have thoroughly insinuated himself into her confidence.

"She is a strong young woman," Darcy observed. "She is a credit to the upbringing of her parents and the love of her sisters. I know that she feels particularly close to you, Miss Bennet. You should be proud of her."

"I am. You described her as strong. Despite her outward appearance of strength, she has a tender heart and a large capacity for love." Elizabeth, she knew, was also naïve and innocent, the perfect combination for suffering heartbreak.

"Those that she loves have every reason to be happy."

"Yes, they do. Mr. Darcy, Elizabeth has never fancied herself in love before. She is unschooled in the relationships between men and women, and anyone who seeks to win her affection would be wise to remember that."

Darcy looked uncomfortable, but said nothing.

"I trust that is something you will remember."

He was quite aware that Jane was suspicious of his motives. Darcy looked at her for a moment. "I will, Miss Bennet." He bowed to her and then walked away.

Jane, not completely satisfied with their conversation, watched him go with feelings of growing uncertainty.

ELIZABETH AWOKE THE NEXT MORNING well rested and happy. She had spent a pleasant evening renewing her relationship with Mary, and she was glad of it. They had promised that they would spend more time with each other in the future, and Elizabeth anticipated their meetings with pleasure.

Contributing to Elizabeth's joy that morning was the fact that she was expecting visits from both Jane and Mr. Darcy, the two people she most wished to see. Just at that moment, one of them knocked on her door. The knock was not the firm, quick one she associated with Mr. Darcy.

"Come in," said Elizabeth cheerfully. She sat up and adjusted her pillow.

Jane entered the room and walked over to give Elizabeth a kiss. "Lizzy, good morning!" Seeing her in good health removed some of Jane's discomfort about not spending the previous evening with her. "How do you feel? You look very well." She removed her bonnet and gloves and sat in the chair next to the bed.

"I am very well. Thank you for coming." She had to confess that spending time alone in that room was tedious, though she knew it could not be helped. She lived for visits from her family and, of course, from Mr. Darcy.

"There is no place I would rather be, my dear sister," said Jane affectionately. "How was your evening with Mary?"

"Oh, I have so misjudged her character. She is such a good person and has such a gentle heart. I fear I have never treated her as well as she deserves."

Elizabeth felt that she had underestimated Mary's intellect and sweet soul.

Though Mary could be pedantic and tiresome at times, her behavior was a philosophic effort to make herself known to others. Regrettably, her behavior could only be interpreted as prideful and, therefore, would repel the very people she was hoping to attract.

Elizabeth was resolved to improve her relationships with all her family. Though she could not approve of her two youngest sisters' behavior, they did have many good qualities that deserved her respect, and they could only benefit from an increase of attention on her part.

"Mary has changed since your accident. She is kinder, more attentive to everyone, and a pleasure to be around. She was very afraid for you as we all were. I am pleased to know that you two are growing closer. We all need each other very much."

"My whole family has become very important to me since my accident. You must tell me about your evening. Did you dance with Mr. Bingley?" asked Elizabeth with a teasing smile. "I must know all about it!"

"I did. He is such a wonderful man. If you had to be anywhere but at home, I am glad you are under his care and protection. He dances so gracefully, has pleasing manners, and always has something kind to say to everyone he meets."

"Tell me more!"

"I shivered when he took my hand and led me to the dance. It was thrilling to spend even those brief moments with him as we went down the dance. I did not want him to let me go. We spoke while we danced, and it is not just that he is intelligent, but the sound of his voice seemed to penetrate my whole body. I felt as if I were a part of him. We spent as much time together as we could. Indeed, I had no interest in anyone else."

"Do you love him?" Elizabeth was certain that she already knew the answer. Jane had never spoken of any gentleman in such terms.

"Yes, I confess I do love him."

"I am so happy for you, though I must admit I am not surprised. The expression on your face every time you speak of him betrays the feelings you have for him. I completely approve your choice. He is a good man."

After a pause, Jane continued. "And we spoke of your friend."

"My friend?" Elizabeth's confusion dispelled when she realized who the friend in question must be. Her face lit up with a smile.

Jane laughed. "Please tell me about Mr. Darcy."

"You are quite right. We have become good friends. He comes to visit me throughout the day, and we talk and laugh together. I find him to be quite a handsome man, full of good humor and serious thought." Looking up at Jane, whose face held a somber expression, she added, "You are not angry with me, are you?"

"I could never be angry with you. I do not want to see you get hurt, that is all." Jane smiled at Elizabeth and then reassured her. "Mr. Bingley has nothing but the highest regard for Mr. Darcy." Jane paused for a moment. "Mr. Darcy and I spoke of you last night."

"What did you say?"

"I can tell that he likes you very much. I know it is inappropriate for me to tell you that, but since I know, I want you to know."

"I know that he likes me. Do you think it could ever be more?"

"You deserve to be happy, and I think he could make you so. I just do not want you to raise your expectations and be hurt, that is all."

"Why do you think I will be hurt?"

"It is just that he is so wealthy and comes from an important, established family, and we ... " Jane's voice trailed off.

"I know, but nothing like that seems to be important when we are together."

The young ladies were interrupted by a knock at the door. Jane looked at Elizabeth, who shared a knowing glance with her.

Darcy was granted leave to enter the room. "Oh, forgive me," he said on seeing Miss Bennet. "I did not mean to interrupt. Please excuse me." He began to step out of the room.

"Mr. Darcy, you are very welcome to stay," said Jane. She could not help but notice how Lizzy's face lit up when he entered. She decided it was a little too late to be warning Lizzy not to fall in love with Mr. Darcy.

"Thank you, Miss Bennet," he said as he walked back into the room. "Good morning, Miss Elizabeth."

"Good morning, sir."

"I was just telling my sister about the pleasant evening we enjoyed at the assembly last night."

Darcy looked pleased. "Yes. It was a wonderful gathering. Meryton seems filled with kind, friendly people."

"Did you dance often, Mr. Darcy?" asked Elizabeth. She wrinkled her brow as a feeling of jealousy passed through her heart at the thought of Mr. Darcy dancing with anyone but herself. More cheerfully, she added, "I venture to say that you must be an excellent dancer."

"Do you think so? I cannot say. You will have to decide for yourself at the next ball." He laughed. "In answer to your question, I danced with three of your sisters, with Miss Lucas, Miss Maria Lucas, and Miss Bingley. They are all very pleasing young women. I was sorry you were not able to attend. Do you enjoy dancing?"

Jane noticed that Mr. Darcy seemed genuinely fond of Lizzy, and she hoped that her impression of him was wrong. If his intentions were not honorable, it was within his power to hurt Elizabeth very much, and Lizzy did not seem to want to guard herself against the possibility.

"Oh, yes, very much. I enjoy moving up and down the set with the music. There is such a feeling of freedom in it for me, like the wind blowing through my hair when I walk in the evening breeze." Elizabeth smiled shyly. "And particularly when I have a pleasing partner."

Jane cleared her throat. "Well, I think I should be going. Lizzy, I will give your love to our family." Jane gave Elizabeth a kiss, and then with a glance at Mr. Darcy added, "And, Lizzy, promise me that you will rest."

"I will. You will come again tomorrow, will you not? I would very much like that. I would enjoy finishing our conversation."

"As would I." Jane grinned. "Good day, Mr. Darcy."

"Let me see you out, Miss Bennet." Fortunately for Darcy, Anne chose that moment to return to Elizabeth's bedchamber, bringing with her a book. Jane stepped back so Anne could seat herself on the other side of the room.

"I thank you, no. Please keep Lizzy company." After smiling at her sister, she left the room to search for Mr. Bingley and bid him good day.

WHEN JANE HAD CLOSED THE door and Anne's attention was called away by her book, Darcy sat down in the chair that Miss Bennet had just vacated.

"Your sister loves you very much, Miss Elizabeth." He had observed their interactions on several occasions, and the affection the sisters felt for each other was apparent in the sparkle in their eyes when they spoke to each other, the gentle words they used, and in Miss Bennet's constant attention to Elizabeth. It was a pleasure to behold, and he resolved in his heart to be a better brother to Georgiana.

"What shall we talk about today?" Elizabeth asked in a playful manner.

He chose to answer her with his own question. "What think you of books?"

"My father had a good library, and we were always encouraged to read, therefore, I have read histories and poetry, letters and prose. I find that I prefer Shakespeare's dramatic plays to any other."

"Which is your favorite?

"I know it may not be proper for a young lady of genteel breeding to say so, but my favorite is *Hamlet*." She favored him with a teasing smile, daring him to rebuke her taste.

"I had not expected that you would like such a dark play. Pray, which part is your favorite?"

Darcy was impressed with many of the qualities he found in Elizabeth. Now, he added intelligence to that list of virtues. He was in great danger of being thoroughly and completely in love with her. Could he marry her despite family and the social demands that found her to be wanting in those aspects of status and fortune that would be expected of the woman who would become the mistress of Pemberley?

"I do not have a particular part I like more than others, but I am drawn to think about the nature of Hamlet and Ophelia's relationship. Hamlet was prevented from marrying her because he was expected to marry a woman who would provide an increase to the kingdom because of her place in her own society, or would promote the cause of peace between two countries betwixt whom some tension existed."

"Are not those good reasons to marry?" He was uncomfortable with the fact that Hamlet's motives and his own appeared to be similar, and he expected that in her next breath Elizabeth would condemn them both.

"I do not think so. Ophelia was a good woman who genuinely loved Hamlet. She was not interested in being queen, and she cared not for the riches and prestige such a marriage would provide her. All she wanted was Hamlet. And because he was weak and would not stand up against his uncle, a man he already knew to be evil, he broke her heart. She died because of it, and he spent the rest of his short life being miserable. Had he married her, none of the other problems in the story would have happened. While it would have made for a less interesting play, certainly Hamlet would have enjoyed great benefits from being loved by such a woman as Ophelia."

"I had never considered Hamlet from that point of view before. Tell me, why will you marry?"

She bowed her head and did not look at him when she answered. "I will marry only for reasons of the deepest love and affection."

Chapter 6

Jane left Elizabeth's bedchamber and descended the stairs into the hall. She was walking towards the entryway when she heard his voice. She could not help but smile when Mr. Bingley drew near her.

"Miss Bennet, have you been visiting your sister?" He colored when he realized how silly his question had been. He sighed inwardly.

"Yes, I was. Mr. Darcy joined us."

"I am not surprised at that. I know he intended to go to her this morning." He hesitated and then glanced at her with a questioning look. "Will you join me for tea?"

Jane had not anticipated this. She had been hoping for just a few words with him. "I would be grateful, sir."

Bingley ushered her into the drawing room and sent a servant for tea. After they were seated, Miss Bennet emptied her heart of the burden of gratitude that she felt for Mr. Bingley.

"Sir, let me thank you again and again for caring for Elizabeth. Because of your kind attentions and solicitude, she will soon be in full health and able to return home. I am filled with gratitude and only wish there was something I could do for you in return. I wish I could express all that I feel. You are everything to us…and to me."

He looked at her intently for a moment, as if deep in thought. Little did she know he was rallying his courage.

"Well, there is something that you can do, Miss Bennet."

"Oh, please tell me."

"You said I am everything to you…"

Jane waited a moment, but he did not continue.

"That is true, sir."

"Well...I want you to be everything to me."

The tender expression on his face and his barely audible whisper spoke of love, and her heart leapt for joy at this acknowledgment of his attachment to her.

"I will."

Jane lost all notice of time and, before she knew it, had been with him over an hour. By the time she left Netherfield, she could think of nothing else.

DARCY CONTEMPLATED WITH EXCITEMENT THE prospect of being with Elizabeth that afternoon. She bade him enter with a happy voice, and he once again enjoyed a welcoming smile from Anne. Darcy moved to the chair next to her bed at her invitation, and once they had completed the usual salutations, they resumed their conversation. "Mr. Darcy, please tell me about your home."

"I share my time between my townhouse in London and Pemberley, my estate in Derbyshire, which is near a little market town called Lambton." Darcy saw a look of recognition on her face. "Do you know it?"

"My aunt is from Lambton and has told me all about the place. She has nothing but the fondest memories of her life there. Is Pemberley a beautiful home?"

Elizabeth moved herself beneath the bedclothes so that she was as near Darcy as she dared. This did not go unnoticed by the gentleman. He sat on the edge of his chair and leaned towards her as he spoke.

"It is, and I am certain that someone who enjoys being out of doors as much as you could spend hours wandering the grounds of Pemberley. There is a stream and a small lake next to the house and verdant woods surrounding the whole place. It is peaceful and is a refuge for me from the cares of the world."

Images of a beautiful house and delightful grounds filled Elizabeth's mind as she contemplated what it must be like and how she would feel exploring new places and, perhaps, doing so with him.

"And do you live there quite alone?"

"My sister is there in the summer months, but she spends most of her time in London where she can enjoy the benefit of masters."

Elizabeth noticed the proud look in his eye. It was obvious that he cared very deeply for his sister. Elizabeth wondered how the lives of her family would have been changed if they had such a loving, caring brother in their family. It was easy to feel envious of Miss Darcy until she recollected that her interest in Mr. Darcy was not fraternal, but something entirely different.

"She must be quite accomplished."

"I am very proud of her, but she is shy and has been since the death of our father."

"It must be difficult for you to be responsible for the education and development of a young woman at such a delicate time of life."

"I can only do my best, and fortunately, Georgiana is patient with me. I fear that sometimes I overwhelm her, for she is quiet and will not always express her thoughts. I often feel she is trying to live up to expectations she believes I have for her, but she is everything I could want in a sister."

"I am certain she loves you very much." She added silently, *for who could not?* "And is London, then, your primary residence?"

Elizabeth realized all the impertinence of her question, but her mind and heart sought knowledge of Mr. Darcy for which her good manners could not answer.

"I consider Pemberley to be my home, and when I settle down, it will be the place to which I shall bring my wife." He nervously cleared his throat.

She hesitated for a moment when he spoke of a future wife. Was that meant for her benefit? Did he know the desires of her heart?

"Do you not go to London for the season and all its gaieties?"

"When I am required to attend."

"Required?"

"Required. I feel as though I am on display for all the mothers who seek a good match for their daughters. It appears that my only attraction is wealth and a good name." Darcy exhaled and stared at the floor. "I wish…"

There was a pause, and after each moment, Elizabeth expected that he would finish his thought. She realized that he was not going to continue speaking, but she was unwilling to let the subject drop.

"Mr. Darcy, for what do you wish?" She boldly reached out her hand to him and felt his fingers surround hers. She experienced the same closeness with him as she had the day they had spoken of their parents.

Darcy marveled at the softness of her skin and was pleased that she would make such an overture of affection.

"For what do I wish?" Looking up, he met her gaze. "The unexpected."

During the ensuing silence, Elizabeth reflected on what he just told her. He caressed her fingers, and it took a moment for her to gather her thoughts.

"The unexpected," she repeated, drowning in his intense gaze. "Is it really unexpected that you could be loved for who you are rather than what you own and where you live?"

Darcy knew he must go. He knew he could not spend another moment with her, or he would blurt out a proposal of marriage, one that he felt would be disastrous. It violated the principles by which his father had raised him and would go against the expectations of his family.

He slowly raised her hand to his lips and gently kissed her fingers.

"You are too good." He stood and slowly left the room.

ELIZABETH WAS NEARLY OVERWHELMED WITH emotion as she watched Darcy leave. The touch of his hand, the gentleness in his voice, and the meaning of his words all spoke of the deepest affection for her. It was sad that he believed that finding a woman who would love him was unexpected. She wished that she would be his choice. She knew she could be that woman, the one who would love him for who he was and for no other reason. It would be easy for her, for she already did.

HAVING SUBMITTED PATIENTLY TO ALL of Mr. Manning's recommendations for bed rest, Elizabeth found herself anxious to be outside again. Knowing that the gentlemen were away, she resolved on leaving the house for a short time.

Her maid was shocked when Elizabeth announced her intentions.

"Miss Elizabeth, please do not. Your head! Mr. Manning's instructions! Think of your health. Please, Miss."

"Nothing will be better for me than fresh air and exercise. I shall be gone for only a short while. You must help me." She arose from the bed and began to dress.

"What if something were to happen to you? Please, let me bring you some tea or a glass of wine or a book, but please do not go out."

"You have been such a help and a comfort to me, Anne, and I do not want you to be distressed on my behalf, but I must go out." She could not remain indoors another minute. She had no complaints about Netherfield or the way in which she was being treated. Indeed, she was all gratitude, but only inclement weather normally kept her indoors, and it was so pleasant outside that she knew she must enjoy it, if only for a few minutes.

"Do you insist on this, Miss Elizabeth?"

"I do."

Anne gave way to Elizabeth, though against her better judgment. "Very well, but do not stay away for long, I beg you. Where will you go? How shall I find you if you become ill?" Anne's apprehension was growing.

"Oh, Anne," laughed Elizabeth, "I am certain I will not be ill."

Elizabeth said all she could to reassure Anne, but Anne's fears were not quieted by her assurances.

Having said all she could, Elizabeth stepped out onto the porch and looked around her. The woods to the north seemed inviting, so she told Anne that she would walk for a little while in that direction.

"I will return in no time at all."

She had been indoors far too long. The feel of a warm breeze and the sounds of birds in the trees strengthened and refreshed her. She felt animated and rejuvenated as she walked through the woods around the house. Recalling a place a short distance away where she knew a stream was to be found, she steered her path in that direction.

THE WATER HAD NEVER LOOKED more clear and inviting. Sitting on a rock, Elizabeth put her hand in the stream, allowing the water to pass through her fingers, and rejoiced in the sensation. She lost herself in the pleasure of being outdoors, unconscious of the passing of time. Quite inattentive to everything around her, she did not notice the approach of a gentleman.

ANNE COULD NOT LET MISS Elizabeth leave the house without feelings of misgiving and regret and nervously paced back and forth in the entryway listening for her return. After not too long a time, she heard footsteps approaching and thought, with no small relief, that Miss Elizabeth had returned, but it was Mr. Darcy who entered the house.

"Good afternoon, Anne." Anne appeared to be fretful and uncommonly pale.

"What is the matter?"

He was fearful that Elizabeth had taken ill once again. Anne's agitated manner was clearly alarming.

"It is Miss Elizabeth, sir. She has left the house to walk about the grounds. I tried to dissuade her, but she would not listen. She has been gone these ten minutes at least."

"Do you know where she went? Did she say where she might go?"

"She said she was going to walk into the woods to the north. I am sorry, but she would not be prevented from going."

"We do not want to give Mr. Bingley any cause for alarm. Please wait in Miss Elizabeth's room, and I will go after her."

Wending his way in the direction that Anne had indicated, Darcy's thoughts were in turmoil. How could he forgive himself if something should happen to Elizabeth?

He took a deep breath to calm himself and then laughed. There was, perhaps, no way of preventing such a circumstance, for that same independent spirit that possessed her before her fall possessed her still, and he imagined she could not long endure the restriction of her room. He would find her and return her to Netherfield, offering every argument for the need for her to comply with Mr. Manning's directions and would apologize to that man for Elizabeth should her indiscretion become known.

It was not long before he reached the water. Looking downstream, where the brush and woods were clear, he caught sight of a vision he would never forget. Sitting on a rock next to the stream, with her hand in the water, was Elizabeth. The sunlight glistened on her dark hair, and exertion had lent a delightful appearance of liveliness to her complexion. She was an image of beauty and loveliness.

He was able to observe her for a few moments without being seen. He knew it was wrong not to make his presence known to her, but he could not help but admire the gracefulness of her movements and the look of contentment that suffused her face.

He gently spoke her name so as not to alarm her.

She looked up and favored him with the most radiant smile he had ever beheld. He gloried in the fact that it was all for him.

How he loved— He stopped himself in the middle of the treacherous thought. However true it might be, it was not permissible for him to love her.

"Good afternoon. I understand that Netherfield became a little too confining for you today." He approached her slowly and then sat on a rock beside her.

"Indeed it did, sir. Did you come in search of me, or do I owe the pleasure of meeting you to coincidence?"

He knew she was teasing him, and he felt his resolve melt away. She looked lovelier and her disposition was more cheerful and playful than he had ever witnessed in her.

"I came upon Anne in the entryway as I returned to the house, and she told me of your escape. I immediately came after you." He paused for a moment, matching her gaze. "She is very worried about you, as am I."

Elizabeth smiled at him.

"I recall that Mr. Manning's instructions to you were to remain in bed awhile longer." He looked at her with a raised eyebrow, as if to playfully scold her.

"I am sorry, sir, and you are correct, of course, but I could not endure another moment without some fresh air. I rarely spend every day indoors, so you must know how impatient I was for exercise."

"You are forgiven, but are you certain you are well enough to be so thoroughly disregarding Mr. Manning's orders?"

"I am, sir. You need not worry yourself."

"I believe you, for I have never seen you look lovelier than you do now."

She blushed in a becoming way.

"And you, sir, look very well yourself." She favored him with cheerful laughter.

"You cannot know how pleased I am with your recovery. I was so worried. I was so...uncertain."

She was silent for a moment, taking in the scene before her. There was a small bird bathing in a pool of water on the edge of the stream, and the breeze moved in a lazy manner through the trees, causing them to nod their approval to a perfect day.

"I owe it all to you, I believe. Anne told me all you did for me. At first, I confess, I was uncomfortable," she instinctively reached out her hand and touched his arm, "but I am not any longer."

"I have something I ought to return to you. It was next to you when you fell. I have kept it and have been carrying it with me ever since."

Her face brightened with curiosity as he showed her the purple ribbon.

"That is from my bonnet! Is it your habit to carry ribbon around with you, sir?"

He paused and looked deeply into her dark, fine eyes. "No, but I have been unable to part with this one."

She could not respond. Just then, the breeze carried a lock of hair onto her face, and as she raised her hand to brush it back, he reached out in a quick motion and held it. Time seemed to stop for a moment as he peered into her eyes. She felt her pulse quicken and was grateful that she was sitting down.

"It is my favorite color."

She sat motionless, and felt, rather than saw him lift her hand to his lips and kiss it.

The beauty of the place, the idea that she was alone with him and the feel of his lips on her hand, caused her heart to bound, and she nearly trembled from delight. He had been carrying her ribbon with him all this time. It could only mean that he returned her love.

He opened her fingers and placed the ribbon in her hand. Instead of releasing it, he raised it to his lips and placed a lingering kiss on the inside of her wrist.

She sighed her approval. She felt his fingers on her neck and chin, and her heart stopped beating as his breath warmed her cheek.

"Elizabeth," he whispered, "I..."

He could say no more.

Their lips met in a gentle caress, and as she closed her eyes, her heart went out to him, and she knew from that moment she would be bound to him forever.

Silently, Darcy took Elizabeth's hand and helped her to her feet. By unspoken agreement, they turned and began a slow walk to the house. He offered her his arm and she took it, nestling close to him.

Her silence as they walked together spoke of the depth of her feelings for him. She had opened her heart, nay, her whole soul to him, and she now looked to him as the protector of all that was good in her. The gift of her love came with a heart unsullied by previous attachment. He was the only one she had ever loved, and there would never be another. She received his love purely and innocently, understanding no other way for love to be offered. No regret furrowed her brow. No mistrust dimmed her mind. All that she had and all that she was belonged to him

ANNE HAD NOT RETURNED UPSTAIRS as Mr. Darcy had requested, but was waiting for them in the entryway. She joined them as Darcy escorted Elizabeth back to her room. He opened the door, and Elizabeth stepped into her bedchamber.

Meeting Elizabeth's eyes with a look that spoke of love and yearning, he closed the distance between them. She took his hand and placed the ribbon in it. Without taking his eyes off her, he kissed the ribbon and put it in his pocket near his heart. He took her outstretched hand, and kissed her fingers, lingering over her hand for just a moment, and then without a word, turned and left the room.

OH, HOW HE LOVED HER! Oh, how he wanted her!

Darcy's mind was in a state of confusion as he stumbled down the hall and into his room. He collapsed into a chair and experienced all the guilt and self-reproach that had been building inside him since he met Elizabeth by the stream. Kissing her was a liberty he should not have taken, for it violated every sense of honor he held dear.

Echoing in his ears was the sound of his father's voice pronouncing her unsuitability. He would never forget his last conversation with him.

Darcy had been attending his uncle at Matlock when he received word that his father had summoned him home. It was very unlike his father to request anything, so it was with a great deal of concern that he left Matlock for Pemberley. It was a trip of only one day, and he arrived in good time. He went immediately to the study where his father was usually to be found.

The study was empty, but Mrs. Reynolds had learned of his arrival.

"Master Fitzwilliam! Welcome home, sir. It is a pleasure to see you."

"Yes, thank you. I was summoned by my father, but he is not here, he — "

"Forgive me. Your father is in his bedchamber."

"His bedchamber?"

"He was very ill. We were all very worried about him."

"Is that why he called me home?"

"Yes. Go to him directly."

Darcy hurried to his father's room. He paused for a moment to catch his breath, and then knocked on the door.

His father responded. "Come in, Mrs. Reynolds."

Darcy opened the door to find his father in bed, looking frail against a background of pillows and blankets.

"It is I, Father! I came as soon as —"

"Fitzwilliam!" said the elder Darcy as he recognized his mistake. "It is a pleasure to see you, my son. Thank you for coming."

"What is the matter? Why do you take to your bed?"

"I wanted to see you; that is all."

Darcy was not convinced. His father had spent a lifetime avoiding him.

"What is the reason for my summons?"

"I was quite ill when I sent for you. I was certain I was going to die. I wanted to speak with you."

"Father?"

"I feel much better now. So much so, that I am planning to leave my room tomorrow. You have traveled a long way, and I have interrupted your pleasures. You deserve to know."

"To know what?" Darcy took a chair and seated himself near the bed.

"It had been my intention to tell you about my will, to reveal to you where your mother's jewels are stored for safekeeping, and to pass along words of advice to help you as you faced the prospect of being the master of Pemberley."

"There is no reason for this, Father. I am certain —"

"Please, let me speak. I will be brief. In my will, I have left the entirety of the Pemberley estate and all that I am possessed of to you. Georgiana will have her mother's jewels and a dowry of thirty thousand pounds. I know it is customary for tokens of thanks to be extended to faithful servants and tenants, but not knowing beforehand who would be worthy of such consideration, I leave it to you to make whatever gifts you feel are appropriate.

"The desk in the study is ponderous and heavy, but if you will slide it forward, you will find that it rests on a loose floorboard. Beneath this board is a strongbox containing your mother's jewels. I believe that Georgiana is too young to be responsible for her mother's legacy. Perhaps you will give them to her someday in the future when she is settled.

"I have an able steward, Fitzwilliam, who has promised me like service to you as I have received from him, and Mrs. Reynolds, dear soul, is quite capable of managing the household. But remember, Fitzwilliam, Pemberley will never be complete until it possesses a mistress. Have you considered the matter of marriage?"

"I enjoy the company of young women, but I have never met anyone with whom I would wish to spend my life."

"My son, you must choose wisely. The woman you marry will determine the measure of happiness or despair that you will experience in this life. It is difficult to know matters of the heart beforehand. My only advice is this: Marry your equal. Wed yourself to a woman of beauty, rank, and fortune. She must be possessed of a worthy family whose society will be advantageous to you and by whose interest your fortune and influence will be promoted. Do not be carried away by the violence of emotions that some would call love. Attach yourself to a woman who will not disappoint and with whom you can be seen with pride on all occasions. Do not let passion interfere with your future.

"Georgiana's prospects for an equal alliance will be endangered if you do not choose such a woman. What man would attach himself to a family where vulgarity reigns? Remember Georgiana!" The old man paused for a moment. "But you will remember her. You have always loved her, even when I… I am satisfied. She will be well cared for under your protection."

Darcy's father kept his promise and left his bedchamber the next day. He and his son were always together during the days that followed, and for the first time in his life, young Darcy knew what it was to have a father. Longing to be loved by him, he promised himself that he would never do anything of which his father might not approve.

Within a short time, the elder Mr. Darcy was fully recovered and persuaded Darcy to return to Matlock. Sadly, two weeks later, Darcy received his father's final summons to Pemberley.

DARCY'S FATHER HAD TOLD HIM that if he married below his station, he would soon lose respect for his wife and be unable to bear her society. He would then fall victim to the vices of the world as he tried to comfort himself from the knowledge that his domestic happiness had been overthrown. The question of an heir had to be addressed as well. How could a woman of inferior birth produce an heir worthy of the honor and prestige of Pemberley? Elizabeth's mother was vulgar, and the family was perpetually scandalized by the behavior of the two youngest Bennet sisters.

The elder Mr. Darcy had said that he need look no farther than his own family for proof. His cousin, Colonel Fitzwilliam's elder brother, the viscount, had married beneath him, shunning women of rank and nobility to attach himself to the daughter of a tradesman. He claimed that he loved her, and she him, but it had ended in misery. Without mutual respect or lasting affection, they were two strangers living in the same home. He was unwilling to move in her circles, and she was unable to move in his. After the ardor of first love passed, they were left without common interests or respect for each other. Their unhappiness was common knowledge, as was the fact that the viscount kept a mistress. Darcy did not want that for himself, and he certainly did not want that for Elizabeth. He would not allow her to be hurt.

Darcy had been motivated by a desire stronger than duty and obligation when he kissed her. The love he felt for Elizabeth had driven reason away. The anguish he felt in knowing that he could never have her exceeded that which he felt at the time of his father's death.

One doubt in particular plagued Darcy's mind. Did not these words of caution come from a father who had left his children alone for months on end, year after year, since the death of their mother?

Darcy's heart ached for Elizabeth. In her, he knew he would find love and acceptance, but the gulf between them was unsurpassable. Feeling that he had never been acceptable to his father, he suffered under the belief that he could not disappoint him any further, and a marriage to Elizabeth would be just such a disappointment. His father never would have approved of her. He would not involve Elizabeth in endless ruin.

He knew his resolve weakened when in Elizabeth's presence and that he had no strength to resist the love she offered him. With that kiss, Elizabeth had shown that she was ready to pledge herself to him. For her sake, he could not remain at Netherfield. He must leave her, and do so without seeing her again. He would not become the man Elizabeth's sister accused him of being. He would not trifle with Elizabeth.

She would not understand, of course. The love she had for him was all too apparent, but a short period of pain was far preferable to a lifetime of heartache. Resolved to his decision, though agonized by it, he summoned his valet and told him they would be leaving for London early the next morning.

ELIZABETH REJOICED IN THE PASSION and tenderness of Mr. Darcy's kiss. This was an intimacy she had never known. The desire she felt for him nearly overwhelmed her, and she basked in the memory of the delight she felt when his lips touched hers. She would willingly proclaim to the world that she loved him. Never had she imagined that such feelings were possible.

Elizabeth knew that she would not see Darcy again until the next day, but she was content. He loved her, and that was all she cared about.

Chapter 7

Darcy was in agony the next morning. He had slept very ill, having been awakened repeatedly throughout the night by vicious dreams. The most distressing, and most often repeated, was the one in which he experienced all the joy of marrying Elizabeth, but when he turned to kiss her after the ceremony, she was in tears, accusing him of betraying her. These visions were intermingled with lectures from his father on the expectations he had for young Fitzwilliam when it came to matters of marriage. "Do not settle for an unequal alliance." Those words echoed in his mind.

Bingley, on the other hand, had slept very well, with pleasant dreams of a happy future with Miss Bennet. There was no guilt or pain to disturb his slumber. Refreshed and ready for the day, he was up early, and intended to go downstairs and await the others in the breakfast room.

Darcy exited his room just as Bingley was passing by. The two friends greeted each other, though their manner of speaking was markedly different. Whereas Bingley was cheerful and pleasant, Darcy was nervous and distracted.

"You are up early, Darcy. Join me in the breakfast room, where we can have tea while Cook prepares our meal." So saying, he put his hand on Darcy's shoulder as if to usher him into that room.

Darcy stiffly resisted this entreaty and shrugged Bingley's hand away.

"Forgive me." There was only the slightest hint of an apology in Darcy's voice. "I am leaving for London almost this instant."

Bingley was surprised to learn that his friend meditated a quick removal to Town, for Darcy planned his journeys carefully and never left unannounced.

"Why? You have not been here three weeks, and yet you are leaving?" This was unfathomable to him. Bingley was persuaded that Darcy was in love with

Miss Elizabeth and could not understand why he would want to leave her now.

"Business has come up that calls me away, and I desire to see Georgiana." How pathetic that he should use his own sister as an excuse to further his deception.

Bingley followed Darcy to the entryway, where the latter began pacing in front of a window watching for his carriage. Bingley's eyes followed Darcy's progress back and forth across the floor.

"Business? Have you received an express from Town of which I am unaware? Come, man! Please stay. I will invite Georgiana here. Let her join us at Netherfield. You need not go. You must stay! I insist. I —"

"NO!" Darcy's response was delivered heatedly.

Bingley could not recall a time when Darcy had raised his voice to him and so was shaken by this rebuke. Before he could respond, however, Darcy spoke again, this time more subdued.

"Please forgive me, but Georgiana must remain in London."

"Very well, but had I not encountered you in the hall, would you have left without a word to me?"

Darcy looked away and did not answer.

Bingley, who was in pain for his friend, was immediately disconcerted by Darcy's intended incivility.

"When will you return?"

"Soon, I hope." Darcy did not know if that were true or not. He had to stay away from Elizabeth until he could conquer his feelings for her. Perhaps he could never return, for he knew full well what her feelings were for him.

Darcy turned his back on Bingley, straining to hear any sound that might signal the arrival of his carriage and the end of the uncomfortable interview.

Given the early hour and Darcy's agitation, Bingley was struck by a terrible thought.

"Have you told Miss Elizabeth that you are leaving?"

Darcy looked at him for a moment, his grave countenance answering Bingley's question. A carriage was heard rounding the house.

"I...I must go."

"What? You have not spoken with her?"

"I have not. I cannot."

"You cannot? I thought...I thought you cared for her."

Bingley could not understand why Darcy would leave Miss Elizabeth and began to suspect that Darcy was not just leaving Netherfield but running away from her.

"Have you quarreled with Miss Elizabeth; have you had a disagreement? Please, you cannot leave her without some conversation! Why are you being so cruel? Do you not love her? You cannot tell me that you do not!"

Darcy's voice was a rasping whisper as he made an honest confession. "Yes, I do love her."

Bingley was shocked and made no answer as Darcy turned and fled from the house and into his waiting carriage. He left without saying another word. He was gone.

Bingley watched the coach drive out the gate. "Darcy, what have you done?"

ELIZABETH PATIENTLY AWAITED MR. DARCY'S visit. She could honestly say that she was fully recovered from her fall, and while desirous to return to Longbourn, she had promised Jane she would not remove until Mr. Manning released her from his care.

Mr. Darcy usually came to visit her by now, but she was not concerned. He would come as he always did. She wanted to know more about his childhood and his years at school, and desired to tell him everything she could about her family. She hoped for just a moment that they would be left alone, that having some errand or other, Anne would leave the room.

Elizabeth responded to a knock at her door, knowing full well by the sound that it was not Mr. Darcy.

Mr. Bingley hesitantly entered the room. "Good morning, Miss Elizabeth. Good morning, Anne."

"Good morning, sir."

Anne discerned an expression of strain in Mr. Bingley's eyes. She could sense his discomfort and wondered what was disturbing him. She also noticed that Miss Elizabeth seemed entirely unaware that anything might be the matter.

"Good morning, Mr. Bingley," answered Elizabeth. "It is a pleasure to see you."

"It is a beautiful day today."

"Yes, it is. Anne opened the curtains for me early this morning."

"I am delighted to see you in such obvious good health. Do you know what Mr. Manning's plans are for you?" It was only on rare occasions that Bingley had been required to carry ill tidings to another person. He considered himself unequal to the task, particularly in this instance. As painful as it would be, he had to tell her the truth about Darcy's departure from Netherfield.

"He is to come this morning. If he determines that I am well, which I am, he will allow me to leave in two days. Everyone here has been so kind to me. I shall be sorry to leave."

"Miss Elizabeth, I have something to tell you that is upsetting to me, and I fear your disapprobation."

Bingley crossed the room and stood near her bed. He had not spent much time in company with her, so while he was aware of her attachment to Darcy, until that morning, he had not known the extent of it.

"I will always approve of you, sir. What is your news?"

Bingley turned away from Miss Elizabeth. "Mr. Darcy left for London very early this morning."

Elizabeth was not prepared for this news. She was not prepared for anything other than Mr. Darcy walking through the door of her bedchamber.

"That cannot be so. Are you certain? Did he say when he would be back?"

"He only said that he would return soon. Did he not come to bid you farewell?"

"No, I had no idea that he was leaving. I had expected to see him this morning." She paused for a moment, searching her mind for some explanation. "Did he leave any message for me?"

"No, he did not."

Bingley could see the brightness fade from her eyes.

"I see."

Unwilling to remain in the room and witness her unhappiness, he used Miss Bennet as an excuse to leave.

"I believe your sister is coming today. I will bring her to you as soon as she arrives."

Elizabeth looked up at him. The pain on her face was unbearable to witness.

With a bow, Bingley left the room to await with dread the arrival of Miss Bennet. She was very protective of Miss Elizabeth and would neither understand nor tolerate Darcy's cruelty to her sister.

A SERVANT LED JANE TO the drawing room where Mr. Bingley was sitting. She observed that he seemed oblivious to the noise and activity of the house, and she dismissed the servant before she could be announced. She wanted to spend a moment studying Mr. Bingley's features but became concerned when she noticed that he appeared somewhat agitated.

"Mr. Bingley, are you well?"

Bingley turned at the sound of her voice. "Forgive me for not receiving you properly. You are very welcome to Netherfield, Miss Bennet."

"Thank you, sir. May I take the liberty of asking what is troubling you?"

"I am pained and distressed, not only for myself, but for others, as well."

"May I be of any —"

"It is a very unfortunate business and has caused me great concern. Mr. Darcy left Netherfield early this morning without seeing Miss Elizabeth or leaving any message for her."

"What? I do not understand. Why would Mr. Darcy do such a thing?" An icy feeling rushed through Jane's heart. This is what she had feared most. She knew that Elizabeth loved Mr. Darcy with her whole heart. She would be devastated. "Does Elizabeth know?"

"Yes. I have just returned from informing her."

"You should have allowed me to tell her!"

Jane's face was flushed with anger and resentment. She had warned Mr. Darcy, yet he had done this. How was she to help Elizabeth heal from this blow? She blamed herself for not doing more to discourage Elizabeth's interest in Mr. Darcy and for trusting everyone at Netherfield to care for her.

"Miss Bennet, please —"

"I must go to Elizabeth immediately."

Mr. Bingley followed Jane as she left the drawing room and moved quickly up the stairs. Taking a deep breath, she knocked on the door to Elizabeth's bedchamber.

"Lizzy, it is Jane. Please allow me to come in."

Elizabeth did not answer

Jane turned to Mr. Bingley. "Would you please excuse me?"

"Yes, of course."

Jane watched him retreat to the staircase before opening the door.

"Lizzy?"

Jane was immediately distressed. Anne had been dismissed and Elizabeth was not in her bed. Jane rushed into the room to find her sister near the dressing table, struggling with pins and buttons in an effort to dress herself. Large, silent tears poured from her eyes. Her whole body trembled.

Jane put her arms around her and murmured comforting words. Elizabeth returned the embrace and slowly began to relax.

"Mr. Darcy is gone," Elizabeth whimpered. "He offered no explanation. He just left Netherfield this morning without a word to me. I do not understand what happened or what I said to make him go away. Jane, I want to go home."

"But what about Mr. Manning's —"

"I do not care for Mr. Manning's opinion! I cannot remain here any longer."

"Of course, Lizzy." Jane sympathized with Elizabeth's desire to leave and would not refuse her.

"Please, help me."

"Here, turn around…"

While helping her dress, Jane's thoughts raged against Mr. Darcy. She would never forgive him if anything happened to Elizabeth because she was leaving without Mr. Manning's consent.

"Lizzy, please rest here for a moment. I will call for our carriage," Jane said as she assisted her sister to a chair.

Jane descended the stairs and found Mr. Bingley waiting for her in the hall.

"It was never my intention to assume your place, Miss Bennet. Please forgive me for informing Miss Elizabeth of Darcy's departure, but I felt she ought to know as soon as possible. How is your sister? Is there anything I can do?"

"She is not well, sir, and insists on removing to Longbourn. Please call for our carriage."

"I am familiar with Mr. Manning's instructions. She is welcome to remain here."

"She is determined and will not be swayed, nor will I make any attempt to persuade her otherwise."

Bingley was not surprised. "I will call for your carriage and send Anne to pack her trunk."

"Thank you, but we must leave at once. Please send the trunk around later." Her voice softened. "I regret that we are to leave under such circumstances. I know you meant no harm."

He nodded, grateful for one kind word from her.

"You must be aware of Elizabeth's attachment to Mr. Darcy — an attachment that she felt was reciprocated. It would appear to me that he was merely trifling with her affection."

Feeling a need to defend the integrity of his friend, he made a feeble effort to speak in his defense. "Darcy said he would return soon." Bingley regretted making that statement the moment he had expressed it.

"That is of small comfort to Elizabeth, sir!"

Jane turned and went upstairs to assist Elizabeth. Thankfully, she had heard nothing of Jane's exchange with Mr. Bingley.

As the young women descended the stairs, Elizabeth leaned heavily on Jane's arm, causing the latter to understand that perhaps Elizabeth was not as strong as she had believed.

Elizabeth was aware of nothing around her. Jane, attending to her sister, ignored an apology that Mr. Bingley was attempting to make as they left the house.

IT WAS NOT UNTIL THE carriage approached the halfway point to Longbourn that Elizabeth spoke.

"Thank you for taking me home. I could not have remained there. I could not... Oh, Jane!" A sob racked her body.

Jane knew not what to say. She was grateful to have been at hand, and knowing Elizabeth's temperament as she did, she was certain that Elizabeth would have fled Netherfield on foot. "What can I say to comfort you?"

"I do not understand. I know he loves me."

"Please do not say such things. If he truly loved you, he would not have gone."

"He does love me, Jane!"

Jane dared not respond to this assertion. She was fearful of speaking of Mr. Darcy in a manner that might cause her sister to defend him. She had nothing pleasant to say about the detestable Mr. Darcy, but knew Elizabeth was too deeply touched by him to be able to listen to her opinion.

"I feel so cold and alone, like a part of me is missing. I do not recognize my own reflection in the glass."

Jane assisted Elizabeth to her room and saw her safely into bed. Unwilling to leave her alone, Jane sat with her through the night. Occasionally, she drifted off to sleep but woke with every movement and sound that Elizabeth made. Twice, she laid herself on the bed to comfort Elizabeth while she cried. Not since their father's death had Jane witnessed such sorrow. Only one who loved with her whole heart could suffer so much under the pain of losing the object of that love.

DURING THOSE MOMENTS WHEN ELIZABETH was sleeping, Jane had time to reflect soberly on the events of the day. She had regrets of her own. She was angry with herself for being unkind to Mr. Bingley. Were she in Elizabeth's place, she would have wanted to know immediately about Mr. Darcy's departure. Mr. Bingley was correct in breaking the news to Elizabeth, but had she been there, she was certain that he would have agreed that it was her place to do it.

The possibility that Mr. Bingley might think ill of her was troubling, but it helped her to understand her own feelings. She had liked other men, but there was no other man that made her feel the way he did, and if she had her wish, she would never be parted from Mr. Bingley again. Now it might be too late. He had good cause to be offended by her words. She wished it was in her power to apologize and restore his good opinion, but all she could do was hope — hope that he would come to see her and hope that she could obtain his forgiveness.

THE NEXT MORNING, BINGLEY CALLED at Longbourn. His acknowledged purpose was to be assured that Miss Elizabeth was well and had not suffered any reversal because of her early departure from Netherfield. His true motive was to ascertain Miss Bennet's feelings towards him. He was uncomfortable enough in this regard, particularly after her cold parting the day before. In all their other meetings, she had been warm and encouraging. Perhaps he was presumptuous, but he could no longer prevent himself from attempting to positively engage Miss Bennet's affections. He had suffered a long night, despairing that she would think ill of him. For his own peace of mind, he decided he would go early to Longbourn. He could not endure another night of uncertainty.

JANE HAD NOT EXPECTED TO see Mr. Bingley so soon but was pleased that he had come.

"Miss Bennet, I hope I am not intruding."

"You are very welcome to Longbourn. It is a pleasure to see you again."

They were quiet for a moment. All that passed between them was a look, but it was enough. Her fears of the prior evening were silenced.

"May I inquire after your sister? Has Mr. Manning seen her yet?"

"Yes, he came this morning. Be assured that she is well." She saw him visibly relax. "Mr. Manning sympathized with her impatience to return to Longbourn and was very kind."

"I am delighted to hear that."

"Elizabeth keeps to her room, but I will let her know that you asked after her. Mr. Bingley, I must apologize for being ungracious yesterday. I am angry with Mr. Darcy, but I know you are not responsible for his actions."

"Say nothing of it, for I join you in your anger with Darcy. I truly thought he cared for your sister."

Bingley arose and paced around the room. All the way from Netherfield, he had argued with himself as to how she would receive his addresses. Miss Bennet seemed better pleased with him than he would have thought possible.

It must be wrong, it must be too soon, but he would not turn back now. He returned to his place next to her.

"Miss Bennet, I have enjoyed our acquaintance very much, and though the circumstances under which it began were unfortunate, it has given me the greatest of pleasure."

She looked at him expectantly.

"The purpose of my visit this morning is twofold. First, it is to assure myself that your sister is well. The second," he paused for a moment, "is to seek your consent to court you. My intentions are honorable. I want to win your love and your hand."

Jane recalled Elizabeth's thoughts on marriage. "Only for reasons of the deepest love and affection." Was that enough? Was that not what Elizabeth felt for Mr. Darcy? Mr. Bingley was that man's friend and very much influenced by him. Could she trust Mr. Bingley? Should she trust him? He was very unlike his friend. Whereas Mr. Darcy masked his feelings, Mr. Bingley was open and sincere. In his whole countenance, there was an expression of honesty and integrity. He was not a complicated man. His tastes were simple and his manners pleasing.

"I welcome your attention, sir, and you have my consent."

IT WAS LATE IN THE afternoon when Darcy arrived at his London townhouse. He was grateful to escape the confines of the carriage, and being unable to move about, his agitation had only increased.

Georgiana heard his entrance and ran from the music room to meet him. Like her brother, she had dark hair and eyes. She was usually quiet and reserved, but all reserve vanished with the return of her brother.

"Fitzwilliam, welcome home! I was not expecting you so soon. Why did you not write to let me know you were coming?" She reached up to kiss his cheek.

"Urgent business called me back."

"I hope that your business can be concluded to your satisfaction and that we will be able to spend some time together." She danced around him, relieved him of his coat, and seated him by the fire.

"Thank you, Georgiana. How have you been? How are your studies?"

"I am enjoying my new music master, Mr. Henry, very much. He says I am making great progress on the pianoforte. Every day I become more comfortable sight-reading new music. Mr. Gladstone is also pleased and says I learn quickly. Mrs. Annesley undertakes the rest of my education. I am struggling with French, but I am certain I shall master it one day or other."

"I am happy to hear it. Is there any way in which I might assist you?"

"No, I thank you. I am content with my situation, but please tell me if you will about Miss Elizabeth Bennet, the young woman you mentioned in your recent letter."

Darcy winced. "There is not much to say, at least not anymore."

"Not anymore? What happened?" It was unusual for her brother to confide in her, and what he had said of Miss Elizabeth astonished her. The idea that he might be in love was welcome to her, and knowing her brother as she did, there was no doubt in her mind that any woman to whom he would attach himself would be someone that she could also love.

He sighed as the memory of Elizabeth sitting by the stream came to his mind. "Miss Elizabeth is a beautiful young woman of about twenty years of age. I enjoy her conversation and the tender affection she has for me. Unfortunately, I cannot feel the same for her."

"You cannot? How can this be?"

"I cannot marry her, so I have departed from Netherfield."

"Why can you not marry her? You obviously love her."

"And why do you think I love her, Miss Darcy?"

"Because, sir, you would never have told me about her if you did not. You never tell me about how or what you feel, so I know it would take something of great moment for you to be as open with me as you were in that letter."

"Of course, you are correct."

Georgiana had never met a young woman who did not believe herself to be in love with her brother, and while she doubted such shallow feelings in Miss Elizabeth, she felt it would be impossible for her not to return the affections of her brother.

"She has no dowry and no connections…"

"I do not understand. If you love her…"

"… and because of this, she does not meet the expectations of society as a suitable wife for the master of Pemberley. It would be an unequal alliance, and would be damaging to your own marriage prospects. Our father warned me against such matches."

Georgiana had been young when her father died and so knew nothing of his opinion of marriage, but to deny love for reasons of money seemed incomprehensible.

"You once told me, on an occasion when you were not hiding your feelings, that you wished to be loved for who you are and not what you have, yet you insist on marrying a woman who has wealth and property. You insist on marrying someone for what she has, not who she is? Are you not rich enough? Does fortune and consequence bring you that much pleasure that you would turn your back on a woman that you so fully love?"

Darcy stared at her, scarcely able to comprehend her words. He should be angry with Georgiana for speaking to him in such a manner, yet he could not. She was turning his words against him, and doing so with sharp clarity.

"You must marry for reasons of love and for no other consideration, Fitzwilliam."

Darcy started, recalling when he had last heard similar words, and by whom they had been spoken.

Georgiana had never spoken to her brother thus in her life. "That is what is unequal about your attachment to her. If you truly loved her, nothing else would matter." A distressing thought chilled her. "Does this mean I am expected to marry into fortune and consequence to uphold the Darcy name?"

A look of horror crossed her features, and she stared at him with a disbelieving expression on her face. Unwilling to stay another moment, she stood and began to leave the room.

Suddenly, she felt herself being pulled back. Darcy had grasped her arm to keep her from departing. "Georgiana, I am sorry."

"No, you are not sorry! If you were, you would return to her at once!" Her heart was heavy with feelings of compassion for Miss Elizabeth. "On what terms did you leave her?"

"I left without seeing her."

She could tell from the expression on his face that he was begging her to understand him, but she could not.

"Fitzwilliam, how could you be so cruel?" With that, she pulled her arm free and ran from the room.

JANE REJOICED IN HER NEW understanding with Mr. Bingley. He was the answer to every hope that she ever had for happiness. She could feel the depth of his affection and knew that their happiness together would be assured. They were alone and at leisure, so she determined to learn more about him.

"Mr. Bingley, there is still so much I wish to know about you. Please tell me about your family."

"I have two sisters. You have met Caroline, and I have another sister, Louisa, who lives in Town with her husband. Both my parents have passed away."

"I am sorry."

"I loved my mother very much, for she was all understanding and kindness. I wish I could say the same for my father. He was not an easy man to love. He was not fond of children. We were an inconvenience to him, I think. He expected us to be his equals and to behave in a way foreign to children. I am afraid that I disappointed him."

Jane touched his hand for a moment to let him know that he could trust her.

Bingley received her assurance with a smile. "He acquired a large fortune from trade, and it had been his desire to retire to an estate in the country, but he died before he could fulfill his dream. I had mixed feelings at his death. Part of me was relieved that I no longer had to live up to his expectations, and part of me felt guilty for feeling so. The only pain that I experienced was remorse for not having been on better terms with him. I hope to be a better father to my children."

Jane felt her ire rising against his dead father. Knowing the kind of man that Mr. Bingley was, how could she be tolerant or patient with a father who did not love such a deserving son?

"My mother died shortly thereafter, just as I became of age. The North held too much pain for me, so I set my sights on Town."

"Do you like London?"

"I found, while London was agreeable, that I did not enjoy spending all my time there. By chance, I heard that Netherfield was available. I think it took just a half-hour to come to an agreement with Mr. Morris. I feel better now than I have in a long time. The country agrees with me very well. Now it is your turn. What more can you tell me about your family?"

The smile faded from her lips. "You already know a great deal about them, but there is one person I have never mentioned. My father died three years ago from a sudden illness. It was horrible. I shall never forget that evening but I think that Lizzy was most affected by his passing. She was his favorite, and they spent hours together talking and debating over books. I was surprised when he left Longbourn to me. It should have been hers.

"Managing the estate has been difficult for me. The men resent receiving directions from a young woman, so I often have to be content with work that is delayed or not satisfactory. I have one tenant who is refusing to pay the rent. He says I must make improvements to his dwelling, yet it does not require any improvement. I am sometimes at a loss as to what to do."

Bingley knew he could help her with that problem and with every other trouble in her life. Someday soon, he would make his proposal. In the meantime, he would give her the time she needed to know him more fully. He had already made his decision about her.

Chapter 8

Bingley was pacing in front of an upper floor window awaiting the arrival of the Bennet family. They were to dine and spend the evening at Netherfield. Caroline was out for the evening, so he would be left alone with the family, which suited his purpose nicely. He wanted to display for the Bennets all his civility and good manners and obtain the regard and affection of the whole family. Finally, the carriage arrived and he saw Jane alight first, followed by the others. He ran down to greet his guests. A servant had opened the door to the family, and he met them in the entryway.

"Welcome to Netherfield. I am so pleased that you could come. I know we shall have a pleasant evening together."

Jane made the introductions. "Mr. Bingley, do you remember my sisters, Catherine and Lydia? And you know my mother and Mary."

"You are all very welcome. And where is Miss Elizabeth?"

"She did not feel well enough to come. I beg that you will excuse her."

Jane had hoped to persuade Elizabeth to join them, for she wanted her to know more of Mr. Bingley, but Elizabeth refused, saying she was not well. When Jane offered to send for a physician, she objected, saying she would remain in her room. Jane knew this had nothing to do with the health of her body but spoke of the pain of her heart. Jane's mood darkened for a moment as she was reminded of Mr. Darcy, but she conquered the feelings, refusing to allow them to intrude on her time with Mr. Bingley. She was not completely comfortable leaving Elizabeth alone and had considered staying behind with her, but that thought was erased as she remembered that she was the reason for Mr. Bingley's invitation.

"I am sorry. Please let me know if I can be of any service to her."

Bingley offered Jane his arm and led her towards the drawing room. The rest of the family followed behind.

"You are very kind, sir. May I inquire after Mr. Darcy?"

"I have not heard from him since he left." He stopped their progress and turned to face her. "You must allow me to apologize again for his behavior."

"I cannot allow that. You are not responsible for his actions." She brushed her fingers along his arm to punctuate her assertion.

He felt all the reassurance of her touch, and cherished the intimacy of that moment. "He was a guest in my home. I cannot excuse him or his insult to your sister."

"I hope that Elizabeth will soon forget about him." Jane felt it was time to change the subject to one less dangerous. "Thank you for inviting us this evening. You have made me very happy."

ONCE IN THE DRAWING ROOM, it was necessary that Mr. Bingley share his attention with the whole family.

"Mrs. Bennet, thank you for accepting my invitation. I am pleased to have your family here at Netherfield with me. "

"We are grateful to you for your kindness." Mrs. Bennet greedily cast her eyes around the room. "You have fitted this room up so nicely. Wherever did you get that wall hanging?"

"It was a gift from my sister. This is the valley surrounding the small town in which I grew up, a place of no consequence."

"I have never seen anything so delightful." She paused, and looked around the room. "Is not Mr. Darcy here tonight?"

"No, ma'am. He left for London earlier this week. He had business there and wanted to visit his sister." Jane could see a momentary look of embarrassment on his face. It was apparent to her that Mr. Bingley was uncomfortable with any discussion of his friend, and Jane had already concluded that Mr. Darcy had neither business in Town nor a special desire to see his sister.

"Mr. Darcy is quite handsome, Mr. Bingley. I do hope he will soon return. Is it true that he has a large estate in Derbyshire?"

"He does, ma'am, a magnificent place called Pemberley."

"Did he see much of Lizzy while she was here?"

Jane did not know what to say to turn her mother's thoughts. She could tell that Mr. Bingley was growing anxious. He must know that she would not have mentioned the relationship between Mr. Darcy and her sister to their mother. Mrs. Bennet's questions could not be construed as anything other than impertinent curiosity.

"I do not know that —"

Jane knew she must intervene. "Mr. Bingley, how do you like Meryton?"

He was relieved at the interruption. "I have been there only once. Mrs. Thomas, my housekeeper, reports to me that it is a delightful place. Do you often go into Meryton?"

"Yes, we have an aunt who lives there, so my sisters walk into town twice or three times a week to visit her. I go as I am able."

"It must be pleasing to have relations living so near. My father was an only child as was my mother, so I have no aunts or uncles."

"Well, sir, perhaps you could join us sometime. We would be happy to share our aunt with you."

"I would be very happy to join you."

Mrs. Thomas announced that dinner was ready. Bingley escorted Mrs. Bennet to the dining room, and then seated himself next to Jane.

In London, the days passed slowly for Darcy. Georgiana's interest in Miss Elizabeth was insatiable, and she frequently persuaded him into talking about her. This was not a simple task, for as often as he would freely speak of Miss Elizabeth, at other times he would resist all inquiries and say nothing. It was not long, however, before she knew a great deal about her and was able to gauge the level of affection she had for her brother. Georgiana observed that her brother had changed as a result of his relationship with Miss Elizabeth. He seemed to be gentler and more affectionate, and she was pleased with the change. She could only credit Miss Elizabeth for it and resolved to keep questioning her brother.

Alone in his library, Darcy poured himself a drink and allowed his thoughts to wander. The longer he was separated from Elizabeth, the more his mind was drawn to her. He remembered holding her hand while painfully relating the story of his parents' deaths. She was gentle, kind, and compassionate and was unconcerned by his wealth and status. Her only interest lay in him as a person, and that interest had quickly grown. She possessed all the attributes he could wish for in a wife, yet he had left her and had done so without saying a word. How she must despise him! How her sister, Miss Bennet, must despise him!

Though he had left her, he felt Elizabeth's loss exceedingly. He called it a loss because she was lost to him. Although he loved her, he knew that any alliance between them was doomed. Her unsuitable relations would be a continual embarrassment.

He set his glass down and moved to his desk upon which were two letters, one from his steward at Pemberley and the other from an acquaintance, Mr. Tilden. That missive was an invitation to a small dinner party in honor of his daughter, Miss Clara Tilden. She was accomplished, young and beautiful, and had a fortune of twenty-five thousand pounds.

Darcy had known Miss Tilden since her coming out ball two seasons ago. She was pleasant enough, though she spent too much time trying to please. Darcy wished that Elizabeth had been blessed with such a fortune, then they would have been an equal match, and his father would have approved. With these thoughts, Georgiana's words came back to him. Was he interested in Elizabeth or were property, social position, and family connections his main concern?

Darcy accepted Mr. Tilden's invitation. He intended to arrive before any of the other guests in the hope of spending time alone with Miss Tilden. If he could see something attractive in her countenance, wit, or manner of speech, perhaps he could make himself believe that Elizabeth was not the only woman he could love.

DARCY ARRIVED AT THE TILDENS' home a half-hour early. A servant showed him into the drawing room where the family was waiting.

"Mr. Darcy, welcome. Please allow me introduce you to my daughter, Miss Clara Tilden."

"It is a pleasure to meet you again, Miss Tilden. Thank you for your kind invitation."

Miss Tilden's eyes were blue, and her hair golden blonde, so very different from Elizabeth, who, though not as elegant, possessed even greater beauty, for she...

He recovered himself, but it was too late. His thoughts had drifted too far. Miss Tilden had spoken, but he had not heard her. "I am sorry. I was momentarily distracted. You were saying?"

Darcy felt hot with embarrassment and was ashamed that his discomfiture was so generally noticed. Mr. Tilden eyed him with curiosity, and Miss Tilden seemed offended by his rudeness. She paused for a moment, considered him with a frown, and then spoke once again.

"I said that it has been a long time since we met, Mr. Darcy."

"Indeed, it has."

"May I inquire after your sister?"

"She is quite well, I thank you. Have you been in Town long?"

"My father brought me to Town about a month ago, and I have been busy renewing old acquaintances. I have attended the theater and the opera. I spent a Sunday afternoon in Kensington Gardens and have enjoyed many of the delights that society offers. My father insists that I be known to the world, though I would prefer to remain in the country. I prefer quiet and seclusion, but if I had remained behind, I would not have had an opportunity to see you now." Miss Tilden was kind enough to blush.

Darcy did not believe this for a moment, and his mind wandered to Hertfordshire, where there was a young woman who did enjoy the country. It took only a moment to ascertain that Miss Tilden, for all her beauty and elegance, would never possess the lively disposition and unaffected charm of Elizabeth. The discovery was mortifying, for Miss Tilden was everything for which a gentleman might wish.

"I, too, prefer the country to Town, Miss Tilden, but this is where my sister resides, and business does call me here from time to time. How do you spend your time in the country?"

Elizabeth enjoyed nothing better than being out of doors. Although he knew she spent time in Town with her aunt, he was secure in the knowledge that she had never lived anywhere but at Longbourn. All she had ever known was the country and its simplicity, and he . . .

". . . and paint in the morning when the sun first rises, giving an early light to the countryside. The grounds around Tilden Manor are beautiful."

Darcy's mind had once again traveled the distance to Longbourn. She was in the middle of a speech, and he made every effort to appear attentive and interested in what she had to say.

"Mr. Darcy," said Mr. Tilden, "if you will follow me, I can show you examples of Clara's painting."

"Thank you. It would be a pleasure."

Darcy followed the father and daughter out of the room, giving him a chance to examine Miss Tilden more closely. She was tall and slender with beautiful blonde hair pulled back in a braid that crowned her head. She moved gracefully and her figure was well formed. She spoke gently and with respect and deference towards him. He recalled another woman that had not treated him with such deference but considered him to be her equal. Perhaps his opinion of Miss Tilden would improve once he knew her better, but then Elizabeth had not required any improvement. No part of his feelings for her were learned.

Darcy admired Miss Tilden's art, much to the lady's satisfaction. He was willing to concede that she painted well. Her father was quite obviously proud of her achievements, and he deserved to be. Her landscapes were exquisite. Mr. Darcy thought of another young woman who did not draw or paint, but who seemed to be gifted in the art of loving and caring for others, an accomplishment he doubted Miss Tilden possessed.

After examining Miss Tilden's art, they returned to the drawing room, where she began the conversation.

"I believe that your estate is in the country. Please tell me about your home, Mr. Darcy."

"Pemberley is the name of my estate in Derbyshire. It was built in 1627. The central section was attacked by Cromwell's men, but it was rebuilt in the same style. There is a stream, a lake, and extensive grounds, and the tenants are all pleasant fellows. I have refurnished a room for my sister that she will see for the first time when she returns to Pemberley. It is to be a surprise for her. I have never had to worry about new furniture before. Our home is lovely, but it certainly lacks a woman's touch."

"I am sure your sister will be pleased with what you have done for her."

Miss Tilden was an only child and had no experience with the love and affection of a brother or sister. She could only imagine the feelings Mr. Darcy had for his sister. Miss Darcy wanted for nothing, she was certain. There was little she would not do to secure the attention and affection of such a generous man as Mr. Darcy.

Darcy smoothed an imaginary wrinkle in his waistcoat. "Please tell me about your home in the country."

"Tilden Manor is not as grand as Pemberley, but I dearly love it. My grandfather had it built during his lifetime and removed his family there on its completion. The manor possesses several natural streams that are well-stocked, and the library is superior to any I know."

Darcy had no doubt that if the streams were not stocked and the library not filled with books, all it would take would be a little interest from him and they certainly would be.

"How long will you be in Town?"

"For a few months. My father has some business to transact. He has enclosed the commons around Tilden Manor and is going to make agreements with new and current tenants and wants his solicitor to prepare the documents. He is also in negotiations for a small farm near Tilden Manor to which his old steward, a longtime friend of the family, will retire."

"You seem to be conversant in the issues surrounding Tilden Manor."

"It is to be mine someday, so I feel that it is important to know what is going on, and my father agrees."

"He is quite right. Of course, when you marry, your husband can assume those duties."

"Yes," she smiled at him, "he will."

THE NEXT MORNING, DARCY WAS reading the newspaper when he was accosted by his sister. She was full of curiosity to know how his evening had passed.

"Did you enjoy your time with the Tildens?"

There was no question in her mind that Mr. and Miss Tilden hoped for an alliance with the Darcys. From what Georgiana knew of Miss Tilden, she was certain that her brother could never love her. She was convinced that he was in love with Miss Elizabeth and so felt no qualms in warning her brother about the intentions of the Tildens. Her brother was a troubled man, and she felt a need to protect him.

"It was pleasant enough."

Glancing up, he met Georgiana's eyes and felt himself grow uncomfortable under her scrutiny, and when she asked how he found Miss Tilden's company, he avoided her eyes altogether.

"She is a pleasing young woman."

Georgiana frowned. Their opinion of Miss Tilden did not coincide. "I am sure you had ample opportunity to converse with her. Of what did you speak?"

"She told me about her home and of her stay in London. Like me, she enjoys the quiet and seclusion of the country."

"Strange that Miss Tilden should call on me earlier this week. She asked many questions, all of which concerned you. In my opinion, my dear brother, she is courting you. How would you feel about a match with Miss Tilden?"

Darcy pondered the question for a moment, and then coolly responded. "I am not certain that this is a conversation I would like to have with my sister, but if you must know, she is an accomplished woman, blessed with many advantages. The man who marries her should consider himself fortunate."

"In other words, she is everything Miss Elizabeth is not, except that you do not love Miss Tilden, and you do love Miss Elizabeth."

"Perhaps you should return to your studies." His lips had not closed before he regretted his words, but it was too late, she had left the room.

NOT LONG AFTER HER FAMILY had departed for Netherfield, Elizabeth realized that she did not wish to be alone. She was disgusted with what she felt was her weakness in refusing to go, but she could not bear to enter that house again and be surrounded by *his* memory.

Why would Mr. Darcy leave just when she had opened her heart to him? He had kissed her, and she now felt violated. She loved him, and the pain of his leaving her without a word after all they had shared hurt deeply.

Maybe it was better that she was alone. She could cry undisturbed.

DARCY THOUGHT IT A GREAT contradiction to be back in Hertfordshire. He had gone to get away from Elizabeth, to free his heart from the hold she had over him, and now he was going back. In a letter, Bingley urgently pressed for his return. He felt that Darcy had been unjust to both himself and Miss Elizabeth when he left Netherfield without a word. Darcy resolved not to allow the slight to injure their years of shared friendship, so when Bingley issued him an invitation to return, Darcy agreed.

To be honest, he could no longer resist the temptation to be near Elizabeth. It had been several weeks since he left, and he had begun to wonder if he had imagined the degree of their attachment. Perhaps she had never loved him as he thought she had. If he could just see her and know he was no longer important to her, to know that she did not care for him after all, perhaps then he could find peace.

The carriage ride seemed interminable. The usual sounds and motions of a traveling carriage, to which he had become inured with practice, seemed to overwhelm his patience. He could neither read nor sleep nor entertain himself with pleasant thoughts.

The carriage pulled up in front of Netherfield, and Darcy was immediately welcomed by Bingley.

"Darcy, you are here, at last! Welcome!"

"Thank you, Bingley." Darcy was exhausted and not equal to his friend's energetic welcome.

"How was your trip?"

"It was much more tiresome than I remember."

As they turned and walked into the house, Bingley hoped that Darcy's ill humor could be attributed solely to being weary from traveling.

"I will have your things carried to your room at once. Perhaps you would like to rest a bit after your journey."

"Yes, thank you." Darcy was relieved by the prospect of quiet and solitude. It would allow him to gather his thoughts and tame the chaos in his mind.

As Darcy walked up the staircase, he remembered the visits he had made to Elizabeth. Instead of going to his bedchamber, he walked to her room and took his usual place in the chair next to the bed. He remembered talking to her as she slept, not knowing when or if she would wake up. He had been captivated by the fullness of her lips and recalled how her dark hair fell down around her face. He could see her hands clasped together and remembered his relief when he learned that she had finally awakened. He would never forget the laughing sound of her voice or her soft touch. In that short time with Elizabeth, he had learned what it was to love and be loved.

BINGLEY ANTICIPATED WITH PLEASURE SHARING the news of his understanding with Miss Bennet, and unable to wait any longer, he went in search of his friend. Bingley did not find him in his room, and after the pause of a moment, acted on suspicion and walked down the hall towards Miss Elizabeth's former bedchamber. He looked in to see Darcy sitting by the bed deep in thought.

"Do you wish to have your things moved to this room?"

Darcy was startled to hear Bingley's voice. "No. I..." There was an uncomfortable hesitation, a feeling of uncertainty. "I thank you, no." Darcy rose and walked past Bingley and down the hall to his usual room.

Bingley watched Darcy's retreating form and then turned to the object of Darcy's attention, Miss Elizabeth's bed. Knowing full well Darcy's feelings for her, he could not say he was surprised to have found him there. Despite his absence, it was clear that Darcy's feelings for her were unabated.

Bingley decided he would inform Darcy of his new understanding with Miss Bennet at a later time.

DARCY CHANGED HIS CLOTHES AND wrote a note to Georgiana announcing his safe arrival in Hertfordshire. Later, Bingley heard him enter the library.

"Please sit down, Darcy, and tell me how you are feeling. You do not appear to be well."

If Bingley had to describe Darcy, he would call him stricken. Darcy was not a man given to mirth, and what liveliness he had displayed in the past had given way to a depression of spirits. He was a man in distress.

"I am tired, that is all. The trip seemed to be particularly trying this time." Darcy collapsed into a chair opposite Bingley.

"And why is that?"

"My mind is not at peace…but I do not wish to talk of that now. I have missed you, my friend. How are you? Are you well?"

Bingley doubted his sincerity. He knew that Darcy was always uncomfortable in any discussion that concerned him, and today he seemed more agitated than usual.

"Is there anything I can do to help ease your mind?"

"I think not."

"Please, remember that I am always at your disposal. You know you may come to me with whatever concerns you." They continued a moment in silence until Bingley spoke. "I have something to tell you."

"What is your news?" Darcy picked up a newspaper from a table and began to peruse the first page.

"I have asked for and received permission to court Miss Jane Bennet."

The room became silent. Darcy returned the newspaper to the table. "I do not know what to say."

"You do not have to say anything. Just be happy for me. I love her."

Darcy could not let his statement go unchallenged. "But do you know her well enough to take such a bold step?"

"I saw much of her while Miss Elizabeth was here, and even more since you left, and I am certain of my feelings for her." He felt a little suspicious of Darcy's motives, sat back in his chair and crossed his legs.

Darcy took a deep breath. "You have known her for only a short while, Bingley." He arose and began to pace the floor.

"Yes, and by securing her consent to court her, I can seek to know her more fully and in an open manner above speculation and public examination. I will not hide my intentions. If she refuses me later, then so be it, but I shall not lose the opportunity to win her hand."

"Are you certain you are making a wise decision? What did your sisters say?"

"I did not consult with them. They will not approve my choice, but that is nothing to me. I am seeking my own happiness and that of Miss Bennet."

"Why do you not think they would approve of Miss Bennet? She seems pleasant enough."

"They do not believe the Bennets are fashionable or wealthy, and they despise their connections."

Darcy continued his walk up and down the room. "There is truth to that. Do you not think it worth considering?"

"What is that to me? I love Miss Bennet, and I want to be with her." Bingley was growing more upset every moment, and Darcy's incessant pacing of the room was irritating.

"A man in your position should have no problem finding a wife who is the daughter of a wealthy, landed gentleman and can provide you with a proper dowry. That kind of marriage will remove, once and for all, any doubts others may have about you being a gentleman."

Darcy eyed Bingley carefully, not knowing how far he dare press the point. He knew Bingley was much less concerned with appearances than he. "The stigma of having acquired your wealth through trade will be gone forever. Your income will increase, and you will be able to move easily in society, respected by those whom you will call your peers."

Darcy spoke deliberately, not wanting to raise Bingley's ire, but hoping to persuade him that his choice was not advantageous. It was a relief for Darcy to speak openly of his objections. If he could convince Bingley that Miss Bennet was not worthy of his love and affection, perhaps he could be more reconciled to his belief that Elizabeth was not an appropriate match for him.

"Miss Bennet is the daughter of a gentleman, and though she has no dowry, she does have an estate. We will immediately have property to give to an heir."

"Perhaps, but the estate is a poor one, and it comes with four unmarried daughters and an unpleasant widow who would immediately become your responsibility. On your marriage, it would become your estate, but do you really think Miss Bennet will turn out her mother and sisters? They will be with you forever. There will be no place for a son to inherit for many years. The two youngest daughters are quite ill-mannered. Their marriage prospects are extremely low. Do you really want to have the care of them for the rest of your life should they live to be old women?"

"Darcy! You are heartless! No, I do not expect that Miss Bennet would turn out her own family nor would I ask it of her. I am happy to care for them as long as they require it. The daughters will come into one thousand pounds each on the death of their mother. They are not that poor."

"Think about it. It is wrong!"

"Darcy!"

Bingley was cut to the heart. Darcy's arguments were superficial, and he had never thought his friend so shallow. Bingley had come to love all the Bennets. The income from Longbourn would continue to support the family. He would not have to spend three-pence, but none of that mattered, for he would do anything to have Jane and would marry her if she had nothing at all.

With a look of hurt and dismay, Bingley left the room.

BINGLEY RETIRED TO THE PRIVACY of his dressing room where his thoughts turned to Miss Bennet. He reflected with pleasure on the time he spent with her at the Meryton assembly and concluded that he would like to give a ball at Netherfield. While it would offer entertainment for everyone invited, the sole purpose of the evening would be to provide an opportunity for him to be with Miss Bennet. He longed to dance with her again. Such a ball would give Darcy a chance to see how lovely she truly was. Every grace that a woman possessed was enhanced as she moved down the dance. Darcy would be forced to admit that he was wrong about Miss Bennet.

Happy with his decision, Bingley sought out his housekeeper, informed her of his plan, and requested her help in planning the ball.

"When would you care to hold it, sir?"

"Tuesday week."

"I am certain that you would not care to be bothered with all the mundane tasks and activities associated with planning a ball; therefore, please leave everything to me. I will consult with you when decisions need to be made."

"I cannot imagine being of any assistance to you, so I leave it all in your hands. I completely trust your judgment."

"Shall I send round your invitations?"

"Thank you, yes, though I will deliver one myself to the Longbourn family."

"Very good, Mr. Bingley."

THE RIDE WAS PLEASANT, THE air refreshing, and birds and animals abounded on the road to Longbourn. Bingley had invited Darcy to accompany him, but he refused. Bingley was uncomfortable without Darcy's approval of his relationship with Miss Bennet, for he had always relied on his advice. Feelings of uncertainty clouded his happiness the closer he came to Longbourn.

Chapter 9

"Hill! Who is at the door?" cried Mrs. Bennet.

"It is Mr. Bingley, ma'am. He desires to call on you and Miss Bennet."

The thought that he had come expressly to call upon Jane gave Mrs. Bennet a great deal of satisfaction.

Hill brought Mr. Bingley to the sitting room, where all the Longbourn ladies were at their work. They stood on his entering the room.

"Mr. Bingley, you are very welcome. Do sit down, sir." Mrs. Bennet gestured to a place on the sofa where Jane was sitting. "We are very pleased that you have come."

"And I am happy to be here. Miss Elizabeth, I am pleased to hear of your improved health."

"Thank you, Mr. Bingley. We are all well, sir."

"Mrs. Bennet, the purpose of my call is to issue an invitation to you and your daughters. I am giving a ball at Netherfield and would be honored to have your company."

There was a general cry of approval amongst the ladies.

"Oh, Mr. Bingley! We would all love to attend, I am sure. Jane, this is a particular compliment to you."

Bingley was a little confused as to the meaning of her remark, but he did concede that it was true. If it were not for Miss Bennet, there would be no ball.

Jane blushed in a becoming way. He glanced at her, caught her eye, and their glance held. All the doubts that Darcy had inspired in him were removed. He loved her, and he would not give her up, not for anything that Darcy said.

The ladies expressed the pleasure they anticipated. There was a great deal of talk about gowns and shoes, flowers and jewelry, none of which were important to Bingley. Only Jane mattered to him. She felt similarly disposed, and wished to spend some time with him alone. She invited him to walk out in the garden with her.

Mrs. Bennet seconded her eldest daughter's invitation. "Yes, show Mr. Bingley around the various walks. I am certain he will be pleased with the hermitage. The garden is so pleasant at this time of year."

Bingley stood, offered Jane his arm, and together they left the house. Elizabeth looked on with great pleasure.

ONCE OUTSIDE, MR. BINGLEY BEGAN the conversation.

"Miss Bennet, it is such a pleasure to see you."

"The pleasure is mine, I assure you. Thank you for your kind invitation. You have made my sisters very happy." She looked up at him. "You have made me very happy."

"May I take this opportunity to ask you for the first two dances?"

"I would be delighted." Jane took his arm and drew herself near him. He placed his hand over hers and had the pleasure of seeing her smile.

"There is something that you ought to know. Mr. Darcy has returned to Netherfield at my invitation."

"Oh, my!"

"Does Miss Elizabeth speak to you about Darcy?"

"I do not wish to betray a confidence, sir, and so am not certain how to answer you."

Bingley led her to a bench near a tree where they sat down together. "Please forgive the question. I did not mean —"

"I will say that she is distraught. I think what troubles her most is that she believed he returned her affection."

Just the thought of what Elizabeth was suffering caused her resentment towards Mr. Darcy to grow warmer. Jane knew not how she could ever be in company with him in any tolerable state of composure.

Bingley shook his head. "Let me apologize again and again for his behavior, and please know that if I could change the past as far as he is concerned, I would, but I would not change one minute of the past as far as you are concerned."

Jane's heart was filled with gratitude for the affection that he made no effort to hide. She had complete confidence in him, and gave him credit for every good quality that a man might possess.

JANE ANTICIPATED THE BALL WITH impatience. The weather had been particularly wet and there had been no opportunity to further her courtship with Mr. Bingley. It took all of Jane's serenity and steady temper not to become frustrated. The day arrived at last, and before she knew it, she found herself in the carriage and on her way to Netherfield.

DARCY AWAITED THE ARRIVAL OF the Bennets with nervous anticipation. He sat at a window on an upper floor watching the carriages and viewing the guests entering the house. Every moment he expected to see Elizabeth. He had been unwilling to speak of her to Bingley, and had, therefore, heard nothing of her since he had left Hertfordshire. He wanted to learn if she still held him in any regard, for the thought of being entirely rejected by her nearly overwhelmed him.

"LIZZY, I AM GLAD YOU agreed to come with us." Elizabeth took Jane's arm as they descended from the carriage.

"I did not have a choice. Mama said I would never find a husband by sitting at home. I wish I could make her understand that I am not looking for a husband."

"Oh, Lizzy."

"I thought Mr. Darcy loved me. I know he did. What can I say to him if we meet tonight?"

"How can you say such things after he left you without a word?" They had reached the top of the stairs, and Jane halted their progress until Elizabeth was done speaking. Her words were not suited for curious ears.

"No man has ever made me feel the way he did. When we talked, he spoke to me neither as a subordinate nor a superior, but as a trusted friend. I felt caressed by the sound of his voice and warmed by his touch. I love him. I will love him forever."

Elizabeth turned away from her. "If he does not want me, then there must be a reason. I know that I do not wish to live my life hoping that he will someday change his mind, but he is all I desire, so I conclude that if I cannot have him, I do not want another."

How had Elizabeth come to love Mr. Darcy so deeply that she felt she could never marry anyone else? Jane began to wonder if she herself knew what it was to love.

"Jane, do you think I must see him tonight?"

Once again they were walking. Jane did not know how to answer Elizabeth. She wanted to believe that Mr. Darcy would have enough compassion for her sister to stay away, but his actions were more associated with selfishness than selflessness. At that moment, Jane saw Mr. Darcy approach and knew how to answer her sister's question.

"Yes, Lizzy," whispered Jane, "for he is coming this way."

DARCY'S HEART WAS POUNDING AS he approached the sisters. Elizabeth was as beautiful ever.

"Miss Bennet, Miss Elizabeth, thank you for accepting my friend's invitation. You both look very well tonight."

Elizabeth felt her chest tighten. He seemed unchanged. Despite the fact that he might appear austere to some, Elizabeth knew how gentle he could be. She remembered how he had held her hand when she unburdened her heart. She could not discount the tenderness she had seen in his eyes or the passion of his kiss.

"Thank you, Mr. Darcy." Jane answered for both of them.

Elizabeth rallied her courage. "How was your trip to London?"

Darcy knew what she was thinking. She had to be wondering why he left. She must be alluding to it.

"It was not very successful, I am afraid."

"You went away so suddenly..." Elizabeth wanted to say more, but could not. "Excuse me, sir. I must attend my mother and sisters."

Darcy watched Elizabeth move to where her family stood and Miss Bennet addressed him.

"Mr. Darcy, please forgive my sister. She has been very distraught lately. Quite recently something — or perhaps I should say someone — hurt her very deeply."

"I am very sorry to hear that, Miss Bennet."

"Are you?" cried Jane.

Darcy could not answer. Excusing himself, he left her and walked to the other side of the room. She eyed him with no small feeling of resentment.

HAVING GREETED HIS GUESTS, IT remained now for Bingley to welcome his beloved Jane to Netherfield. He found her standing alone on one side of the ballroom. For a moment, she did not appear to be herself, but he noticed that she immediately brightened on seeing him approach.

"Miss Bennet, I am so pleased to see you." Bingley took her hand and kissed it. "You look beautiful tonight."

"Thank you for inviting me, sir. Netherfield is such a lovely place for a ball.

You have outdone yourself."

"I would have to say that Mrs. Thomas has outdone herself. All I did was issue an invitation."

"Then please thank her for me. Are all your guests arrived?"

"Nearly all. I have been looking forward to this evening with great delight." Bingley paused. "Do you remember your promise of the first two dances?"

"Yes I do. How could I forget?" Jane lowered her voice. "You must know that I have been looking forward to tonight. I have been so eager to see you."

Jane wanted to confess more. She wanted to express her love to him, and the appreciation she felt for his affection, but, of course, now was not the time. These sentiments filled her heart, though, and she could detect in his every word and touch a feeling of shared intimacy.

"I have taken on extra servants in hopes that my guests will not make too many demands on their host that might take him away from you."

"Very thoughtful, sir."

Bingley glanced at Elizabeth as she walked past him. She seemed pale, fretful, and not at all easy. It was disturbing but not surprising. He had hoped that she would take pleasure in such a gathering of friends and neighbors, but it appeared to him that she wished she were miles away.

"I am concerned about Miss Elizabeth. She does not seem herself. Has the apothecary seen to her? I know that Mr. Manning has returned to London."

"I believe Elizabeth is recovered. Mr. Jones no longer comes to see her." She gave him a worried look. "She is not the same. She has yet to walk out of sight of the house." But this seemed to be the least of it. Something inside of Elizabeth had faded. There was no laughter and neither was there any joy or animation. She was sullen and quiet all the time. "I believe she is still nervous being alone outside since the accident. After all, what happened was horrifying. What if you had not come along when you did?"

"You should thank Darcy for that. I might have ridden past and not seen her. He was off his horse and by her side before I noticed she was there."

"Yes, Mr. Darcy…" Jane's voice trailed off. "What really happened while she was here?"

"He fell in love."

"Then why do this? Why break Lizzy's heart?"

Bingley was fairly certain that he knew why, but had not the heart to tell her.

DARCY HAD EYES ONLY FOR Elizabeth, and on finding her standing alone, could not prevent himself from speaking.

"Good evening, Miss Elizabeth."

A look of recognition dawned on her as she slowly turned to face him. Her heart stopped for a moment when she saw his beloved form and heard her name fall from his lips.

"Good evening, Mr. Darcy."

"I am pleased to see —"

"I recall that you said that you visited with your sister while you were in Town. How is Miss Darcy?"

"My sister is well. She is progressing in her studies and is enjoying London."

"I am pleased to hear it."

Her throat was growing thick and she could hardly speak. Indeed, she knew not what to say and concluded that for her own peace of mind she must get away from him. It was his presence. She could not endure his presence...the memories... It was too much.

"Mr. Darcy, please excuse —"

"Miss Elizabeth, have you resumed your habit of walking out in the countryside?"

"I have not." She closed her eyes and felt them begin to burn.

The music stopped for a moment as a new set was forming. She tried to turn away, but again he stopped her.

"Miss Elizabeth, will you do me the honor of dancing the next two with me?"

"I..." She knew she would be undone once she felt his touch. She knew she should refuse him but could not. "Yes, Mr. Darcy, I will."

They moved down the dance, their hands touching and lingering. Each touch seemed to awaken a further desire in her. They did not speak during the set, for which she was grateful.

The yearning in her eyes cut through him. He understood this to be a further testimony of the love she held for him. He felt his resolve nearly shatter every time their eyes met. He felt cursed. Why could he not act on the feelings of his heart? He could not imagine a woman more suited to be his wife, yet she was not suitable, at least according to the dictates of his father.

The music came to an end. Unwillingly, he released her hand. Just as unwillingly, she let hers fall carelessly to her side.

"Thank you," said Elizabeth, with lowered eyes.

"My pleasure." He cleared his throat. "I wish..."

She could barely hear his words. In the next instant, he was gone.

Jane apprehensively witnessed Elizabeth and Mr. Darcy dancing. No good could come from such an intimate encounter. Jane knew that Elizabeth would be unequal to it. When Jane observed Mr. Darcy walk away from Elizabeth, she joined her sister.

"Why did you dance with him?"

Jane put her arm around Elizabeth's shoulder and reproached herself for allowing her to have been left alone. She had not imagined that Mr. Darcy would approach Elizabeth, let alone ask her to dance. Once again, she felt she had failed her sister. Whatever he was about, it was all meant to hurt Elizabeth, whether by design or not.

"He asked me, and I could not refuse him. I did not want to refuse him." Jane led Elizabeth off to the side of the room.

As they were walking, Elizabeth continued. "Just now, as he walked away, I heard him say, 'I wish . . .' Oh, Jane, you do not know how much I also wish."

Knowing that Mr. Bingley loved her, Jane could easily imagine for what Elizabeth wished. What was wrong? Elizabeth and Mr. Darcy were so well suited to each other. Elizabeth would temper him with her playful and lively manners, and she would benefit from his vast experience and knowledge of the world. They truly belonged with each other. What had happened?

Jane could no longer express her anger with Mr. Darcy. It would only hurt Elizabeth for her to speak poorly of him. All she could do was comfort Elizabeth and be grateful for her own Mr. Bingley.

Sir William Lucas had observed Mr. Darcy and Miss Elizabeth dance. After the set, Sir William hoped to engage Darcy in conversation.

"Mr. Darcy, dancing is such a fine entertainment for young people. I noticed that you are adept in the art yourself."

"Do you enjoy the amusement, sir?"

"I was very fond of the activity. Lady Lucas and I would dance for hours at every assembly, but my dancing days are over now, though I like to watch. I saw you dancing with Miss Eliza Bennet. She certainly is the jewel of the country, would you not say?"

"She is beautiful, sir." *A jewel. Yes, she is a jewel.*

"As is her sister, Miss Bennet. It will be a fine thing when she is married to Mr. Bingley. A fine thing indeed."

"Excuse me?" Darcy was shocked. He knew of Bingley's understanding with Miss Bennet, but was not prepared to hear from those outside the relationship that it had progressed forward enough that their marriage was considered as certain.

"It is assumed by everyone that they will soon be married. I am sure that all that remains to be done is to draw up the settlement and arrange for the wedding breakfast."

"I was not aware. Please excuse me." Darcy walked away from Sir William who watched his receding figure with satisfaction, knowing how much pleasure he must take in the happiness of his friend.

Darcy was shocked by this revelation. He had to talk to Bingley. For Bingley's sake and for his own, he had to convince him that it was wrong to marry Miss Bennet.

He found his friend deep in conversation with that lady. He observed them for a moment before interrupting them, seeing with wonder the ease and familiarity with which they spoke, and witnessing in the exchange of knowing glances and casual touches a relationship of true intimacy.

At his friend's insistence, Bingley excused himself from Miss Bennet, and he and Darcy left the room.

BINGLEY RETREATED WITH DARCY TO the library. Darcy, being uncomfortable with the task he was about to undertake, found the air in the room to be rather stifling, and so threw open the sash to allow for some fresh air.

ELIZABETH COULD NO LONGER ENDURE the confinement of the ballroom. Having danced with Mr. Darcy, having touched Mr. Darcy, her mind was full of him. Unable to bear the feelings she was experiencing, she went out on a balcony to be alone in the night air.

A tear escaped her eye as she recalled each step they took during the dance. She had been able to detect his familiar scent and the memories it conjured up of the time he held her and kissed her. Her mind was aflame with anguish, and she promised herself that she would never again submit to being in his company.

She longed to be at home, but she was constrained to remain at Netherfield, for it was dark. In former times, the walk home would have been nothing to her. She had been out in the dark often enough, but now she dared not go. She was afraid, and did not trust herself to be out of sight of refuge.

She knew if she asked to be sent home in the carriage, Jane would accompany her, and no matter how much she suffered, she would not intrude on the happiness her sister found in Mr. Bingley's company.

Her reverie was disturbed by voices coming through an open window, and without knowing it, she found herself drawn into a conversation between Mr. Bingley and Mr. Darcy.

"What kind of accidental information, Darcy?"

"From Sir William Lucas. Your marriage to Miss Bennet is widely assumed."

"I told you that she gave me her consent to court her."

"And we talked about that. Do you intend to propose marriage to her?"

"I do..."

Elizabeth was not surprised to hear this.

"...my mother's ring comes to me tomorrow from London. I intend to ask her at the earliest opportunity."

"Bingley..."

Elizabeth knew she should not be listening to this, but could not help herself. Bingley was to propose to Jane as early as tomorrow!

"Be happy for me, Darcy."

"Bingley, are you absolutely certain that you wish to attach yourself to the Bennet family? What about the younger sisters and their scandalous behavior? How do you think that will end? What about their mercenary mother, with whom it is an embarrassment to associate? Surely, you cannot believe that you will be untouched by these things! What about her connections?"

"What about them? She has an uncle in trade and another that is an attorney. I am willing to acknowledge shortcomings in the younger girls, but remember, they lost their father at an early age. Mrs. Bennet should be a stronger mother to them, but I am certain that with Jane's good example and my assistance, we can influence the girls towards better behavior. Mrs. Bennet is merely looking out for the welfare of her daughters. Her manner may be coarse, but it is sincere."

Elizabeth inched closer to the window.

"But you could marry the daughter of a gentleman from an established, reputable family. You could take away the stigma of trade from your fortune. If you marry Miss Bennet, you will never be able to assume your rightful place in society."

"So you have told me. Miss Bennet is the daughter of a gentleman and my fortune does come from trade. I accept that fact even though my sisters do not. Our sons will be born as gentlemen. I cannot ask for more."

There was a pause, and then she heard Bingley's voice again.

"But I can and will ask for more. I will ask that I am loved and respected regardless of fortune, and I know that this is how Miss Bennet feels about me. I am going to marry her!"

Elizabeth was shocked. Is this what Darcy thought of her?

She ran off the balcony and down a hall until she came to a dark staircase. She sat down and cried softly. Why did she ever have to fall that day? Why did she ever have to be so long at Netherfield? Why did she have to love Mr. Darcy?

THE MORNING AFTER THE BALL was one of remorse and regret for Darcy. He felt angry and embarrassed by his own behavior. He had walked away from Elizabeth in mid-sentence and quarreled with Bingley.

Two words, "I wish," had escaped his lips in Elizabeth's hearing. Yes, he wished that her prospects were better or that it did not matter to his father that they were not.

Darcy had never had such a disagreement with Bingley before. In the past, he had always been able to persuade Bingley to adopt his opinion, but for the first time, he would not be influenced. Indeed, Bingley's resolve seemed strengthened with each argument that Darcy put forward. It was Bingley's opinion that Jane Bennet would fulfill all the desires he had for marriage, and those points in which Darcy considered her to be wanting were irrelevant to his happiness.

The choice of a wife was an important matter, but was it worth a rift with Bingley? Miss Bennet was a very pleasing young woman and was in no way irksome or greedy like her mother. If Bingley was able to ignore the expectations of society, Darcy would have to confess that he could not make a better choice.

After he had announced his intention to ask for Miss Bennet's hand, Bingley had thrown Darcy's feelings for Elizabeth back in his face. That had been the worst of it. Bingley had told him that his objections to his marriage with Jane had nothing at all to do with Miss Bennet, but were his own objections to a match he wished to form with Miss Elizabeth. Bingley had said that if all he was concerned about was wealth and connections, he was not worthy of being loved by Elizabeth. Darcy recognized the truth of Bingley's words and fled the library for the solitude of his room

In the monotonous silence of his bedchamber, Darcy reflected on the events of the evening. He had accomplished one thing. He knew that Elizabeth did not hate him. This provided some comfort, but his mind was not at peace. He had cut himself off from two of the people he loved most in the world. With feelings of isolation and loneliness, Darcy spent a tortured, sleepless night.

DARCY AROSE FROM HIS BED while it was still dark with a pitted, icy feeling in his stomach. He acknowledged that he had committed an unforgivable transgression. He had betrayed a friend. No, he had betrayed two. Trying to dissuade Bingley from a marriage with Miss Bennet was unjustifiable. It was evil. Breaking with Elizabeth violated every sense of justice he held dear. He discovered at the ball that she still loved him. Treating her as he did, he deserved not her love but her hate and contempt.

If he felt any shred of decency towards Elizabeth and Bingley, he knew he must leave Netherfield. His presence caused only pain, upset, and grief, and certainly neither Elizabeth nor Bingley deserved further harm at his hands.

He had been prepared to leave early, but now he descended the stairs to leave immediately. In the silence of darkness, he escaped from Netherfield and was now on the road to London. He had made no farewell, and now as he listened to the rattle of the carriage, he realized that perhaps he would not see either of them again.

BINGLEY AROSE EARLY WITH A discontented mind, and as he dressed, he thought about all the disadvantages under which he would suffer by being at odds with Darcy. It was unfamiliar ground for him, and he felt unsure of himself. He relied very much on Darcy's opinions and sought out his counsel on all matters of importance.

Bingley resolved that he would speak with Darcy that morning and would employ every power he possessed in the hopes of changing Darcy's mind. In marrying Miss Bennet, he knew he was pursuing the best course for happiness.

As Bingley passed through the hall into the breakfast room, he came upon his housekeeper. "Good morning, Mrs. Thomas. Would you please send me word when Mr. Darcy comes down? I will be in the library waiting for him." Bingley began to move in that direction when his progress was arrested by her reply.

"But, sir, did you not know that Mr. Darcy left early this morning for London?"

"For London?"

"Yes, sir. I offered to bring him tea, but he told me he could not wait, that he must leave, even at that instant. I am sorry. I thought he must have told you."

"Did he seem well?"

"He appeared to be agitated and upset. He left in a violent hurry."

"Thank you, Mrs. Thomas."

She left him to go about her duties, and Bingley stared for a long moment at the space she had occupied. Darcy's sudden departure was wholly unexpected, and he felt himself resentful at the implications. He had not imagined that their disagreement would result in any type of breach between them, yet Darcy had left without a word. He was filled with regret that Darcy had left so precipitously but would not blame himself. He was resolved that he would marry Miss Bennet, even against Darcy's wishes and without his blessing.

Bingley moved behind his desk, penned a brief note to Darcy, and then took down a book. Although reading was out of the question, by leafing through the pages, he was accomplishing his real intent, which was to put off a visit to Longbourn until it was late enough in the morning that a call there would not be unwelcome.

He was not long amused by the book, however, and took to pacing the floor by the fire. His thoughts wandered between Longbourn, where he thought with pleasure on the happiness he would experience when Jane accepted his ring, and the road to London, where he thought with irritation about Darcy. He was grateful to be interrupted by a servant who carried a parcel from Town. Bingley knew what he would find. It was his mother's ring.

He ordered his horse and prepared to ride to Longbourn. Today, he would give the ring to Jane. They had spoken of it. His proposal would be a formality. In no time, they would be married, and she would be not only his friend but also his companion and lover. There could be no greater happiness.

Netherfield

Darcy,

I am distressed that you chose to leave Netherfield without so much as a goodbye to your friend. I can only assume you were deeply hurt by our conversation. We have never differed on any point before. I have always changed my opinion to yours and followed your counsel implicitly, but this time I cannot.

I find no greater happiness than the thought of Jane Bennet as my wife. You know why I think she would be more than suitable for me, and I know your objections to the match.

I apologize for my part in our dispute. I know I must have hurt you with my allusions to Miss Elizabeth. It was wrong of me. Your situation with her is none of my business. I hope you will be able to forgive me.

I would like to ask you to stand up with me when Miss Bennet and I marry. I hope you will agree to come.

You are my best friend and I remain yours.
Charles

Chapter 10

Jane woke up the next morning refreshed after a night of pleasant dreams. The ball had fulfilled her every expectation. She had danced with Mr. Bingley twice and was in conversation with him for much of the evening. He had also been very solicitous of Elizabeth's comfort and had finally persuaded her to dance. Jane recalled the way she felt when Mr. Bingley kissed her hand when she departed from Netherfield. She was so happy! If only Elizabeth . . .

Suddenly recollecting herself, she remembered that her sister had gone to bed quite upset. Upon entering Elizabeth's room, she found her looking out a window.

"Oh, Lizzy," said Jane soothingly. She sat on the bed next to Elizabeth and put her arm around her. Elizabeth smiled faintly but did not speak.

Elizabeth had arisen feeling quite disturbed, and her unhappiness was obvious. She had been undone during her dance with Mr. Darcy and now found herself quite angry and disillusioned after overhearing his conversation with Mr. Bingley.

"I am distressed by my feelings for Mr. Darcy. I am so confused."

Jane sighed and nodded her head to encourage Elizabeth to continue speaking.

"You were right. I should not have danced with him." Her breath caught in her throat for a moment, and she had to pause. "But I cannot completely banish him from my heart, and indeed, I do not want to." She would not tell Jane what Mr. Darcy had said concerning their family or how Mr. Bingley had defended them.

Jane reached out to Elizabeth and held her tightly. She felt Elizabeth's tears on her neck and began to murmur endearments.

Elizabeth knew that she had to accept that Mr. Darcy held her in no special regard — not now, not after hearing his conversation with Mr. Bingley. She was shocked at his attitude, not so much with respect to herself, but that he would have the presumption to try and dissuade Mr. Bingley from seeking Jane's hand. Elizabeth was proud of Mr. Bingley. He had stood up to his friend, and he would not be swayed in his affection for her sister. Mr. Bingley was truly a good man, and Jane would be happy with him.

Jane did not fully understand all that was troubling Elizabeth. "Your heart will mend. Please rely on me to take care of you. I love you very much, and I will do anything for you."

"You are too good, Jane."

They were interrupted by a knock at the door. It was Mrs. Hill.

"Excuse me, Miss, but Mr. Bingley has called for you. I have shown him into the drawing room."

"Thank you." Turning to Elizabeth, she asked, "Will you come with me, Lizzy?"

"Go to him, Jane. I will join you when I have composed myself."

"Are you sure? I will gladly stay with you." She knew that Mr. Bingley would not be angry if she remained awhile with Elizabeth. He was not unsympathetic to her plight, and knew full well that Jane was Elizabeth's only source of comfort.

"No. I will be fine."

JANE ENTERED THE DRAWING ROOM and felt her breath leave her at the sight of Mr. Bingley. As her love for him grew, he appeared to her to be more handsome each time she saw him, and today was no different.

"Good morning, Miss Bennet. I hope I have not called too early." She came up to him and he took her hand.

"Good morning. You know very well that I am always pleased to see you, regardless of the hour."

"Will you walk out with me into the garden?"

"I would like that very much."

Bingley closed the door quietly behind them as they exited the house. He spoke after a pause of several moments.

"Will you...will you sit with me?"

She nodded and they walked together to a bench that was protected from the house by a large tree. Bingley took her hand and kissed it but would not release it.

"Miss Bennet...Jane...I have come to see you with a purpose this morning."

114

He had rehearsed this moment in his mind many times, most lately on the ride from Netherfield, but now he could not remember what he had determined to say.

She smiled brightly at the sound of her name and suspected what was to come. He had never used her Christian name before, and her anticipation was excited.

"And what purpose might that be, sir?"

"I have come here to express to you my love and to tell you that you are dearer to me than anyone. I love you so very much. I want you to know that I treasure each moment we have ever spent together, and I am looking forward to the time we will share in the future. Please grant me that future. Please accept my pledge to care for you and cherish you for the rest of my life. Please accept me as your constant companion. Please consent to be my wife."

Jane looked at him joyfully. While she had expected his addresses, the open avowal of his love brought her happiness she had never known. These were the very words she wanted to hear. This was the future in which she wanted to live, she by his side, happier with him than she could ever be alone.

"Yes, I will," she whispered, grasping his hand with both of hers. "I will be so happy to be your wife."

Bingley brought out the small box that contained the ring.

"This ring, Jane," he said, her name rolling off his lips, "belonged to my mother. Please accept it as a token of my love for you."

"Oh, Charles! I do, I do accept it!" His name fell naturally from her lips, and she felt as comfortable with it as she was with her own.

He slipped the ring on her finger with a feeling of satisfaction. It fit perfectly.

"I must tell you how much I love you. I have never felt more fulfilled or content with my life than I have since I met you. There is nothing I desire more than to be your wife. Thank you for wanting me. Thank you for your love. I have never been so happy!"

She held her hand up so she could admire the ring in the morning sunlight. It was a brilliant diamond ringed by pearls. Bingley's mother's name and wedding date were engraved inside the shank of the ring. It was beautiful, and knowing that it had belonged to his mother, whom he had dearly loved, increased its importance.

He released her hand and caressed her cheek. Sensations were spinning through her body, and she found herself holding her breath. He leaned into her and softly kissed her. She responded as he deepened the kiss. She was lost in the feeling of his lips on hers, the touch of his hand on hers, and the beating of her heart. She knew she belonged to him and resolved at that moment to spend the rest of her life making him happy.

DARCY FOUND HIMSELF PACING THE floor of his study in London with a letter in his hand. It was another invitation from the Tildens to join them for dinner on Saturday of the next week. He was at odds with himself as to what he should do. It was obvious that his recent behavior toward Miss Tilden had been considered encouraging enough that her father wanted him back in her company. Darcy had no doubt that Miss Tilden would accept his attentions with pleasure.

Miss Tilden was accomplished in the usual sense of the word, playing and singing extremely well. She spoke French, a language that he himself knew, and she enjoyed the theatre and the opera. In fact, she seemed to enjoy all the things that he did. Coincidence, or conspiracy? She was rich and well-liked in the fashionable circles of London. Except for Lady Catherine, who insisted that he should marry his cousin, Anne, his family, as well as his late parents, would approve of Miss Tilden. Should that not mean that he approve of her, as well?

Darcy returned to his desk and penned a note accepting their kind invitation

BINGLEY HAD TASTED JANE'S LIPS as long as he dared, knowing full well that it was time to return to the house. He released all but her hands, relishing in her acceptance of his love, and rejoicing in the thoughts of what the future would bring.

"Jane…"

She loved hearing the sound of her name on his lips. It was his right to so address her, she knew, and she was glad of it.

"…shall we go back into the house so I may speak with your mother?"

"I like hearing you say my name, Charles."

"Then let me say it again, Jane."

BINGLEY WAS NOT AT ALL concerned about approaching Mrs. Bennet. He knew she would give her consent to any man who wished to marry one of her daughters, and he had to restrain himself from resenting her for it. How could a mother so easily part with a daughter, let alone give her up to any man that presented himself?

Jane left Bingley in the drawing room, and after sending Hill to bring her mother to him, retired upstairs.

Mrs. Bennet was slightly annoyed that Jane should send Hill to summon her, for she was quite comfortable sitting in her dressing room. With a frustrated sigh, she set down her work and followed Hill downstairs to see what her disagreeable daughter was about. She was not expecting to find Mr. Bingley alone and apparently waiting for her. He stood as she entered the room and bowed to her.

"Mrs. Bennet, good morning. I am delighted to see you." As he spoke, he took determined strides towards her.

She was surprised at his action. "And I, you, Mr. Bingley. Where is Jane? Hill said she wanted to see me."

"I am sorry. There must be some confusion, for it is I who wished to speak to you. May we sit down?"

Mrs. Bennet sat herself down and began to fidget with her handkerchief. "Very well. What may I do for you?"

"I wish to speak of your eldest daughter, Miss Bennet. I wish —"

"Oh, Jane!" interrupted Mrs. Bennet. "She is the loveliest girl in the country, do you not agree? She has by far the sweetest disposition of anyone I know, and is five times as pretty as any of my other girls. The others can be quite wild on occasion, especially Lizzy, but not Jane." She paused to smile at Mr. Bingley. "Jane is as gentle as a lamb."

Bingley began to smile to himself as he listened to Mrs. Bennet's recommendations of Jane, but his smile faded when he discovered her opinion of Elizabeth.

"Mrs. Bennet, I find all of your daughters to be pleasing young women, but I agree with you. Miss Bennet is beautiful and has the disposition of an angel."

Bingley's thoughts returned to that first moment when he had seen Jane in that very room. She had appeared to him to be a gift sent from heaven to make his life happy. Without knowing anything about her, he had made up his mind regarding his own future, and had only hoped he could persuade her to share it with him.

"I am sorry, Mr. Bingley. I believe I interrupted you just now."

"Miss Bennet has accepted my proposal of marriage, and I am seeking your blessing on our union."

"Mr. Bingley! I am so excited! This is just what I had hoped for her, to marry a young man as handsome and as ... well, of course you have my blessing! Of course you will marry Jane! Let me call her down! Hill! Hill!"

UPON LEAVING MR. BINGLEY, JANE had gone directly to Elizabeth's room.

Sharing her news with her dearest sister had been her first thought.

"I am so happy! You will never guess why!"

"Whatever is the matter, Jane? Are you well? You seem quite flushed!"

"Mr. Bingley has proposed! We are to be married! He is speaking with Mama right now!"

"Oh, Jane, that is such happy news!"

"I do love him so, Lizzy, and he loves me."

"Of course he does, and how could he not?" Elizabeth sat on the bed again and pulled Jane down to sit beside her.

"Oh, do not tease me. Look at the ring he has given me. It belonged to his mother."

"It is beautiful. When will you marry?"

"We have not discussed a date yet, but I hope in the next few weeks. There is no reason to wait. Besides, the shorter the time, the less of a fuss Mama can make." The girls laughed.

"Not to mention that your Mr. Bingley will not choose to wait, either, I suppose. I am so happy for you!" They embraced each other once again.

"Lizzy, I would like you to stand up with me. Will you?"

"Of course, I will."

Just then they heard a knock, the door was opened, and in walked Hill.

"Miss Jane, your mother would like to see you in the drawing room."

"I must go to her. I am certain she is with Mr. Bingley. I wanted you to be the first to know of my happiness."

"I am happy for you, Jane. Now run along. Mr. Bingley is waiting for you."

Jane followed Hill from the room and left Elizabeth alone with her thoughts. Yes, Mr. Bingley would make Jane very happy and she him. They were a well-suited couple. Elizabeth thought with anger on Mr. Darcy. How dare he try to interfere with Jane's happiness! How dare he speak to another person of his feelings for her family! Yes, her mother and sisters had some failings, but they were not proud, arrogant, and hurtful like Mr. Darcy!

Elizabeth's thoughts went back to the time at Netherfield when he took her hand while he spoke of his parents. He had seemed so vulnerable, so childlike, as his grief was played out on his face. His touch was a comfort to her as she told him of her own sorrow, and at that moment, she had felt that nothing could ever come between them. How wrong she was! He had disappointed her and had now tried to hurt Jane. How happy she was that he had failed to separate Mr. Bingley from her sister!

She was grateful that she would never see him again! She was grateful that she did not have to think of him anymore.

But how would she ever quit loving him?

JANE WAS NERVOUS AS SHE walked down from Elizabeth's bedchamber to the drawing room. She had no doubt of her mother's approval, but it was with no small sense of relief that Jane could hear her mother's voice from the bottom of the stairs excitedly explaining to Mr. Bingley how happy she was and how happy Jane would make him.

Mr. Bingley stood as she came in the room.

"Jane," began her mother, "you should know that I have given Mr. Bingley my blessing to marry you." Mrs. Bennet pulled Jane into an uncomfortable hug. "I am so happy, you have no idea. You shall be married from Longbourn Church just as soon as possible. I am sure there is no reason to wait."

"Thank you, Mama. I believe Mr. Bingley wishes to marry as soon as may be."

"There can be no objection to that at all, I am sure. I shall visit you every day at Netherfield, of course. We shall be so merry. We will plan to go to London and stay with my Brother Gardiner and shop for your trousseau. We will get —"

"Mama! We shall do no such thing." The thought of being separated from Mr. Bingley now, when all her happiness was assured, was too much. "Whatever I need can be purchased in Meryton. Besides, there is not enough time to wait for the warehouses in London if we are to be married soon."

"Perhaps, then, you should wait a little while longer." Mrs. Bennet felt that wedding clothes were nearly as important to a new marriage as the parson who performed the ceremony.

"Mama, there is no reason to wait."

"Indeed, ma'am," seconded Bingley with a smile, "I would wish to marry your daughter just as soon as possible."

"Oh, very well. If it must be, then so it must. We will make do the best we can." Jane was grateful to have found her mother to be so persuadable on such a point and gave all the credit of it to Mr. Bingley. "I am so happy, Jane! I knew you could not be so beautiful for nothing. Mr. Bingley, you must stay for dinner."

"I would be delighted. There are few things I would like better."

"I shall go tell Cook to make a special dinner."

Jane smiled at Bingley and he put his arm around her waist to draw her close to him. He could not help himself. He leaned down and kissed her nose. Jane giggled just before he captured her lips with his.

CALDWELL STREET, LONDON

Dear Mrs. Bennet,

I am writing to accept your kind invitation to visit at Longbourn. It will be a pleasure for me to meet you and your daughters.

I will be accompanied by my daughter, Constance. She is fourteen years of age and a very amiable and well-mannered girl.

We are both very pleased with the prospect of seeing you all. Please extend my best regards to your family.

Sincerely,
Thomas Grinly

"GIRLS! GIRLS! I HAVE WONDERFUL news. A cousin of mine, Mr. Thomas Grinly, is coming to visit."

Mrs. Bennet's daughters answered their mother's call and assembled in the drawing room. Mary became spokesman for the group. "Who is he, Mama?"

"He is a widower with a fourteen-year-old daughter named Constance. He lives on a fine estate in Wiltshire with an income of three thousand a year and has been visiting in London these past two months. I have never met him but know of him by the report of your aunt, Mrs. Gardiner. They are cousins. I was pleased with what I heard, so I invited him to stay at Longbourn after his visit to Town is complete. Mrs. Gardiner persuaded him to accept my invitation to join us at Longbourn before his long journey home."

"What is he like? What did my aunt say about him?" asked Jane.

"Oh, I am sure he is not half so handsome as Mr. Bingley, Jane, but... I have such high hopes!" cried Mrs. Bennet.

"High hopes of what, Mama?" asked Mary.

"Why, of his marrying one of you, of course."

"CHARLES IS JUST WHAT A young man ought to be, Lizzy. He is filled with kindness towards everyone, and I have never heard him speak ill of another person." The girls were sitting alone on Elizabeth's bed. The house was asleep and all was quiet.

"Then you two are very similar in thought and disposition, for I have never heard you speak spitefully of anyone. You are a good match. I am so happy for you."

"Thank you, Lizzy."

"Are you at all afraid of the changes about to come to pass in your life?"

The candles in the room colored the fabric of her bedclothes with a softened glow.

"I shall miss you very much, but I am not afraid of marriage or apprehensive of living with Charles. We shall call often, and we are to hire a steward to take my place here and to ensure that all our tenants are well cared for." Jane took Elizabeth's hand. "You are not angry that I am leaving, are you?"

"Of course not." Elizabeth paused for a moment. "You know, my dear sister, Mr. Bingley is a very handsome man."

"Yes, he is," agreed Jane with a laugh.

"It will be quite advantageous to us all to have you so well settled. Do you think your marriage will throw us into the path of other rich men?"

Jane laughed again. "Well, I suppose you and my sisters will be thrown into the path of at least one rich man when Mr. Grinly calls next week."

"Oh, yes. Mama will not let me forget. It seems I am chosen to be his next wife, but I do not want to think about it. Perhaps Mary will do just as well. I would prefer to remain at Longbourn."

"In all the excitement of my own wedding, I have been thoughtless of what you must be feeling. Please forgive me. I do not know why Mr. Darcy treated you as he did, but I am sure he must have loved you."

In the afternoon of the day before Jane's wedding, a carriage was heard driving into the yard. Mrs. Hill brought their visitors into the drawing room.

"Mr. and Miss Grinly, ma'am."

They all stood to greet the visitors, and Mrs. Bennet welcomed them very graciously to Longbourn.

"Thank you, madam," said Mr. Grinly. "We are delighted to be here. I hope we did not arrive at an inconvenient time."

"Of course not, sir. We are glad that your trip was completed in safety and that you are here with us now. We have been looking forward to your arrival with much anticipation."

"Thank you. That is very kind."

Mr. Grinly surveyed the party around him. He had to confess to being a little anxious at first about accepting the invitation from Mrs. Bennet, but she and her daughters had received such a warm recommendation from Mr. and Mrs. Gardiner that his fears were allayed. Upon seeing them for the first time, his immediate impression was that the Bennets were very agreeable people with whom he would enjoy becoming better acquainted. Another advantage of the visit would be that his daughter would have the companionship of young women nearly her own age.

"Allow me to introduce my daughters. This is my eldest, Jane, and this is Elizabeth, and Mary, and Kitty, and Lydia."

"It is a pleasure to meet you, ladies," said Mr. Grinly as he bowed to them. "And may I introduce my daughter, Constance."

Elizabeth observed that Mr. Grinly had no striking features about him. One would not call him handsome, but he had an air of confidence that spoke of a man of strength and character. He was of medium height, with lively blue eyes and light hair. From both his appearance and the age of his daughter, Elizabeth concluded that Mr. Grinly must be nearly forty years of age.

Miss Grinly had a blossoming figure and rosy cheeks. She was nearly as tall as Elizabeth, but she did not favor her father in looks, for she had dark hair and brown eyes. She was shy and very reserved. It was obvious to all that she enjoyed the love of her father and returned it with equal fervor.

"Oh, you must be so tired," said Mrs. Bennet. "Please, come and sit down. Mary, ring for tea."

"You have a beautiful home, Mrs. Bennet," complimented Mr. Grinly as he led his daughter to a sofa. "You must enjoy it very much."

"We do enjoy Longbourn and are pleased that you appreciate its beauties. How did you leave the Gardiners?"

"We saw them two nights ago, and they were very well. They are such delightful people. Constance enjoyed their children very much. Is not that right, my dear?"

"Yes, Father, they are lovely children." She spoke so quietly that she could hardly be heard from across the room.

Jane smiled at her. "I hope you are well after your long journey, Miss Grinly."

Jane did not receive a response to her inquiry into Miss Grinly's wellbeing due to an interruption by her mother.

"Mr. Grinly, my brother and his wife visit above twice a year and always at Christmas. She is from Lambton, you know, a little town in Derbyshire. My brother, my sister, and I grew up here in Hertfordshire. The Gardiners met through an introduction by her father who was in Meryton on business. They tell me it was love at first sight."

"Well, they are a very handsome couple and appear to uncommon advantage together. My cousin and Mr. Gardiner are two of the most pleasant people I know."

A moment of silence prevailed. Before it could grow awkward, Elizabeth took it upon herself to speak.

"Miss Grinly, did you enjoy your trip through London?"

"Yes, ma'am, very much." Constance felt nervous and out of place in front of the elder Miss Bennets. She had not spent much time in the company of young women who were older than she, and she had to confess to feeling a little nervous around these new friends.

Elizabeth realized she would receive no more answer than that. Wishing to encourage Miss Grinly, she continued. "We have an instrument here if you like to play or sing. Mary practices every day, and I am sure she would be willing to share her music with you. The garden is very beautiful at this time of year, and you are welcome to walk in it whenever you want. We have many books in the library that are also at your disposal should you care to read. I confess that reading is one of my favorite pastimes."

"I only play a little," whispered Constance. "I prefer to draw."

"I do not draw at all, but I would like very much to watch you if you do not mind."

The faintest of smiles crossed Miss Grinly's lips. "I would like that. Thank you."

"You have come at a wonderful time," said Mrs. Bennet. "Jane is to be married tomorrow, and you are both invited."

EVERY SEAT AT LONGBOURN CHURCH was filled with family, friends, and well-wishers come to witness Jane and Bingley's marriage. The atmosphere was gay, and everyone was happy. All of Meryton knew this was a love match, and that knowledge made the occasion even sweeter for those in attendance.

Bingley was standing at the front of the church awaiting Jane's arrival. The day of which he had dreamt since first meeting her had finally arrived. Jane had not yet entered the church, so he took the opportunity to look around him to see if Darcy had come. He had not heard from him since his abrupt departure from Netherfield. As time progressed, it became more and more apparent that he would not hear from Darcy, so he asked another friend, Mr. Graham, to stand up with him.

All in attendance grew quiet as Jane entered the church. She caught sight of Bingley standing by the altar. His blue eyes flamed with desire for her. She felt herself grow weak and leaned more heavily on Elizabeth's arm.

Jane was surprised that Bingley had chosen Mr. Graham to stand up with him. She was certain that Mr. Darcy would have had that honor, but as she watched Bingley gaze at her, Mr. Darcy was quickly banished from her thoughts.

JANE AND BINGLEY KISSED EVER so gently as the final words pronouncing their union echoed through the church. With Jane on his arm, Bingley led the way through the church where they received the compliments of their friends and neighbors.

Bingley placed his free hand over Jane's and felt himself flush at the feel of her skin. They shared a knowing glance as they exited the church, the kind of look that only couples who truly love can understand. Bingley handed her into the carriage, and they were off to Longbourn for the wedding breakfast.

They had not spoken to each other since she entered the chapel except for the words they repeated during the ceremony. They had communicated everything with their eyes, the brush of a shoulder, and the touch of a hand. The intense feelings of love and emotion that were engendered by the service hung thickly in the air.

Once the carriage pulled away from the church, Bingley moved over to sit next to Jane. He gently caressed her cheek and smiled into her loving eyes. Jane sat still, glorying in his touch, and watched as he bent down slowly and kissed her, firmly and without reserve.

"Charles, I love you."

Chapter 11

Darcy arrived at the Tildens' home in good time for the dinner party and soon found himself walking arm-in-arm with Miss Tilden towards a public park across from her home. It was the very situation he had hoped to achieve. If there were any possible way in which he could obtain a favorable insight into her character that would allow him to attach himself to her, it would be on occasions such as this.

"It is always a pleasure to see you," said Miss Tilden.

He felt her lean against him as they walked along a sheltered path to which she had steered their progress

"Thank you for the kind invitation. I enjoy being with you and your family very much. Have you had any adventures since I last saw you?"

"Adventures? No, but I have been to a concert."

Darcy was certain that a question such as that would have been rewarded with some light-hearted playfulness from Elizabeth. He believed that Miss Tilden would assume he would not care for such behavior and consequently he would receive no teasing from her. In former times, this would have been true, but Elizabeth had taught him better. There were few things more enjoyable than being the object of Elizabeth's pleasantries.

"Which concert was that?" He led them onto an avenue occupied by other couples rambling in the fresh air, suddenly unwilling to continue alone with Miss Tilden.

"It was a thrilling performance by an Italian soprano. She sang a variety of songs from different operas as well as traditional love songs. It was a remarkable experience. I am quite envious of her talent."

He could not tell if she was sincere, or if she was fishing for a compliment.

Thinking it better to err on the side of safety, he spoke accordingly.

"Please do not underrate yourself, Miss Tilden. You play and sing very well."

"Thank you. I do so enjoy listening to a good tenor. Do you sing, Mr. Darcy?"

"I? No, I never learnt. My only foray into the arts was a brief period of acting while I was at school. My father did not approve, and so I gave it up."

"Fathers can be so tiresome," sighed Miss Tilden.

Darcy recalled the pain he felt when first informed of the death of his father, and feeling his loss as he did now, he considered him to be anything but tiresome.

"Please, do not be weary of your father. Mine died five years ago, and how I wish he were still alive."

A moment of embarrassed silence followed his remark. He was uncomfortable with what he considered to be her indelicacy, and she was painfully aware that she had displeased him.

"Oh, I am sorry. I did not know. Please excuse me. Please, do not think that I do not love my father."

He glanced at her but said nothing.

"If I may speak frankly, though, I believe my father regrets that I was not a son. He is eager to find a match for me and for me to bear the future heir of Tilden Manor during his lifetime."

Darcy softened towards her when he heard this. He could easily sympathize with anyone who felt they did not live up to the expectations of a parent.

"I am sorry that he finds any regret with you. And you? How do you feel about his efforts at marrying you off? I suppose that you will go to the highest bidder?"

Miss Tilden laughed. She had a cheery voice, though not quite as pleasant to listen to as was Elizabeth's. Elizabeth . . . Darcy tried to catch himself in the thought, but it was too late.

He cut off any response that his companion may have been inclined to make. "Miss Tilden, I think we should return to the house."

She looked up at him and wondered at the sudden appearance of sadness in his eyes. They did not speak again until they arrived at the house, and he offered to assist her in ascending a small flight of stairs.

They were met in the entryway by Mr. Tilden, who had been pleased to send them off together into the park and now eagerly searched their faces for any sign of attachment. Determined that the night should not pass away without some progress in that quarter, he concluded that he would speak with Mr. Darcy alone about the hopes and dreams he had for his daughter. "Did you enjoy your walk, Clara?"

"Very much, Father."

She noticed her father's glance at Darcy and excused herself.

BOTH MEN WATCHED MISS TILDEN'S receding figure as she walked down the hall. When she was out of sight, Mr. Tilden invited Darcy to join him in his study.

Mr. Tilden's study contained a large desk, several family likenesses on the walls, and many rows of books on finely finished shelves. The desk was very ornate but was too large for the room. The books were all very handsome, but appeared to be unread.

"Mr. Darcy, may I get you a drink?"

"No, I thank you." Whatever Mr. Tilden was about, Darcy wanted a clear head to deal with him, and he did not want to be off his guard later when conversing again with his daughter.

"I want you to know how much we enjoy your company here in our home. Clara tells me she is very pleased with your visits." Mr. Tilden poured himself a glass of port.

"She is a pleasant young woman, sir. You should be proud of her."

"I am, of course. Thank you." Darcy was not convinced.

Mr. Tilden continued. "I asked you in here specifically to talk about her. I am curious to know how deep your concern for her runs."

Darcy began to grow uncomfortable. The truth of the game he had been playing suddenly became clear to him. Here was a father who believed that Darcy's intentions ran in a way that would lead to marriage with his daughter. While Darcy had tried to convince himself that this was his wish as well, he suddenly realized that he was caught in his own finely spun web of self-delusion.

He could only listen as Mr. Tilden continued to speak. "I have been blessed in my life with many advantages, and have been able to provide for Clara accordingly. She has a dowry of twenty-five thousand pounds and at my death will inherit Tilden Manor. I am seeking a good match for her, sir."

These are the very things he had thought he wanted to hear. This is why he had left Elizabeth. This is why he had been visiting with the Tildens. But now . . . Where was the joy? Why did he suffer under a feeling of apprehension? The decision to marry was to bring the relief one feels upon arriving home after a long journey, but all he felt was a chill. There was no warmth or happiness. What was wrong? He had done everything his father had told him to do.

Darcy's attention was drawn back by the sound of Mr. Tilden's voice.

"I am seeking a worthy alliance for her, though I know that it might seem presumptuous to extend my efforts to such a one as yourself. I would like you to know that I am willing to add an additional ten thousand pounds to her dowry should you feel it appropriate. I know that money matters are important in bringing about successful matches, and I would not want her prospects jeopardized. Clara is a sweet girl, but I know that it takes more than sweetness to bring about a good marriage."

The horror of Mr. Tilden's proposal struck Darcy forcibly. Here was a man trying to sell his daughter! What if that daughter could not be happy? Who was the fortune hunter, and who was the hunted?

Darcy imagined what his life would be like if he married Miss Tilden. The sound of her voice pronouncing his name would become revolting. In an effort to avoid his wife, he would be separated from his beloved Pemberley by continual absence. He would have no respect for his own children. He realized that he would do to them what his own father had done to him. He would abandon them. If he followed in his father's footsteps, he would be as isolated and alone as his father had been. If he lived up to his father's expectations, he would end up just as miserable. The truth dawned on him at this moment of realization with bone-chilling clarity. For his own sake and for the sake of his children and their consequent happiness, he must marry a woman he could love and respect. And the woman that he loved was Elizabeth Bennet.

Darcy could barely maintain his seat as a searing heat passed through his mind, convicting him of his foolishness. He had left Elizabeth. He had willingly parted from her, denying himself the very love he sought. What pain had he inflicted on her? If she had thought of him in the same way he now considered her, what agony she must be suffering. Dare he flatter himself that now, after all the sorrow he had caused her, she would accept him? The bile rose in his throat as he experienced a feeling of self-loathing. His mind revolved between the taste of Elizabeth's lips and the vileness of Mr. Tilden's offer. What had he become that he could turn from the first and fall victim to the second?

Recollecting himself, Darcy attempted a graceful retreat.

"I do not know if I am in a position to know my own heart on the matter. I should not wish to marry without love."

"Of course not, Mr. Darcy. It is just important to love the right woman." Mr. Tilden paused to let the effect of his words sink in. "Shall we join the others?"

There was no question in Darcy's mind who was the right woman.

LATER THAT EVENING, DARCY SAT glumly in the library of his townhouse staring blankly into a glass of brandy. Today had been his closest friend's wedding day, and he was not there. He knew he had disappointed Bingley and was ashamed of it. While it was true that Bingley could have married with greater status and prestige, he had chosen to marry for love. What greater gift could there be for a man than a woman who loved him? Too late, Darcy had come to realize the value of such a gift.

Bingley had every right to be happy, and Darcy envied him his joy, for he knew he himself had every reason to be miserable. Perhaps today he could have been married to Elizabeth. He had been wrong in trying to separate Bingley from Miss Bennet. He had been wrong to leave Elizabeth. He had been wrong about himself. As a man who had always tried to do right, the magnitude of his errors of late left him humiliated and confounded.

London

Bingley,

Let me congratulate you on your marriage. I wish you joy and happiness with Miss Bennet, who by now is Mrs. Bingley. You, of all people, truly deserve to be happy.

Please allow me to apologize for my behavior. I know I have offended you, and I deeply regret it. My motivations in trying to persuade you against marrying Miss Bennet were self-serving and wrong. You deserved better counsel in your decision than I gave you, and you were right in refusing to be persuaded. The firmness of mind and steadiness of character that you exhibited in your determination to marry Miss Bennet are a testimony of your natural goodness. Mrs. Bingley has been very fortunate in her choice of husband and I have no doubt that she will make you as happy as you will her.

I know that I have offended Miss Elizabeth, and I pray that she and your wife may someday forgive me. Parting from her is the worst mistake I have ever made.

Please extend my best wishes to your new bride.

Sincerely,
F. Darcy

He folded the letter and marked it for express post. It would go out tomorrow and hopefully by nightfall, Bingley would once again think on him kindly.

MRS. BENNET RECEIVED MANY COMPLIMENTS on Jane's wedding breakfast and was particularly gratified by the comments of Lady Lucas who told her she had never seen so elegant an affair. Mrs. Bennet had made it as elaborate as possible so that no one could forget her triumph in marrying Jane off to Mr. Bingley. She also felt quite pleased with herself for having arranged the match in the first place, for had she not insisted that Elizabeth remain at Netherfield, who knows what might have happened?

"Mrs. Bennet," said Mr. Grinly, "allow me to offer my sincerest congratulations on the marriage of your daughter. She looked beautiful, and I have never seen anyone so happy. It must be a great comfort to you to have a daughter married to a man who truly loves and admires her."

"It is a pleasing thing, to be sure, to know she is so well settled. Mr. Bingley has five thousand a year, at least. She will have such carriages, jewels, and pin money that I cannot even begin to imagine. I am so happy."

"Surely, madam, she married him not for his money but for his affection." Mr. Grinly was convinced that Jane was no fortune hunter. The manner in which she looked at her husband spoke of love and esteem, not avarice.

Elizabeth, who was sitting at a writing table in the drawing room, sympathized with Mr. Grinly's incredulity at such a statement, but it came as no surprise since she was no stranger to her mother's opinion of marriage.

"Yes, she loves him, and he loves her, I am sure," said Mrs. Bennet.

Mr. Grinly was shocked at her callous view of marriage. He remembered his own dear Julia with fondness. How she had loved him! The advantages he could offer meant nothing to her. He could not help but fall in love with her the first time he saw her. The way Julia had looked at him, that particular expression of tenderness in her eyes, had captured his heart. As he grew to know her, he realized what a treasure she was. She had been a poor tradesman's daughter with no dowry or property, and her father was old and sickly, but he had been pleased to give her away. It seemed, though, that she had been his lifeline, for not long after they married, he died. Now his Julia was gone, having left him with a daughter. Constance was the true image of her mother, and when he looked at her, his heart was filled with both joy and pain: joy, because of the love he felt for Constance, and pain, as he reflected on the loss of Julia.

Julia had asked him before she died to marry again for his own sake and for Constance. He told her that she would be his only love. Julia responded by saying that she hoped he took so much pleasure in being married to her that he could not do without love in his life. "Please, do not spend your life alone.

Do not leave Constance without a mother." One of the hardest things he had ever done was promise her that he would try. It was the beginning of the full realization that he would soon be without her.

That had been eight years ago. Never once had he found a woman that he imagined her equal.

"I believe that love should be the primary motivation for marriage," said Mr. Grinly. "How can life be pleasant where one partner cannot respect or esteem the other? To me, any alternative would be unendurable."

Elizabeth raised her eyes to Mr. Grinly, pleased to find that he shared her opinion of marriage. She had been impressed with everything about him, and this only made her appreciate him more. Mr. Grinly was correct. She would only marry a man she could respect, one for whom she felt the deepest love and affection, and if not, she would remain at Longbourn. She knew that Mr. Bingley would allow her mother and sisters to live there as long as they wanted, for the rest of their lives, if necessary. Because she had bestowed her love on Mr. Darcy and had been mistaken about him, she knew very well that in her case, it might be necessary.

NETHERFIELD WAS EMPTY AND JANE and Bingley were alone. Everyone attached to the household was gone except for Mrs. Thomas, who refused to let the Bingleys be without the comfort of dinner and a warm fire. She discretely kept to the servants' quarters awaiting their summons should they need her.

Jane was sitting in front of an ornate mirror brushing out her hair. It was odd to be sitting in such luxury and to know that this would be her life from now on. At Longbourn, she had never known the pleasure of her own maid.

She felt nervous with anticipation. She had changed into a silky, white nightgown, and the way it moved over her skin caused her to shiver with delight. It was plain, without any ornamentation. It was simple, like her love for Charles.

Jane heard his knock at the door and smiled. "Come in."

Bingley closed the door behind him but remained at the far side of the room, seeking in her eyes the permission he felt he needed to approach her.

"Good evening." He was obviously tense and uncertain. *As am I,* thought Jane. For both their sakes, she felt it best that she lighten the mood.

"My name is Mrs. Charles Bingley."

"And I am Mr. Charles Bingley. I am very pleased to make your acquaintance."

"No more than I, sir."

Bingley saw with pleasure the sparkle of delight in her eyes. "I am told that

I was married today. Could you possibly be my wife?" He took a single step towards her.

"I do not know," she said inching closer to him. "Perhaps if you were to describe her to me, I could tell you whether I have seen her."

"My wife is extremely beautiful. She is tall and has lovely blonde hair that pours over her shoulders when she lets it down. Her laughter is like music. I love the sound of her voice. I love everything about her."

"What else can you tell me?" She again moved closer to him.

"She has beautiful blue eyes that illuminate her face when she smiles. They seem to speak of the joy that she feels in being alive."

"If she is married to you, I can understand why she might feel such joy."

She watched him step nearer to her. Only a very few steps remained between them.

"I should mention her skin. It is soft and delicate."

Jane moved again towards her husband. "Have you ever kissed her?"

"I have. I can still remember the taste of her lips and the way I felt when I took her in my arms. It is a pleasure of which I could never tire."

Bingley reached out his hand to her and she took it. He encouraged her forward until she was standing next to him.

"If I knew where she was, I would touch her like this."

Bingley outlined her lips with his fingers. She rested her hands on his arms and looked at him.

"Would you like to kiss her again?"

"There could be no greater happiness."

BINGLEY WOKE UP TO THE distraction of something passing over his face. With his eyes closed, he reached up to brush it away and found himself holding a lock of Jane's lightly perfumed hair. He drew in a deep breath to enjoy the fragrance and all the memories it inspired, memories of such love and passion as he would never forget.

Jane was an angel. Had he thought her beautiful before, those thoughts were nothing in comparison to reality. How he loved her! She fulfilled his every conceivable desire with the magic of new discovery. He would cherish and love her for the rest of his life.

THAT AFTERNOON, THE BINGLEYS WERE drinking tea in the drawing room and discussing the details of their wedding.

"Charles, why did not Mr. Darcy come to our wedding?"

"He was called away on urgent business."

"Business?"

"Well…"

"But if that were the case, how did Mr. Graham know to come to stand up for you?"

"Darcy knew he would not be able to come. We did not…"

Jane did not understand his behavior. Bingley was always forthcoming and open, but now he seemed so hesitant and reluctant. "Charles, is something troubling you?" Bingley was truly distressed and she could only conclude that there had been a gross misunderstanding between her husband and Mr. Darcy. "Well, I am sorry he could not come, but it was very unkind of him. How could he allow himself to be called away? What could possibly have been the problem?" She thought for a moment. "Did you quarrel?"

"We did have a disagreement."

"What did it concern?"

There another was a pause. "Must we talk about it?"

Bingley knew if he spoke the truth, his wife would be forever prejudiced against Darcy, though certainly it would not be without just cause. Bingley cherished hopes that Darcy would witness his happiness with Jane and change his opinion of her.

"Very well." She stroked his cheek. "But it does seem odd that he would not come." She took his hand and kissed it, then held it against her cheek. "He is a strange man by way of a friend."

Bingley was quiet for a moment. His eyes were closed, his brow was furrowed, and he found himself forced to agree with her. What kind of a friend was Darcy? "He attempts to look after me."

"But?"

"But I would not listen to his advice."

"What was the advice that caused all this difficulty?"

"He did not…he said I should not…he recommended that…that I not marry you." He followed this strangled sentence with a sigh.

"He said that?"

He answered with a slight nod of his head.

"But why?"

Bingley's pain was evident in his voice. "He thought I should marry a woman with a large dowry, a woman of fashion and society, one who could bring me wealth and status."

"I am not that kind of woman, Charles, as you well know." Feeling some alarm, she added, "You do not regret marrying me, do you?" Jane drew back from him. She knew how heavily Bingley relied on Darcy's advice.

Bingley felt her efforts to move away and held her close. "Not at all! I told him that I wanted to marry someone who loved me and whom I loved in return, and that every other consideration was irrelevant in the face of this desire. I do love you, Jane, and all I wanted was to be with you forever."

He felt her relax. "How could Mr. Darcy call himself your friend, but say all of those things? No wonder he stayed away. He thought I was ruining your life!" She paused as a realization dawned on her. "That is why he left Elizabeth! He felt she was not good enough for him, so he broke her heart. Cruel, cruel man! I hope I never see him again!"

Bingley thought about what she had said. All of it was true. Darcy had tried to take Jane away from him and had hurt his new sister, Elizabeth, whom he admired very much. He and Darcy had been friends for many years, but in just a few weeks, Darcy had managed to injure the two women most important to him. What kind of a friend was that?

LONGBOURN WAS RELATIVELY QUIET WITH its inhabitants either absent or pursing their usual diversions in silence. Constance and Mary were reading, Kitty and Lydia had gone into Meryton, and Mrs. Bennet was sitting at her needlework. Elizabeth had left the house, saying that she was going to walk in the garden. Mr. Grinly, having arrived at a good stopping place in the book he was reading, determined on following her example.

Mr. Grinly reflected on the wedding of the day before, and he compared it to his own fifteen years earlier. It had fulfilled every wish he had for happiness. Then Julia died and his life had been clouded ever since. Constance was his only real source of joy, but if he were to be honest, he would have to confess that he was not happy. Perhaps Julia was right. Perhaps he should marry again.

MR. GRINLY WAS WALKING AWAY from the house when he espied Elizabeth seemingly lost in thoughts of her own as she progressed across the lawn. He noticed how attractive she looked with the sun shimmering through her dark hair, and he paused for a moment to watch her before resuming his walk. She heard his approach and greeted him with a wave.

"Good morning, Miss Bennet. You certainly have a pretty garden at Longbourn."

"Yes, I enjoy it very much. It is a beautiful day for walking. Where is Constance?"

"She is in the drawing room with a book." Elizabeth's voice was pleasant, her face and eyes were animated, and she appeared to take a real interest in him. It was a pleasure to be with her.

"I must tell you how much I like her, Mr. Grinly. She is such a sweet girl."

"Thank you. I confess that I enjoy every minute I spend with her."

Elizabeth began walking again, and he fell into step beside her. "I know you have not been in Hertfordshire long, sir, but how do you find the country so far?"

"I feel very much at home here. The air is refreshing and the colors are so vibrant. There is a great feeling of vitality and freshness to the whole place that I like very much." He once again noticed Elizabeth's beauty and realized those same words could be applied to her as well.

"I am glad you like it. I never tire of the beauties of Hertfordshire."

They progressed a little further. "The wedding was beautiful, was it not?"

"Yes, it was. My sister was such a lovely bride, and Mr. Bingley looked very handsome. It is a joy to behold two people so very much in love."

"I am certain they will be happy."

They continued on in silence, but Elizabeth did not mind it, for she was not uncomfortable around Mr. Grinly. In fact, he made her feel quite at ease. She felt that he placed no demands on her as might make her feel obliged to talk or behave in a certain way.

"Tell me," began Elizabeth, "did you like London?"

"I liked it well enough. I have not been to Town in several years. It is larger and there are more people than I remember. There are many new buildings, and the parks add such charm to the neighborhoods. Although it was exciting to be there, I confess that I do prefer the retirement of the country. I enjoyed the time we spent with Mr. and Mrs. Gardiner very much."

"I enjoy staying with my Aunt Gardiner, but I also confess to preferring the country. Did you find amusement in the public places and the assemblies?"

"No, I did not want to leave Constance alone. She is not yet out in society, and I felt that the public dances were not appropriate for her. We attended the theatre and concerts, which we both enjoyed very much and will provide hours of conversation for us during the evenings at Sappingford."

"Sappingford is your home?"

"Yes, it is a modest estate in Wiltshire. I have lived there all my life."

"What is the country like?"

"It is very hilly and covered in trees. I take great pleasure in watching the sunset from the top of a knoll near our home. Constance and I frequently walk there in the evenings. The closest town of any significance is Westbury, which is about an hour's ride by coach. I sometimes feel that Constance must be terribly lonely. She does not enjoy much female companionship, and I am sure she would benefit from associating with other young women more often than the monthly assemblies allow."

"She is a beautiful young lady. You must be proud of her."

"I am, very much so."

"If I might ask, how old was she when her mother died?"

"She was only six years old."

"I am so sorry," said Elizabeth gently.

"Constance has only fleeting memories of her mother and these grow fainter with time. I cannot imagine growing up without a mother. There is only so much a father can do for a daughter, you know. I try my best, but I feel as though I fail her. I do not always understand her."

"I am certain that your love for her is sufficient to provide her with everything she will need in life."

"It is difficult knowing what is right. Oftentimes, I feel quite helpless."

"Helpless? Forgive me, sir, but Constance's manners, understanding, and conversation speak to the contrary. You should feel more confident, Mr. Grinly, for you are bringing her up very well. Anyone who sees her must know that. It is obvious to me that you are an excellent father." She spoke warmly, perhaps more so than she intended, but it pained her to see him undervalue himself. He was a good man and deserved her praise and respect.

He was grateful for her assurances. His natural feelings of inadequacy as a parent delighted in any form of encouragement. He also understood them to be perhaps a sign of some regard on her part, a feeling that was not at all unpleasant.

They exchanged a look and a smile and continued on in silence.

Chapter 12

Elizabeth was working quietly in the drawing room when Constance came up to her. Her behavior was more shy and diffident than usual, and Elizabeth believed that something must be bothering her. Set on relieving her uneasiness, she offered Constance her hand.

"Miss Grinly, please come and sit with me."

"Miss Bennet, I know that you and your sister, Mrs. Bingley, are quite close."

"Yes, we are," replied Elizabeth cautiously.

"It must be a great loss to you to have her living so far off."

"Netherfield is only three miles away. I shall see her very often."

"I mean ... well ... here I am, Miss Bennet ... a perfect stranger ... occupying her room." Rallying her courage, Constance finished her thought. "I suppose I am a little uneasy by it. I do not wish to make you uncomfortable."

"Miss Grinly, since we are friends, you must call me Lizzy."

"Thank you, Lizzy."

"Constance, please do not feel that you are intruding. I am very happy that you can make use of Jane's room, for if not, where would I find such a friend as you?" Elizabeth pulled her into a warm embrace.

This uncertainty had been a cause of worry to Constance, but she now felt much more like herself again. She had grown close to Elizabeth and had found in her the friend she wished she had in Wiltshire.

Elizabeth could sense Constance's regard and returned it equally. The young lady was as gentle and considerate as Jane, which endeared her to Elizabeth even more.

CONSTANCE WANTED A FRIEND DURING her stay at Longbourn, and while all the Miss Bennets were very kind to her, she felt as if she did not quite fit in. Catherine and Lydia were wild after officers, and Constance felt awkward participating in an activity she felt was improper, as well as considering herself too young to be forming an attachment. Mary's attitude of preaching against pleasure was not endurable for any length of time. It seemed impossible to get to know her. That left Elizabeth, who was six years her senior.

"Tell me about your home, Constance," asked Elizabeth. "Your father mentioned that it is a place called Sappingford, in Wiltshire."

"Yes. It is a lovely old home, though too isolated for my taste. I spend much of my time alone. I do have friends, but I see them only at the assemblies in Westbury."

"Has your father considered remarrying? It might be a comfort to you if there was another woman in the home."

"It would be if she loved me."

"I doubt very much that your father would marry someone who did not like you. Besides, it would be a strange person who could not."

"My poor father misses my mother so much. I wish I had been the one who had died and not my mother. So much happiness is missing from his life. If he were to remarry, it should be for his sake, not mine."

Constance was always concerned about her father's well-being. She had reflected on his loneliness many times before, but it always led to feelings of melancholy. Hoping to avoid such emotions now, she changed the subject. "Who made that pretty needlework framed by the entryway?"

"That old thing? I did, if you must know. I made it for my father when I was about your age. He hung it in his library. After he died, Jane moved it out here. She said it was too pretty to hide."

"Would you teach me to stitch like that? I never learnt."

"Certainly. I would be delighted."

THE NEXT AFTERNOON, MR. AND Mrs. Bingley called at Longbourn and it was Jane's first visit as a married woman. A few days earlier, it was her home, but now she felt like a stranger. It is just a house, she thought to herself. Mrs. Bennet met them in the entryway as soon as they were announced. "Mr. Bingley, Mrs. Bingley, welcome to Longbourn!"

"Thank you, Mama," said Jane as she stepped up to kiss her mother's cheek.

"I am so glad you are here! Come into the drawing room so we can all talk. Jane, you look beautiful. Come along, Mr. Bingley."

Mrs. Bennet was all pleasure and happiness. Jane, in having captured such a wonderfully rich man as Mr. Bingley, was now her favorite daughter, and she took great pride in her own efforts at insuring they were a match. Mrs. Bennet was still receiving compliments from friends and neighbors about the wedding breakfast and took no inconsiderable pleasure from it. On seeing Jane for the first time and being able to call her Mrs. Bingley, her joy was nearly absolute. All that remained to make it complete would be an attachment between one of her daughters and Mr. Grinly. She was determined that he would not leave the country without taking one of them to wife.

Jane's four sisters were in the drawing room. Bingley quickly stepped up to them, and with a bow and a flourish, said, "Ladies, allow me to introduce my wife, Mrs. Charles Bingley."

The ladies clapped their approval, and Elizabeth smiled at the blush on Jane's cheeks.

"And I am your new brother, Charles Bingley, at your service."

The girls rushed up to them to greet Jane as Mrs. Bingley and claim Mr. Bingley as their brother. It was a wonderful moment for Elizabeth, who observed Jane glowing with happiness.

Elizabeth was the last of the sisters to present herself to Mrs. Bingley. "Jane, congratulations! Is Mr. Bingley taking good care of you?"

Jane could not hide her joy. "He is the most wonderful man!" And in a subdued tone, she added, "I know that Papa would have liked Charles."

"Yes, I know he would have."

THE WHOLE PARTY RETIRED TO the drawing room. Jane found herself next to Mr. Grinly and took it upon herself to begin the conversation. "Well, sir, how are you enjoying Longbourn?"

"I have experienced nothing but enjoyment and relaxation since I have been here. The country is a healthy change from the fuss and dirt of London."

"But there are many diversions in London. Lizzy and I would often stay with our aunt. She takes us to the theatre, the opera and the outside concerts, amusements that are sorely lacking in Hertfordshire. The shops and stores are delightful."

"You are right. There are many good things about London." He paused for a moment. "Will you remain long at Netherfield?"

"Yes, we consider ourselves quite at home there, and it is such an advantage for me to be settled so near my friends and family. I could not be more content."

"Netherfield is a beautiful home. Mrs. Bennet took Constance and me over to the house one day to see the park. I hope you are pleased with it."

"I am, and I am glad that you like it. It is so wonderful living there. Mr. Bingley spoils me with luxuries I have never known. Every day is so new and exciting for me."

"There is no greater pleasure than basking in the love of your partner in life. I wish you joy."

"Thank you. Will you be long in the area?"

"Our plans are not yet fixed. We spent six weeks in London and the surrounding area. Our visit to Longbourn has been very agreeable. Your mother is a gracious hostess, your sisters are very pleasant young women, and Miss Bennet has been especially kind to Constance. It is a delight for me to watch them together. She is teaching her some needlework, and every day Constance tells me how much she enjoys Miss Bennet and about all the things of which they talk. It warms my heart to see it."

"Elizabeth's goodness makes her a favorite with everyone."

Mr. Grinly did not reply, but his mind had not wandered far from the subject as his attention turned towards Elizabeth's side of the room.

Jane observed an expression of tenderness on his face as he looked at her sister. "She has a lively personality. When anyone is with her, they cannot help but feel happier. She brightens any room she is in with her laughter and gentle smile. She is my best friend."

Recollecting himself, he turned his attention back to Jane. "That is quite a recommendation. She is a delightful young woman."

It was Mrs. Bennet's turn to make an observation. "Mr. Grinly, you must tell Mrs. Bingley about your beautiful home in Wiltshire. Jane, it is a remarkable place called Sappingford and is worth three thousand a year!"

"Mother! Please!"

"I am only saying what is true. Am I not, Mr. Grinly?

Mr. Grinly laughed. "I am partial to Sappingford as the handsomest home in the country."

Following this exchange, Hill called Mrs. Bennet to the dining room, and the others were left alone. Once she was gone, Jane turned to Mr. Grinly. "I apologize for my mother, sir. She had no right to say those things, but you need not be uncomfortable, for you are among friends."

Elizabeth nodded her assent, very willing to admit Mr. Grinly as a friend.

"Thank you, Mrs. Bingley. Please do not make yourself uneasy."

The Bingleys were to remain to dinner, and in the afternoon, Jane had the pleasure of seeing Elizabeth speaking quietly with Mr. Grinly and Constance for a considerable time. Jane could not hear what they were saying, but she watched them closely and understood from her sister's countenance that she was well satisfied with the conversation.

JANE WAS SITTING QUIETLY IN the small sitting room at Netherfield when Mrs. Thomas mentioned to her that Mr. Bingley had received an express from Town. Wondering who might have sent it and if it were good news or bad, she went in search of her husband. She found him in his usual place in the library, sitting behind his large desk, and knowing that she was always welcome, she entered the room.

"Mrs. Thomas said that you received an express from Town. Is anything the matter?"

She slipped behind his chair and began to rub his shoulders.

Bingley made an unsuccessful effort not to be distracted by her gentle hands. "I hardly know. It is from Darcy. Perhaps you would like to read it."

Jane read the note quickly as she walked around to the front of his desk and sat down on one of the large chairs. "What does this mean? What does our marriage have to do with Elizabeth?"

"It was my opinion that he was in love with your sister, and that the objections he voiced concerning our marriage were really arguments that he was using to persuade himself that he did not care for Elizabeth."

"And do you really think that he still loves her?"

"I do."

"I know that Elizabeth was in love with him. Indeed, she still is despite the hurt he caused her, but what right does he think he has to play with her heart in such a way that causes her pain?" Jane was furious at the arrogance of Mr. Darcy.

"He has no right at all. It was wrong of him." Bingley hesitated for a moment. "If I were to invite him back to Netherfield, do you think she would see him?"

"I do not know if I want to see him, and his coming back will certainly hurt Elizabeth. How will she heal if he is here to remind her of all they shared together?"

"Very well. I shall not invite him, but if he truly loves her, he will not stay away."

A NEW SOURCE OF DELIGHT opened itself to Mr. Grinly. After several days of indecision, he had formed a resolution, one that promised great joy. He was going to propose marriage to Miss Elizabeth.

Mr. Grinly quietly arranged spending time alone with her each day in the garden, and they were always together in company in the evenings. He had continued to observe her developing relationship with Constance, and he was not unmindful of the pleasing effects of her charms over him.

Every time he looked at Elizabeth, his heart awakened in further recognition of her merits and accomplishments. While she could never replace Julia, she would be a good companion and would have a remarkably positive influence on Constance, the very circumstances to be desired in a second marriage.

He liked Elizabeth very much, but did not know if he would call it love. He felt nothing like the depth of feeling he felt for Julia, and while the years had tempered those raw feelings, it would take time for them to be replaced with love for Elizabeth. It would happen, and in the meantime, they would be very close friends. Undoubtedly, she did not love him, but she did love Constance, and as his love for her began to bloom in time, so too would hers for him. Their relationship would continually grow and progress to a stronger, safer place.

ELIZABETH HAD GROWN QUITE FOND of Constance. Each afternoon they would sit together in the drawing room, and Elizabeth would teach her how to stitch. Constance was an apt pupil and would someday be very proficient with a needle if she continued to practice. She had also noticed that Mr. Grinly began to pay her more attention. He was a very kind man and in some ways reminded her of Mr. Bingley. He had a gentle personality that was not easily disturbed by the silliness of her mother and sisters. Despite their nonsense, Mr. Grinly treated them calmly and with respect. Elizabeth had to admire him. He was so full of love for his daughter that it brought to mind how much she missed her own father.

"Miss Bennet, I want to thank you for the kindness you have shown my daughter," said Mr. Grinly to her after Constance had left them to seek another amusement. "She tells me that she enjoys your company immensely and has proudly shown me the needlework that you are teaching her. Thank you for taking the time to be with her. I am exceedingly grateful, and I know that she is, also."

"She is a pleasing, well-mannered young lady. I cannot help but like her."

"She is my treasure. It pains me that she knows so little of her mother. Constance reminds me of her."

"What happened to her mother? I mean, if it is not too painful for you tell me."

"She died following a carriage accident. The horses suddenly bolted and the driver could not regain control. They flew down a road until the wheels hit a tree and the carriage overturned. The driver jumped off suffering only slight injuries to his legs, but Julia could not escape. She was thrown against the inside of the carriage as it hit the ground and received a blow to her head. When she was removed from the carriage, she was curled up around Constance, who was miraculously unhurt. Although Julia regained consciousness for awhile, her injuries were too severe, and she died within a few days."

A tremble of sadness passed through Elizabeth as she considered the unhappy fate of poor Julia Grinly. She could not hear such a tale of tragedy without a great deal of sympathy for Mr. Grinly.

When he finished speaking, Elizabeth turned to him and put her hand on his arm. "Mr. Grinly, I am so sorry. I do not know what to say. How terrible it must have been for someone to come and tell you that your wife was gravely injured. I cannot imagine. How you must have suffered!"

Their eyes met and their glance held as she favored him with a smile of encouragement.

"Time has softened the pain, but I worry about Constance. It is not good for her to be alone. I hired a companion for her once, but they were never close, and Constance seemed more distressed by her than comforted."

"You have done your best to bring her up. Your love for her is quite evident."

Mrs. Bennet had determined that Mr. Grinly should marry Elizabeth. She observed them in the garden from an upper window, they had just parted, and Elizabeth was alone. Determined to find out all she could, Mrs. Bennet left the house to speak with her.

"Lizzy, I saw you and Mr. Grinly walking in the garden. Of what were you speaking?"

"Of nothing, Mama, we were just talking."

"I am sure that he likes you. Make every effort to please him and perhaps he will make you an offer."

Elizabeth glared at her mother. Unwilling to respond to such an affront, she turned and ran into the house.

"Miss Lizzy, come back here!"

Darcy knew that his mind and heart belonged to Elizabeth, but he was now faced with the question of how to regain the affection he had so callously thrown away.

Bingley had not responded to his letter. Darcy had hoped for an invitation to Netherfield, but was now beginning to doubt the possibility of receiving one. He remembered Miss Jane Bennet's words to him about Elizabeth, and she was now Mrs. Bingley so she would no doubt influence her husband's decisions. He did not want to think of her as his adversary, though he could hardly blame her for wanting to protect her sister. He determined that he would have to go to Hertfordshire without an invitation and stay at the inn. Before he had any chance at all of winning Elizabeth's hand, though, he would have to be reconciled with Bingley and confess his wrongdoing to his bride.

MR. GRINLY DID NOT KNOW what to do. He and Julia had been of one mind concerning marriage. They had discussed it, planned on it, and were secure in each other's affection long before his formal proposal. Her father's consent had been a matter of course.

With Elizabeth, it was very different. He was uncertain as to how she would respond to his addresses. To be sure, they had not known each other long, but he felt as though he knew her heart. His devotion to her was increasing. Once he set his heart free, he was surprised at how quickly it had come about.

Mr. Grinly knew Elizabeth spent the mornings in the garden, and he determined to meet her there. It was without difficulty that he found Elizabeth in a secluded place reading a book.

"Good morning, Miss Bennet."

"Good morning. It is a beautiful day, is it not? Would you care to sit down?" She gestured to the seat next to her as she closed her book. Taking this as a sign of encouragement, he joined her and cleared his throat.

She gave him a questioning look. It seemed as though he wanted to say something, yet he hesitated. He had never been uncomfortable with her before.

"Miss Bennet, I have been hoping for an opportunity to speak with you alone." He paused. "I have come to feel a deep regard and affection for you."

Elizabeth struggled to understand him. Affection?

"Sir?"

"Elizabeth, I know that I may not be what you imagined in a husband, but I offer myself to you." He stood up and paced in front of her for moment, then stopped and faced her. "I know we could be happy together. Constance needs you, and I need you. I give all that I am... and all that I have... to you, and beg that you will consent to be my wife."

Elizabeth could not speak. When the effects of her first astonishment wore off, she recalled how her father had teased her by saying he would never allow her to marry because he always wanted her to stay at Longbourn with him. She thought about Mr. Darcy, the kiss they shared, and the passion she felt for him. She remembered the blush on Jane's cheek at the end of her wedding ceremony when Mr. Bingley had repeated the words, '... with my body, I thee worship.'

Grinly was encouraged that she had not immediately answered, certain that such an answer could only be a negative.

Elizabeth's mind was in turmoil as images of Mr. Darcy tumbled about in her mind. Could she worship Mr. Grinly with her body? Was she free of Mr. Darcy?

No, she could not and was not.

"Mr. Grinly," she said with a voice barely audible, "thank you for your offer. I am flattered to know that I have inspired such feelings in someone who I regard as much as I do you."

But why could it not have been Mr. Darcy? She felt a blush overwhelm her features.

"As for marriage..."

"Miss Bennet," interrupted Mr. Grinly. He sat down with her again. "Please, I do not want you to decide now. It would not be fair. I have had time to consider this, and you have not. Perhaps we may discuss the matter at another time after you have had a chance to reflect on it?"

Although she was certain her mind would not alter, she felt she owed him a carefully framed answer and was grateful for the reprieve that would allow her the time she needed to formulate such a response.

"Yes, thank you."

She allowed him to take her hand, and he kissed it. She opened her heart in anticipation of his touch, but her thoughts were drawn to another time, another kiss, and another man.

From an upper window, Constance watched her father cross the lawn. She had expected that Elizabeth would accompany him back to the house, but she was not with him. This did not bode well.

Mr. Grinly had informed his daughter of his intention to ask Elizabeth to marry him, wanting to know how she felt about the prospect of having Elizabeth as her stepmother. Constance liked Elizabeth very much. Nay, she could say that she loved her, and she assured him of that.

Constance had only vague memories of her mother, images of being loved very much by her. Life had been cruel the day she was taken from the world. If only Elizabeth would accept her father, she would love her as much as she did him.

RETURNING TO THE HOUSE, MR. Grinly went immediately to his daughter, knowing she would be expecting to hear from him as to his success with Elizabeth. Constance was anticipating his visit, and immediately answered his knock at her door. "Father?"

He stepped into the room and closed the door behind him. "I received neither a favorable nor unfavorable answer from Miss Bennet. She told me that she held me in regard. She seemed to hesitate, though, and before she could continue, I asked her to think about my offer and suggested that we would talk about it at a later time, to which she agreed."

Constance embraced him. "Do you think she will accept?"

Mr. Grinly held his daughter close. "It would be a big change for her. I am so much older than she, and we live so far away. I know she is particularly close to her sister."

"She must love you. How could she not?"

LEFT ALONE IN THE GARDEN, Elizabeth had time to think about what had occurred. As astonishing as Mr. Grinly's proposal was, she could now look back over the course of their relationship and see the increasing intimacy into which she had been drawn. He had never behaved in any manner that would make her uncomfortable, and she would have to confess that she always enjoyed his company. She was satisfied that she had done nothing to encourage his suit and had done nothing to discourage his friendship.

She was not insulted by his offer, and she would even admit that a portion of her vanity was gratified by the attention, yet it was painful. She did not want to hurt him but she knew he would be disappointed.

Mr. Grinly was offering a home and a daughter. Constance was a lovely girl, but it seemed an unlikely responsibility for her to assume the education and development of a young woman only six years her junior. Constance's sweet disposition had endeared her to Elizabeth, and she knew that they could be friends, but Wiltshire was so far away.

Elizabeth passed unseen into the house and went up to her room, pleading indisposition when she was called down to dinner. She knew Mr. Grinly would be distressed by her absence, and perhaps her mother would be angry, but she could not face him, not until she had spoken with Jane.

ELIZABETH WALKED TO NETHERFIELD BEFORE breakfast the next morning. She had been unable to sleep, and she had to see Jane. There was nothing else to be done.

The cool morning air was refreshing. She had felt confined and restricted in her room, unwilling to leave it for fear of encountering Mr. Grinly. This was the farthest she had been from home since her fall, and now she was going back to the place where it all began.

"Good morning, Miss Bennet," said Mrs. Thomas as she opened the door. "Welcome to Netherfield. May I inquire after your health?" She ushered Elizabeth towards the sitting room.

"I am well, thank you. Is my sister awake?"

"Yes, but Mrs. Bingley has not come down yet. I will send word that you are here."

Jane must have been nearly dressed because Elizabeth did not have to wait long. On Jane's appearance in the sitting room, all the anxiety that had been building inside her burst, and she ran to Jane and dissolved into tears.

"Oh, Jane!"

Jane held her without saying a word, and gently hushed and caressed her into silence. "Will you tell me what is wrong?"

"I do not know what to do or how to feel!"

"What do you mean?"

"Mr. Grinly proposed marriage to me yesterday." She nestled herself in Jane's embrace and felt her eyes begin to burn once again.

"What did he say?"

"Everything! He said we would be happy together. He said Constance needed me. He said that he needed me. He said he would give me everything he had."

"I can tell by your tears that you did not accept him."

"I did not reject him completely. He asked me to consider the offer, and that we would talk about it later, to which I agreed. Please tell me how to refuse him."

Jane was grateful that the refusal had not been made. She knew that Elizabeth was quite distraught and was probably not thinking clearly, yet she was faced with such an important decision, perhaps the most important of her life. Jane knew that her sister's happiness was at stake and determined that she must give Elizabeth her best counsel.

"Do you think that is wise?"

"What do you mean?"

"To refuse him."

Elizabeth's head begin to ache. "Do you think I should accept him?"

"Do you like him?"

"Well… I… He is a pleasant man, I confess, and I do love Constance, I truly do, but Jane — "

"You will come to love him in no time at all. You will move away from Longbourn and the society of our mother and sisters to your own home. The three of you will settle very comfortably in your own family party at Sappingford."

There was a long, uncomfortable silence.

"But, Jane, I do not love him. I do not know if I could ever love him."

"Why not?"

"Because I am still in love with Mr. Darcy."

Jane shook her head in frustration. Mr. Darcy had hurt Elizabeth more than she had thought possible, and now her attachment to him might cause her to give up the best chance for happiness she might ever have.

"I see. Has Mr. Darcy made you an offer?"

Elizabeth frowned. "No, you know he has not."

"And has he given you any reason to believe that he will come back? Does he love you?"

"No. I have not heard from him, but I know he loves me," said Elizabeth firmly. She wiped her eyes and tried to focus on the conversation. Jane was behaving very strangely. It was as if she were trying to convince her to accept Mr. Grinly.

"Is his behavior consistent with someone who loves you?"

Elizabeth did not answer.

"What about a letter? Has he sent you a letter?" Jane was not about to tell her of Mr. Darcy's note to her husband. Elizabeth would be encouraged by it, and she would hold onto her feelings for Mr. Darcy. In the note, Mr. Darcy had said nothing about coming back to her, just that he was admitting a mistake.

"I know he loves me! I know he does!"

"Does he? Does he express his love for you by not coming back into Hertfordshire? There is nothing to prevent him. He is his own master."

Tears poured out of Elizabeth's eyes. "Why are you doing this? Why are you saying these things?"

"Regardless of what you may feel, Mr. Darcy is not worthy of your love. Here is Mr. Grinly, a man who will love you and who has asked for your hand, and you are ready to refuse him. And for what reason? Because you nurse an affection for Mr. Darcy that is not returned."

Jane felt her own heart breaking. She had never used such language with Elizabeth, and she knew that she was causing her considerable pain. Yet what else could she do? She could not allow Elizabeth to walk away from Mr. Grinly's offer because of an infatuation for Mr. Darcy.

Elizabeth could not respond. Her heart was pounding as if it would escape her chest. She sat resolutely silent with her eyes clenched shut, rocking herself back and forth on the sofa.

Chapter 13

Darcy went in search of Georgiana and found her in the music room studying a new song. He stood in the doorway and looked at her. Stepping out of the role of brother and guardian, he admitted to himself that she was a handsome young woman, and though she had a serious disposition, she was pleasant and lively with those whom she knew well. She seemed to have grown overnight. How had it happened?

He spoke her name softly so that he would not startle her.

Georgiana set down her music and turned to him with a smile. "Fitzwilliam, I did not hear you."

"I am sorry if I am disturbing you." He put his arm around her shoulder. "You are sixteen, my dear, and will soon be out. Have you given much thought to marriage?"

Georgiana glanced at her brother with a surprised look. "Marriage? I do not give it any thought at all. Why do you ask?"

"You have a large dowry. Thirty thousand pounds is no insignificant sum. You accused me of not being willing to pursue my affection for Miss Bennet because she has no dowry. The opposite is true for you. There are few larger. I am afraid that in the coming years you will meet young men who will appear to be trying to win your affection, but are really interested in marrying you solely for your fortune. Please be cautious, and do not be fooled by these men. A man who would marry you for your money will never love you. Oftentimes, I regret that our father was so generous with you because your dowry will always be of interest to unscrupulous men. I know it is my duty as your guardian to protect you from such men, but I cannot safeguard your heart. Should you give your affection to a fortune hunter, I may prevent the marriage, but I cannot

150

prevent the broken heart and pain you will suffer.

"What I have to say now is very private, but I trust your discretion." Darcy paused, and Georgiana looked at him expectantly. "During my last visit at the Tildens, Mr. Tilden drew me into his study to discuss his daughter."

"What did he say?"

"He told me about Miss Tilden's dowry of twenty five thousand pounds and wanted me to understand that he would approve of a marriage between us. He told me he wanted a good match for his daughter and that he would add an additional ten thousand pounds to insure success. Georgiana, he was trying to bribe me into marrying his daughter."

"Does Miss Tilden know this?"

"I am certain she had no idea of what we were speaking, but I would suppose that she is aware that her father will do anything he can to secure a match for her. I cannot tell you how disgusted I was. Had I ever felt any inclination for Miss Tilden, I am certain I would no longer. I want you to know that I will never do anything like that to you."

"I will remember your advice, and I shall take pity on poor Miss Tilden. I assume she will not be allowed to make her own decisions regarding her future. Thank you for allowing me the opportunity to make mine. I suppose that makes a woman like Miss Bennet very fortunate."

"In what way?"

"Without a dowry, she must know that the man who would propose marriage to her must truly love her."

MR. GRINLY WAS WORRIED AS he paced in the drawing room. A servant told him that Miss Bennet left the house early on foot, though he did not know where she went. Now it was the afternoon, and she was not back, yet her family did not seem to be concerned about her. The behavior of Miss Bennet compared to that of her younger sisters, and even her mother, was very different. He suspected that the gulf in thoughtfulness and consideration was just as great. They seemed oblivious of her absence. He did not know whether it was appropriate for him to speak to Mrs. Bennet about it. To own the truth, he had hoped to talk with Miss Bennet today and hear her answer to his proposal, but that could wait. As long as she was safe, there would be plenty of time for talking.

He took his place in a chair by a window that overlooked the paddock. Satisfying himself that there was no one out front, he resumed his book and resolved to be calm. Breaking his resolution ten times in as many minutes, he was still surprised when a lone rider approached the house. The man was a liveried servant carrying a letter. Mr. Grinly heard a knock, a brief conversation, and then the man mounted his horse and rode off. Having worked himself into a near panic, he resolved to speak with Mrs. Bennet immediately, but before he could remove from his chair, Mrs. Bennet herself entered the room.

"Mr. Grinly, I am so sorry. I am certain... at least... well, perhaps you have been waiting for Elizabeth. She spent the morning with Jane at Netherfield. A servant just came to inform me that she has fallen ill and will not return until tomorrow."

"I hope she is not seriously ill."

"There was no mention of it. I suspect she just wanted to spend some time with Jane, that is all."

"But would she not have said that in her note?"

"I see that you do not know Elizabeth well at all." He detected resentment in her voice. "She walks here and there and goes running off for the longest time. Why, before Jane was married, she spent two weeks at Netherfield after falling and striking her head on a rock. I told her that she should be careful, but she never listens to me. I told her she must not behave so recklessly if she wants a man to like her well enough to marry her. She must —"

"Mrs. Bennet," interrupted Mr. Grinly, who had difficulty in hiding his displeasure. "Miss Bennet is a lovely young woman, and I am certain she will have no trouble in attaching any young man in whom she should take an interest."

"You are very kind, sir. Perhaps if you read the letter yourself, you will be at ease and not worry over Elizabeth." She handed him the note and walked off. He found that it reported just what Mrs. Bennet had said. Returning to his chair, he wondered how a mother could say such things about her own daughter.

Mr. Grinly again opened his book, but could not concentrate. He was not satisfied that there was not something seriously wrong with Miss Bennet. He did take comfort that she was with her sister and only hoped that he was not the cause of her distress.

AFTER DISPATCHING THE NOTE TO Longbourn that announced Elizabeth's indisposition, Jane returned to her bedside. She was in agony over the words she had used with Elizabeth. In her effort to crush Elizabeth's hopes for a marriage with Mr. Darcy, she had seriously shaken Elizabeth's spirits. To comfort her, Jane climbed onto the bed next to her as she used to when they were children.

"I am so sorry. Please forgive me," Jane whispered. "I only want the best for you, and now I have distressed you." Jane caressed Elizabeth's cheek and brushed her fingers through her hair.

Elizabeth did not immediately respond, but felt her strength return as she was comforted by the affection and love of her dearest sister. At length, she spoke. "Perhaps I should marry Mr. Grinly. I know he is fond of me. He is a kind man, and possibly, we could be happy together. I wish I loved him more and Mr. Darcy less."

"FATHER, WHERE IS ELIZABETH? HAS she returned?"

Mr. Grinly was convinced that Elizabeth's absence was directly related to his proposal. Why else would she go to Netherfield so unexpectedly? He saw the look of worry in Constance's eyes. "Mrs. Bennet received a note from Mrs. Bingley a short while ago. Miss Bennet went to Netherfield this morning and has fallen ill and will not be returning today."

"Is she going to be well?

"I know that Mrs. Bingley will do everything in her power to insure her sister's health and happiness." Mr. Grinly sat down on the sofa and took Constance's hand as she sat down with him. "I hope this has nothing to do with me. I hope that my proposal has not distressed her."

"Perhaps she needs this time away from us to make a decision. I cannot imagine that she would not love you."

LONDON

Dear Bingley,

I hope you are happy and well. I have no doubt that you are. I confess that I am distressed because I have not heard from you. Perhaps my last post was misdirected. I rather believe, though, that you have chosen to ignore it. I cannot blame you. It is my fault that a breach has arisen between us, and I deeply regret it. It is painful to me in every way.

I admire your strength of character. You withstood all my attacks and did what you knew to be right. Miss Bennet is very fortunate to have gained the love of such an honorable man as you and I apologize for my interference. What I thought was right for you was only my own selfishness. There is not a kinder and gentler woman than Miss Bennet, and your marriage to her will bring you the highest degree of satisfaction and pleasure. You are married now. I should call her Mrs. Bingley.

I know our friendship is ruined, and I am sorry for it. I promise I will never fail you again should you ever decide to renew our acquaintance.

Sincerely,
F. Darcy

A SHAFT OF LIGHT PEEKING through a gap in the curtains announced to Elizabeth that a new day had begun, a day that had arrived too quickly. Jane had stayed with Elizabeth for a large part of the night, and she had slept well, but was now faced the prospect of discussing her future with Mr. Grinly. What that future should be she hardly knew. All that she could say with certainty was that she was completely bewildered.

After a late breakfast and exhausting every excuse she could think of to delay the inevitable, Elizabeth declared that she must return home. Jane insisted that she use her carriage. "I will come with you if you would like. I know the others cannot give you much comfort."

"No. I can see no reason to take you from your dear husband. If Mr. Grinly truly cares for me, he will wait for his answer until I am ready to give it."

"Whatever your decision, I will support you in it. Whenever you wish to come to Netherfield, allow me to send the carriage for you. Please do not ever feel that you must walk."

"To make you happy, I will. Goodbye, Jane." Elizabeth smiled a farewell while Mr. Bingley handed her into the carriage.

THE RIDE BACK TO LONGBOURN passed quickly for Elizabeth. Alone with her thoughts, she was able to compose herself. She reviewed her conversation with Jane, who had told her that Mr. Darcy was not worthy of her love, that he had rejected her, and that she owed him nothing. She advised her to forget him and not spurn the offer of a good man with whom the future would be bright and with whom love would surely grow out of mutual respect and esteem. As Elizabeth approached Longbourn, she felt surrounded by a feeling of peace.

She arrived home to a quiet house. Mrs. Bennet, Kitty and Lydia had all gone into Meryton. As Elizabeth was passing through the hall, Constance happened upon her.

"Elizabeth! You have returned!" Elizabeth could see tears well up in her eyes and reached out to embrace her. "We were all so worried about you! Will you not tell me what happened?"

Elizabeth had just a moment to reflect on the irony of a comparative stranger welcoming her home with more enthusiasm than she could expect to receive from her own family. This thought brought Elizabeth both pleasure and pain as she remembered whose daughter Constance was and what Elizabeth could expect from her in the future — if there was a future.

"I am sorry. I did not mean to alarm anyone. I am well enough now. How are you?"

"Relieved that you are back. My father has been very concerned since the night you did not come down to dinner."

Elizabeth could make no response, and the serenity she had achieved on the ride to Longbourn quickly faded into confusion.

Constance observed Elizabeth's change of countenance and led the conversation in another direction. "I must say it has been quiet here without you."

"Quiet? In this house?" laughed Elizabeth.

"Well, you are right. It is much noisier than Sappingford."

"It must be very lonely for you there."

"It is, some of the time, but it would be so much happier there if you..." Constance covered her mouth with her fingers. She was about to bolt from the room when Elizabeth gently held her arm.

"Constance, please do not go. Come and sit with me."

Constance allowed Elizabeth to guide her to a sofa where they sat together and were silent while Elizabeth determined what should be said. "Your father told you about his proposal of marriage, did he not?"

"Are you angry that I know?"

"Of course not. You have had him all to yourself for a long time. Your father is very wise to have spoken to you about me. It concerns you almost as much as it does me, really. If I were to marry your father, it would mean many changes for you."

"I am ready to share him, Elizabeth. He told me that you have not given him an answer yet and that he asked you to wait before you do."

"That is true."

"Is that why you left yesterday and did not come back? Did he distress you?"

"He did not make me angry, but I was very upset. His proposal was... It was so unexpected. All evening my mind was in turmoil. I did not know what to say to him. The next morning, I rose early after a sleepless night and walked to

Netherfield to see my sister. The prospect of facing your father was daunting to me. I was so distraught that I made myself ill. Rather than send me back to Longbourn, Jane asked me to stay with her."

"Why were you so upset?"

"I recently met a man who I believed loved me, and I loved him, but he disappointed me, hurt my sister, and betrayed his best friend. He has not come back, nor do I expect to see him again. Last night, Jane persuaded me to believe that he was gone forever, and it was difficult for me to accept that."

"Do you still love him?" That Elizabeth's heart might be engaged elsewhere was something Constance had not considered.

"I do not know anymore."

"Does that mean you cannot love my father?"

"No. It does not mean that at all."

"My father was distressed yesterday when you did not come back. He sat by the window, waiting for your return. When the servant came with the note from Mrs. Bingley, he was relieved that you were with your sister, but was further pained. He was convinced that his proposal was the reason you did not come back. It appears that he was correct."

"I did not mean to hurt anyone and especially not your father. He is a good man. You are so lucky to have him."

"He is a good man, Elizabeth, and he will love you and care for you the way you deserve. You will be happy at Sappingford. My father and I do not want to change you, just love you and join our lives with yours.

"I have much to learn, and if I had my choice, I would learn it from you. I admire your cheerfulness and your smile. You cannot imagine how grateful I am for the kindness you have shown me. I never learned to do needlework until you taught me. I do not know how to play the pianoforte. We have one at home that my father says is very fine. You could teach me, and we could play together, and I will show you how to draw."

"Oh, Constance!"

"If I can love you for all these things as your friend, imagine how much my father will love you as your husband. I know that Wiltshire is a long way from Hertfordshire, but I am sure we can travel here often and invite your family to Sappingford. We want to share your life, not take it away from you."

Elizabeth could see that Constance spoke with all the sincerity of an honest heart. As the idea of a closer connection between them unfolded, she knew she would welcome this relationship. "I am concerned because your father is so much older than I am, and I am only six years older than you. Would he begin to treat me as a daughter and not a wife? Would I want to treat him as a father? I feel daunted at the responsibility of helping to raise a young lady of fourteen. I feel I have nothing that I can teach you."

"My father loves you. He is older than you, but not so much older that your relationship with him would ever change. I do not want you to be my mother. That is not what I need. I need a friend who will love me even when I am angry and upset, who will be patient as I continue to mature, and who will be my confidante after I come out and am introduced to young men. I need someone who can teach me how to love, and that will happen by example, by the way you love my father and he loves you."

"Your view of our life together is a happy one, to be sure. Do you think it would really be true? Does he really love me enough to put up with my moods and impertinence?"

"He would put up with anything to have you, but from what I know of you, there would be very little to 'put up with,' as you say, and very much to love."

Elizabeth suddenly felt confined and uncomfortable. "This is all so new, and I do not know that I love him. I do not think that it would be fair to marry him if I do not."

"He told me that he knows he is not what you expected in a husband. That is why he did not want your answer right away, so that you would have a chance to think about it. If you do not love him now, could you?"

"He is a good man. He has not told me if he loves me, but I believe he might."

"He does. I know he does."

"What will be our plans, if I were to accept your father?"

"He knows that you want to be married from Longbourn Church with all your friends and family. After the wedding, I will stay here while you and Father tour for as long as you want. Then you will return for me for our trip to Sappingford and your new home."

"It all sounds very nice, Constance."

At that moment, Mr. Grinly came into the drawing room. "Am I intruding?" He was surprised to see Elizabeth, but did not let the emotion show on his face.

"No, Father, please come in. I was just leaving. Why do you not entertain Elizabeth while I ask Mary to play the pianoforte for me?"

ELIZABETH AND MR. GRINLY REMAINED silent until Constance left the room. When he was certain they were alone, he took a few steps towards

Elizabeth, but stopped in unspoken acknowledgement of the turmoil he saw in her eyes. "I am pleased to know that you are well and have returned home. I feared that I was responsible for your indisposition. My only consolation was that you were with your sister."

"Please forgive me for making you uneasy. Please —"

"Elizabeth." She turned away from him at the sound of her name. "To be honest, I was surprised at the indifference of your family regarding your absence."

"I am sure they mean well."

Elizabeth hesitated. Was now the time to talk with him? They were alone, to be sure. Her mother and sisters were away. Constance had left and Elizabeth knew she would not be seen again until sought by her father. Elizabeth could hear the sound of Mary's instrument and knew she would not be a disruption. There would be no better time.

"Would you care to sit with me?"

He sat down next to her and began to hope. If she were bent on rejecting him, she would not allow him to be in such close proximity.

Elizabeth closed her eyes and chased away her anxiety. "Sir, I have given much thought to your proposal." She stood and walked away from him towards a window. "I had to leave. I had to speak with Jane. I did not know what to do or how to answer you, and during my conversations with her, I became very distraught, and she insisted that I remain at Netherfield for the night. I am sorry to have worried you, though I must say I am gratified at the same time. I take pleasure in knowing that somebody cares about me."

"I care very much, Elizabeth." Their eyes met, and their gaze held.

"Constance informed me that she is aware of your proposal."

"I felt that she should know. I am sorry if that offends you. It was not my intention to —"

"No, you were right. The marriage of her father would cause an impact on her life and bring so many changes that it is entirely appropriate and kind of you to include her in your decision. We had quite a conversation concerning you."

Mr. Grinly joined Elizabeth at the window. "I fear for her, for she is alone, but seeing you with Constance has taught me to know that you would be not only a loving wife to me, but a friend to her. I love you, Elizabeth, and I cannot help loving you even more for Constance's sake."

Elizabeth became flushed with embarrassment. It was the first time he had professed his love.

Mr. Grinly took her hand, which she willingly surrendered. "Elizabeth, I promise to love you for the rest of my life and beyond. I promise to treat you with kindness and respect. I am certain that you do not love me equally, but I know that you will. I know that we will be happy together. Please accept my hand in marriage."

Thoughts of Mr. Darcy came to Elizabeth's mind. In the briefest instant, their relationship passed before her eyes. She remembered the expression on his face when he first saw her awake and when they talked about their parents' deaths. The memory of his kiss was immediately followed by a recollection of the pain he inflicted when he left her and tried to take Mr. Bingley away from Jane. All of it danced in her mind. Mr. Grinly was offering her everything Mr. Darcy would not, longing for her to be with him the way he had not, wanting her in the way he did not.

"Yes, Mr. Grinly," she whispered, "I will marry you."

THE NEWLY ENGAGED COUPLE TOOK advantage of the relative solitude of the drawing room to speak of their future together and of all the happiness they anticipated in each other's society. Elizabeth questioned him about her new home, and Mr. Grinly replied in particular detail. He described the grounds and country around Sappingford as the prettiest in the kingdom and rejoiced in the pleasure she anticipated at the prospect of living there. He assured her that Sappingford would be at her disposal to decorate as she liked and hoped that she would soon feel quite at home there. Elizabeth could not imagine how such a fine home could be improved and was certain that she would be very comfortable.

With each word they spoke, Elizabeth experienced a thrill of excitement at the prospect of her marriage. That led to questions as to when the precise moment was that he fell in love with her, a question he was very eager to answer.

"I first noticed your gentle manner with Constance. I could not but be moved by witnessing the particular attention with which you favored her. Every day I heard new reports from her about the manner in which you taught and entertained her. Constance told me she loved everything about you. As you are aware, she is generally shy and reserved, so I was surprised to hear her voice such sentiments about anyone, though in your case," he smiled, "they are wholly deserved."

"Mr. Grinly, please..."

"I watched you whenever I could, to learn for myself how you interacted with my daughter, and what I witnessed truly pleased me. At first I saw you as friends, but it occurred to me that you were treating her with the same care, gentleness, and kindness that were characteristic of your relationship with your elder sister. Your behavior and what I heard from Constance convinced me that your relationship with her was not that of just an acquaintance, but one of sincere regard and attachment. Constance blooms when she is in your company. All shades of reserve are put aside, and I see true joy in her countenance. Do you recall the occasion of Mrs. Bingley's first visit to Longbourn after her marriage?"

"Yes, I do."

"I was seated near her. You were across the room with Constance, and so I was free to talk with your sister. I remarked to her on the improvements I had witnessed in Constance as a result of your kind attentions to her. Mrs. Bingley spoke of the nature of your relationship together and pronounced you to be her best friend. She said that every room was made cheerful by your laughter and happy disposition. I looked over to you, you were laughing, and I realized that I felt the same way. The same charm with which you captured Constance's heart was working on me, and as I observed your relationship with her with its warmth and tenderness, I realized that I wanted that for myself."

Elizabeth listened with a smile. Every word he spoke confirmed to her how important she was to him and filled her with gratitude for his assurances of love.

He raised her hand to his lips and kissed her fingers. "Perhaps I spoke too soon, but I believed that you would never consider me as a prospective husband until the thought was first placed in your mind, and I determined that I would place that thought there. I was disappointed, but not surprised, when you did not answer me immediately. Indeed, I feared that such an answer would be a resounding rejection. The suspense of not knowing my future, then finding that you were ill at your sister's home and that I was the probable cause of it, made last night one of the most miserable of my life."

She turned away from him. "I did not mean to hurt you. It was all so new and unexpected. I had to talk to Jane. All I could think about was speaking with Jane."

Mr. Grinly stepped behind her and put his arms around her. Grateful for his touch, she folded her arms, resting her hands over his. "It must have been a difficult time for you, Elizabeth. The suddenness of my application must have troubled you, and I perfectly understand your need to speak with her. I just wish I had known with a certainty where you were and that you were safe and cared for."

"I was safe and cared for, but I was so confused. I did not know what to feel. Jane and I spoke all day and into the night. I was very upset, and she refused to allow me return to Longbourn that evening."

"Your mother gave me the note that Mrs. Bingley sent, announcing that you would not be returning, and I was comforted by the knowledge."

"Jane and I continued to discuss your proposal, our future prospects, and the expectations for happiness that I could reasonably expect as your wife. I became comfortable with the idea of being sought by you. Jane spoke very favorably of the match, and in just a little time, I began to take the greatest pleasure in the thought of being married to you. When I returned to Longbourn, Constance came upon me and we sat together in the drawing room for quite a while. She shared with me the hopes and dreams she had for me, and assured me of your love and affection. I was concerned about how much younger I am than you and how that might affect our relationship. I was also uncertain how I might accomplish my role as a friend and teacher for Constance, who is at a very delicate time of life."

She favored him with a smile and continued.

"When you came in and poured out your heart to me and again proposed, I was prepared to hear you. I knew that my own happiness would be secured by marrying you, and I committed at that moment to make certain that I ensured your happiness."

He kissed her hand. "You cannot imagine how happy it makes me to hear that."

Chapter 14

Their conversation passed to lighter subjects.

"Where would you like to go on a bridal tour, Elizabeth?"

"I confess that I have not thought of it."

"Other than the Gardiners, I do not know who we might visit. Is there anywhere in particular you would like to go?"

Elizabeth had not given any thought to a tour of any kind, but after thinking for a moment, she recalled a wish from her childhood. "Would you be willing to take me to the sea, perhaps into Kent?"

"I would be very happy to take you there."

This conversation took place in the drawing room in front of a large window overlooking the grounds of Longbourn. The couple continued to discuss the minutest details of their relationship. It was a subject of insatiable interest to them.

"Elizabeth, will you please call me by my Christian name, Thomas?"

He wished to hear her pronounce his name, but the request masked another purpose. He felt that her acquiescence would be a further indication of the ease and comfort she felt with him. Despite her apparent pleasure in having accepted his suit, the difficulty she had experienced in determining to accept him was troubling.

"Yes, Mr. Grinly," she laughed, and then she looked up at him with a full heart. "Yes, Thomas, I will."

He released the hand he had been holding and caressed her cheek. She smiled and closed her eyes, basking in the warmth of his touch. She opened her eyes when he withdrew his hand and saw a look of passion that filled her with expectation. In an energized moment, their lips came together. At first, it was a light touch, for he was uncertain what her response might be. He did not want to make her uncomfortable, but when she put her hand on his shoulder and leaned into him, he wrapped his arms around her waist and held her close. The relief he experienced as she encouraged him removed the anxiety and uncertainty he had felt in wondering if she had truly decided in his favor.

Elizabeth released herself from his embrace and turned away from him with downcast eyes. She had longed and hoped for that same feeling of passion and desire that Mr. Darcy had created. She wanted so desperately to feel that same hunger for Mr. Grinly, knowing that if she did, she could honestly give herself to him, but he did not elicit that same desire and she was left feeling nothing.

UNFORTUNATELY FOR THE COUPLE, BUT fortunate for propriety's sake, they heard the front door open and Mrs. Bennet and her daughters come into the house. Elizabeth and Mr. Grinly separated, just as her mother walked into the room.

Mrs. Bennet had seen them together through the window and had witnessed their embrace, and the expressions of embarrassment that now colored their cheeks left no doubt as to their situation. She sat down in a chair opposite them and increased their embarrassment by studying them closely. "Do you two have anything you wish to tell me?"

Mrs. Bennet could barely contain her excitement. It was a pleasure to think of having two daughters well married to rich gentlemen. She congratulated herself on having invited Mr. Grinly to Longbourn and only wished there were another cousin to introduce into the family.

Mr. Grinly rose to his feet. "Madam, may I speak with you in private? I have something I would ask of you." Elizabeth rose as if to leave the room.

"Lizzy, my love, please do not run off. Mr. Grinly, is what you have to say to me anything that Lizzy may not hear?"

It was, perhaps, inappropriate for a woman to witness her future husband request the consent of a parent, but he would say nothing that would offend. Indeed, it was an opportunity to express his feelings further for her in his address to her mother.

Mr. Grinly took Elizabeth's hand. "During my visit to Longbourn, I have experienced greater joy than I have ever known by being in the company of your family, and particularly with one member of it to whom I have become seriously attached. I have spoken with her and have learned that she reciprocates the affection I have for her, and she has pledged herself to me for the rest of her life. I have asked for Elizabeth's hand in marriage, and she has accepted me, and I am seeking your consent to our union and your blessing on it."

Elizabeth was touched by this declaration and squeezed his hand.

Mrs. Bennet squealed with delight. "I knew how it would be. Lizzy, I am so happy for you. Mr. Grinly, I know that Lizzy will make a proper wife for you. She will be nothing to Jane, of course, but just the same, I am so pleased that she will be settled so well."

"I assume that I have your consent?"

"Yes, you certainly do. Here, let me give you a kiss." He endured it admirably. "I am so happy! Lizzy, I am going to go into Meryton to tell my Sister Philips, Lady Lucas, and the Longs all about your engagement. I will go by Netherfield, too."

"Mama, will you please let me tell Jane? I want her to hear it from me." This was important to her, for just as Jane had broken the news of her engagement first to Elizabeth, she desired the opportunity to be the first to announce hers to Jane.

"Oh, very well. I will call for the carriage and set you as far as Meryton."

"Thank you, Mama." Mrs. Bennet went off to get ready.

Elizabeth turned to Mr. Grinly. "Thomas, I would like you to be with me when I tell Jane of our engagement. Will you?"

"Yes, love, I will." Elizabeth acknowledged him with a kiss on his hand. "We should tell Constance. She will be delighted. Will you go up to her with me?"

"Yes, Thomas, I would truly like to be there when she first hears our news." She knew that Constance would eagerly approve of their engagement and anticipated with pleasure the joy she would express on learning of it.

MR. GRINLY AND ELIZABETH LEFT the drawing room. As they approached the stairs, he noticed that they were quite alone. "Thank you for accepting me."

"It is my pleasure, sir." He drew near her and soon felt his lips on hers.

Elizabeth felt herself to be very happy, but in that moment of exultation, her joy was darkened as a memory of Mr. Darcy intruded. She felt herself grow very sad, very quickly. Mr. Grinly's kiss reminded her of Mr. Darcy, and her eyes began to burn and she could not hold back a sob. She clung to Mr. Grinly, grateful that she was not alone with such thoughts.

Mr. Grinly increased in her esteem by his response to her distress. He did not ask her what was wrong or try to determine its cause but merely held her, stroked her hair, and was silent.

She relaxed against him and squeezed her eyes shut. Nearly as fast as it came, the feeling passed, and she was able to compose herself again. "I am sorry."

"Shh…"

She determined that she would never again think about Mr. Darcy or let him ruin her happiness with Mr. Grinly.

"Thank you." Elizabeth wiped her eyes. "I will be fine."

Convinced that Mary would remain at her instrument for a good deal longer, Constance felt secure in leaving her there and retiring to her own bedchamber. She knew that her father would seek her out after his interview with Elizabeth.

Elizabeth and Mr. Grinly stepped together into the room, their faces brightened by smiles.

"Yes, Father?"

"Constance, Elizabeth has consented to be my wife."

Constance jumped off the bed and ran to her father. "I am so happy for you! Elizabeth, thank you so much! Thank you! I know we will all be happy together!" She turned to Elizabeth and gave her a kiss.

"We will, Constance," agreed Elizabeth. Constance's satisfaction with the engagement served to increase the joy Elizabeth felt. It confirmed to her that her decision to marry Mr. Grinly was correct.

"When shall you be married?"

"We have not really discussed it, but if there are no objections," she turned to Mr. Grinly, "within the month. I can see no reason to wait. We shall be the happiest family in the world!"

Mr. Grinly was very much in agreement, and the few minutes that they waited for the carriage were spent answering all of Constance's inquiries about her father's proposal and Elizabeth's acceptance of it.

Elizabeth and Mr. and Miss Grinly walked briskly from Meryton to Netherfield. It was a relief to be out of the carriage and away from Mrs. Bennet's constant chatter about fine weddings, lace, and satin. They walked up to the entrance to Netherfield with Elizabeth on one side of Mr. Grinly and Constance on the other. Mrs. Thomas opened the door.

"We are come to call on Mr. and Mrs. Bingley."

"Of course, Miss Bennet. Please, come in."

The party followed Mrs. Thomas into the drawing room where Jane was at her work. She rose at their entrance. "You are all very welcome to Netherfield."

"You know Mr. and Miss Grinly, of course," said Elizabeth. "Jane, I have good news. Mr. Grinly and I are to be married."

Jane embraced her sister. "Lizzy, how wonderful! I know you will be so happy."

At that moment, Mr. Bingley came into the room. "Welcome, Elizabeth. Good morning, sir," he said, addressing Mr. Grinly.

"Mr. Bingley," said Elizabeth shyly, "let me introduce you to my betrothed, Mr. Thomas Grinly."

"Betrothed? Congratulations! What a pleasure, sir, and welcome to the family." A hearty handshake for Mr. Grinly confirmed his goodwill. Constance received her congratulations with delight, and was every moment more and more pleased with the prospects of belonging to such a family.

Jane invited them to sit down and then sent for tea. "While we are waiting, may I speak with you, Lizzy?" She spoke in a serious, urgent voice, not consistent with the mood of the occasion.

"Of course, what —"

"Please come with me," whispered Jane.

"Very well. Please excuse me, Thomas." Elizabeth rose from the couch that she was sharing with Mr. Grinly and followed Jane from the room.

Mr. Grinly watched them leave, disconcerted by their sudden exit. He hoped that Mrs. Bingley would accept and approve of him. He knew that Elizabeth relied heavily on her opinion.

ELIZABETH AND JANE REMOVED TO a small sitting room and sat down together.

"Lizzy, I am sorry to take you away from your Mr. Grinly, but I must talk with you. I am very happy for you and so pleased that you came to a decision. I want you to know that I think it was the correct one. I like Mr. Grinly, and I know you will be very happy with him. He loves you. I can tell by the way he looks at you."

"Thank you. I am sure we will be happy." Jane's confidence in her happiness was a great comfort to Elizabeth.

"Lizzy, I will miss you! You will be living so far away from me."

"Thomas said that you will all be invited to Sappingford and that we would travel into Hertfordshire often. Will you write to me?"

Jane laughed. "Only if you promise to write to me."

"You know I will."

"I know how upset you were yesterday and how strong your feelings were for Mr. Darcy. Are you sure you love Mr. Grinly as you ought?"

"I do care for him, and I know that I will soon love him."

"Have you no thoughts of Mr. Darcy?" Jane felt that this conversation was more for Elizabeth's benefit than her own. She wanted Elizabeth to speak aloud the words that would put Mr. Darcy in her past and Mr. Grinly in her present and future.

"I have come to your way of thinking, Jane. If Mr. Darcy loved me, I would be preparing to marry him, not Mr. Grinly. I shall soon cease to think of Mr. Darcy at all."

"Then I am happy for you." Jane took her hand. "I am sure Mrs. Thomas has tea ready by now. Let us go back in. We do not want to keep Mr. Grinly waiting for you any longer that we must."

Mr. Grinly was anxiously awaiting their return, hoping for some indication of how their conversation went by the expressions on their faces. When the ladies walked into the room, they both looked at him, one with a smile and the other with a look of affection. He was satisfied. All would be well.

NETHERFIELD

Darcy,

I appreciate your recent letters, and I do accept your apology. Let us speak of it no more.

You must believe me when I tell you how happy I am. Jane fills my life with love and makes each day a precious experience for me. I only hope that someday you will be as blessed as I have been.

Unfortunately, Mrs. Bingley is still rather angry with you. She feels that you were trifling with Elizabeth. I am confident, because of circumstances that have just occurred, that this, too, will soon be forgotten.

It is to this effect. Elizabeth has consented to marry Mr. Thomas Grinly of Wiltshire who is a distant cousin. Mrs. Bennet invited him to Longbourn and he has been there since my wedding. While it was a short courtship, Jane believes that Elizabeth is genuinely attached to him. It is obvious that Mr. Grinly loves her very much.

Mrs. Bingley extends an invitation to you to come to Netherfield. She knows I miss your company. It is conditional, for she has assured me that you will be asked to leave the house immediately if you make any attempt to endanger Elizabeth's happiness with Mr. Grinly. Though you are my lifelong friend, my first allegiance is to my wife and her family, particularly Elizabeth, whom I admire very much. Please come to us, but I beg of you, stay away from Elizabeth.

With regards, &c.
Charles Bingley

A FOOTMAN BROUGHT DARCY a letter, and he began to smile in anticipation when he saw the directions. It was from Netherfield. It could only mean one thing. Bingley had accepted his apology and wished to renew their friendship. He quickly tore open the seal with an expectation of pleasure. The letter was short and did not take long to read.

"NO!!" he screamed. "NO! No, no, no..."

GEORGIANA HAD BEEN WORKING QUIETLY in the drawing room when she heard her brother's cry. She ran to the library and breathlessly entered the room. "Fitzwilliam, what is it? What is wrong? Please tell me!" She was shocked at the sight of her brother sitting at his desk. Agony was written on his face.

"Georgiana..."

His head fell onto his arms.

"Georgiana! Georgiana!"

If she had never known fear before, she did so now. Never had she witnessed such an outpouring of emotion. Never had she seen him so distraught.

"Oh, Brother, what is it?"

She ran behind his desk and embraced him. She was startled when she felt herself suddenly encircled by his strong arm and crushed against his chest.

"Georgiana," he whispered.

"Fitzwilliam, please..."

He released her and pushed her back an arm's length. "You shall know all." He handed her the crumpled letter.

She took it from his hand, smoothed it out, and began to read. It was astonishing, and she never would have thought it possible, but Fitzwilliam had somehow offended Mrs. Bingley. Mr. Bingley and her brother had been friends forever. What could this possibly have happened?

She continued reading, and her own heart nearly stopped. "Elizabeth has consented to marry Mr. Thomas Grinly..." Miss Bennet was to be married!

It was no small wonder that he called out.

"I am so very sorry." Georgiana stepped behind him and put her hands on his shoulders. She could feel the tension in his body.

"I do not know what to do. I do not know what to do," he repeated. "I love her."

He was then silent, and the ensuing pause was horrible to Georgiana.

In a voice filled with anger, he continued. "I have failed her, and I have failed myself! She cannot love him, for I know she loves me, yet I have driven her into his arms. He will take her from Hertfordshire, she will forget about me, and I shall never see her again." Darcy buried his face in his hands.

Georgiana could feel his body quake with emotion. She had never seen such pain before nor experienced it herself. How was she to relieve his suffering? What could she do for him? The truth was awful. She could do nothing. There was no telling how long he would suffer because of his actions and mourn Miss Bennet's loss. Indeed, she was now dead to him, the only woman he ever loved.

"I blame myself and my own stupid pride! Had I followed my heart, had I done what I knew to be correct, rather than striven to live up to the expectations of other people — our parents, our dead parents — if I had done this, she would be mine, and I would be filled and made whole because of her." A sob racked his body. "I realized my mistake too late, forever too late."

Georgiana knew he was no longer aware of her presence. She looked at him with tear-filled eyes until it became too much for her. She quietly slipped out of the room, unable to bear his anguish any longer.

ELIZABETH WAS LEANING ON MR. Grinly's arm as they walked through the garden at Longbourn. She felt liberated from the pain of her affection for Mr. Darcy, knowing that she had relinquished him. The air was fresh, the sun invigorating, and she felt loved.

"Elizabeth, have you ever been into Kent?"

"Except to go to London to stay with my aunt, I have never traveled beyond the neighborhood of Meryton. I have heard that Kent is a beautiful place."

"It is. Many years ago, Julia and I went..." Mr. Grinly interrupted himself. "I am sorry."

Elizabeth pulled on his arm to stop their progress. His eyes were fastened on the ground as he tried to recover from embarrassment. "Thomas," Elizabeth began in a soothing voice, "I am very sorry that your wife died, but please do not be afraid to speak of her to me. I am not afraid that you will love me any less."

Those words were exactly calculated to calm his misgivings. He took her hands and kissed them. "Indeed, my love, I know nothing about 'less' when it comes to loving you."

She smiled her approval and felt that with every minute she spent with him, her confidence increased and her commitment deepened.

DARCY SPENT A TORMENTED NIGHT reviewing his relationship with Elizabeth. It started off well enough, to be sure. Watching over her and caring for her while she was at Netherfield had been an exquisite pleasure. He remembered loving her even while she slept, entranced by her beauty and the delicacy of her skin, and then she had awakened and confirmed the desire that had inflamed him. Her eyes, her laugh, the sound of her voice, all spoke to his heart. He could see love in her eyes and a return of the passion he felt for her.

He awoke with a start from a familiar dream. He had returned to Netherfield, and she had met him once again by the stream, his eyes following her progress as she approached him with outstretched arms. Just in the very moment when he reached out to take her hand, her image faded, and he could see nothing. Every night it had been the same.

He had never opened his heart to anyone the way he had to Elizabeth, but with her, it had been so natural. He remembered the comfort he received from holding her hand. She strengthened him. She excited every good thought that came to his mind, and to be worthy of her love, he resolved to be a more attentive brother, a loyal friend, and to put aside cynicism and distrust. He had resolved to do all these things, and he had utterly failed.

Why had he let her go? Now he was desolate and felt her loss immensely. How could he face the future with the pain that he felt? How could he despise himself enough for turning against her? All she wanted was to love him. There was not sufficient hate in the world to describe his self-loathing

Knowing full well that he deserved every wretched feeling he would be called on to bear, Darcy left London for Hertfordshire. He told himself he was going to repair his relationship with Bingley, but he knew he was going there to see Elizabeth. He wanted to know if she really loved Mr. Grinly.

Darcy had answered Bingley's letter and was now on the road to Netherfield. It was a noisy ride. Each time he grew comfortable or became lost in thought, a rock would dash against the underside of the carriage or the coach would jar its way over a rut. All he wanted to do was sleep. All he could do was remember.

"WELCOME TO NETHERFIELD, DARCY. IT is good to see you again."

"Thank you, Bingley. It is good to be here." Darcy hesitated. "I realize that I am not to mention, at your particular request, my transgressions, but you must allow me to beg once again for your forgiveness and apologize for my arrogant interference in your affairs."

Jane walked up behind her husband in time to hear Darcy's speech, though he did not notice her.

"All has turned out as it should. Let us put the subject behind us."

"How is your wife? Is she —"

"I am well, thank you. How was your journey, Mr. Darcy?"

"It is pleasant to be out of the carriage." He could not meet her eyes. "The roads were a bit rough this trip. Mrs. Bingley, thank you for inviting me back to your home."

"You are welcome, Mr. Darcy."

Bingley ushered them into the drawing room, and after they were seated, Mrs. Bingley turned to her guest.

"So, Mr. Darcy, how long do you expect to be with us this visit?"

"At least until Eliz... your sister's wedding." He looked away, feeling the weight of Jane's scrutiny upon him. "Mrs. Bingley, I beg that you will please forgive me for all that I have done to offend you and your family."

"And just what is it that you have done, sir?"

Darcy shifted nervously in his seat. "I have been proud, assuming myself to be better than my fellow man. I have been narrow-minded, believing that my way of living is the correct way for everyone. I have been weak, unwilling to commit to your sister because of the fear of offending a parent who is long dead. I have been deceitful and blind, and I have caused hurt and pain to an innocent heart. I do not believe I can truly be forgiven of these crimes. Despite your willingness to invite me here, I must have fallen in your esteem, and how could I not? Bingley, my friend who relied on me and trusted me, now has cause to doubt both my sincerity and integrity. And what is most painful to me, and what I will always regret, is that I was loved by your sister, yet I rejected that love. I have lost her. She will belong to another man, and I will spend the rest of my life regretting her."

"Mr. Darcy, I do honestly forgive you. Charles loves me, despite all my deficiencies..."

Darcy cringed at that comment.

"...and my sister's heart has healed, and she will soon be wed to a generous man who cares deeply for her. I believe that anyone seeing them together will realize what a good match Mr. Grinly is for Elizabeth."

It was impossible for Darcy to respond to that in a manner that would be agreeable to Mrs. Bingley, so he remained silent.

Mr. Darcy's feelings for Elizabeth were plain. Jane had imagined that when he left Netherfield, Mr. Darcy had conquered his feelings for Elizabeth, and that he and Mr. Grinly could associate without any danger to her sister. She knew that Elizabeth's love for Mr. Grinly was not what it should be and was now afraid that any suggestion from Mr. Darcy that he held any affection for Elizabeth would endanger her relationship with Mr. Grinly. Jane now knew it had been a mistake to invite Mr. Darcy back to Netherfield.

"What have I done?" she whispered.

The gentlemen did not hear her.

IT WAS A BEAUTIFUL DAY to be out of doors, and as Elizabeth took great pleasure in sharing her happiness with Jane and in walking with Mr. Grinly, she prevailed on him to call again at Netherfield. Constance had joined them, but lingered as far behind as she could. Though inexperienced in the ways of love, she was certain that her father and Elizabeth would have things to say to each other that they would not wish for her to hear, and Constance would do anything she could to promote their happiness. Truly, their happiness was her own.

"ELIZABETH, WHAT WOULD MAKE YOU the happiest woman in the world?" Mr. Grinly kicked a rock off the pathway in front of him as they walked together towards Netherfield.

"Other than being married to you?"

"You have no idea how pleased I am to hear you speak thus." His voice was warm and affectionate, and had they been truly alone, he would have responded to that comment the way it deserved.

"I have always wanted Jane to be happy. She is my best friend and favored companion... Oh, but do not worry, I believe I shall learn to like you, also," she teased. He laughed with her. "She sacrificed her own pleasure to be of use to our family, and now that she is married to Mr. Bingley and is so happy, I do not know for what I could wish. I know that the rest of my family will be well cared for by Mr. Bingley, and I am to be married and happily settled myself, so I am content. Thomas, just love me. That is all I want." They walked on for a moment in silence. "But what about you, Thomas? What would make you happy?"

"I am already happy. To have met you and to be loved by you brings me more joy than I had imagined I would ever feel. If there is not a smile on my face, there is one in my heart. When I see how close you are with Constance, my joy is complete. There is nothing else for which I could wish." He turned to face Elizabeth, taking her hand that she freely offered. "Well, there is one thing, I believe."

"And what would that be, sir?"

"A brother or a sister for Constance."

A blush overspread Elizabeth's cheeks. "I wish for that, too."

He offered her his arm, and they resumed their walk towards Netherfield.

THE HOUSEKEEPER LED ELIZABETH, CONSTANCE and Mr. Grinly through the wide hall and into the drawing room where they expected to see Mr. and Mrs. Bingley. Elizabeth had entered Netherfield in good spirits. As Mrs. Grinly, she knew she would be loved and cherished. Her whole future looked bright. She knew she had made the right decision, and because of that, would soon forget about...

"...Mr. Darcy!"

"Miss Bennet!"

Chapter 15

A flash of white light passed through Elizabeth's mind as the color faded from her cheeks. Her first instinct was to run away, but her feet would not move. She could not turn away from Mr. Darcy. She raised one hand to cover her open mouth and with the other, gripped more firmly onto Mr. Grinly's arm. Her breath caught in her throat as she understood all that Darcy conveyed with his eyes. The love and the raw passion he felt for her were expressed in that look. He did love her! He did want her!

Darcy thought he had steeled himself against the time when he would see Elizabeth with Mr. Grinly, but their sudden appearance at Netherfield taught him the futility of that effort. He was assailed with jealousy, anger, and hurt. He had a desire to lash out at Elizabeth and demand an explanation for why she would not marry him, until he remembered that it was he who had abandoned her.

Just before Elizabeth turned away, Darcy recognized and acknowledged the look she had given him. Elizabeth did not love Grinly. She had greeted him with such an expression of passion and delight that he knew she still loved him. He ached to touch her and make her a part of him. Her skin, her lips, her delicate hands — all — all were meant for him. Never had he loved her more than at this instant of reunion, and never had his heart been rent as it was when the look of joy faded from her face.

Elizabeth caught sight of Mr. Grinly watching her with a look of astonishment. Her heart sank. She was betrothed to Mr. Grinly, not to Mr. Darcy. She was honor bound to Mr. Grinly, but at that moment, she realized she could never be his. She turned away, her vision blurred by the tears that were forming in her eyes.

Constance was looking at Elizabeth, expecting that she would introduce her to Mr. Bingley's friend, when she was stunned by her reaction. It could only mean one thing. It could only be one person.

"It is him!"

MR. GRINLY WAS STARTLED BY the intensity of Darcy's reaction to Elizabeth. Without a doubt, a gentleman should rise when a lady entered the room, but Darcy had exploded from his seat. Mr. Grinly was alarmed when Elizabeth released his arm. And how was it possible that Constance knew that man?

Jane and Bingley exchanged worried glances. They had hoped to orchestrate this meeting by giving each party advanced knowledge of the other. Now, Elizabeth and Mr. Darcy had been thrust into each other's company when neither was prepared. It was obvious that Mr. Grinly had no idea who Mr. Darcy was and what he had once been to Elizabeth. Constance's recognition of Darcy confused Jane because she was certain they had never met.

Jane stared at Elizabeth, willing her to look her way, but Elizabeth's eyes were fixed on Mr. Darcy. Jane could see that those eyes were filled not only with pain but also with a love for the man that had not waned over time. Regardless of what Elizabeth may have stated before, her heart was not free of him.

Asserting herself as mistress, Jane proceeded with the civilities. "Mr. Darcy, please allow me to introduce you to our cousin, Mr. Grinly, and his daughter, Constance. The Grinlys reside in Wiltshire and have been visiting in Hertfordshire since my wedding. Mr. Grinly, Mr. Darcy is my husband's good friend."

Darcy was shocked by Mr. Grinly's appearance. He was old, so much older than Elizabeth or himself. How could she be wedding herself to a man twice her age? He cleared his throat. "I am pleased to make your acquaintance, sir, and you, also, Miss Grinly."

"I am happy to meet you, Mr. Darcy." Grinly was certain he was not, but could not say why, other than that Elizabeth had reacted very poorly when she saw him.

Constance honored Mr. Darcy with a low curtsy. Rising up, she touched Elizabeth's arm.

Elizabeth realized that everyone was looking at her. She heard Constance when she saw Mr. Darcy and realized that she must have guessed his identity. Elizabeth did not know if Constance had told her father that such a man existed, but she was certain that he would now know that Darcy meant much more to her than a common acquaintance.

"Mr. Darcy…" Elizabeth's voice wavered. A chill passed through her body and anguish flashed in her eyes as she spoke the words that condemned her. "Mr. Darcy," she repeated, "Mr. Grinly and I are to be married."

ELIZABETH'S ANNOUNCEMENT CAME AS NO surprise to Darcy, but somewhere in his heart, he had harbored a self-deluding hope that it was not true. He looked at her with all the intensity of emotion he could spare from the agony he was enduring. His eyes locked onto hers. "You have my congratulations, Miss Bennet."

Mr. Grinly looked from Elizabeth to Darcy and back again, wishing for anything that would break their gaze and put an end to whatever was passing between them. Elizabeth had never looked at him with such an expression of longing and desire, and now she was bestowing those passions on another man.

Jane noticed Mr. Grinly's discomfort and attempted to intervene on his behalf. "Lizzy."

Elizabeth did not seem to hear her. Her eyes were fixed on Mr. Darcy.

Once again, Jane called her name, this time more firmly.

Elizabeth slowly turned her head towards her sister, her eyes not leaving Darcy until the last moment. "Yes?"

"Mr. Darcy has just this moment arrived from London, and I believe he would like to freshen up. Perhaps we can continue this visit another time when he has had a chance to rest from his trip." Jane stepped close to Elizabeth, struggling to gain her attention. "Would you and Mr. Grinly care to join us for dinner tomorrow?" She would say or do anything to get Elizabeth away from Netherfield.

Elizabeth did not know how to respond. She realized that she had been engaged in self-deception when she accepted Mr. Grinly, but now her faith and honor bound her to him. She looked at Mr. Darcy, whose expression was one of shock and disbelief. His face looked pale. He did not look well. Oh, how her heart went out to him!

"I…yes…thank you, Jane."

Mr. Grinly spoke to Elizabeth in a low voice. She turned her head slightly to hear him.

In heated jealousy, Darcy watched as Mr. Grinly whispered quietly to Elizabeth in an intimate manner. Though Darcy could not hear what Mr. Grinly told her, she made that obvious by her next statement.

"We should be returning to Longbourn, Jane. We will see you tomorrow."

Elizabeth's eyes turned once again towards Darcy, and every emotion of love, passion, and yearning that she ever felt for him returned with a force that nearly took her breath away.

Jane stepped between Elizabeth and Darcy, but her presence seemed not to matter. She took Elizabeth's hand and led her from the room. "I look forward to it. Please give my love to Mama. Goodbye, Miss Grinly. It was a pleasure to see you again."

"Thank you, Mrs. Bingley."

Mr. Bingley saw them off at the door.

DARCY COLLAPSED ONTO THE SOFA. He had held his breath from the moment Elizabeth left the room until he heard the front door close. Inhaling deeply, Darcy closed his eyes and turned his head away from Jane to conceal his tortured emotions from her. He had seen Elizabeth! The fact that she was marrying anyone but him was torment enough, but that she was not marrying for love caused an even deeper wound. It was obvious to him that Elizabeth was not in love with Mr. Grinly and never would be. Despite all the hurt he had caused her, the look of regret in her eyes had been unmistakable. She still loved him!

Darcy stood and walked to the window. He could feel Mrs. Bingley's eyes on him as they followed his progress across the room.

"Mr. Darcy, are you unwell?"

"I…I do not know."

"The damage has been done, sir. It was apparent to me, and I fear to everyone in the room, that my sister still loves you."

"And I have never ceased loving her. I had resolved to return to Hertfordshire before I received your husband's letter announcing her engagement. I was to leave the very next day." He looked out the window again. The beauty of the garden was lost to him. "I did not know what to do. It was not my intention to hurt her further. I suppose I came to punish myself for my foolishness."

Jane's frustration spent itself in a burst of emotion. She quickly crossed the room and placed herself directly in front of Mr. Darcy.

"And what about Elizabeth?" she cried angrily. "Did you come to punish her as well?"

The suddenness and violence of her attack left him speechless. All he could do was shake his head and step back from her.

"I am sorry. Please forgive me, sir."

"Believe me, madam, I have asked myself that same question, and I have no answer for it other than to charge myself with selfishness and an unwillingness to let her go."

"What will you do now?"

What will I do now? "Your sister," said Darcy sadly, "does not love Mr. Grinly."

"I am certain my husband told you that we would withdraw our invitation to you if you did anything to disturb Elizabeth's happiness."

"He did."

"You have done that."

"I did…"

"Your presence here has ruined her happiness with Mr. Grinly, and I grieve for it." Jane invited Mr. Darcy to sit near her on a sofa.

He took his place, though perhaps a little uncomfortably at the restraint of sitting compared to the freedom of walking around the room as an outlet for his frustration.

"It is my fault, though," continued Jane. "I encouraged her to accept Mr. Grinly when it was apparent that she should not. I overcame her objections to the match, and though she confessed to me that she was still in love with you, I told her you did not care for her anymore."

"I do care for her. I love her."

"I consented to my husband's request to invite you back to Netherfield. Perhaps if she had not called today, perhaps if she had not seen you again, all would be well with her. So you see, her unhappiness is my doing."

"If it is still your wish, I will leave immediately."

"Please, sir, do not! She will be expecting to see you tomorrow. Do not leave her wondering what her own feelings may be. Tomorrow I will ask her again, and if she tells me she loves you, I will do everything in my power to ensure that she does not marry Mr. Grinly. She could not be happy. I was wrong before, but I will not be wrong again."

"And if she does not love me?"

"Then you will have to leave. Mr. Darcy, I am left not knowing how to repair the damage I have created in her life. There will be scandal and upset if she terminates her engagement to Mr. Grinly, and there may be a lifetime of regret and misery if she does not. What has changed, sir? Why are you back?" This question had bothered her from the moment he stepped from his carriage.

Darcy felt nothing but gratitude for the opportunity this question provided to explain himself. "I spent my whole life trying to live up to my father's expectations for me. As he has been dead for five years, you can see what a futile effort that has been." He got up from the sofa and walked back to the window.

"When I attempted to persuade Bingley not to marry you — please forgive me for that — I was voicing my own objections to an attachment I had formed for your sister. Bingley saw right through the charade."

"So you did love her. I cannot imagine that your father would not have approved of Elizabeth."

"My father told me that I could not be happy in an unequal alliance as to family, fortune, and position in society. I have since learned that none of those has any claim on happiness."

"And how did you learn this?"

"An acquaintance recently offered me £35,000 if I would marry his daughter. She is an attractive, pleasant young woman from a prestigious family, and it would be the kind of match of which my father would have approved."

"But I thought you loved Elizabeth." Neither she nor Elizabeth could offer any such advantages. No wonder Mr. Darcy thought she was unworthy of being Bingley's wife.

"I was horrified when he made the offer. He knew I did not love his daughter, and I reminded him of that. He said it took more than love to make a good marriage. At that moment, I realized that love is all that is necessary and that my father was wrong. I knew I had hurt your sister, and I despised myself for it. I wanted to return to Hertfordshire, and I wanted to know if your sister would give me another chance and if, after all the pain I had caused her, she still loved me. Because I had not received an invitation from Netherfield, I intended to come to Meryton. The night before my departure, I received Bingley's letter announcing your sister's engagement. You cannot comprehend what I now suffer."

"Indeed I cannot, but it seems to me that brought it all on yourself." Mr. Darcy was a complicated man. Had he exerted himself more and been more considerate of others, either Elizabeth would be his or neither of them would be suffering from such misery.

Jane passed quietly out of the room to search for her husband. She felt the need for the reassurance of his love. She was grateful to him for loving her, and his affection was dearer than ever to her as she understood all that he had sacrificed to marry her.

ONCE OUT THE DOOR OF Netherfield, the Longbourn party formed up with Elizabeth on one side of Mr. Grinly and Constance on the other. At a distance from the house where conversation would be desirable, there was only silence. Elizabeth could not speak, Mr. Grinly would not speak, and Constance dared not speak.

It had taken only a moment for Mr. Grinly to ascertain that not only was Mr. Darcy more than an acquaintance to Elizabeth but that her heart belonged to him. He could not imagine a person looking more stricken than Elizabeth on seeing Mr. Darcy. Her pale skin had become white, and her eyes were filled with anguish.

For her part, Constance knew from Elizabeth's reaction that Mr. Darcy was the man to whom she referred when she spoke of someone who had disappointed her. Constance kept looking at Elizabeth for some sign of reassurance from her that all would be well, but Elizabeth would not return her glance.

Elizabeth's feelings for Mr. Darcy were a mass of confusion. He had left her, hurt her, and given no explanation for his behavior. It was perfectly natural for her to accept a proposal from a respectable man like Mr. Grinly, but why did she feel so awful, as if she had committed some kind of betrayal?

The answer was painful. Against her will, she was passionately in love with Mr. Darcy, and she realized she did not love Mr. Grinly at all. In that moment, she repented of every feeling of distrust and resentment she ever felt for Mr. Darcy. In that instant, it all meant nothing. All that mattered was him.

DARCY FOLLOWED MRS. BINGLEY OUT of the drawing room and climbed the stairs to his bedchamber. He wished to be alone with his thoughts. Lying on his bed, he pulled Elizabeth's purple ribbon from the place he always kept it, in the pocket nearest his heart. He laced the ribbon through his fingers and held it to his lips, reproaching himself for the pride and uncertainty that had cost him Elizabeth. Was there any chance that she would break her engagement to Mr. Grinly? Was there any chance at all?

ELIZABETH LITERALLY FLED FROM MR. Grinly when they reached the entryway at Longbourn. How she longed to confide in Jane! There was no one else with whom she could talk about her feelings. Finally persuaded that Mr. Darcy did not return her love, she had accepted Mr. Grinly in the hope of forgetting him, in the hope of being loved, in the hope of some semblance of a happy future.

Now everything changed. Seeing Mr. Darcy brought back all the feelings she had for him. She remembered how she felt when he kissed her. The instant she saw that look of passion in his eyes, she knew he still loved her. He must have known of her engagement. She was certain Jane would not have invited him back without informing him. Why did he come back if not to claim her?

But could she allow that? Did not honor bind her to Mr. Grinly? Surely, it must. She knew that to reject Mr. Grinly would be to hurt him in nearly the same manner he had suffered when his wife died. It would do the same to Constance, who might never understand. How much pain would she cause them? They had done nothing at all to deserve it.

Her own family would be embarrassed if she ended her engagement. Poor Mama! She had told the whole of Meryton. Could she rely on Mr. Darcy to make her an offer? Could she base her future on such an expectation? He had disappointed her before. She had felt abandoned and rejected because of him, but all of that seemed forgotten the moment their eyes met.

How much would Mr. Darcy suffer and how much would she suffer if she tried to live a life without him? If she could not be whole without Mr. Darcy, then marrying Mr. Grinly would be tragically wrong. How could she be a good wife knowing she loved another? How could she give herself to Mr. Grinly knowing she wanted Mr. Darcy?

She collapsed on her bed with all the pain of a tortured mind and cried until there were no more tears. When she was herself again, it was night, and the room was dark. She crawled under the bedclothes and pulled them close around her chin, praying for the insensibility of sleep.

ELIZABETH KNEW SHE WOULD HAVE to face Mr. Grinly and Constance. She would have to give them some explanation as to why she ran up to her room the previous night without another word to them. Elizabeth was certain that Mr. Grinly would find some way to excuse her actions. Having slept badly and feeling poorly for it, Elizabeth crept down to the drawing room to await the inevitable. To her surprise, Constance was already up. She appeared to be struggling with some needlework.

"Good morning, Constance." Elizabeth sat down next to her.

"Elizabeth, I must ask you. Was that him? Is Mr. Darcy the man who loved you?"

"He is," whispered Elizabeth.

"He still loves you, I think."

Elizabeth could not respond.

"If you leave me, I do not know how I shall bear it." Constance set down her work and laced her fingers together, clasping her hands tightly. "I watched you look at him. You do not look at my father in the same way." Constance started to cry softly. "I could see it in your eyes. You love him." Constance could not bury a sob. She burst into tears and ran from the room.

ELIZABETH WALKED TO THE WINDOW. Her mind returned to that exact, unexpected moment when she had come upon Mr. Darcy at Netherfield. Before seeing him, her heart felt free in the knowledge that he was gone from her life. Now Mr. Darcy was back, and she felt that her freedom had been taken away. There was no denying how she felt about him, and now that she had seen him and the love and passion in his eyes, she knew she could never forget him.

Her mind revolved in circles between the shock of her revived feelings for Mr. Darcy, the pain she caused Mr. Grinly, and the knowledge that Mr. Darcy loved her. The circle tightened around her and she felt trapped in the vise-like grip of self-reproach for having been weak. If Jane accused Mr. Darcy of trifling with her, is that not what she had done to Mr. Grinly and Constance?

She whispered his name. "Mr. Darcy."

Just at that moment, Mr. Grinly entered the drawing room, soon enough to hear Elizabeth pronounce that man's name.

"No, Elizabeth, it is I, Thomas."

"Oh . . . I . . ." She sighed. "Good morning, Mr. Grinly."

He winced at her formality. He stepped next to her, cringing when she unconsciously moved away from him. She did not look well, and it appeared as though she had slept very little and was emotionally spent. Mr. Grinly clenched his teeth at the thought of her crying the night away over Mr. Darcy.

"Good morning," he said with an air of cheerfulness that he did not feel. "Did you sleep well? I missed you last evening. You did not come down from your room."

"I was not well, but I will be fine. I felt ill after our walk back from Netherfield."

"Constance and I were worried about you, and I am worried now." His daughter had just come to him in tears, directly from her conversation with Elizabeth. Mr. Grinly now knew about Mr. Darcy's connection to his intended and was fairly certain he understood her feelings towards the man. He wondered whether it was something she could overcome.

"I am sorry."

"My only concern is for you," he paused, "and us."

Elizabeth turned away from him as a shiver ran up her spine. It was a reminder of her weariness of body and mind.

"Oh…" she whispered.

Mr. Grinly saw that she looked pale and seemed unsteady on her feet.

"Elizabeth, are you unwell?"

"I…I feel a little lightheaded."

With a quick motion, Mr. Grinly put one arm around her waist and lifted her to a sofa. "Let me call for tea." He rang the bell and requested that tea be brought to Miss Elizabeth as quickly as may be. Sensing Mr. Grinly's urgency and seeing that Elizabeth was out of countenance, Mrs. Hill hurried from the room on her errand.

"You are putting yourself to too much trouble for me, you…"

He touched her hand. "Please let me care for you. Please allow me to do this." She acquiesced with a nod.

Throughout the whole course of their relationship, he had always felt that she held an advantage over him, but now she was at a disadvantage, and he wanted her to be assured that he would and could take care of her and that it was a privilege to be allowed to do so.

They sat in silence, Elizabeth looking at her folded hands in her lap while Mr. Grinly examined her face and sympathized with the distress he saw there. At last, she spoke. "I am so sorry; you must believe me." Her eyes began to tear up. "It was not my intention to cause anyone pain — especially not you, especially not Constance."

"Shh… Please do not say such things. It will only upset you, and there is no need for that."

Hill returned with the tea service, and Mr. Grinly dismissed her. Elizabeth moved as if to pour out the tea, but he gently held her arm and withstood her weak effort.

"Please, let me serve you."

Mr. Grinly cheered Elizabeth into a faint smile with all his delicate attention. Rarely was she treated in such a way by anyone other than Jane. "Do you feel any better?"

Elizabeth had not experienced such tenderness from any man since her father died, and she had to confess that she liked the gentle treatment she was receiving. His concern for her was genuine, his love of her obvious.

"I do, but I am so very tired."

"If you were to retire to your bedchamber, do you believe that you could rest?"

"Thomas, I fear I have upset Constance —"

"Constance has revealed to me the substance of your conversation. She is upset, but I have calmed her fears. Be assured that she loves you as much as she ever did."

"And you, sir, must be uneasy. You must have suspicions…"

Although intending to comfort her, his next words only added to her misery. "I have every confidence in your regard for me."

She felt a tear trickle down one cheek. "I seem to do nothing but offend." She wished herself a thousand miles away and briefly considered whether it might not be appropriate to seek an invitation to her aunt's home in Town until she could sort out her feelings. She quickly discarded the thought. She owed it to both men — and to herself — to resolve the issue, and she had learned from Mr. Darcy that running away only made matters worse.

"Do you believe you could rest if I were to assist you to your bedchamber? I will make your excuses to the rest of your family."

"You are very kind to me."

"Kind? I would do anything for you." Mr. Grinly took her hand, helped her to her feet, and guided her to the foot of the stairs. He watched her progress until she turned and was out of sight. Only then did he allow himself to despair of the future he hoped to have with Elizabeth as his wife.

"Oh, Mr. Grinly!" cried Mrs. Bennet. "Good morning, Constance. It is a beautiful day, is it not?" The Grinlys were just returning from a walk around the front of the house. Mrs. Bennet had espied them from the entryway and met them at the front door.

"It is," replied Mr. Grinly, feigning cheerfulness. He and Constance had been discussing the state of affairs with Elizabeth, and the conversation had not brought comfort to either. "Will you join us for another turn around the garden?"

Despite her eccentricities, Mr. Grinly liked Mrs. Bennet. Though loud and often silly, he believed that she was capable of genuine love for her daughters, and he felt she cared for him, too. This knowledge made the morning's meeting with Elizabeth all the more painful. He could envision the circumstances whereby he could lose Elizabeth and, in turn, her whole family.

"No, thank you. But is not Elizabeth with you? That girl is always running off. I can never —"

"Mrs. Bennet, please!"

She was silenced.

"Forgive me," said Mr. Grinly penitently. He took Mrs. Bennet's arm and led her onto the lawn. "I saw Miss Bennet early this morning. We took tea together, but she is not well and has returned to her bedchamber. I expect to see her later in the afternoon when we leave for Netherfield."

"Oh, yes, the Bingleys have invited you for the evening. Will Constance attend too?" Mrs. Bennet realized that although she had declined an invitation to join the Grinlys in the garden, she now found herself walking with them.

"No. Constance will remain with Mary."

"Very well. I am sure we will be glad to have her with us."

Mrs. Bennet liked Constance very much, although she could not understand why she was quiet and shy, so unlike her own daughters. Be that as it may, she was a pleasant addition to their family party, and any relation of Mr. Grinly's would be very welcome.

SHORTLY BEFORE THE CARRIAGE WAS summoned, Elizabeth joined her family in the drawing room. Mr. Grinly's kindness had removed much of the apprehension she felt as a result of seeing Mr. Darcy the day before. He had not accused her or blamed her. She had been able to rest and did feel stronger, though not altogether recovered. She tried to enter into conversation with Mr. Grinly and forget that in a few short minutes, he would hand her into his carriage and she would be driven to Netherfield where she would come face to face with Mr. Darcy.

THE DOOR WAS FASTENED SHUT, the step raised, and the carriage was off. Elizabeth sat quietly across from Mr. Grinly. They both felt ill at ease and made every effort not to appear as though they were avoiding each other's sight.

Elizabeth was not comfortable. She knew Mr. Grinly's hopes for her, for they talked at length about their future and the joy they would experience together. Those hopes were ruined. She would never know happiness without Mr. Darcy, and she could never know it with Mr. Grinly. Her heart screamed in defiance of the calm exterior that she maintained, and only a tear betrayed the silent turmoil that burned within her.

Mr. Grinly sat quietly and pretended not to notice her distress.

Chapter 16

Elizabeth and Mr. Grinly arrived in good time for the evening's engagement. Jane had gone to as much effort as possible to make her home pleasing and inviting, knowing there would be a charged atmosphere as soon as they arrived. She had noticed, without surprise, that Mr. Darcy had been on edge all day.

Elizabeth, mindful of her place as an engaged woman, resolved that if it were at all possible, she would neither look at Mr. Darcy nor speak to him. She hoped that he would not address her beyond the normal civilities.

Darcy and Bingley stood on the appearance of the lady and gentleman in the drawing room, where they all had gathered awaiting word that dinner was ready. Determined to give no encouragement to Mr. Darcy, Elizabeth kept her eyes on Mr. Bingley.

"Good afternoon, Lizzy. Welcome to Netherfield, Mr. Grinly!" Bingley was all cheerfulness.

Jane came over to Elizabeth and kissed her cheek. While embracing her, she whispered into her ear, "I love you, Lizzy. Do not worry. Everything will be well."

Darcy did not know if he would be able to speak. The pain in his heart had created a lump in his throat. Elizabeth looked as beautiful as he had ever seen her. He knew she must be pained, perhaps even more so than he, for she was here with the man she loved and the man to whom she had promised herself; much to her misfortune, they were not the same person.

Now that she was here, Elizabeth wished she had feigned illness to prevent this meeting with Mr. Darcy. Her heart was all his, and she ached nearly to tears with the agony of knowing she could not have him. Unable to resist the temptation, she raised her eyes to him and her misery increased when she saw him return her look with one of equal pain and longing. She immediately withdrew her gaze.

Mr. Grinly witnessed the exchange between Elizabeth and Mr. Darcy. His first impressions were confirmed. Mr. Darcy was intimately connected with Elizabeth. His first thought was to force an early end to the evening and get Elizabeth away from Darcy. His next was to persuade Elizabeth to leave Hertfordshire as soon as may be. They could be wed in just a few days and immediately leave for Kent.

Mr. Bingley invited them all to sit down. "Mr. Grinly, I am told you are from Wiltshire. I have never traveled that far west before. Is it much like Hertfordshire?"

"A little, though I believe there is more farmland in Hertfordshire, and as a consequence of being so far from London, the population in Wiltshire is not so numerous."

"I have never been to the West, but I would have to say that my favorite county is Derbyshire. Are you familiar with that country?"

"I am not."

Elizabeth could not refrain from looking at Mr. Darcy on the mention of Derbyshire. It brought to her mind the images of his home that she had conjured up during their conversations.

Jane saw the exchange between the two with pursed lips. The tension in the air was thick, and she admitted that this dinner would not allow anyone to appear to advantage, but making such an invitation had seemed the only way to diffuse the previous day's meeting. She realized now that all she had done was delay the inevitable.

Elizabeth knew that her resolution to remain silent was impossible, but certainly, there was merit in trying to appear composed. She made an effort to turn the conversation away from anything connected with Mr. Darcy. "Mr. Grinly has lately been in London visiting my Aunt Gardiner."

"She is a pleasant woman," commented Mr. Bingley. "I am fond of all her family. Their children are lovely. Did you like them yourself? How did you find London, sir?"

Darcy coolly observed Mr. Grinly watching Elizabeth. Clearly, Mr. Grinly was familiar with her discomfiture, and he wondered how much he knew of her situation or her feelings towards himself. Very likely Elizabeth had not spoken a word of it to him. He was certain Mr. Grinly would not have brought her to Netherfield if she had.

"The Gardiners are some of the most likeable people I know, and their children are beautiful. Constance is quite fond of them. I particularly enjoyed Mr. Gardiner's company and spent time with him inspecting his warehouses. He is very intelligent and quite successful. As to your other question," said Mr. Grinly clearing his throat, not at all pleased with the idea of having to say so much, "it has been several years since I was in Town, and it has certainly grown larger. Despite the richness of the society there, London is plagued with much poverty. It is sad to see. My daughter and I took in the theatre, the opera, and visited with my deceased wife's relations."

Mr. Grinly saw Darcy look up at him, and he regretted that he had mentioned anything to do with Julia. Somehow, it made him feel vulnerable, which made no sense, as he had always drawn strength from her. He felt the eyes of all in the room on him, everyone's eyes except Elizabeth's. "I was married previously, sir, many years ago. Julia died in a carriage accident."

"Mrs. Grinly's death was heroic, though tragic," said Elizabeth. "She saved the life of her daughter, Constance, whom you met yesterday. She is a lovely girl and would have made her mother proud."

Darcy wanted Elizabeth to speak to him. He wanted to hear her call him by name. He knew that she was avoiding him. He did not know whether she was uncomfortable only because of Mr. Grinly, or perhaps she was making an effort to conquer her attachment to him.

"Do you often walk by the stream near here, Miss Bennet?"

Elizabeth made an attempt to swallow through her dry throat. She met his gaze and spoke quietly. "I have not been there since...since that time...when I was ill. It would be too much for me...I mean, too far."

"I am sorry. It is such a beautiful place. The water is so cool and refreshing. I was never happier than the last time I visited there."

Elizabeth closed her eyes. What was Mr. Darcy doing? Was he deliberately tormenting her? This was certainly no way to recommend himself, but perhaps that was not his desire. Perhaps he considered her lost and was punishing her for accepting Mr. Grinly. She felt her anger rising.

Mr. Grinly could address Elizabeth intimately, as no man there could, and he took advantage of his privilege to reinforce his claim on her. "Elizabeth, perhaps we can walk to the stream tomorrow, and you can show me all the fine prospects." He could not suppress a brief look of triumph over Mr. Darcy.

Elizabeth's eyes flashed at Mr. Darcy, but her voice was sweet and conciliatory towards Mr. Grinly. "You would not like it, Thomas. It is a dreadful place that evokes dark feelings and brings to mind painful memories."

JANE KNEW SHE MUST ACT. She stood in a decided manner, excused herself, left the drawing room, and went into a small sitting room. She summoned a maid to go to the drawing room and request that Elizabeth join her there.

The gentlemen thought it strange that Jane would choose to withdraw just as they were preparing for dinner, but their surprise and concern was almost beyond their ability to conceal when Elizabeth was called away. She followed the maid into the sitting room. Jane took her hand and led her to a sofa. "Oh, Lizzy, this is too much for you."

"What is Mr. Darcy doing here? I was never so surprised as I was when I saw him here yesterday. I had thought he was in London."

"I made a terrible mistake. I agreed to allow Charles to invite him here. With your engagement to Mr. Grinly, I thought there was no danger. I am so sorry."

"I admit that I did not realize the depth of my feelings for Mr. Darcy. I have made a terrible mistake. I am to be married to a man I do not love, and now, having seen Mr. Darcy again, I feel I can never love Mr. Grinly. All I feel is obligation." Her situation was hopeless, absolutely hopeless.

"To what was Mr. Darcy referring when he mentioned the stream?"

"While I was at Netherfield, on a day when everyone was out, I left the house for fresh air and exercise. I went to the stream, sat near the water and reflected on my relationship with Mr. Darcy."

Elizabeth paused for a moment, feeling as if she were once again by the stream. "He returned to Netherfield that day before the others and Anne informed him that I had left the house. He came after me. I do not know why he chose to go to the stream, but he found me there, and sat with me, and we talked. Jane, he kissed me."

"Lizzy!" cried Jane. Recollecting that it was her purpose now to comfort Elizabeth and not to rebuke her, she immediately regretted her tone. "I am sorry. That was unkind. I am just astonished, that is all." Jane struggled for the right words. "How did you receive his advances?"

"I welcomed them with all my heart. I loved him, and he loved me. After Mr. Darcy left Hertfordshire, I hoped I would not still love him. I had pledged myself to Mr. Grinly for the rest of my life, and I wanted to be happy with him. I had come to your way of thinking." Jane winced at this. "But when I saw Mr. Darcy yesterday, I knew all my efforts to forget him had been in vain. I want to believe that he came back for me. Is that true?"

"I have spoken with Mr. Darcy. He says he loves you."

"Please tell me. What else did he say?"

"He believes that you do not love Mr. Grinly. He has come back for you."

Elizabeth sat back on the sofa and leaned her head on Jane's shoulder. "Mr. Darcy hurt me when he left without a word. He tried to persuade Mr. Bingley not to marry you and said that our family would shame him. What am I to do? I do not believe I can expect that same behavior from Mr. Grinly. I know he is devoted to me, whereas Mr. Darcy, though he told you he still loves me at one time at least, felt I was not good enough for him. How can I trust that his love for me will not be as transient now as it was before? I realize now that I have loved Mr. Darcy the whole time. Is that wrong?"

"I do not believe that falling in love with a person is either right or wrong. It just happens. I am certain that you did not choose it. When I saw Charles, I knew that I would love him. I did not make a choice."

"But I want that choice. I am tired of feeling powerless. If I am to love Mr. Darcy, I want to choose to love him, not be forced into it because my passion is stronger than my reason! How can I rely on Mr. Darcy's love for me? He left me once. I was ready to give him everything, but I heard him say that I was not enough. How do I know that he does not still feel that way? How much does he love me? How do I know he will not hurt me again?

"If you ask him," continued Elizabeth, "for my sake, to leave Hertfordshire and never come back so that my peace of mind can be restored and I can reconcile myself to Mr. Grinly and fulfill my obligation to him, do you think he would do that?"

"Oh, Lizzy." Jane brushed the hair back from Elizabeth's face and stroked her cheek. "I will do whatever you want me to do. Do you want to marry Mr. Grinly? Do you want me to ask Mr. Darcy to leave?"

Elizabeth recalled the desire in Mr. Darcy's kiss, the look of love in his eyes, and the way she felt when he held her in his arms. Elizabeth paled at the thought of never seeing him again, but if she were honest, she would have to say that she simply did not trust him. Had it all been a lie? She was in agony now because of Mr. Darcy and would always feel the pain of his rejection. He had done that to her. Is that what love does? If so, she would not wish this misery on anyone. She knew Mr. Grinly could never inflict that kind of pain on her because she did not love him and never would.

"Yes," she said through her tears.

JANE SPENT A FEW MINUTES with Elizabeth, comforting her, drying her tears, and making every effort to bolster her weakened spirits. Jane understood Elizabeth, and knew that she did not want to see Mr. Darcy. She would not ask Elizabeth to return to the drawing room nor would she ask her to face him again.

Mrs. Bingley rang for a servant. "Please order Mr. Grinly's carriage to be brought around immediately."

"Lizzy, I will ask Mr. Grinly to take you back to Longbourn. Talk to him. Trust him. Allow this moment to be the beginning of a new understanding between you." She knew the best chance for Elizabeth's happiness with Mr. Grinly would be a relationship based on trust and integrity. Now was the time to prove his mettle. "Charles and I will speak with Mr. Darcy. I will relate to him briefly the substance of our conversation and your firm decision in favor of Mr. Grinly. We will ask him to leave Netherfield, and I will send you word at Longbourn when he is gone."

"Very well. Please send Mr. Grinly to me. And Jane, thank you."

THE DEPARTURE OF THE LADIES brought an end to all conversation in the drawing room. As host, Bingley felt it his obligation to say or do something that would ease the tension in the room, but he was at a loss as to what that should be. It was clear to him that Darcy had surrendered all appearances of disinterestedness and had set himself as a rival to Mr. Grinly for Elizabeth's favor. This violated the condition of Darcy's invitation to Netherfield and could lead only to more trouble.

Neither Darcy nor Mr. Grinly spoke. Darcy's attention seemed to be focused inwardly. His eyes were fixed on the floor in front of him and the only sign of the struggle he was enduring was an occasional shake of his head, as if he were scolding himself for some misdeed. Bingley could easily imagine on what those regrets centered.

Mr. Grinly appeared to be focused outwardly. The majority of his attention was directed to the door through which the ladies had passed. He was not at all familiar with the house, and it seemed as if he were trying to peer through the walls that he might see where Elizabeth was and what Jane might be saying to her.

Darcy had recognized Elizabeth's confusion and had to agree that the conversation had gone far enough. He knew that his comments had distressed Elizabeth, but he believed that they brought to her mind all that he meant to her, and that even now she was pleading with her sister to help her break her engagement to Mr. Grinly. He thought with satisfaction on Mrs. Bingley's commitment to prevent Elizabeth from marrying without love, and if tonight's display did not show that Elizabeth did not love Mr. Grinly, then he did not know what would.

Mr. Grinly quickly ascertained that Darcy loved Elizabeth, but wondered what had happened. Was it true that at one time Elizabeth had been his and that he had lost her, or worse, had given her up? In either case, he was unworthy of Elizabeth's love and affection. He did not understand how she could not realize this. Nevertheless, he feared for himself and his future. Elizabeth was quite upset, and the last time that had happened, she left him. Last night, she had not come downstairs from her room. The day of his proposal, she had fled to Netherfield. With every agonizing moment, he felt as if he were losing her.

JANE STEPPED SLOWLY AND RESOLUTELY into the drawing room and all eyes turned to her. She was met by three different emotions from three very different men. Her attention was drawn immediately to Mr. Darcy, and she was feeling all the discomfort and self-consciousness of her own situation in having to dismiss him from Elizabeth's life. Needing reassurance, she looked to her husband. His face held an expression of support and determination mingled with concern. She had always relied on his love and would need it now more than ever.

The only word that Jane could use to describe what she saw in Mr. Grinly was anguish. His relationship with Elizabeth had started off with uncertainty, though it had quickly become stronger, at least until Mr. Darcy returned. For the rest of her life, she would reproach herself for inviting Mr. Darcy back to Netherfield.

"Excuse me." Jane's voice cut through the silence, "but I would like to speak privately with Mr. Grinly. Would you please follow me, sir?" She motioned towards the door and, as he stood and began to walk towards her, she preceded him through it and down a short hallway.

Jane turned to face him. "Elizabeth is unwell. I have ordered your carriage. Please take her home."

"What is the matter?"

"She has chosen her future, Mr. Grinly, but it was a difficult decision and will yet be painful for her. Please be patient."

"I will. Thank you. May I go to her now?"

Jane nodded to him and then left him at the entrance to the sitting room.

MR. GRINLY STEPPED INTO THE room and stood near Elizabeth. Her cheeks were stained with tears and her eyes looked red and swollen. Mrs. Bingley had asked him to be patient. He would be. He would not demand anything from her. "May I sit with you?"

She nodded.

"Are you unwell? Mrs. Bingley told me that you wish to return to Longbourn."

"You must hate me, sir," she whispered.

Her eyes were cast down and her fingers laced in her lap. Her lips were pursed together as she sat stiffly on the couch. She knew he had every right to condemn her, but hoped he would not. She would prove to him her resolve to love him in every way she could, and she would start now.

"No, I do not. You must not say that."

There was a moment of silence. "I have not told you all. I did not tell you everything about my fall and recovery here at Netherfield. While I was here, Mr. Darcy came to visit me every day. I fell in love with him. I thought he loved me, too. I know he did. I was never as happy as I was when I was with him."

Grinly was not surprised by this confession, and having steeled himself for the likelihood of hearing it, he showed no sign of emotion on his face or in his voice when he responded to her. "I thought so."

"My heart and mind were full of him. I expected to receive his addresses. Mr. Bingley held a ball here one evening after I was well again. He was very much in love with my sister, and I heard him and Mr. Darcy discussing Jane. I was on the balcony outside the window of Mr. Bingley's study. The sash was open, and I heard him tell Mr. Darcy how he felt about my sister. He loved her and intended to propose marriage to her very soon. Mr. Darcy objected to the match. He told Mr. Bingley that Jane was not rich enough. He condemned my mother and sisters, saying that they would be a burden to him. He told Mr. Bingley that he could easily attach a gentleman's daughter and connect himself to a family that would remove the stigma of trade from his wealth."

She looked up at Mr. Grinly, begging for his understanding and acceptance. "Jane is in possession of Longbourn, and she is a gentleman's daughter, yet Mr. Darcy felt she was not good enough for his friend. Can you imagine how I felt — I, who have nothing at all?!"

"Oh, Elizabeth."

"Now he is back," she cried softly. "My sister told me that she has spoken with Mr. Darcy. He knew of our engagement before he arrived. He told her he still loves me."

Everything made sense to him now. Her reaction to his proposal, coming so soon upon the heels of the pain Mr. Darcy had caused her, would be natural. Of course, she would seek out her sister. The startled look on her face when she saw Mr. Darcy the previous day and Constance's penetration into Elizabeth's distress were all understood.

"My proposal came at a very unpropitious time, I see. Why did you accept me?"

"Sir, I…I did not love you. I hardly knew you."

Grinly felt as though he had been hit in the stomach. Had he been so blind to her feelings?

"After much consideration, your offer became very attractive to me. The life you wanted to give me seemed so pleasing. I thought I could forget Mr. Darcy. I thought I would never see him again. I was certain we would all be happy together. I wanted nothing more than to go into Wiltshire to a new home and family."

Elizabeth had never seen a countenance as pale as his appeared to her. The blood had drained from his face, and he was left without any color at all. She repented of the pain she was causing him, but knew that to deceive him would be worse. How had her life become so complicated? She turned to face him and touched his arm. "But, sir, I know we will be happy. I know I will learn to love you."

He looked at her for a moment. *'I did not love you…I did not love you…I did not…'*

Grinly quickly stood in an attempt to hide the feelings of desperation and sadness that were overwhelming him. He knew she had just offered herself to him. It was not a question of whether he wanted her. The difficulty was in reconciling himself to the fact that in accepting her and thus securing his own happiness, he would be sacrificing hers. She would be content with him, but her heart belonged to another, and was it not wrong to prevent her from loving that man, even if it meant that he himself was to suffer? He did not doubt the sincerity of her offer, but he did doubt its wisdom. There would always be something in their life together, something he could not provide for her, an emotion he would be unable to inspire in her – passion. He approached her and knelt down. He had to be strong for her, though his eyes burned with the heartbreak and finality of his decision.

"Miss Bennet, allow me take you home."

DARCY WATCHED MR. GRINLY FOLLOW Mrs. Bingley out of the room and instinctively knew that she was taking him to Elizabeth. That Elizabeth was distressed was not in doubt. That she was overwhelmed by her feelings upon seeing him was certain. Once again, she had been wounded, first by his absence and now by his presence.

But that would soon change. No doubt Grinly's summons from the room would result in the termination of any relationship he had with Elizabeth. He was grateful to have gained Mrs. Bingley's confidence. She would be a strong influence over Elizabeth at such a delicate time. He was sorry for Mr. Grinly, but there was no possible alternative.

Darcy started at the sound of Mrs. Bingley's voice. "Sir, are you well?" She had observed him closely as she entered the room and knew her task was going to be painful. She took a seat next to her husband and slipped her hand into his. Bingley gave her a quick look, as Jane usually shied away from public expressions of affection. He squeezed her hand and drew a smile from her.

"Mr. Darcy, you must have seen that Elizabeth is very upset. Her distress results from a combination of feelings, including a strong affection that she has for you. Until you arrived here yesterday, she thought she had overcome that emotion, and while she would dearly wish to surrender to those feelings, she is afraid. You broke her heart, sir, and she does not trust you." She spoke emphatically. "I will reproach myself for the rest of my life for inviting you to Netherfield."

Darcy was surprised by this assertion. He had understood that Mrs. Bingley was an ally in his effort to win Elizabeth from Mr. Grinly.

"Elizabeth confesses that she is not in love with Mr. Grinly, but she acknowledges that she has obtained something from him that you were not able to provide."

"And that is?"

"Devotion. Elizabeth is of the opinion that Mr. Grinly will never hurt her. She is shaken as a result of this contradiction in feelings, both loving you and unable to trust you. Because of this, I now recognize the impertinence of saying that I would assist you in bringing an end to her engagement with Mr. Grinly."

Darcy closed his eyes and felt darkness overwhelm him. Her words were almost lost on him as his mind recoiled from the knowledge that Elizabeth was rejecting him for fear of being hurt. He cursed himself for the susceptibility to guilt that caused him to listen to the words of a dead father and to reject the pleadings of a living heart. His behavior towards Elizabeth was reprehensible and warranted the severest rebuke. A rebuke he was ready to receive, but losing

Elizabeth was something for which he was not prepared.

"It is Elizabeth's desire that you leave Hertfordshire. She believes that this is the only way for her to recover her peace of mind. She is committed to her engagement with Mr. Grinly and even now is assuring him of her desire to become his wife. Mr. Grinly realizes that she does not feel all that she ought, but he is confident that he will earn her affection. I am sorry, Mr. Darcy. I know you love her, but you gave her up, and now she belongs to another."

"Mrs. Bingley, how is it possible for you to allow your sister to knowingly enter into a loveless marriage? I made a mistake. I freely admit it. I was afraid. I was living in the shadow of my father and the expectations he placed on me. I have hurt everyone around me, and I beg to be forgiven. I beg for the opportunity to love Elizabeth as she ought to be loved."

"Before my conversation with Elizabeth, I might have agreed with you, but this is her decision, not mine." Jane delivered the final blow. "If you truly love her, you will leave her."

He could not speak.

"Elizabeth will regain her happiness secure in Mr. Grinly's love. Mr. Darcy, if you seek her happiness, help her secure it by removing yourself from her life." Jane knew he had no choice but to go. If he resisted, he proved that he did not love Elizabeth, a confession she knew he could not make.

Darcy stood, and after a glance at Bingley, a friend whom he would probably never see again, he looked at Mrs. Bingley. "I do love her, madam, and I will make every effort to secure her happiness even if it destroys my own."

He strode half way across the room, and then paused for a moment in front of the door through which Elizabeth had passed. Bidding her a silent farewell and knowing he would never see her again, he walked with a defeated step into the hall and up to his room to prepare for his departure.

ELIZABETH SAID NOT A WORD on the trip back to Longbourn. The ride seemed longer than usual. She was not comforted by her decision to honor her engagement to Mr. Grinly. Perhaps she should ask Mr. Grinly for a long engagement, for a chance to free her mind and heart of Mr. Darcy. Eventually, the pain would lessen, and she would take pleasure in her new life as Mrs. Grinly. She thought they could be happy together, and someday they would. She would never forget Mr. Darcy or the passion she felt for him. Even now, it was all she could do not to stop the carriage and run back to Netherfield and into his arms. Why did it have to hurt so much?

Mr. Grinly knew her mind was in turmoil. He sat back on the bench, keeping as much distance between them as possible, allowing her all the space that could be afforded so she could be alone with her thoughts. He knew that solitude would be her only relief.

He also knew that he needed solitude as well, but he could not indulge in its luxury. Constance would soon need him, and he must be strong for her. She had been his strength through the dark hours of loneliness at Sappingford. He had hoped that Elizabeth would soon be the source of needed strength for Constance, and in return, he would supply love and affection to his new wife, but he would not allow Elizabeth to marry him if she did not love him. He would not condemn her to a life of regret. It would only lead to misery for all of them.

On their arrival at Longbourn, Mr. Grinly handed Elizabeth out of the carriage and followed her into the house. She walked to the bottom of the stairs and beckoned to him. She raised a hand to his cheek and looked deeply into his eyes, and then gave him a faint smile. He took her hand and kissed it.

Mr. Grinly watched her as she climbed the stairs, turned the corner, and out of his sight.

"Goodbye, Elizabeth."

Chapter 17

Darcy wrote dozens of business letters each week. He could express himself well in all matters of his estate, in contracts, in purchasing new property, and in all money matters. Alone in his bedchamber in the middle of the dark night, he could find few words. In this letter to Elizabeth, he wanted to express his love and beg her forgiveness. He knew he should not be writing it. It was not appropriate that he should do so, and Mrs. Bingley would be angry if she knew of it, but he could not leave Elizabeth behind in Hertfordshire without being in her presence once more, even if it were only in a letter.

For the last time, he kissed the purple ribbon and then slipped it into the envelope. She would understand its import. He hoped she would keep it and from time to time think of him. He would never forget her or stop loving her.

He was to leave for Town before dawn, and at such an early hour, there was no one to see him off except the groom. He did not want to see Bingley. The pain of losing both his friend and Elizabeth in one blow would be exacerbated by a parting with him. Elizabeth and Mrs. Bingley's tie of blood would be stronger than his and Bingley's tie of friendship. As he stepped into his carriage, he handed the servant the letter and instructed him to deliver it immediately to Longbourn.

ELIZABETH ROSE EARLY THE NEXT morning filled with resolve and determination to start her life anew with Mr. Grinly. She had spent the whole night thinking about her situation. She would shower on him every attention and prove her commitment.

As she entered the breakfast room, she was met by Mrs. Hill. "A letter arrived quite early this morning for you from Netherfield."

"From Netherfield?"

"A servant was here at first light, but as you seemed rather ill when you came in last night, I thought it best not to wake you. Please forgive me if I — "

"No, no, you were quite right. I have been ill," conceded Elizabeth. "Thank you for bringing it to me."

The missive was directed to "Miss E.B. at Longbourn." There were no other markings on it that might identify the sender, but she knew the handwriting did not belong to Jane.

Hiding the letter in the skirts of her dress, she hastened out the front door, crossed the paddock, and took a seat on a little bench within a copse of trees. Her breathing was labored, and her hands trembled as she attempted to break the seal, so much so that she dropped the letter.

It occurred to her that it must be from Mr. Darcy and that she should not break the seal, but should present it unopened to Mr. Grinly as a sign of her commitment to him. She would ask him to read it and relay to her any message that Mr. Darcy might have for her. If it was another plea to her to reconsider his suit, it was something that she should not read and by which she should not be influenced.

Yet Mr. Darcy had been such a friend to her and perhaps had saved her life. And what of all they had shared? Did that not mean something? Did she not owe him the consideration to read what he had to say to her?

She opened the letter.

Netherfield

Dearest Elizabeth,

I am returning this ribbon that has been with me from the beginning of our acquaintance and that you allowed me to keep after those precious moments we spent together near the stream.

I loved you then, and I love you now. Please forgive me for allowing fear and uncertainty to come between us. Please forgive me for the pain I caused you. I hope that one day you will remember me with kindness.

I wish you every happiness in your new life with Mr. Grinly. He must be a good man if he was able to obtain your affection.

I remain, &c.
Fitzwilliam Darcy

HE WAS GONE. MR. DARCY was gone. She always thought he would be there, somewhere, and that perhaps she might see him from time to time. It was a silly notion, of course, for she would soon be living in Wiltshire. By returning the ribbon, he had released her and surrendered her to Mr. Grinly. Her heart ached for Mr. Darcy, for she knew very well how he must feel. She would not show the letter to Mr. Grinly but would destroy it. She would keep the ribbon as a memento of the love and happiness she once felt and never expected to feel again.

CONSTANCE WAS IN HER ROOM waiting for Elizabeth who usually came by this time to help her dress. Today, she had dressed alone. Constance was impatient to see her friend and to be assured that all was well. She had retired before Elizabeth and her father returned from Netherfield and so did not know the outcome of that meeting.

The knock at the door was not that of Elizabeth but her father. She smiled a greeting to him as he entered the room.

"Constance, we will be leaving Longbourn tomorrow for home."

"And Elizabeth?"

"Elizabeth and I will not be wed. She will not be coming with us." *I did not love you...* The pain was still fresh.

"She loves him, does she not?"

"Yes." He put his arm around Constance and she leaned her head against his shoulder. "I knew that she did not love me, but I hoped that, in time, she would. I cannot break the engagement, but it is out of my power to make her happy, and it is impossible for me to do anything that will make her otherwise."

"Will she end it? That might be damaging to her reputation."

"I have to trust that Mr. Darcy will preserve her. I cannot do anything more than absent myself from her life."

"I wanted so much... I wish..."

"I have also wished. Constance, I am so sorry. This is not what I intended for us."

"Have you spoken with her?" She felt hollow at the prospect of returning to Wiltshire without Elizabeth.

"Not yet, but I cannot put it off any longer." He rose to leave. "We will depart early and breakfast on the road."

"Yes, Father."

ELIZABETH SLIPPED MR. DARCY'S LETTER into her pocket, and after sitting on the bench quietly for a half-hour, she was enough recovered to be able to go into the drawing room and wait for Mr. Grinly — for Thomas, she reminded herself. She wanted to come to a firm understanding with him and arrange to be married as soon as possible. He would take her into Kent, and then they would travel to Wiltshire. Elizabeth would ask him if they could take Constance with them so that there would be no reason to return to Hertfordshire. She would miss seeing Jane, but there was no other way.

From her place in the drawing room, she heard heavy footsteps, and concluding that it was Mr. Grinly, she calmed herself as best as she could and then rose when he came in the room.

"Good morning, Thomas.

"Good morning, Miss Bennet."

She frowned at his formality but assumed that he felt distant from her because of her behavior the previous night. She was going to close that distance. "Will you sit with me, sir?"

"No, please, forgive me." There would always be the fear of intrusion if they remained in the house. "Perhaps we can go out into the garden?"

"I would like that."

They walked in silence as he followed her to the bench where she was sitting the day he had proposed. It was protected from view of the house by a large tree. Mr. Grinly chose not to sit, but leaned against the tree.

He knew not how to begin. He knew not how to tell her that he loved her but could not marry her. He wanted to tell her —

Elizabeth interrupted his thoughts. "I would like to be married as soon as possible, Thomas. I hope you will agree."

Mr. Grinly was astonished by this revelation. It was a resolution that he would have welcomed yesterday, but today he had better knowledge, and though it was a tempting offer, it could not sway him. He knew his decision was correct.

"Miss Bennet..."

She could see a tide of pain wash over his face. A sense of foreboding sprang up in her mind.

"...I know that you still love Mr. Darcy."

Elizabeth raised her hand as if to interrupt him, but he forestalled her. "Please, let me continue. Your heart belongs to another man." He paced away from her. "I fear that if we were to marry, you would come to regret your decision and would soon resent Constance and me. It will be impossible for me to secure your lasting happiness."

Elizabeth suddenly felt heavy and would have been unable to stir from the bench had she desired it. The enormity of what he was saying was nearly incomprehensible.

"Thomas, you can secure it! I will be happy with you. I will!" She closed her eyes for a moment. "What you say is true, but it does not mean I do not respect and esteem you. I am committed to you. I have promised myself to you, and I do want to marry you. I have chosen you, Thomas. In time, I will forget about Mr. Darcy as I am surrounded by your love and Constance's affection. My feelings for him have brought me nothing but heartache. I know that you will not hurt me and that I am safe with you."

As she spoke, her strength returned and her courage rallied. She rose up and stood directly in front of him. "I will love you, Thomas, and I am truly sorry I do not now because you are a good, worthy man deserving of my affections. We shall be very happy together. I know we shall."

He stepped away from her as he felt his resolve weaken. Every instinct called out to him to take her in his arms, hold her, and love her just as much as he could and to be satisfied with whatever affection she could give him in return.

"Miss Bennet, I know that Mr. Darcy hurt you, but it is only those for whom we feel the most love, only those who are most dear to us, who can truly hurt us, but that does not mean we cease to love them."

"Which is to say that I have hurt you."

"Remember the joy that Mr. Darcy brought you and the way you felt whenever you were with him. Think of the passion that is in his eyes when he looks at you. Forgive him. Love him. That is where your happiness is to be found, and that is where you belong." He never imagined that the ultimate expression of his love for her would be to give her up to another man.

She struggled to catch her breath, but could not.

"I am begging you, Elizabeth, to agree to end our engagement — to end it for the sake of the happiness of us all."

Why did the feeling she was experiencing remind her of rolling down the hill with Jane when they were girls? It seemed as if she were falling and could not stop herself.

"I know it will cost you some embarrassment and for a time will be uncomfortable, but in the end, it will be the best for all concerned." He ceased to speak and turned away from her.

"I am so sorry, Mr. Grinly. I beg that you will forgive me."

"There is nothing to forgive. You have done nothing wrong."

"Yes, I have. I have raised expectations in you. I know what you must be feeling. I know that Constance will be deeply wounded. How shall I bear knowing that I have done that?"

"I have already spoken to Constance and explained my sentiments. She is saddened, but composed, and is in agreement with me."

"To what did she agree, sir?"

"That we cannot bring you the fulfillment and pleasure your life deserves, and because of that, you and I should not marry."

"What you truly mean," Elizabeth said bitterly, "is that I cannot bring you the happiness you deserve."

"No, not if your heart belongs to another."

He knew it would hurt, but he wanted Elizabeth to know that he was fully detached from any expectations. He wanted her to be free to accept Mr. Darcy.

"Very well."

IT WAS DONE. ELIZABETH WAS no longer to be married. She sat in stunned silence, wondering how it was possible that so much of her life could change in just an instant of time. She must have slipped into a reverie, because it was with a start that she heard him speak to her.

"…and may I ask one thing of you?"

"Yes…of course…anything."

He sat down next to her on the bench. "You must allow me to be the one who informs your mother. I can imagine how she will react, and you do not deserve that. You must allow me to do this. You must give me this opportunity to help you."

"You take too much upon yourself, sir."

She reached out to touch his hand by way of emphasis but, recalling their change in situation, withdrew it with an embarrassed look.

"I think not," replied Mr. Grinly in a gentle tone of voice. "Constance and I will leave for Wiltshire in the morning. You will talk to her, will you not?"

"I will. I could not let her leave without speaking to her." Elizabeth watched him stand and walk slowly back to the house.

When he was gone from her sight, she could not hold back her tears. The shock of one moment being engaged to marry and the next moment unshackled, though not free, was overwhelming.

THE PASSAGE OF TIME TO Mr. Darcy was irrelevant today. His worries were not centered on the length of the trip from Hertfordshire to London, but on the rest of his life. Never having given his heart to any woman, he now found it lost, and as the distance between himself and Netherfield grew, he knew a part of him, what he recognized as the best part, remained behind.

When he told Mrs. Bingley of his love for Elizabeth, he never imagined that his ultimate act of love would be giving her up. He had hoped to win her back. He had hoped that love was enough, but she had sent him away. She had consigned them both to a life without love — he, because he was not allowed to love her, and she, because she did not love Mr. Grinly. Peering through the darkness that surrounded his mind, he knew he would never see clearly again.

RECALLING HER SITUATION, ELIZABETH WIPED her tears and walked into the house. Mr. Grinly was in the drawing room talking to her mother. Elizabeth drew up near the door, though she remained out of sight of both, and listened to what passed between them.

"In choosing a wife, Mrs. Bennet, it is my desire to provide myself with a companion I can love and respect and who returns that love and for that woman to be a friend to Constance." Before she could make any reply, he quickly asked, "May I sit down?"

Mrs. Bennet was not pleased with his gravity. Though she knew him not to be of a lively disposition, this serious talk was making her uncomfortable. She invited him to sit in a chair opposite the sofa on which she sat.

"Because of these desires, and as a result of serious conversation with Miss Bennet, we have agreed to end our engagement."

"What? You cannot be serious! You cannot end the engagement! What kind of talk is this?"

"Indeed, I cannot end it, but Miss Bennet can, and I have persuaded her that she must, and she has agreed that it should be done."

"Mr. Grinly, please! I will talk to Lizzy myself. There must be some mistake. I will tell her that she shall marry you!"

"That is impossible."

"Why is it impossible? It must be possible."

"I cannot in good conscience marry your daughter."

"What? Good conscience? What has that girl done to offend you?"

"I believe it is impossible, madam, for Miss Bennet to offend anyone. However, it is not in my power to bring her the happiness she deserves. She will be miserable with me and would soon regret marrying me."

"Lizzy is a good humored sort of girl. There will be no unhappiness, of course there will not. I will talk to her. I will bring her to reason."

"Madam, it is not she with whom you must speak. This is my decision, not hers. Her delicacy of mind alone allows her to acquiesce. I am resolved. For her welfare and that of my daughter and myself, I cannot marry Miss Bennet. It is impossible."

"She shall be ruined! We shall all be ruined!"

"She has not been compromised. Her virtue is intact, and she will love again and be loved by someone who can truly care for her. I agree that there may be some uncomfortable moments, but your true friends will stand by you and console you in your disappointment."

"You cannot be serious! Why cannot you make her happy?"

"I beg of you," Mr. Grinly said earnestly, "that you do not make this any more uncomfortable for Miss Bennet or myself than it already is. The decision has been made."

"Oh, Mr. Grinly!"

Elizabeth chose this moment to enter the room. "Mama —"

"Lizzy, I am done with you from this day forward! I do not know what you have done to make Mr. Grinly reject you, but it must have been something awful!"

Elizabeth silently agreed with her mother in this regard.

"Mrs. Bennet, you must not blame her. It is wholly my decision."

"Mr. Grinly," said Elizabeth, "you should not, I mean, I —"

"Elizabeth, please." He looked at her earnestly, begging her with his eyes not to speak further.

She was sorry to be the cause of all the pain and discomfort he must be feeling. Mr. Grinly was correct, though. Ending the engagement was the only way he and Constance could hope to arrive at happiness in the future. For herself, she held no such expectations.

"Elizabeth, I am done with you. You have disgraced us all!" Mrs. Bennet stormed out of the room.

ELIZABETH TOOK HER MOTHER'S SEAT on the sofa. She had no tears left for crying, though she felt all the sorrow that often accompanies such tears. She felt shamed and embarrassed and could only imagine what life would be like at Longbourn until her mother had vented every feeling she had on the subject. In all likelihood, it would be no time soon.

Mr. Grinly sympathized with Elizabeth. He was no longer able to prevent forming an ill opinion of her mother. He had been striving to love her, and he was willing to make many allowances, but he would not countenance cruelty to Elizabeth. He first broke the silence. "Miss Bennet, perhaps you should stay with Mrs. Bingley until your mother's anger has abated. Would you like me to arrange for an invitation?"

"No, but thank you," Elizabeth answered with a weak smile. "I want to be the one who breaks the news to Jane. I am grateful to you, for in speaking to my mother, you have preserved me from some of her immediate disappointment, but I cannot ask you to do more."

He looked at her silently.

"I will go speak with Constance now, sir. I will ask her to walk out with me."

"I will leave you. I know you would wish to speak with her alone."

It would be a conversation he would like very much to hear, but by his very presence, it would not take place. Elizabeth and Constance had a close relationship. It would be uncomfortable for both of them, but it was an experience that should not be denied them. They had shared so much together, and they would very likely never meet again.

"I will go to her now." Elizabeth was on the point of leaving the drawing room when Mr. Grinly called her back.

"Miss Bennet…Elizabeth…" his voice softened. "I cannot leave Longbourn without saying…"

She colored, looking at him expectantly. He seemed embarrassed, which only contributed to her anxiety.

"Elizabeth, I must express my admiration for you. You have brought such joy to my life since I have been here and —"

She could not help but interrupt him. Hearing such things from him would be unbearable. "…and pain," she concluded for him.

He thought for a moment. "I do suffer, but that does not change how I feel about you. I would give anything for matters to have worked out differently."

How could she respond to such a profession?

"I wish you every happiness, Elizabeth — every happiness imaginable."

"Mr. Grinly, that is my hope for you. And I also hope someday you will forgive me."

Elizabeth left the drawing room, knowing that this was the last conversation she would ever have with him. Ascending the stairs with no little apprehension, she reached the top with her courage nearly failing her.

ELIZABETH WAS CERTAIN THAT CONSTANCE knew who was knocking and so was not surprised when she was not immediately invited in. There was a little time between her knock and Constance's opening the door — a hesitation, as if a decision was being made or a resolution determined.

Constance opened the door. She said nothing to Elizabeth and then walked back to the bed and sat down.

"I am sorry for disturbing you," said Elizabeth.

"Your visit is unexpected. I did not believe that I would see you again." Constance turned nervously away from Elizabeth. She felt very agitated.

"I suppose that your father has informed you that we —"

"Yes, he did! Yes, my father told me that you..." She stopped with a horror-stricken look on her face.

Elizabeth refused to be offended by her abruptness, knowing that she must be frustrated by all the changes occurring in her life, but before she could consider it further, Constance ran to Elizabeth and embraced her.

"Oh, Elizabeth. I did not mean to be harsh. Please, forgive me. Please." Constance was torn between feelings of resentment for Elizabeth, as a daughter might feel for her injured father, and feelings of compassion, such as a friend might feel for another who was suffering.

"There is nothing to forgive." Elizabeth's voice was full of compassion and gentleness. "I was wondering if we could talk."

"Yes, I would like that."

"Then would you be willing to walk out in the garden for a little while?"

THE LADIES EXITED THE HOUSE in silence and progressed across the lawn to the back of the garden where they were assured of privacy. Elizabeth was particularly anxious to avoid the notice of her mother.

"I know that your father has informed you that we have ended our engagement."

"He has, but I do not understand why it must end. Why cannot you marry my father?"

Constance strove to keep her mind busy, for if she thought too much about her feelings, she might begin to cry, and the thought of crying in front of Elizabeth was dreadful. Previously, she would have taken comfort from Elizabeth, but now she felt it would be a sign of weakness. She must be strong for her father.

"You and I have touched briefly on my relationship with Mr. Darcy, so you may have some idea of my feelings towards him."

"I believe that you love him."

"When I agreed to marry your father, I thought that I no longer loved Mr. Darcy. I thought that he was out of my mind and heart, but he was not. It is your father's opinion that if we were to marry, I would not be happy. Your father believes that I could never love him, and that I would soon come to resent both him and you." Elizabeth wondered why doing the right thing was so difficult and why innocent hearts must suffer.

"I cannot believe that you would ever resent me. I know you would not."

"I do not believe that I would."

"So, you do not love my father."

"No. It would be very unfair to your father for me to marry him without being deeply attached to him. He is a wonderful man, and I cannot bear the thought of making him unhappy."

"Does this mean you are going to marry Mr. Darcy?"

"Last night I was given the chance to reconcile with him, but I did not. He hurt me very badly, and I was determined to keep my obligation to your father, so I sent Mr. Darcy away without seeing him again. It was cowardly and unkind of me."

"Oh, Elizabeth. You will be alone! I was so happy in the thought of us being a family."

"I am so sorry. I feel terrible. I have hurt everyone, it seems."

"I am worried about you. Will anything ever change between you and Mr. Darcy? I mean, if you love him, should you not be with him?"

"He has left Hertfordshire, and I do not expect to ever see him again. I cannot imagine that he would want to see me even if he could, not after last night."

They walked on a little further until they reached a familiar tree and bench. Elizabeth sat and invited Constance to join her.

"But, Elizabeth, have neither of you heard of forgiveness?" Constance was incredulous of the idea that two people who loved each other so fervently should not be together.

"Your father asked me the same thing."

"My father was correct. Elizabeth, please promise me, I beg of you, that if you ever see Mr. Darcy again, that you will forgive him, and that you will tell him that you do."

Elizabeth smiled at the earnestness of Constance's plea and was touched by her sincerity. "I will, just for you."

"No, do it for you and for him."

Elizabeth was struck by a singular thought. Is that all it took, that she seek Mr. Darcy's forgiveness and grant him her own? Was it that simple?

Returning from their walk, the young women encountered Mrs. Bennet in the entryway. Sensing her anger, Constance excused herself.

"Elizabeth Bennet," shouted her mother, "There you are! Sit down!"

Mrs. Bennet pointed angrily at a chair. Elizabeth sat down and prepared for the worst. "Lizzy, you have spoiled your best, your only chance, for happiness! You have ruined everything! You —"

"Mama, I —"

"I will not be interrupted! If you go on refusing every offer of marriage that comes your way, you will never get a husband! You will end up an old maid and will die in this very house unless Mr. Bingley turns you out beforehand, and who will take care of you then? I told you I have done with you, and I will be as good as my word! Think of the disappointment you caused Mr. and Miss Grinly. Do they deserve that kind of treatment? No, they do not! Your behavior is…"

Elizabeth sat patiently while her mother continued to rant. Every reference to the pain that she caused Mr. Grinly cut deep inside her. It was a punishment to listen to her, but she felt it was well deserved.

When Mrs. Bennet had exhausted her strength for expostulation, Elizabeth sought refuge in the silence of her own bedchamber. The wish of her heart was to speak with Jane. Perhaps Mr. Grinly was correct. Perhaps she should go to Netherfield for a few days.

Elizabeth was many hours lying restless in her bed before she was blessed with sleep. Though finding difficulty in falling asleep, her weariness caused her to remain late abed the next morning. When she finally went downstairs, she was informed by Mrs. Hill that Mr. and Miss Grinly had departed.

A deep feeling of sadness nearly overwhelmed her as she considered the pain and upset that the Grinlys must be carrying with them on their journey. She felt their loss as much as they did hers. In Constance, she had found a sister and a friend. Although she had been unable to attach herself to Mr. Grinly, it did not mean that she wished for circumstances to turn out as they had. Any woman loves being admired by a kind and generous man, and Mr. Grinly was both.

Chapter 18

Elizabeth regained strength after breakfasting on toast and drinking chocolate. As soon as she could, she slipped out of Longbourn unnoticed and began the walk to Netherfield. The closer she came to Jane, the closer her feelings moved to the surface of her heart, and by the time she reached the front door, she could no longer hold back her tears. Elizabeth rang the bell and was greeted by Jane herself.

"Lizzy, I thought I told you I would send the... Lizzy! What is wrong? Come here." Jane pulled Elizabeth against her and held her until she stopped crying. Without a word, she gently led Elizabeth into the small sitting room and placed her on a sofa. "Please tell me what is wrong."

"Oh, Jane! I have caused them so much pain!"

"Who have you hurt? I am certain you did not intend it." She brushed a curl from Elizabeth's face.

"Mr. and Miss Grinly left this morning for Wiltshire."

"Were they not to remain at Longbourn until your wedding?"

"There is to be no wedding."

"What happened? Surely you did not quarrel..."

Again there was a painful pause.

"We agreed to end the engagement. We..."

Jane waited silently for Elizabeth to continue.

"Mr. Grinly persuaded me to believe that because of my attachment to Mr. Darcy, we could not be happy together. He feared that I would come to resent him."

Jane's arm was around Elizabeth, and she continued to hold her. "Why does he believe you would resent him?"

"I know I do not love Mr. Grinly, and because of Mr. Darcy, I do not believe that I ever could. He is correct. We would not have been happy together."

Jane was troubled by one part of Elizabeth's narrative. "You said he persuaded you. Do you mean to say that you would prefer that he had not?"

"He felt very strongly, and I could not deny the love I have for Mr. Darcy."

"I am so sorry."

"It is for the best." Elizabeth spoke with much more confidence than she felt. "I wish Mr. Grinly every happiness. I feel most deeply for Constance, though. She is so disappointed. We had so many plans for what we would do together. I think that hers is the greatest loss of all."

THE SISTERS' CONVERSATION CONTINUED UNTIL Mrs. Thomas interrupted them with a tray of lemonade.

"I beg your pardon, ma'am." Mrs. Thomas addressed herself to Jane. "But Mr. Bingley insisted that I bring you some refreshment." She set the tray down on the table nearest Jane.

"Thank you, Mrs. Thomas, and please tell Mr. Bingley that we have not forgotten about him."

"Jane, you have such a sweet husband."

"I love him dearly." She poured out two glasses of lemonade and gave one to Elizabeth.

Elizabeth continued. "I knew that the Grinlys were to leave this morning. Mr. Grinly told me so yesterday, but when I came down, I was still bewildered to learn that they had actually left, that they were gone. For good or for ill, they have been such a part of my life these past weeks that I hardly know what to do with myself now."

"Lizzy, ever since your fall, you have experienced a tumult of emotions, more so than is natural for any one person to experience in so short a time. You should not feel bad because you do not feel like yourself."

"I feel so empty, so hollow. I feel as though my life has no direction or purpose any longer. Despite the fact that ending my engagement with Mr. Grinly was the correct decision, I still miss him and Constance. My heart aches when I think of Mr. Darcy. At the end of my conversation with Mr. Grinly, when all was decided, he said something that has affected me deeply."

"And what is that?"

"Mr. Grinly told me to forgive Mr. Darcy."

"He said that?" Jane was not surprised to hear it. During her conversations with Elizabeth, she had become acquainted with Mr. Grinly and felt that one of the positive attributes he possessed was integrity. Ever since he made the decision to let Elizabeth go, he had promoted her relationship with Mr. Darcy.

"Yes. He said that only the people we love most have the power to hurt us, but if they do, it does not mean we cease to love them."

"I had not thought about that before, but I suppose it is true."

Elizabeth was silent for a moment as she focused on Jane's last words. Yes, it was true, and something else was also true. "I love him, Jane. I love Mr. Darcy."

Jane felt responsible for Elizabeth's engagement to Mr. Grinly and consequent separation from Mr. Darcy. She remembered how she and Elizabeth used to talk about love and marriage, and how Elizabeth had always told her she would only marry someone with whom she was in love. She had persuaded Elizabeth to deny that love, and now Elizabeth was suffering for it. Jane wanted to change the subject to one less tender. "How is Mama taking the news?"

"Not very well. She blames me and is being rather unpleasant."

"Then why do you not stay at Netherfield with us until the storm has blown over. Would you be willing to do that? I will send a servant to Longbourn for your things and to inform Mama that you will be with us for now."

"Thank you, Jane. That is most kind. I would like that very much."

DARCY STUMBLED THROUGH THE DOOR of his London townhouse after a slow and difficult ride from Hertfordshire. The silence of the house was deafening. Georgiana was not at home, and neither his housekeeper nor any of the servants were prepared to receive him.

He stepped heavily through the hall towards the solitude of his library, his body weighed down with grief. He could describe the emotion he felt in no better term than mourning, for it seemed as though someone close to him had died. Darcy sat in silence for hours before he heard a light knock at the door. If he did not respond, he knew no one would dare come in, so it was with no little surprise and quickly mounting anger that he saw the knob turn and someone prepare to enter.

"Leave me!" He struck the desk with an open hand, the sound punctuating his command.

The unwelcome intruder was no less startled by his violence than he was by the appearance of Georgiana.

"Fitzwilliam," she said in a faltering voice, "I did not mean...I am sorry that...I..." She turned and fled the room. Georgiana was not accustomed to her brother raising his voice and the prospect was frightening.

Darcy sprang from his chair and ran to her, gently calling her name. She was reassured by the softened look on his face. Taking her elbow, he led her back to the library.

"Georgiana, I did not mean to frighten you. I am so sorry. You are always welcome here. Please, come and sit with me. There is no fire, but I have a blanket with which to warm you." Chastising himself for the bad temper that led him to abuse her, he assisted her into a chair by the empty fireplace. He took the promised blanket and covered her.

As he sat down next to Georgiana, Darcy realized just how injured he was as a result of losing Elizabeth. If his behavior towards Georgiana was a sample of how he might act in the future, his life was going to be one of misery.

Georgiana was quick to forgive him. She knew he was suffering and would say nothing to disrupt what she knew to be delicate emotions. Instead, she stated the obvious. "Fitzwilliam, I was not expecting you home so soon."

Grateful for her generosity in not mentioning his affront, he quickly answered. "I had not anticipated such an early return, but I found that I had no reason to remain in Hertfordshire. Indeed, I found that my presence was unwelcome."

Despite the blanket, a chill passed through Georgiana. She knew why he had gone to Hertfordshire, and if he were back so soon, nothing good could have come of his trip. She pulled the blanket close around her. "I can see that you are not well. What may I do for you?"

Darcy shook his head with a bitter laugh. "There is nothing you can do. There is nothing anyone can do. I have lost her. Elizabeth is to marry another man."

Uncertain how to respond, she gave him a weak smile and a nod as encouragement to continue speaking.

His voice was rife with frustration. "Elizabeth loves me. I could see it in her eyes, and her sister confirmed it when we spoke privately."

"Did you meet her...her..."

There was a moment of silence as Georgiana searched for a delicate way to ask the question.

"...her future husband? Are those the words for which you are searching but will not speak? You will not offend me. I have punished myself enough. No one else can injure me." His head dropped against his chest. "Yes, I met him. Mr. Grinly is quiet and unassuming, and she does not love him!"

His words echoed in the quiet room.

Georgiana was incredulous. "Then why? Why is she marrying him?" From what little she knew of Miss Bennet, allowing for the fact that all she knew of her was from her brother's report, she did not think that she was the kind of young woman who would marry where she did not love.

"To escape me. It is my opinion that she wants to leave Hertfordshire and all her friends and go off to Wiltshire with this man in order to free herself from the attachment she feels for me, perhaps even to punish me."

"She should marry you! She will only be hurting herself. Does she not see that? How can she expect to be happy marrying a man she does not love?"

"Georgiana, I do not believe that she expects to be happy."

"Are all her hopes for happiness truly that blighted?"

"Oh, how I hurt her! She does not love Mr. Grinly, and therefore he cannot hurt her. She is safe with him."

"That is so sad."

He could say no more, but stepped over to the sideboard and poured himself a glass of brandy. The heat of the liquid was like fire in his throat as he quickly drank it down, but compared to the flames burning in his mind and heart, it accounted for nothing. He reached again for the brandy.

Georgiana pushed her blanket aside and moved to join her brother.

"Do not be foolish, Fitzwilliam," she whispered as she took the glass from his hand. "It will only make it worse."

For a moment, he was quiet and just looked at her. "You are correct, and you were also correct when you told me to return to her. I will follow your advice because I know the price I am paying for not having listened to you before."

She pulled him into an embrace and heard a groan of despair rumble deep in his chest. She could not imagine what he was feeling, but his anguish and raw emotion were painful to witness. She felt helpless. There was little or nothing she could say or do that might console him or ease the burden he carried.

"It is late. Go to bed, Georgiana."

When he was alone, he eyed the brandy and fingered his glass, but thinking of Georgiana, he set it down again and retired to his own bedchamber for the night. He knew he had no hope of sleep, but there was, in fact, nowhere else for him to go.

ELIZABETH WAS GRATEFUL TO ESCAPE both Longbourn and her disagreeable mother, and it was with the greatest relief that she found herself installed at Netherfield in the bedchamber she considered to be her own, the room where she recovered from her fall. She chose it as the best place to pour out her heart with thoughts of Mr. Darcy. Jane assumed that Elizabeth was very fatigued, and that it was for this reason that she spent so much time above stairs when she was not out of doors.

Every day the weather was fine. Elizabeth wandered around the grounds of Netherfield just as her mind wandered through the streets of London in search of Mr. Darcy. One day while walking some distance from the house, she came upon a turning in the path and caught sight of a tree root raised up from the ground. Though she had no recollection of her accident, she fancied that this must have been the spot where she fell, that this was the place where she was unknowingly introduced to Mr. Darcy's notice, that right here he had come upon her and held her while awaiting Mr. Bingley's carriage. Perhaps next to that small green shoot was where he found her ribbon. He had kept her ribbon with him from that time forward as an endearment and a remembrance. Now he had no need for it. It was too late. He had returned the ribbon, and at her bidding, was gone.

THE DAYS PASSED SLOWLY FOR Elizabeth. Every morning, she walked out, either going past the tree root or sitting on one of the rocks in the stream thinking of Mr. Darcy. The water flowed gently through her fingers. She wondered if he ever thought of her and wondered if she would ever stop thinking of him. She wanted news of him and wished to learn if he were at peace. She harbored no bitterness towards him, only love and longing.

In the deepest moments of despair, she would imagine him walking into the drawing room while she was at her work. She would look up at him and their eyes would meet. Soon their hands would come together, and then their lips. Sometimes these feelings became so vivid that she was nearly in tears by the time the emotion passed.

JANE WAS BECOMING EVER MORE concerned about Elizabeth. She had hoped that the passing of time would begin to heal Elizabeth's heart, but it seemed that every day her spirits were no better. Jane carefully watched over Elizabeth, always aware of where she was, when she left the house, and when she might be expected back again. Her desire to protect Elizabeth was further excited each time she came upon her sitting alone in silent tears.

Elizabeth's melancholy was painful for Jane to witness. She had always been so lively and enthusiastic, full of life and vigor with a smile and a cheerful word for everyone, but all that was gone now. In their place were sadness and heartache. Agonizing over every moment that Elizabeth was alone, Jane spent as much time with her as she could, often accompanying her on her walks.

They had been pursuing their way in companionable silence when Jane put her hand on Elizabeth's arm and began to speak. "Lizzy, what can I do for you? I know you are not happy, and it pains me to see it. Is there not anything I can do for you?"

Elizabeth attempted to put on a happy air, not wanting Jane to suffer for her lack of spirits, but it was a futile effort. Jane was so familiar with her moods and tempers that there was very little she could conceal from her.

"You are doing everything. I love being at Netherfield with you and your adorable husband."

"Yes, my husband is adorable, but I love you very much, and I want to know what I can do to make you happier."

They walked on a few paces while Elizabeth determined how or whether she should open her heart to Jane.

"I do not know if I am allowed to express such feelings as I have. I do not know if it is appropriate for me to…" She paused. "Oh, Jane, I am afraid. I fear that you will not approve of me."

Jane smiled at her. "You can tell me."

"Very well." Her eyes started to burn, and she turned abruptly away in embarrassment. "I want to be with Mr. Darcy!" She looked back at Jane. "I want to be his wife."

Jane was not surprised by the emotion or the declaration. She put her arms around Elizabeth and held her close.

"Does Mr. Bingley ever hear from him?" asked Elizabeth. "Where is he? How is he?"

"We have not heard from him since…" She could not finish. The memory was too painful.

"…since that night," said Elizabeth bitterly. "I was in error. I made a grave mistake."

Jane watched apprehensively as Elizabeth's countenance darkened. She struggled to formulate a response. "But he hurt you, and you said you did not trust him. Your behavior was reasonable. You should not censure yourself."

"You may say that, but the fact remains that I love Mr. Darcy, and yet I am not with him." A tear trickled down Elizabeth's cheek. "I know I shall never see him again."

Elizabeth could speak no further, and they walked on in silence. Upon gaining the house, she withdrew to her bedchamber, and she was not seen for the rest of the day.

JANE HAD NOT NEEDED ELIZABETH'S confession of her desire to be married to Mr. Darcy to believe that her depressed state of spirits was the result of the love she harbored for him. Now, being in possession of Elizabeth's open avowal of such a desire, Jane considered herself to be at liberty to affect a reunion between the former lovers. Truthfully, Jane knew there was little she could do herself, but a great deal might be accomplished with some exertion on the part of her husband.

Jane found Charles at his accustomed place in the study, behind a noble desk of the finest wood. She believed that the solid strength of his desk was mirrored in the man sitting behind it. In him, she had trusted her heart, her happiness, and her hopes, and from him, had gained everything.

"Charles, do you have a moment for me?"

Bingley looked up with a smile at the sound of her voice. "I have a lifetime for you, my love. Please come in."

He rose, met her halfway across the room, and assisted her to a sofa that, with two other chairs, formed a small sitting area in front of the fire. He sat beside her and took her hand.

"I am very worried about Elizabeth. She is not happy, and time is not healing her heart."

"I join you in your apprehension. I have noticed that she does not look well. She eats so very little, and when I see her in the morning, she appears tormented and exhausted. She no longer laughs."

"I now know what we can do for her."

"Do you? And what is that? You know I will do anything for her."

Jane leaned her head on her husband's shoulder as he sat back on the sofa. Sitting and talking with him in such a manner as this was one of her dearest pleasures.

"She has confessed to me that she is still in love with Mr. Darcy."

"But have we not always known that?"

"Yes, we have, but the situation is different now. She has made a decision. It is her desire to be with him, to marry him. It is a studied desire that has not arisen from the impulse of the moment, but is the true feeling of her heart."

Bingley said nothing, so Jane went on.

"She has conceded that she made a mistake in sending him away, and I believe her. If she were not in love, she would act more like herself, but she is not. She is truly attached to Mr. Darcy, and I feel called on to help her in any way that I can. Unfortunately, I cannot do much for her," she paused, "but you can."

"What would you have me do?"

"I would like you to write to Mr. Darcy."

Bingley was silent, considering the implications of resuming contact with his friend whom he had deliberately cut off in an effort to protect Elizabeth's fragile relationship with Mr. Grinly. Would it not seem insincere to resume a correspondence with him? Yet, his intentions had been honorable, and the engagement was now broken. "I have had no contact with him since he was last here. I had thought, well, that we could not continue...for Elizabeth's sake...that we could not remain friends."

It was Jane's turn for a moment of reflection. Even worse than encouraging Elizabeth to marry Mr. Grinly she was preventing her husband from maintaining a relationship with his friend. As she looked back, she could not countenance her behavior in any way that satisfied her. "I am sorry. It was wrong of me. Please write to him and extend to him my warmest regards and an apology."

"An apology?"

"Yes. I know he feels that I am his greatest enemy, and I want to correct that impression. I am not. I want to be his friend. Oh, Charles, I am so sorry. I had no right to separate you from your friend. It was cruel and was based on a mistaken assumption of the needs I felt Elizabeth had in her relationship with Mr. Grinly, but a commitment to one man should not be based on the absence of attentions from another."

"I know that you did not intend to injure anyone."

"But do you not see? I have injured everyone — Mr. Darcy, Elizabeth, and you!"

"No one blames you."

"Perhaps not, but they ought." She turned her head into his shoulder. "Please forgive me."

Bingley laid Jane back in his arms until he was cradling her head in the crook of his arm. He could tell that she was very near tears. "Jane, what am I to do with you?"

She was silenced by his kiss.

THE FOLLOWING MORNING, MRS. THOMAS sent a servant into Meryton to post a letter written by her master in an effort to heal relationships that had been damaged over the course of the past few weeks.

It read as follows:

Netherfield

Darcy,

I have not heard from you since you left Hertfordshire, and I just want you to know that everyone here is thinking of you.

Mrs. Bingley sends her warmest greetings and begs that I tell you that she hopes you are well. She asks me to encourage you to write and let us know how you are faring and that she would be certain to pass your salutations on to all your friends in Hertfordshire.

You may be unaware, perhaps, that Elizabeth is with us. She and Mr. Grinly ended their engagement, and he has returned to Wiltshire. Although their separation was amicable, Elizabeth is not happy. She has very tender feelings over what I believe is a recent loss.

Please forgive my part in our past differences. Indeed, I can hardly remember over what we disagreed. Let us always remain friends.

Yours, &c.
CB

To say that Darcy was astonished on receipt of Bingley's letter would not adequately describe his feelings. Indeed, he could not utter a sound, but could only read and reread with shocked amazement the news that Elizabeth was not married.

Immediately on the heels of his astonishment was concern. Elizabeth was not happy. It was no small matter to terminate an engagement, and her removal to Netherfield was a statement of the difficulty she was experiencing at home. He had great confidence in the honor and integrity of Mr. Grinly. Whatever had occurred between Mr. Grinly and Elizabeth had happened with her full knowledge and consent.

He knew of nothing in her life that could be accounted as a loss. Was it possible that she had repented her decision? Hope immediately kindled in his heart, hope that she might yet still love him.

From reading the letter, two things must be concluded. First, he had imagined that he would never hear from Bingley again. He had assumed that in an effort to prevent further injury to her sister, Mrs. Bingley would force an end to their friendship, but she had not. Regardless of what precipitated this letter, Bingley would not have written without his wife's knowledge.

Second, when he considered all his acquaintances in Hertfordshire that may wish to hear from him, he could only think of Bingley. Who else could it be? Was it possible that Elizabeth wished to know of him?

There could be no other explanation. It must be Elizabeth.

The darkness that clouded Darcy's mind from the moment he left Hertfordshire began to disperse, and it was all he could do to restrain himself from leaving immediately for Netherfield. Yet it was impossible for him to go. He would not risk it. He could not endure being near Elizabeth unless he was certain that she would forgive and accept him, and it seemed to him incomprehensible that she would, not after what he had done.

Yet that letter…

Elizabeth should not be left wondering. He must seize the opportunity to speak to her and avail himself of Mrs. Bingley's invitation to send a message that would be passed on to her.

What to write? He could not profess the love he felt. She may not be prepared to hear it, and she would only become embarrassed because Bingley and her sister would undoubtedly see the letter before she did. No. All he could do was let her know that she was never far from his thoughts and that he had not forgotten her.

Taking his pen, and after many trials and frustrations, the following letter was ready to be posted to Netherfield.

London

Bingley,

It was such a pleasure to hear from you. I pray that you will forgive my mistaken neglect in not writing sooner. Georgiana is well and asks me to send you her love.

My thoughts frequently turn towards Hertfordshire and the great enjoyment I experienced being with you when you first occupied Netherfield. I have never been happier than I was during those short weeks.

London is a little thin this time of year, but it makes no difference to me. I remain quietly at home. I correspond with my steward at Pemberley regularly, but have no plans for traveling.

I am saddened that anything should have happened to Miss Bennet to make her unhappy, but I am reassured that she is with her sister. She is never far from my thoughts. If there is anything I can do for her, please let me know. I would appreciate nothing more than to be of service to her by any means that are in my power.

Please, thank your wife for all the kindness she has shown me. I am looking forward to the day when we can all be together again.

I remain, &c.
FD

Chapter 19

The next day, Bingley received Darcy's letter and had the pleasure of sharing it with his wife. Jane, more than pleased with the contents, went in search of her sister, knowing she had information that would be gladly and gratefully received. Elizabeth was outside in the garden, as usual, this time sitting on a bench that encircled the trunk of a large tree.

"I have been looking for you." Jane sat down next to Elizabeth, making every effort to suppress her delight.

"You have? I hope I was not hard to find."

"No," laughed Jane, "you are always out here somewhere. Lizzy, I have news that will interest you. I have come to tell you that we have had a letter from Mr. Darcy that should make you very happy. As you know, we have not heard from him since he left Netherfield, but Charles wrote to him, mentioned that your engagement had ended, and that you were staying with us."

"Mr. Bingley wrote to Mr. Darcy? May I ask what Mr. Darcy's response was?"

"Perhaps you would like to read the letter for yourself." Jane offered the envelope to her sister.

Elizabeth's eyes grew wide in response to the surprise she felt on reading his letter. "He sounds well." Her eyes glimmered with happiness.

"Is that all you can say? Lizzy, that letter is for you. He has not forgotten you."

"And I have not forgotten him. Do you think it is true? Do you think he still loves me after all this time?"

"I am certain of it."

Elizabeth rose from her seat and stood in front of her sister. "What should I do, Jane?"

"You and he have suffered through immense heartache and misunderstanding.

I know how strongly you feel about him. I would recommend that you take a chance and send him a note telling him what is in your heart."

"Would that be proper?"

"It may be best that, in this circumstance, propriety be transgressed. Mr. Darcy is as uncertain of you as you are of him. Give him just a hint as to what you feel. Give him reason to hope and then wait to see how he responds."

"Thank you, Jane. I will. I will write to him."

It was a fine morning when Darcy returned from an appointment with his solicitor. His housekeeper, Mrs. Jamison, greeted him. "Sir, Mr. Tilden is waiting to see you. I told him you were out, but he insisted on waiting for your return and would not be persuaded to leave. I am very sorry. I know that you do not like to be disturbed in such a manner as this."

"Thank you for your efforts, Mrs. Jamison." Darcy relieved himself of his hat and gloves. "I suppose the sooner I see him, the sooner he will leave."

Mrs. Jamison laughed.

"I will receive him in the drawing room."

He knew that Mrs. Jamison went to great lengths to insulate him from unwanted callers, so he could only conclude that Mr. Tilden must have been in rare form if he were able to stand his ground against her. There was no doubt in Darcy's mind as to Mr. Tilden's errand, but he was unmoved.

Assuming a proud, dignified air, he proceeded to the drawing room to await his visitor.

Darcy was standing when Mr. Tilden entered the room. He moved quickly to greet him and ushered him to a seat near the fire.

"Mr. Tilden, welcome to my home. To what do I owe the pleasure of this visit?" The conventions of society necessitated lies. Pleasure? Not likely.

"I came to learn the truth for myself. I have heard confusing reports, some telling me that you were in Town, and others confirming that you were in the country, and not having had the pleasure of your company for quite some time, I thought I would take the liberty of calling."

"As you can see, I am here," said Darcy flatly. "I am sorry you were kept waiting. Mrs. Jamison, of course, told you that I was out?"

"Ah…she did," answered Mr. Tilden uncomfortably, "but I am not to be at White's until later in the morning, so I asked if I could wait." Mr. Tilden had no appointment to be anywhere, of course.

"Would you care for some tea?"

"Thank you, but no."

"Well, Mr. Tilden, how long will you remain in Town? It must be nearly time for you to return to the country. I believe Miss Tilden mentioned that your visit was to be only three months." Darcy concluded that it was best to get directly to what he believed was the point of Mr. Tilden's visit, and so was not unwilling to introduce his daughter into their conversation.

"We have no immediate plans for a removal. I bring with me Clara's compliments, Mr. Darcy, her warmest compliments…"

"I thank you, sir, and please extend my…"

"…and a renewal of my offer."

"Your offer, sir?"

"Let me speak plainly. It is my earnest desire to form a match between you and my daughter."

Darcy was taken aback by such a boldfaced attack. He had hoped to escape this interview without giving or receiving offense, but with each word, Mr. Tilden was making that less likely. Marrying his daughter was out of the question.

"Yes, you have touched on that before, but I recall that my response to you was that I did not love your daughter and, for that reason, could not marry her."

"Mr. Darcy, both our families, though untitled, are ancient and honorable. The fortune on each side is splendid. Upon your marriage, you will receive £35,000. Tilden Manor will be Clara's upon my death, and through her, yours. She is a beautiful young lady, highly accomplished, and pleasant company. You cannot possibly have an objection to her."

"No, indeed. There can be no objection to Miss Tilden. She is all that you describe."

"Let me ask you this, Mr. Darcy. Are you engaged elsewhere?"

Once again, Darcy was astonished at Mr. Tilden's impertinence. "No, I am not."

"You spoke of love, Mr. Darcy. That is a meaningless concept these days."

Mr. Tilden's boldness was unprecedented. Darcy stared at him incredulously.

He continued. "You are a man of sense and understanding. You cannot possibly consider that matters of the heart exceed the considerations of fortune, connection, and rank. Who is it that you claim to love? Surely, she would be found wanting in a comparison with my daughter."

Darcy rose to his feet in anger. "Sir, I beg that you will importune me no further!"

Mr. Tilden, not yet discouraged, continued to pursue the matter. "Mr. Darcy, you must satisfy me. Why will you not consent to marry my daughter?"

"Because, as I have said before, I do not love her."

"And as I have said before, it takes more than love to make a good marriage. You must believe me. I speak from experience."

"Mr. Tilden, I am certain that there is nothing but love that can ensure a happy union."

"Consider what you are throwing away. How can you walk away from such an offer?"

"Mr. Tilden, please consider what it is that you are throwing away, or should I say, who. We are speaking of the happiness of your daughter, of a thinking, feeling individual, not a piece of property to be bartered about. Think of her, Mr. Tilden, and stop thinking of me."

"I can see that further conversation with you is pointless." He rose, and bowed stiffly. "I take my leave, sir." And he was gone.

Darcy sat back heavily into his chair, exhausted from the confrontation. Mr. Tilden had recommended a comparison between his daughter and the woman he loved. Darcy had compared the two. And while it would not be fair to criticize Miss Tilden, Elizabeth's superiority was clearly established.

It was only urgent business that could call Darcy away from his home, and his visitors were equally as rare. He had very few acquaintances who made any effort to see him, his reticence having offended many.

But Darcy had every reason to be happy. The indescribable joy he felt on hearing that Elizabeth was not married gave him every reason to hope. The hint in Bingley's letter was obvious. It had been just two days since he sent his missive to Netherfield, and any day now, he hoped to hear something.

As he walked through the hall to the library, his butler petitioned for a moment of his time to inform him that the post had just arrived, and that there was a letter for him. Darcy, feigning composure, calmly accepted the letter, thanked the man, and then walked quickly across the hall. When he knew he was alone, he looked at it to see if it was the one for which he had been waiting.

He could not tell. The directions were written in a fine, flowing, feminine hand, but he had never seen Elizabeth's writing, so he did not know for certain. It was addressed from Netherfield, but there was no name on it. He held his breath as he opened the envelope. The note was not dated and contained just three words.

Please come back.

Accompanying the note was something he recognized. He laced it through his fingers and kissed it. It was Elizabeth's purple ribbon.

DARCY'S EXULTATION COULD NOT BE constrained to the confines of his library. He literally burst out of his townhouse and walked briskly into a nearby park to stride down the walks and avenues. It was a simple note, but he read it over and over again. The ribbon did not leave his hand. It was the most precious gift he had ever received. It was an invitation from Elizabeth to love her once again.

As the excitement of the moment wore off, he began to doubt himself. Perhaps she just wanted to be on good terms with him again. Perhaps it was merely a token of friendship. Then he remembered the significance of that ribbon when they were together at the stream, when he kissed it, and then her. There was no mistaking her meaning then, and there could be no mistaking it now. There could be no two opinions about it. She still loved him.

After taking a few more minutes to compose himself, he returned home and began making the arrangements for an immediate removal to Netherfield. If he left now, it would be after dark by the time he arrived in Hertfordshire. This would be unsafe as well as inconvenient to the Bingleys, and certainly Elizabeth should be given notice of his coming. He would, however, announce to them his imminent arrival, and so he penned two letters.

London

Bingley,

I am taking the liberty of traveling to Hertfordshire in the morning to call on you, and more specifically, to wait on Miss Bennet. She has communicated her wish to see me, and I will answer it immediately.

Please extend my warmest thanks to your wife. I know she has been intimately involved in all the particulars that have occurred to make my presence in Hertfordshire not unwelcome to Miss Bennet.

I wait for the morning with eagerness and impatience, as you may well understand. I look forward to seeing you all.

Yours, &c.,
Fitzwilliam Darcy

The second note was much shorter and more to the point.

Dearest Elizabeth,
    I will be with you before dinner tomorrow. Please forgive me.

All my love,
Fitzwilliam

EARLY THE NEXT MORNING, a servant delivered two letters to Netherfield. Both were given to Mr. Bingley. With pleasure, he read the one addressed to him, which announced Darcy's imminent arrival. Bingley had expected that Darcy would come once his wife told him that Elizabeth had sent him a note. Though he did not know the contents of her letter, he knew it would bring Darcy to Netherfield and had therefore instructed Mrs. Thomas to prepare Darcy's usual bedchamber.

After a moment of deliberation, he decided that Jane would be best suited to deliver the second letter to Elizabeth. He sought out his wife and gave her both letters. They exchanged a kiss, and then she went directly to her sister.

Jane found Elizabeth in her bedchamber. "Lizzy, I have news for you! Two letters have arrived from Mr. Darcy, and one is addressed to you!"

The color drained from Elizabeth's face for a moment.

Jane offered the letters to Elizabeth. "Here. There is one for you, and another for Charles. He thought you might like to read it, also."

"Oh, Jane."

"I will leave you alone to read your —"

"Oh, no!" interrupted Elizabeth. "Please, stay."

Jane smiled and sat down on the bed next to Elizabeth and watched her as she opened the letter and began to read. She could tell by the expression on her face that it brought welcome news.

"All is well! He loves me!" Elizabeth clasped the letter to her heart.

"Of course he does!" replied Jane, embracing her. "How could he not?"

Jane's sense of relief was great. For the first time since Elizabeth's fall, she felt that she had done the right thing.

"He is coming today!"

ELIZABETH SPENT THE REST OF the morning in a nervous agitation of spirits. Always on the watch for a carriage, she waited impatiently in the drawing room, alternately looking out each window.

Finally, for Elizabeth's peace of mind and to give her something to do, Jane encouraged her to walk out for a while. Mr. Darcy could not possibly arrive for another hour or two, and she would send for her immediately upon his arrival. Elizabeth agreed to anything that would help pass the time.

"Where will you walk, Lizzy? To the stream?"

Elizabeth could not hide her smile. "Yes, Jane, I believe I will."

DARCY ANTICIPATED THAT HIS JOURNEY to Netherfield would be tedious and long. Fortunately, he was wrong. The whole time his thoughts were filled with memories of Elizabeth, from his first discovery of her on the path, through all the joy they shared together during her recovery, and when he kissed her by the stream. He was unable to put from his mind the images he had created of what Elizabeth must have felt and looked like when she learned of his sudden departure. Seared into his very being were the events of the night when he last saw Elizabeth. He was jealous at the thought of Mr. Grinly touching her, and knew that as soon as he was able, he would kiss away all remembrances of him from her heart.

In a shorter time than he thought possible, the carriage pulled up in front of Netherfield. Alighting from the coach, he breathed in the fresh scent that he had come to associate with Hertfordshire. His anxiety rising, he approached the door with cautious steps. Before he could knock, it was thrown open by Mrs. Bingley.

"Mr. Darcy, you are very welcome! We have been awaiting your arrival."

"Thank you for the welcome and for all that you have done. I have no doubt that your husband was speaking for you in his letter."

Jane responded with a smile.

He continued. "I am grateful for the invitation." He hesitated and looked around for a moment.

"Elizabeth," said Jane with an amused smile, "is out walking, but she asked me to call for her just as soon as you arrived. Perhaps you will oblige me and go for her yourself?"

"I would be very happy to, as you are well aware."

"Indeed I am, sir. I believe there is a small stream nearby with which you may be intimately acquainted?"

"I am."

"She is there now, sir. Go to her. She has been waiting for you for a very long time."

The meaning of her words and the tone of her voice did not escape him. He looked at her apologetically.

"I promise you that I will never do anything that will ever bring her pain again."

"Thank you for your assurance. Now go."

After watching Darcy quickly descend the steps and hurry off behind the house, Jane returned indoors and thought with pleasure on the future happiness of her sister. That Darcy was the one man who could bring joy into Elizabeth's life was not in doubt, and that both he and Elizabeth finally understood this relieved Jane of a great deal of remorse. The misery of watching Elizabeth suffer over the past weeks had been awful. She knew the next time she saw Elizabeth she would be smiling again, and for this Jane was exceedingly grateful.

DARCY KNEW EXACTLY WHERE TO find Elizabeth, and he moved expeditiously in that direction. He slowed his pace as he came to the small clearing by the stream, savoring the anticipation of seeing her again.

He pushed through the edge of the woods. There she was!

My Elizabeth!

He had never seen a sight so beguiling. She was seated on a rock dangling her fingers in the water. For a moment, he was transported back to the time when this scene had played itself out before. He knew that this time it would end differently.

She was humming a tune to herself as she trailed her hand through the water. She had let her hair down, and it cascaded across her shoulders, partially shielding her face from his view. Her movements were graceful and the sound of her voice was enticing. His breath caught in his throat at the intimacy of what he was witnessing. This was Elizabeth in her true environment, outside and at peace. Her hair would not be down unless she was certain that she would not be seen. Yet, she had told Mrs. Bingley where she could be found.

Elizabeth had done this for him. She knew he would come for her and desired that he find her just as she was — innocently in love, free from deception, and willing to give herself to him in heart and body. He gently spoke her name.

THE WATER APPEARED FRESH AND inviting, and for just a moment, Elizabeth nearly forgot the reason she was there. Nearly.

Mr. Darcy was coming.

She stepped over to a familiar rock and sat upon it, letting her fingers fall into the water. She wet both hands and wiped her face, chilled for a moment as the water dried in the gentle breeze. She took out her hairpins and combed her fingers through her hair. The breeze pushed a few curls across her face.

This time, as well as on all prior visits to this place, her thoughts drifted back to the occasion when Mr. Darcy found her here. She could not recall the words they had exchanged. All she could remember was how he drew near to her and closed the distance between them. Soon he was sitting by her, then touching her hand, then holding her, then kissing her. It was beyond familiarity. It was intimacy. It was need. She needed him, and he had been there.

Once again, she needed him, and he was coming. It was while she was engaged in this happy thought that her reverie was broken by a familiar voice pronouncing her name.

She tensed at the sound.

She was still for a moment, neither speaking nor moving, as she calmed herself. Despite the pleasure she felt at his arrival, there was apprehension and uncertainty. She had been at this place with him before and had left it with assurances of his love, but then he had broken her heart.

"Is it really you?" Elizabeth withdrew her hand from the water and dried it on the skirt of her dress.

"Yes."

"Why are you here?" Her voice was soft, and he strained to hear her.

"I have come to claim you as my own."

Elizabeth felt a diffusion of warmth overspread her body. Summoning her courage, she looked up at him and saw an expression of love and yearning that immediately put to rest any doubts she had of his regard and calmed her fears and uncertainty concerning his intentions towards her.

"Elizabeth, please forgive me. I have been wracked with guilt and torment from the moment I left you. There has been no peace in my life and no hope for happiness until I received Bingley's letter telling me you had not... that you were not..."

"Married," she concluded for him.

"Yes. I know that you have suffered because of my foolish desire to submit to the expectations of other people."

"What expectations were those?"

"I have lived much of my life striving to earn the love and affection of my father. Doing so became a habit that did not end with his death. On the subject of marriage, he was most clear. He did not believe I could be happy if I did not marry a woman of equal fortune, connections, and rank. I had never felt loved by my father. After my mother died, he barely seemed aware of my existence. This was the only request he ever made of me. I longed to be loved by him, and I promised never to do anything of which he would not approve."

"Mr. Darcy, I ask you again, why are you here?"

"I have learned that all that matters in a marriage is love. Having arrived at this knowledge, I resolved immediately to return to this place, beg your forgiveness, and seek to regain your affection. As I was preparing to leave London, I received Bingley's letter announcing your engagement to Mr. Grinly."

She raised her hand quickly to her heart. "Please, sir, do not speak of that. It is painful to me. I hurt Mr. Grinly deeply, and that knowledge weighs heavily on my conscience."

Elizabeth offered her hand to Darcy. He took it and sat down near her.

"You must forgive me, Elizabeth, indeed, you must. I hope that by explaining my actions, I can begin to prove myself worthy of you at last. I am not beyond redemption."

She bit her lip, looked up at him until meeting his eyes and then turned away. Had she not taken his hand with both of hers, he would have thought his suit was hopeless. "I was a fool. I was wrong. I was seeking acceptance from a long dead parent who could do nothing for me, and in so doing, denied to myself the happiness I could enjoy with you. That was not the worst part. You had entrusted your heart to me, and I failed you and left you in pain." He moved as if to take back his hand, but she would not release it.

"I beg that you will forgive me."

"I have long forgiven you, sir," she said as she caressed his hand, "and I now seek your pardon."

"You have done nothing wrong."

"I have been so unwise, so weak and inconstant!"

"Elizabeth, to whom should you have remained constant? To a man you were convinced did not return your love?"

"I had hoped to forget you, but I could not. I did not love Mr. Grinly, but I thought that in time I might. He is a good man, and I love his daughter very much. He offered me a good life and a good home. He was devoted to me, though there were never any feelings of passion. There was no craving or desire, and I realized the night I saw you at Netherfield that there never would be because I was still very much in love with you."

"Then why did you send me away? I would have married you instantly."

"I had pledged myself to Mr. Grinly. I had accepted his offer. You had hurt me. I felt rejected by you, and I was afraid to expose my heart to more pain. Because I did not love Mr. Grinly, I knew he could not hurt me in the same way. When Mr. Grinly realized that I was still in love with you, he insisted our engagement be ended because he could see that I already belonged to you and he could not make me happy."

He took her hand and held it to his lips. "I wept as I left Netherfield. I was overwhelmed by the pain of losing you. It was unendurable seeing you with another man." She felt him shudder as he spoke.

"Fitzwilliam, I knew that you would be pained when you learned I had left Netherfield without seeing you, but I could not have done otherwise. I had not the courage to face you. Please forgive me."

"Please, let us try to put our pain behind us. We both made mistakes. We have both sought and received forgiveness. All that matters now is that we are together."

"Fitzwilliam, what will become of us?"

He caressed her cheek with his fingers, drawing lazy circles over her delicate skin. She closed her eyes to enjoy the sensations he was creating inside her, delighting in the warmth and security they contained.

"Elizabeth," he said softly. Her eyes opened, and she saw him slowly move towards her, and gently resting his arm around her shoulders, he drew her near him, and brushed her lips with his own.

"Elizabeth," he repeated, his lips caressing her cheek as he spoke. "There is no future for me without you." Firmly, and in such a manner as bespoke neither hesitation nor uncertainty, he folded her in his arms and kissed her. His kiss communicated passion and yearning. It spoke of the heartache he had suffered at her loss and of the regret he felt in having hurt her. It was filled with anticipation for a future that would be happy only if it included her. It was a kiss of healing. It was a kiss of love.

She nestled up against him, lacing her hands around his waist and holding him tightly. Out of the relief of having the unknown revealed, the waiting ended, and her love rewarded, she softly cried. "Fitzwilliam," she whispered, "I am so happy."

"I have discovered what it is like to be truly alone, to be cold and desolate," he told her, "and it is frightening. There is no one I cherish as I do you. Your gentle heart, understanding spirit, your witty intelligence, and elegant beauty are things without which I cannot live. I adore you. My whole life depends on you and on your answer to this question. My love, will you marry me?"

Through his kisses, she breathed the answer he longed to hear.

"Yes, Fitzwilliam, I will."

HE HAD DREAMT OF THIS moment from the time that he had received her ribbon. The feelings of being complete, of being whole again, that coursed through his body filled him with an assurance of her love and forgiveness. Never had he understood the depth of his own love for her as he did at that moment.

"I love you, Elizabeth. You are everything to me."

"And I love you. Fitzwilliam, you said that you knew what it was to feel frightened and truly alone. I never want either of us to feel that way again. You must promise me that we will never part. Now that we have found each other, I never want to be without you."

"Elizabeth, I —"

"I never want to be without you again. You must promise me."

"I do promise." He took her hand and looking deeply into her eyes. "I promise never to leave you. My heart aches that you feel you have to ask me. I wish never to be apart from you from this day on. I promise to love you with all my heart. You are my hope and my dreams. My future is yours, and I will endeavor every day to make it happier than you could ever imagine."

"And I give myself to you."

They were each silent for a moment as they considered with happiness the commitment they just made to each other. It was as natural as life itself.

"In a week, I can procure a special license in London, and we can be married. I can leave this very day and —"

"Please, let me come with you to London. There must be something that can be done that will allow us to remain together. There must be a way." She paused for a moment. "I know! I will ask Jane to take me to our Aunt Gardiner in London, and I will be able to see you every day."

They would not spend another day without each other, and soon they would not spend another night.

THE LOVERS SAT QUIETLY BY the stream, enjoying their newfound understanding. Oftentimes, words are not necessary between those who love, and this was just such a moment. In her mind, there was a sense of peace and certainty. In his, a determination to make up for all the pain he had caused by loving her in every way that he could. He had no objection to taking her to London.

Being separated from her for even a day would never be his choice. Indeed, he was thrilled that she wanted to accompany him.

Releasing her hand, he reached up and began to trace the outline of her lips. The look of love in her eyes testified to him that she truly had forgiven him.

No longer needing words to express their love, he kissed her. She felt as if her heart would leap from her body as he kissed her again and again. She slid an arm around his neck and held his lips against hers, glorying in his touch and fulfilled in his love.

He was the first to speak, and she felt his breath on her cheek as he pronounced the words she could not hear often enough.

"Elizabeth, I love you."

Chapter 20

There was no doubt in Jane's mind as to the outcome of Darcy's interview with Elizabeth. They were two people who belonged together, and they had each been taught that by hard-learned lessons. When she saw them approach the house, they were walking very close together and making no effort to hide the fact that they were holding each other's hand. When they caught a glimpse of her, they did not separate or shy away from each other. Jane was pleased. She would allow any liberties between her sister and her husband's friend that were required to make them happy.

Jane met the couple in the entryway. Elizabeth rushed to her and embraced her. "Mr. Darcy has asked me to marry him, and I have accepted."

Darcy walked up to Jane to receive her congratulations, and all three went into the drawing room. Darcy and Elizabeth sat together on one sofa while Jane sat on a chair opposite them. Jane began their conversation after calling for tea. "When will you marry? Please tell me all the details."

"We will marry as soon as possible, Mrs. Bingley. I will go to London to procure a license for us."

"We will marry just as soon as we have the license," added Elizabeth.

"What about Mama? She will have no time to arrange for the wedding."

"Mama will have to be understanding. Brides must be given a great deal of latitude on such matters, you know." She paused for a moment. "I have something I would ask of you, Jane."

"Of course, you know I will do anything for you."

"I want to accompany Mr. Darcy to London. He must be gone a few days, and I cannot bear to be away from him."

Jane smiled at her. "I will be happy to go to London with you. Of course you want to be with Mr. Darcy. Mr. Bingley will accompany us."

"In that case, Mrs. Bingley, I invite you all to stay with me at my house in Town. There is plenty of room, and we shall all be very comfortable."

"Thank you, Fitzwilliam. Thank you, Jane."

"I will leave you two alone while I speak with Charles."

ELIZABETH CROSSED THE ROOM TO the window and looked out over the lawn. Netherfield had never looked so beautiful, yet it was no different than yesterday. She knew her outlook was forever changed because she was certain of Darcy's love. She could barely remember the hurt she had felt the day before. He had extinguished all the pain and loneliness and had filled her heart with a sense of love and belonging. She reached out her hand to him, inviting him to come to her. She bit her lip as she watched him approach. He did not move with haste, but with deliberate, determined steps, his eyes not leaving hers.

He took her in his arms and softly whispered her name. She returned his embrace, feeling confident in his love and affection. He kissed her in such a way that she could not mistake his feelings for her. Her whole body was heated by his touch. She felt her breath begin to fail her.

"Thank you for coming back."

"DARCY, YOU ARE VERY WELCOME to Netherfield," said Bingley.

"Thank you for your invitation."

Elizabeth looked expectantly at her sister. "Have you told him, Jane?"

"Told me what?" inquired Bingley with smile that indicated his good knowledge.

"Mr. Darcy and I are to be married." She did not fear his disapprobation. It was through his means that she and Darcy had been reunited.

"I knew it would happen. I knew you two could not, should not, stay apart."

"Mr. Darcy, we have spoken about it, and Charles and I are very happy to go to London with you. All that remains is for you to tell us when you would like to leave."

"If possible, I should like to leave in the morning."

Elizabeth looked at him with an expression of happiness. Her every wish was being fulfilled. Darcy had returned, they were to be married, and with Jane's help, they would not be separated. It now struck her that her new and sudden engagement to Darcy, following so soon upon the heels of the end of her very public engagement to Mr. Grinly, would appear strange to the community of

Meryton. People might wonder about their motives for marrying. They might speculate as to why Mr. Grinly had left so suddenly. Her removal to London with Mr. Darcy would not be looked upon with favor, and her reputation would suffer as a result. It did pain her to some degree, but it did not overcome the desire she had to be with Mr. Darcy nor her resolution to marry him.

AFTER A LIGHT DINNER, THE friends spent a companionable evening together. Darcy related to Bingley how he had arrived at Netherfield and had been sent by Mrs. Bingley to seek Elizabeth by the stream. While not disclosing the substance of their conversation, he did make Bingley understand that she had accepted his immediate proposal of marriage and that the purpose of their trip to London was to obtain a special license so they could marry as soon as possible.

"Elizabeth," said Mr. Bingley, "I suppose your mother is quite happy in the knowledge that another of her daughters will be well settled."

"Sadly, my mother does not yet know her own happiness and probably will not know it for some time. She has not forgiven me for ending my engagement to Mr. Grinly, and I have been banished from her presence."

"Elizabeth, is there anything I can do to help?"

"You can do nothing, Fitzwilliam. You have made me happy, and that is all I care about."

"But your mother?"

"She will learn soon enough of our engagement and then perhaps she will forgive me. I do not trouble myself over it, and I pray that you will not, either."

AFTER THE SERVANTS HAD REMOVED the tea service, Jane announced that she would be retiring for the night. She was certain Elizabeth would like some privacy with Mr. Darcy, and knew she would enjoy the same with her husband. Jane stepped over to Elizabeth and embraced her. "I am happy for you! He loves you."

"I know he does. Thank you for everything."

The sisters separated and Mr. Bingley led his wife from the room.

ELIZABETH WAS QUITE SURPRISED AT the nervous feelings she experienced upon being left alone with Mr. Darcy. She felt it incumbent on her to speak.

"I…"

"Well…"

They laughed at the coincidence, and hearing Darcy's deep voice removed

Elizabeth's feelings of discomfort.

"Pray, continue, Fitzwilliam."

He shook his head and smiled at her. "Today has been an astonishing day. I traveled from London this morning with a great deal of anticipation at seeing you again, hoping that you still loved me. In the afternoon, you bestowed on me your hand and gave me your love. Now it is the evening and propriety dictates that we separate for the night, yet I do not want to be without you."

"Well, there is certainly no cause for rushing away, is there?" Elizabeth motioned to the seat next to her on a sofa.

Darcy sat down with her, took her hand, and held it with both of his. "Because of you, my heart is made whole. All the pain and anguish of these past weeks is gone. I can scarcely remember it. I have always loved you, even when I thought I should not. I am so happy to be with you now, just sitting and talking." He paused for a moment, and then continued. "Soon after we marry, I would like to take you to Pemberley. I cannot wait until I can take you home."

"That sounds wonderful."

"I am sure we will live happily at Pemberley, and perhaps we will not be alone. I mean, I hope we are blessed with children."

Elizabeth laughed. "Yes, Fitzwilliam, I would like that very much."

Observing Elizabeth struggling to hide a yawn, Darcy helped her to her feet. "I think it is time for us to say goodnight, my love."

"Oh, but I do not want to."

"I am not going anywhere without you. I will be here in the morning when you wake. You must rest for our journey tomorrow."

"Yes, of course, you are right."

Darcy led her through the hall and to the staircase. "You can have no idea how many times I mounted these stairs in anticipation of seeing you. For the first time, I will climb them with you." He put one arm around her waist and held her hand with the other. They ascended the stairs in silence.

They arrived at the door of her bedchamber. "May I kiss you good night, fair lady?"

"I am yours, dear sir."

Their lips touched softly. Elizabeth had been longing for the moment when he would touch her again, and she was not disappointed. She was being held by the man she loved, and as his hands explored her curves and his lips warmed hers, she wished she could remain in his arms forever. She knew that she had attained the happiness she had sought her whole life.

Early the next morning, Mr. Darcy, Mr. and Mrs. Bingley, and Elizabeth set off in Mr. Bingley's carriage. Mr. Darcy's unoccupied conveyance followed behind. Jane had prepared a basket of fruit and bread with which to make their journey more comfortable, and they found no reason to stop along the way but to change horses.

Elizabeth was nearly bursting with excitement. She took great pleasure in the novelty of her trip, beyond the immediate enjoyment of being with Jane, Mr. Bingley and Mr. Darcy. She and Darcy were well beyond the immediate embarrassment of their new situation, and they were not ashamed of showing their affection for each other in the presence of the Bingleys. Sitting beside each other in the carriage, he held her hand and softly caressed her fingers.

The conversation died away as the coach entered the noise and bustle of London. Elizabeth was astonished at the section of Town in which she found herself. The homes were magnificent. Although she had known by general report that Darcy was rich and knew from his description of Pemberley that it was a fine estate, the magnitude of his wealth was evident when they stopped in front of the Darcy townhouse.

Georgiana came to the entryway when she heard her brother's voice. She had known Mr. Bingley for a long time, but she did not know the two young ladies. "Fitzwilliam, once again you have surprised me. I did not know you were coming back so soon."

"I did not realize that my business would be concluded so quickly or in so happy a manner." Darcy began the introductions. "Mrs. Bingley, Miss Bennet, this is my sister, Georgiana."

"Mrs. Bingley," said Georgiana, "please accept my congratulations on your marriage. I have known your husband for much of my life, and you could not have chosen a better man."

"Thank you, Miss Darcy. I do love him dearly."

"Miss Bennet, my brother has spoken very highly of you. I am so happy to make your acquaintance."

Darcy ushered the ladies into the drawing room. Jane was seated with Bingley on a sofa. Elizabeth moved to the far side of the room and placed herself opposite Georgiana and Darcy.

Georgiana was very pleased finally to meet Miss Bennet. She knew her brother loved her and had gone to Hertfordshire to win her hand in marriage. That he could accomplish this task so quickly was reassuring to Georgiana, as it spoke volumes about Miss Bennet's attachment to her brother. She was as beautiful as her brother described and seemed just as amiable as she had hoped. She was delighted with Elizabeth and now strove to make her feel more comfortable and at home. Indeed, Georgiana thought, it would very soon be her home.

Elizabeth began the conversation. "Miss Darcy, your brother has told me about Pemberley. It must be a beautiful place."

"It is. Perhaps someday you can visit us there. There is no place I would rather be. Unfortunately, I must remain in Town to pursue my education. I go there only for the summer months."

"That must make it all the more special for you. I understand that you play the pianoforte very well."

"I do like to play, but I do not play very well. My brother tells me that you sing and play."

"A little, but I would so much like to hear you perform. Will you, while I am here?"

Georgiana seemed flattered by the attention. "If you like."

"Miss Darcy," said Jane, "you must insist that my sister play for you. She is much more accomplished than the world is generally aware."

"Then I will insist. Thank you for the hint. Miss Bennet, I am so happy that you are here!"

Elizabeth was a little surprised at this admission, but was pleased with the warmth of the young lady's welcome. She would soon be her sister and was eager to meet with her approval.

Unable to wait any longer, Mr. Darcy stood. "Please, excuse me. I have urgent business to which I must attend immediately."

Bingley arose also. "Darcy, may I be of any service to you?"

"I thank you, no. Please stay and entertain the ladies. I hope to be back to a late dinner."

Darcy crossed the room to where Elizabeth sat. "I will go now to apply for the license. Would you like to accompany me?"

She hesitated in her response. She wanted to go with hi, but felt that perhaps it would be inappropriate, and under no circumstances did she want to do anything that might embarrass him. She replied in a hushed voice. "You have been very generous to indulge me by bringing me to London with you, for which I am very grateful. I do believe, though, that it would be best for you to attend to these affairs alone. How long will you be away?"

"I will be home before dinner, my love."

"Let me walk with you to the door, sir."

IN THE ENTRYWAY, ELIZABETH AND Mr. Darcy found themselves quite alone, and he took advantage of it by taking her firmly into his arms. She pressed herself against him and gloried in the feeling of love that his embrace afforded her.

With his lips nearly touching hers, he whispered, "I will attend to this as quickly as I can. I love you."

His kiss was surety for its truth. She delighted in the warmth of his lips, and he savored the fullness of hers. With closed eyes, her whole body was attuned to the sensations he was creating inside her. She felt loved, truly loved and wanted.

When his lips left hers, she wanted to tell him that she loved him, but could not speak. Without another word between them, and with only a parting glance, he slipped out of her arms and left the house.

Elizabeth took a step forward to occupy the space he had just vacated and hugged herself, refusing to surrender the memory of the tender feelings of being held by him.

DARCY DID NOT HAVE MUCH experience in being away from Elizabeth since their engagement, and as he left his house, what would be their first home, he realized how much he depended on her. Loving her so fully and completely, and similarly being loved by her, were feelings of a nature he had never experienced. The door of his carriage had not closed before his heart suffered from being out of her presence.

JANE NOTICED THAT ELIZABETH HAD not returned to the drawing room, so after excusing herself, she left Miss Darcy with her husband and went in search of her sister. Elizabeth did not hear Jane come up behind her and started when Jane touched her shoulder.

"When did Mr. Darcy leave?"

"Just now. He asked me if I wanted to go with him, but..."

"...but you did not," finished Jane.

"I know he will come back just as soon as he can, but I do not like to be separated from him."

"There will always be those times when couples must be apart."

"Half the day and all the night. It seems like such a long time."

"You will marry soon, will you not?"

"Yes, but how I wish it could be tomorrow."

Jane sympathized with Elizabeth, knowing how little she liked to be away from Mr. Bingley. Elizabeth had little obligation to her family, thought Jane.

Mrs. Bennet had been offensive, and their younger sisters were equally ambivalent regarding Elizabeth's happiness. Their opinions were not important. Jane knew that there were few opinions that mattered to Elizabeth and that all the people that were truly important to her were already in London. There was no reason for the marriage to be delayed. Nothing would be gained by making a spectacle out of the affair, and their mother would surely insist on that if they married in Hertfordshire.

"Lizzy, why not? Why should you not marry tomorrow? Mr. Darcy will have a license. There is nothing to prevent your marriage and an abundance of happiness to promote the idea. I know you do not wish to be apart from Mr. Darcy, and now you will not have to be."

"But what of Mama?"

"What of her? I am certain that she will be more than willing to forgive you when she learns of your marriage, and I have no doubt that Mr. Darcy would agree to it. We can invite our Aunt and Uncle Gardiner and Miss Darcy. It will be a cozy, simple affair with just the seven of us. You need nothing else."

The thought of being married to Mr. Darcy so quickly brought a flush of excitement to Elizabeth's cheeks. Jane looked at her with pleasure, knowing her suggestion would be to the happiness of both.

"Marrying him tomorrow would be my dearest wish."

ALMOST AS IMPORTANT IN DARCY'S mind as obtaining the license was doing so quickly and returning as soon as possible to Elizabeth. He sensed her discomfort at parting with him and knew her happiness would be restored only when he returned.

While waiting for his turn at the office from whence the license would be issued, he let his thoughts drift back to the first moment when he saw Elizabeth, and absentmindedly drew the purple ribbon from his pocket. As was his habit, he laced it through his fingers and then brought it to his lips and kissed it. His thoughts turned to the last time he held her and kissed her.

Elizabeth was a beautiful woman, more so than any he knew. There was no one whose company he sought more. There was no one from whom he received such pleasure in conversation. The sound of her laughter rang through his mind, and he stilled for just a moment as he remembered the gentle voice that she employed to tell him that she loved him. Her skin was so soft and warm, her fingers a mixture of delicacy and strength. She had endured much because of him, but that special light had returned to her eyes, that endearing liveliness once again animated her features. How blessed he was to know her, and even more so to know that she was his. All that was lacking in his life was their marriage, and that was nearly assured as the clerk handed him the completed license. He took his leave of the building and returned to his carriage.

"Jane, may I ask you a question?"

"Of course."

"How did you feel on your wedding day? I know you were happy, anyone could see that, but what was it like?" Elizabeth took her eyes away from the window to look at Jane.

"It was a beautiful day for me. It was as if every feeling of happiness that I had ever experienced came together on that one day. Sometimes I felt lifted out of my body. I loved Charles so much. I knew I would never want to forget anything about the day, so I made every endeavor to see everything and feel everything. A wonderful sensation of peace settled in my heart when I entered the church and saw Charles waiting for me. I confess that he had never looked so handsome to me as he did at that moment. It is a memory I shall always cherish and that I entertain whenever I am away from him."

"Were you afraid?"

"I was nervous, but not afraid. I will say, though, that when we arrived at that part of the ceremony where we were actually wed, all agitation left me and I knew without a doubt that I had made the correct decision. I did experience a moment of sadness when I thought about Papa. I know Papa would have liked Charles, and he would have liked your Mr. Darcy just as well. I had always thought he would be there when I married."

"I shall miss Papa, also. I take comfort in knowing that he would approve of my marrying for love. That reminds me, though. When Mr. Darcy left me so suddenly that morning at Netherfield, he thought he was acting in accordance with the expectations of his father."

"What do you mean?"

"His father told him he could never be happy in a marriage unequal as to fortune, family, and connections. Fitzwilliam overcame those feelings, but it was hard for him, and then I became engaged to Mr. Grinly and all the sadness happened."

Jane took Elizabeth's hand and squeezed it. "That is all to be forgotten. You and Mr. Darcy have come to a good understanding together. All the confusion has passed."

"You are right. It would have been gratifying, though, to have met with the approval of his parents."

ELIZABETH AND JANE WERE QUIET, lost to the sound of horses and carriages as they waited for Mr. Darcy's return when Georgiana entered the room. "Please forgive me for intruding Mrs. Bingley, but Mr. Bingley has requested that you join him in the library. May I take you to him?"

"I think you must, for I have no idea where in this large house the library might be." Jane looked back at Elizabeth as she walked out of the room, but the latter had returned her attention to the road outside.

Having safely delivered Mrs. Bingley to her husband, Georgiana felt that now would be a good time to get to know Miss Bennet a little better. She returned to the room where Elizabeth was waiting for her brother and sat down on a chair opposite the window. Georgiana cleared her throat, hoping delicately to gain her attention. It was obvious that she had not heard her enter the room.

"Oh, Miss Darcy!"

"Forgive me. I did not mean to startle you. You are waiting for my brother, are you not?"

"Am I that transparent?"

Georgiana laughed. "I know that Fitzwilliam loves you."

"Do you really?"

"He has told me that he does."

"Your brother has told me how much he cares for you, Miss Darcy. He is a good man."

"He is the best of brothers. I do not want to appear impertinent, but I would like to tell you something about him."

Elizabeth looked at Georgiana expectantly.

"I was in London when he received the letter from Mr. Bingley announcing your engagement to Mr. Grinly. I just want you to know that before he received that note, he had already determined on returning to Hertfordshire in the hopes of gaining your forgiveness and regaining your affection. You cannot believe the agony into which he was thrown as he read that letter."

Elizabeth felt that she did understand. "I did not mean to hurt him. I thought he did not care for me."

"Only then," continued Miss Darcy, "when I saw him with that letter, was I able to comprehend what you went through when he left Hertfordshire the first time. May I ask . . . may I ask how you found it in your heart to forgive him?"

"Do you believe that I have?"

"Yes, or you would not be sitting here eager for his return."

"You are right," conceded Elizabeth. "It has been a long road for both of us. I thought he did not love me, and so I agreed to marry a man I did not love. I blamed your brother for hurting me, but I never realized that he might be running from demons of his own. I tried to forget him when I became engaged to Mr. Grinly, but when your brother returned to Netherfield, I knew that I still loved him."

Georgiana nodded.

"Circumstances allowed me to change my mind if I wished, but I sent your brother away. I was resentful, angry, and fearful of being hurt again. Mr. Grinly realized my feelings for your brother and requested that we end our engagement. He felt that he would not be able to bring me happiness. He also told me something else that I shall never forget."

"What is that?"

"Mr. Grinly told me that the only people who can hurt us deeply are the ones that we love. He told me that I belonged with your brother and that I should forgive him. The next morning, I received a farewell note from your brother, and Mr. Grinly returned to his home."

"That must have been horrible!"

"I tried to convince Mr. Grinly that we could be happy and that we ought not break off the engagement, but he was right. My mother was quite upset with me, so I removed to Netherfield and have been there since."

"You must be very close to Mrs. Bingley."

"I am. I spent much time alone walking about the countryside, and every day I found myself returning to the places around Netherfield that held special significance for your brother and me."

"Did you love him then?"

"I did, and I came to realize the depth of my love for him. My sister asked Mr. Bingley to drop some hints in a letter to let Mr. Darcy know I was thinking about him."

"No!"

Elizabeth laughed. "I assure you, it is true. She felt the only way I would be happy was with your brother, so she invited him to Netherfield. I knew before he came that we would be reunited. He asked me to marry him almost as soon as he arrived…"

Georgiana smiled.

"I suppose that piece of news should have waited until your brother announced it." Elizabeth laughed.

"Rest assured, I will act very surprised when he tells me."

"I cannot live without him, Miss Darcy. He invited the Bingleys to come to London with him so that I could join the party. He is so kind. Since I have told you all, I will add that his errand today is to procure a license so that we may marry as soon as possible."

"And how soon will that be?"

"I hope very soon. I shall speak with him tonight, and we will set a date."

"He must have traveled directly to your home to gain your father's consent."

Elizabeth's smile faded for a moment. "No, sadly my father is dead, and my mother's permission is not required."

"I am sorry."

"Miss Darcy, since we are to be sisters, I would be very happy if you were to call me Lizzy."

"I am so excited. I hope I can attend your wedding."

The ease and friendliness of Georgiana gave her a sure place in Elizabeth's heart. She knew she would love Georgiana very much.

Chapter 21

As soon as Darcy entered the house, he was met with a peal of feminine laughter. He was unaccustomed to hearing that in his home. When he peered around the door into a small sitting room, he found Elizabeth and Georgiana deep in conversation. As they did not notice him, he remained quiet to watch how they behaved.

"…stayed with me until Mr. Bingley's carriage arrived," said Elizabeth as she described the circumstances of her fall to Georgiana.

"That must have been awful, Lizzy!"

Still unseen, Darcy could not but smile at hearing his sister call Elizabeth by her familiar name. He wanted them to love each other, and it seemed as if they were well on their way to doing so.

"I was unconscious for several days, but then I woke up. I found out that Fitzwilliam had been coming to see me every day."

Apparently, Georgiana knew of their engagement, because Elizabeth would not have referred to him by his Christian name unless Georgiana had known of it. He had planned to tell Georgiana that evening, but now realized that that was quite a miscalculation. Elizabeth must have unintentionally told her or Georgiana must have surmised. In either case, he was glad, because it seemed to have drawn the ladies even closer together.

"How long did he stay with you?"

"After I was awake, he would come for just a few minutes but sometimes he would stay for an hour. We poured out our hearts to each other. Other than Jane, there is no one who knows as much about me as does your brother."

Darcy was shocked to hear this. He now realized just how much Elizabeth had opened her heart to him, how valuable her confidence was, and he was once again pained at the memory of how he had crushed those precious feelings. *If only... If only... If only...* repeated in his head. Darcy quietly entered the room.

"Fitzwilliam, you are back!" cried Georgiana. "Oh, congratulations, Brother! Lizzy told me you are to marry. I am so happy for you, I truly am! I wish you joy!"

"Thank you, Georgiana."

"When will you marry? Lizzy told me the date is undecided. Please marry soon."

"If you will excuse us, dear sister, I would like to speak with Elizabeth concerning a date right now."

Georgiana smiled and ran lightly from the room.

MR. DARCY TOOK ELIZABETH INTO his arms and rested her head against his shoulder. "I am very pleased that you and my sister like each other."

"She is a sweet girl."

"London has been her home since our father died. I wanted to ask you, but only if you agree, if Georgiana could live with us at Pemberley after we are married."

Elizabeth stepped back for a moment to look at him. Of course, she could not refuse him anything, but she was gratified that he would think of her and request her opinion.

Darcy returned her gaze with a hopeful look on his face. He knew that Georgiana would benefit from being with Elizabeth, and he wanted them to be together.

"That would be delightful."

"Thank you. I am sure we shall all be very happy together."

"There is a point on which I would like to speak with you. I would like to talk about the date on which our happiness together will begin."

Darcy was pleased that she would begin a subject that he had wished to broach with her. He felt his hope rising as he saw the look of firm resolve on her face.

"I have our license right here." Darcy withdrew an envelope from his pocket.

Elizabeth nervously continued. "I would like to marry soon. Very soon, indeed."

"How soon, beloved?"

She lowered her eyes and then turned away from him, as if fearing his rejection. When she did not speak, he put his hand on her shoulder and slowly turned her back towards him. Looking up, and with a voice barely audible, she made her request.

"Tomorrow."

Darcy felt the floodgates of his heart open up with joy. Not only was it what he most desired, but she desired it, also.

"That, my love, deserves a kiss."

She gratefully allowed herself to be taken up in his arms.

"Tomorrow," he whispered.

ELIZABETH AND DARCY WENT IN search of the others. "You are all invited," announced Darcy, "to a wedding…"

There was a murmur of excitement amongst them.

"…tomorrow."

"Tomorrow" was repeated with surprise and delight. Jane went to Elizabeth and embraced her. "Lizzy, I am so happy." She turned to Mr. Darcy. "Sir, you are too good. Thank you for making Elizabeth so happy."

"Trust me, Mrs. Bingley, she can be no happier than I."

"I am so excited," cried Georgiana. "A wedding tomorrow! This is so wonderful!"

They all sat down and listened while Georgiana quizzed the happy pair on their plans for the wedding. Those plans were very simple. They would go to St. Clement's and be married. Elizabeth would immediately invite the Gardiners while Darcy wrote to the clergyman.

The rest of the evening was spent in general conversation with the subject of the wedding something to which they always returned.

LONDON

My dear Aunt,

I have such wonderful news to relate. I am to be married tomorrow, and you are all invited.

I am marrying Mr. Darcy. All our differences have been resolved, and there is nothing but happiness between us. We were to marry at some future time from Longbourn, but Mr. Darcy has procured a special license and has arranged with the rector of St. Clements for our marriage to be solemnized at eleven a.m. tomorrow.

I want to assure you, my dear Aunt, that this early date is a result of our desire to guarantee our happiness, and it should not be construed to be scandalous. I know

*you will come to love Mr. Darcy almost as much as I do. He is looking forward
to meeting both you and my uncle.*

With all my love, dear Aunt.
Elizabeth Bennet

ELIZABETH GLANCED AT THE CLOCK over the fireplace in her bedchamber.
It read one a.m. She had been sitting in front of her dying fire and spent candle,
reading, and she was preoccupied with anticipating the very moment when
she would become Mr. Darcy's wife. This was a moment of which she had first
dreamed many weeks ago while nestled in her bed at Netherfield. She could not
identify the instant when she first realized the wish of her heart, and though
she would not say it came on slowly, she did understand its depth and never
more so than when she and Mr. Darcy shared their first kiss.

She had never kissed a man before. Indeed, it would be a most improper
thing to do, but her mind was less concerned with proprieties than it was with
love and desire. Elizabeth knew she could not give herself to someone whom
she did not love. She had tried to do that with Mr. Grinly. In her heart, she
once again thanked him for making her realize how much she loved Mr. Darcy
and that he loved her enough to let her go. Now, at this early morning hour,
she could say that today was the day of her wedding. While they were growing
up, she and Jane spent much time discussing men and marriage, and today it
was all to come true. Elizabeth never imagined that she would not be married
from Longbourn, but neither had she imagined that her father would not be
there to give her away. Mr. Bennet would have liked Mr. Darcy very well, and
while her father would have struggled to give her up to any man, if he had to
choose, she knew he would have chosen Mr. Darcy.

With such a busy mind, sleeping was out of the question, and having just
completed her book, Elizabeth needed something new to read. She felt certain
she would not be seen and was, therefore, confident about leaving her room.
The house had long been quiet. The whole party had retired at eleven. Surely,
no one would be awake at this hour.

Not knowing the habits of the house, she was unaware of the fact that
it would be unusual for the library door to be ajar. Paying no attention, she
entered the room and cast her eyes around her, first noticing a glow from the
fireplace, then a candle burning on the desk, and to her astonishment, Mr.
Darcy in a black silk dressing gown sitting behind the candle. He was staring

intently into the flame. His hair was tousled and his gown tied without a care for his appearance. The front was open at the neck, revealing the dark curls that covered his chest. He was resting his head on his hand, his fingers curling up the side of his cheek.

A recollection of her situation caused her cheeks to burn. To be seen by him would hardly be modest, yet she could not take her eyes away from him, she could not move herself from the room. Elizabeth had considered her body to be well concealed, but in the dim light of Mr. Darcy's candle, she realized the flimsiness of her nightgown.

Elizabeth had not paid much attention to her own candle. It had burned quite low and went out just at that moment. She was startled by the sudden change in light and gave a muffled cry.

DARCY RECOGNIZED THE SOURCE FROM whence that small cry issued.

"Elizabeth? Is anything the matter?" He took his candle and moved towards her.

"Please forgive me for intruding. I cannot sleep. I was seeking a book."

"I was not able to sleep, either. I find myself filled with anticipation for our wedding…" he paused to look at the clock on the chimneypiece, "…which will be in ten hours."

"I am similarly distracted. Please forgive me for interrupting you. I cannot leave you, though, I —"

"Please, do not go."

"My candle went out," she said almost inaudibly.

Although anticipating the discomfort that such a meeting might cause, in no way would he allow her leave without speaking to her.

Or looking at her. She was beautiful…and tempting. Very tempting.

"Give me your hand."

She reached out to him, knowing full well what she would feel when their hands met.

As he took hold of her fingers, a feeling of warmth and excitement coursed up the length of her arm, as it always did when he touched her. She returned the gentle squeeze he gave her and allowed him to lead her to a sofa next to the fireplace. He took his seat in the armchair beside it.

After sitting down, she turned her head away from him, feeling self-conscious because of her appearance.

"Elizabeth, trust me."

She looked back at him and the look of love and concern on his face removed all her discomfort.

"You should not see me like this, Fitzwilliam."

"And you should not see me like this, yet we have no reason to be shy around each other."

"No, we do not. May I ask, sir, what it is you have been doing in here all by yourself?"

"I have been thinking about you."

Even in the dim light, he could see her smile.

"And what were your thoughts?"

"I was thinking how very much I love you and how proud I will be to call you my wife. I was trying to decide how much I would be willing to share you with the world. I fear that I will want to keep you all to myself for a very long time after we are married."

He moved from his chair and sat next to her on the sofa. She could feel the heat from his body penetrate her nightgown. Their eyes met, held together by longing and passion. Her heart raced at the thought of being held by him.

His breathing nearly stopped when he saw her tongue dart out of her mouth to wet her lip. "Elizabeth," he whispered. He lowered his lips to hers and kissed her. As he broke the kiss, he turned her and she felt his hand cross her shoulders to caress her neck as his other hand slid around her waist. Smiling, she leaned back against his chest and felt his arms encircle her.

"You are my life. I love you, Elizabeth."

"And I love you so very much that I fear my heart will burst." She rested her hands on his arms and waited until her pulse returned to normal. He found her hand with one of his and laced his fingers through hers.

"So, have you decided how much you will be willing to share me?" asked Elizabeth.

"If we stay in London for too long, we will eventually have to entertain visitors in order not to give offense. Normally, I care not for such matters, but I will not allow the world to think ill of you." He changed his position on the sofa to one more comfortable. She settled in against his chest.

"We could travel directly to Derbyshire."

"Yes, but I do not think we want to spend our wedding night in a coaching inn." Her cheeks colored at the implications. "What is your opinion?"

"No, I do not think that would be comfortable for us."

"Very well, we will remain in Town for two weeks. I will show you off to my undeserving friends and family, and then we shall travel to Pemberley."

"I would like that very much."

They were quiet after this, each comfortable in the arms of the other. The night was dark and soothing, and each was blanketed with a feeling of peace and contentment.

Elizabeth was growing tired, and as their conversation lagged, she unknowingly did something she had always longed to do. She fell asleep in Darcy's arms.

ELIZABETH WAS THE FIRST TO awaken. Darcy had shifted his weight, and the motion had interrupted her sleep. She was not sorry for it. She loved being held by him.

His arms were still around her, and she could not move without fear of waking him, a risk she would not take. Relaxing her mind, she let her eyes close once again. As certain as he held her now, she knew he would never let her go.

IT SEEMED LIKE A DREAM. He was asleep and Elizabeth was in his arms, yet it felt so real. He had never known a happier moment!

Elizabeth was curled up with one hand around his waist and the other flat against his chest. Her hair blanketed his shoulder. The warmth of her body penetrated deep inside him and drew from him feelings of gratitude that she loved him so well that she would be comfortable enough to fall asleep in his arms. He watched her lips form into a smile. She was so beautiful when she smiled. Her whole face lit up with an expression of delight, and he recalled the last time those lips had touched his. It has only been a few hours ago, but he longed to taste them again.

"Fitzwilliam, thank you."

"For what, my love?"

"For keeping me warm," said Elizabeth softly. "The fire went out, and I fear I should have been cold, except for you."

At this intimation that Elizabeth might be chilled, Darcy ran his hands over her exposed skin.

"Fitzwilliam, I want to look at you," she said turning in his arms. "I want to see what you look like in the morning before you dress properly for the day. I want the answer to this question, what does the great Fitzwilliam Darcy look like before being attended by his valet?"

"The great Fitzwilliam Darcy?"

"Let me see," she said as she reached for his face. "You have grown a beard.

When I was a girl, sometimes I would see my father before he was shaved, and I would touch his face like this."

Elizabeth gently rubbed her hand across his skin. "And then I would do this."

She leaned against him and slid her delicate cheek across his rough skin. "But, I never did this." Elizabeth kissed him with all the ardor of love and need that she possessed.

Momentarily satisfied but not sated, she broke the kiss. "I have not kissed you in forever, Fitzwilliam. I have missed you."

Darcy began to speak, but was silenced when her lips touched his. Words were not adequate, so he held her close and answered her in the language she understood and with all the passion and desire he felt.

IT WAS TIME FOR HER to return to her room lest they be discovered. The fire had died away, yet there was a glow in the room that announced the approach of daylight.

"Today we shall be married, Fitzwilliam."

"It will be the happiest day of my life. Come, let me take you to your room before the others awaken."

He stood and offered her his hand. Standing next to each other, they peered into a large mirror over the mantelpiece. Smiling back at them was a happy couple filled with love and tenderness. "There is one last thing that I must do. I must kiss Miss Bennet for the last time."

She reached out and began to caress his cheek and favored him with an enticing smile. He responded just as she deserved, and then placing an arm around her waist, guided her from the library and delivered her safely to her room.

He stood for a moment outside her closed door breathing in her scent, which lingered in the air, and lifted his heart in gratitude to heaven for the blessing of having her in his life.

ELIZABETH SAT QUIETLY IN FRONT of a mirror reflecting on her night with Darcy and the many changes that had occurred in her life. There were many attendant consequences surrounding her fall. First, there was Jane and Bingley, and now Darcy and her.

Elizabeth was happy for Jane, but she confessed greater pleasure in her own circumstances. True, it had cost them a great deal, but she and Darcy were finally together. She was so excited about her future with him. He had described Pemberley and the beauty of Derbyshire to her on many occasions, and she was quite eager to see her new home.

And Georgiana! What a companion she would be. While nothing could make up for the loss of her near daily intercourse with Jane, having Georgiana with her would come as near to it as anyone possibly could. She was so full of life and energy. Her heart was in every action that she performed and in every word that she spoke. It was impossible not to be happy around her.

Elizabeth was musing over these pleasant thoughts when she was interrupted by a knock at the door.

"Lizzy, it is Jane. May I come in?"

Jane closed the door and stood behind Elizabeth. She placed her hands on her sister's shoulders and looked at her in the mirror. "Well, today is the big day. You must be very excited. I know I am!"

Elizabeth turned to face Jane as the latter moved to sit on the bed. She watched Jane's eyes grow wide as they both realized at the same time, one with a look of surprise, the other with some embarrassment, that the bed had not been used the previous night.

Jane cleared her throat with a smile. "And how was Mr. Darcy when you left him, Lizzy?"

Having observed her sister and Mr. Darcy, this development came as no surprise. The passion they felt for each other warranted an early marriage in and of itself and without any other consideration.

Elizabeth offered a contrite smile. "I could not sleep, and so I went to the library to pick out a book. Fitzwilliam was there. We talked for a long time, and then we fell asleep together on his sofa. I have just now returned here."

"It is fortunate that you were not discovered by anyone else, dear sister. I can see by the look on your face that you have no regrets, and so I shall trust your discretion and be grateful that you shall be married before dinner." Jane took Elizabeth's hand. "I am so happy for you."

"It means so much to me that you are here and that you and your dear husband will be with us today when we are married."

JANE TOOK A BRUSH AND ran it through Elizabeth's hair until it shined. She hoped that this would not be the last time that she and her sister could be together in such an intimate setting. Unfortunately, that opportunity had not presented itself since Jane's marriage, so she was slow and deliberate in her strokes, savoring the moment.

"Jane, I remember when you brushed my hair every night. It seems so long ago."

"Indeed, it was not. I have not been at Netherfield that long."

"It is true that you have not been married long, but I cannot think of you in any other way. In my mind, you have always been with Charles."

Jane returned to sit on the bed. "We will be leaving from the church to return to Netherfield. Charles has invited Georgiana to accompany us."

"How thoughtful. You are so very kind."

"Do you know what your plans are after your wedding?"

"We are to remain in London for two weeks and then depart for Pemberley."

"Have you not considered visiting in Hertfordshire to announce your marriage to all your friends there?"

"I had not thought about it, but you are right."

"You must stay with us at Netherfield. Our mother and sisters can visit you there. I know that you would not be comfortable at Longbourn. Will Georgiana be returning to London?"

"No, her home will now be with us at Pemberley."

"I am happy for her. You need not stay long in Hertfordshire, though I know we would be happy to keep you forever."

"This all sounds perfect, though I must speak with Fitzwilliam before I can give my full consent to the plan."

"Of course. Let me call for your maid to help you dress." Jane laughed. "I suspect that you will not be doing any more sleeping this morning."

ELIZABETH WAS IMPATIENT TO BE with Darcy, and the task of dressing seemed more tedious than usual. Her maid could sense her eagerness and arranged her hair as skillfully and efficiently as she could. Just as the maid left her room and she was ready to go downstairs, there was another knock at her door.

Fully expecting to see Jane, she was surprised when she found Georgiana standing there. "Good morning, Lizzy."

"Good morning, Georgiana. You look beautiful this morning."

"I was too excited to sleep, so I dressed early and have been waiting until your maid left you so that I could have a few moments of your time."

"Please tell me what I can do for you."

The ladies sat down near the fireplace.

"After our father died," began Georgiana, "Fitzwilliam gave me our mother's jewelry. Some pieces I have kept, others I have had reset, but there is one special necklace from which I will never be parted. My father told me it was my mother's favorite jewel. Let me show you."

Georgiana produced a small case from the folds of her skirt. Opening the lid, she pulled out an intricately crafted gold chain from which hung a pendant with a large red stone. "This stone is a ruby, and Mother wore it on all formal occasions. I know that Fitzwilliam will recognize it. I want you to wear it today. It would mean so much to my brother. I never knew my mother, but there is a likeness of her in the gallery wearing this gem. I will show you when we get to Pemberley."

"Thank you, I would be pleased and honored to wear it. You are very thoughtful, for you must know that I have no jewelry at all beyond this little cross my father gave me."

"Oh no, I did not mean…"

"I was thrilled when your brother asked me if you could live with us at Pemberley, and I was very pleased to agree to the plan."

Georgiana and Elizabeth came together in a sisterly embrace.

"I will bring the necklace to the church. You can put it on there so that it will be a surprise for my brother."

The ladies shared a laugh and then removed to the breakfast room where Mr. and Mrs. Bingley and Mr. Darcy awaited them.

HAVING LEFT ELIZABETH AT HER bedchamber door, Darcy retired to his room and lay down on his bed, savoring the recent memories he had of his beloved.

He was roused by a knock that he recognized to be that of his valet. Darcy had not asked Elizabeth when she planned to go downstairs, but he wanted to be there when she did, so he dressed quickly and quietly. His valet assured him that he looked very well in his dark green coat and that his new bride would approve. Darcy smiled and exited the room.

DARCY WAS RELIEVED WHEN HE arrived in the breakfast room and discovered that Elizabeth had not yet come down. When he had left her, she did not look at all tired, and he did not imagine for a moment that she would try to sleep. As for himself, he had never slept so well nor been so warm and comfortable as he had last night with Elizabeth in his arms, and now he looked forward to not being parted from her on any night for the rest of his life.

He started when Bingley entered the room with Jane on his arm. "Ah, Darcy, so I have caught you gathering wool!" Bingley laughed. "Good morning, sir."

"It is a very good morning, and good morning to you, Mrs. Bingley."

Jane walked over to Mr. Darcy and led him to a corner of the room near a window as if to admire the view. "Mr. Darcy, I trust you slept well last night?"

"I...well, yes, I did. And you?"

"I slept very well, thank you. I saw Elizabeth this morning, and she also had a restful night. Her dreams were very pleasant, and she hopes always to sleep as well in the future. I am certain that you can arrange that for her, can you not?"

"Yes, of course." He could not hide a smile and turned away from her.

Elizabeth and Georgiana stepped into the room. Darcy immediately went to Elizabeth and kissed her hand, and she smiled at him with eyes that sparkled with excitement. She had not had time to purchase any wedding clothes so she chose to wear her favorite gown of white muslin with gold tambour worked into the bodice. Sometimes a woman may feel insecure as to how she appears before others and particularly on her wedding day, but the satisfaction that Elizabeth derived from Darcy's gaze as he looked at her settled all discomfort.

"Good morning, Mr. Darcy."

"Good morning, Miss Bennet. You have no idea how pleased I am at the prospect of not being able to address you as anything other than Mrs. Darcy very soon."

"I know very well how you feel," she laughed. "You will not be surprised to know that I spent part of the morning with both Jane and Georgiana and that all we did was talk about you. You need not fear, though. We did not say too many things that you could not hear."

"Your sister tells me that you slept very well, Elizabeth. I hope it is true."

"I have never been more comfortable in my life."

"Miss Bennet," said Bingley, "I am shocked. Others have slept in that bed before and remarked that the morning could not come soon enough."

"I have no complaints to make, Mr. Bingley, I assure you."

It was time to be off to the church. Darcy handed Elizabeth, Georgiana, and Jane into the Netherfield carriage and then joined Bingley in his own.

"How do you feel, Lizzy?" asked Georgiana as she sat back against the seat of the coach. She was so pleased that her brother was to marry Elizabeth. He deserved to be happy, and knowing how he had suffered when he thought he had lost Elizabeth made Georgiana's satisfaction even sweeter.

"I am so happy. I love your brother and I am honored that he would ask me to be his wife. I will spend my whole life endeavoring to bring him joy and happiness."

THE CARRIAGES RATTLED SLOWLY ALONG streets filled with horses, coaches, and vendors selling their wares. At the height of Elizabeth's anticipation, the party pulled up in front of St. Clement's. The gentlemen rushed out of their carriage to assist the ladies as they alit from theirs. With Elizabeth on one arm and Georgiana on the other, Darcy ascended the steps to the church.

They were met by the pastor who invited them in and explained the order of the ceremony. When his instructions were given and understood, the party advanced towards the front of the chapel. At this moment, the Gardiners arrived, having been delayed some minutes due to the demands of their children.

"Lizzy," said Mrs. Gardiner as she came up and embraced her niece, "please forgive us for being late. The children..."

"Aunt, the important thing is that you are here."

The rector joined them and delicately cleared his throat. "Mr. Darcy, shall we begin?"

Chapter 22

As Darcy took Elizabeth's hand to lead her to the altar, he was struck once again by her beauty. She was the handsomest woman he had ever known. He could not take his eyes from her, and the service was delayed for a moment as he examined every pretty feature and delicate line she possessed.

At last, the couple moved toward the altar until Elizabeth heard a sound that halted her progress.

"Lizzy!" whispered Georgiana.

Elizabeth looked back at Georgiana and raised a hand to her mouth. She asked Darcy to excuse her for just a moment and hurried down the stairs.

"Lizzy, I should have reminded you sooner. Please forgive me."

Georgiana took the ruby from its box, stood behind Elizabeth and fastened it around her neck. She brushed a wisp of Elizabeth's hair out from under the delicate chain. "You are so beautiful. My brother is so lucky to have you!"

"Thank you, Georgiana." The ladies exchanged a quick embrace and Elizabeth turned and resumed her place at Darcy's side.

FOR A MOMENT, A VISION from his past rose up before Darcy as he watched Elizabeth approach him.

The ruby! He had not seen that in years, and immediately his mother's portrait came to mind. He had always considered his mother to be a beautiful woman and took great pleasure in viewing her likeness in the gallery, but with that ruby resting against Elizabeth's delicate skin, every sensation of happiness that he had ever felt passed through him. Unable to contain himself, he moved to meet her.

Elizabeth could easily see that Georgiana had been right. She glowed under his admiration.

He took her hand, slowly kissed it, and then placed it in the crook of his arm.

It was time. They turned to face the rector as he fulfilled their ultimate desire — to be bound to each other forever.

The clergyman, Mr. Joseph Everton, was a young man who had recently come into the office of Rector of St. Clement's. He was not married, though he was courting a young woman of beauty and distinction who he hoped would take his name before long. Weddings, therefore, and especially love matches, were particularly interesting to him.

Although this was a very small gathering, there was no shortage of warmth and affection amongst the seven people present. A powerful feeling of love existed between the young couple and was expressed in the way they looked at each other, the manner in which he held her hand, and the gentle voice he used when speaking to her. This would be marriage in its purest form, a union of the deepest love and affection. Mr. Everton knew he might officiate at many more ceremonies before he experienced such circumstances again.

Seeing that all was in readiness, Mr. Everton began.

"Dearly beloved, we are gathered together here in the sight of God, and in the face of this congregation, to join together this Man and this Woman in holy Matrimony; which is an honorable estate, instituted by God in the time of man's innocency, signifying unto us the mystical union that is betwixt Christ and his church..."

Elizabeth glanced up at Darcy and was pleased to see him smiling at her. All the warmth of the passion she felt from him last night coursed through her body as she recalled his tenderness and gentle manner. She turned her attention back to Mr. Everton, fingering the ruby as she did so.

"...it was ordained for the mutual society, help, and comfort that the one ought to have of the other, both in prosperity and adversity..."

In his life, Darcy had only known prosperity. Many people felt that this precluded the ability to suffer in the face of adversity, but it did not. He felt as any child might have felt on the death of his mother and the neglect of his father. It was now difficult for him to imagine how marriages of convenience could be sufferable when he remembered the joy he felt with Elizabeth.

"Fitzwilliam Darcy, wilt thou have this woman to thy wedded wife, to live together after God's ordinance in the holy estate of Matrimony? Wilt thou love her, comfort her, honor and keep her..."

Elizabeth could not hide a smile. She knew Darcy was committed to her, but there was a thrill in the anticipation that he would make an open declaration. She heard his deep voice proclaim the two words that were the driving force behind all the actions performed by any man or woman.

"I will."

A contented sigh escaped Darcy's lips. A goal for which he had striven was complete. He turned his attention to Elizabeth when he heard Mr. Everton pronounce her name.

"Elizabeth Bennet, wilt thou have this man to thy wedded husband, to live together…"

To live with Darcy was the ultimate wish of her heart. He had promised always to stay by her side, sealing that promise with a proposal of marriage that would allow him to perform it. Never again would she be without him.

"…forsaking all others, keep thee only unto him…"

She could not hear this without a thought for Mr. Grinly. A prayer in her heart went out to heaven that he would be blessed with as much happiness as she now felt.

"I will."

Mr. Everton placed Elizabeth's right hand in Darcy's right hand.

"I, Fitzwilliam Darcy, take thee Elizabeth Bennet, to be my wedded wife, to have and to hold from this day forward, for better for worse, for richer for poorer, in sickness and in health, to love and to cherish…"

Elizabeth was certain that she had not been loved or cherished since the day her father died, at least until that moment when she felt her love kindle for Mr. Darcy and his for her. The comfort of such feelings was indescribable.

"Miss Bennet, it is your turn," whispered Mr. Everton.

"I, Elizabeth Bennet, take thee Fitzwilliam Darcy, to my wedded husband, to have and to hold from this day forward…"

These words were life to Darcy. "To have and to hold." There could be no greater gift.

Mr. Everton gave Darcy Elizabeth's ring. It had been his mother's and now it was to be hers. He slipped it on her finger and repeated the words that defined the way he would treat her.

"…with my body I thee worship…"

At first, she could not meet his eye, but when she did look, she saw an expression of love and tenderness. The order of the ceremony did not require it, but in her mind, she promised to worship him with her body, and it began with a gentle press of his hand.

Mr. Everton addressed the five individuals witnessing the service.

"Forasmuch as Fitzwilliam Darcy and Elizabeth Bennet have consented together in holy wedlock, and have witnessed the same before God and this company, and thereto have given and pledged their troth, either to the other, and have declared the same by giving and receiving of a ring, and by joining of hands; I pronounce that they be Man and Wife together..."

ELIZABETH FELT A RUSH OF excitement course through her body at the words "Man and Wife together." Man and wife. He was her husband and she belonged to him!

She felt his grasp on her hand tighten. Looking up at her new husband, she saw a tear escape his eye.

MAN AND WIFE TOGETHER.

It was not a dream, Darcy thought. Elizabeth was his wife. What a precious moment! What an instant in time never to be forgotten! As he listened to the words of the psalms and prayers read by Mr. Everton, words of advice, counsel, and warning, he recommitted himself to the promise he had made to Mrs. Bingley that he would never do anything to make Elizabeth unhappy. His heart was softened and his spirit made tender as he considered the wonderful charge that had been given him, that of making Elizabeth Bennet...no, Elizabeth Darcy...happy. The emotion outstripped his composure, and he felt a tear run down his cheek.

Gently cupping her cheek, he brushed his lips against hers. "I love you, Elizabeth."

He took her hand and held it against his heart as he leaned into her to kiss her again. This kiss was different from all the others. Before, her kisses had excited feelings of anticipation and longing. Now, he felt the deepest satisfaction in knowing that she was his wife.

THERE WAS TOTAL SILENCE IN the church as everyone witnessed the exchange between Elizabeth and Darcy. While they knew his feelings for her were deep, they did not comprehend the extent of his love for her.

Elizabeth wiped the tear from his cheek and then leaned against him. He wrapped his arms around her and held her while he recovered himself. When she felt his breathing slow and he seemed himself again, she looked deeply into his eyes. "I love you, Fitzwilliam."

"I love you, Elizabeth."

Darcy's vision drifted to the ruby that Elizabeth was wearing. A fresh smile suffused his face. "This belonged to my mother."

"Georgiana told me it was her favorite jewel."

Darcy fingered the stone, watching the light reflect off the facets. "You are far more beautiful than this ruby. You shine for me more brilliantly than any gem."

ELIZABETH AND DARCY GRATEFULLY RECEIVED the congratulations of the small party that accompanied them to church, and while they were as attentive as possible, it was clear to all that their only desire was to be alone. To that end, the Gardiners excused themselves, and the Bingleys and Georgiana escorted Mr. and Mrs. Darcy to their waiting carriage.

Elizabeth shared a private word with her sister, and then Darcy handed her into the carriage. Just before he stepped in, Georgiana approached and gave him a small box that he deftly slid into his coat pocket before seating himself across from Elizabeth.

"Mrs. Darcy."

"Yes, sir?"

"May I sit with you?"

"Would that be proper?"

"Yes, I believe so."

Elizabeth moved over on the bench and extended her hand to him. He took it and sat next to her. At first, they spoke little, but sat quietly together. Words were not required. Her hand was cradled between his and their occasional glances reflected their own feelings of contentment. Her thoughts went back to that final moment at the altar when he had spoken of the gem she was wearing. His expression was penetrating. His fingers felt warm against her skin as he handled the stone. "Fitzwilliam, please tell me more about this ruby."

He turned on the bench to face her. "That ruby belonged to my grandfather's first wife, Cecily, who passed away at a young age. When he was going through her possessions, he came upon a small box that contained that stone. Accompanying the ruby were instructions to a jeweler that it be set in a man's ring, and that the shank of the ring be engraved, 'To Edmund, with all my love, Cecily.' Edmund was my grandfather's name.

"As you can imagine, my grandfather was quite moved by this discovery. Because the stone belonged to Cecily and was a gift to him, he felt it would be disrespectful to his second wife if he were to have the ring made, so when my

264

father was approaching his own marriage, my grandfather gave him the ruby. He said it had been a gift of love, and he told my father to give it as a gift of love to my mother. My father gave it to her in that simple setting and with that chain. My mother highly prized it and wore it as often as she could. You will see when we get to Pemberley that she wore it when her portrait was painted."

"No wonder Georgiana is so attached to it."

Darcy shifted in his seat and brought out the box that Georgiana had given him. "I have something for you that I hope will someday become as important to your daughters as this ruby is to Georgiana."

"My daughters?"

"Yes. When I found you after your fall, a piece of ribbon became detached from your bonnet. You are familiar with how I kept that ribbon with me. As I grew more and more in love with you, the ribbon meant even more to me. While you slept, it was a constant reminder of your beauty. When you awoke, it became a token of your attachment to me."

Elizabeth watched him attentively, heedless of the sounds of horses and carriages or the roughness of the road.

"When I left Hertfordshire, I felt that the only way I could free myself from you and begin to come to terms with your loss was by returning the ribbon. How could I bear having such a remembrance with me when I could never have you? When you returned the ribbon to me, the pain of unfulfilled longing was healed. You would not have sent it to me unless you were offering me the opportunity to regain your love. Even now, I carry it with me wherever I go." Darcy took the ribbon out of his pocket. "You see, I even have it with me now."

Elizabeth smiled.

"The color of the ribbon is purple and that color is found in nature in a stone called amethyst."

Darcy opened the box and displayed it for Elizabeth. It contained a necklace of rectangular cut stones separated by large diamonds in a pattern that repeated itself. "I would like you to have this."

Elizabeth took the necklace out of the box and held it up to the light. The purple stones were dazzling against the brilliance of the diamonds.

"It is beautiful, Fitzwilliam. Where did you find such a treasure?"

"It was not to be found, but was crafted by a friend of mine who is a jeweler."

"So this is your doing? You had this created for me?"

Darcy answered with a slight bow of his head. "The color purple will always remind me of the love you have for me, and that love is symbolized in this necklace. On the day our daughters are married, I hope to place this around their necks and send them off to their futures remembering the love their parents shared, and that love, extended to them, is something they can pass on to their children.

"When you wear this, I want you to think of me and know that you are cherished. When I see this necklace grace your neck, I will remember how I am loved by you. Let this necklace seal our union, and let the love it represents be the foundation for all that we do."

"I will, Fitzwilliam. I will always remember how much you love me."

Darcy brought a hand up to her chin, raised her lips to his and kissed her with all the fullness of his heart. How he loved her! How well it felt to be loved by her!

Elizabeth touched his cheek. "May I wear it now?"

Darcy unfastened Georgiana's ruby and replaced it with the amethyst necklace. "Let this be the first of many traditions we will establish in our family."

"Thank you, Fitzwilliam. Thank you so very much."

Darcy settled back in the seat and held her, her head leaning on his shoulder. With one hand, she touched the necklace and reflected on the generosity and love of her husband, and with the other, she held one of his.

He felt her body form against his as a heavy silence enveloped the carriage and hushed the sounds of the road. In what seemed to be the passing of just minutes, the coach came to a gentle rest.

Elizabeth looked up at her husband. "We are home, Fitzwilliam."

"Yes, my love, we are."

MR. AND MRS. DARCY WERE alone. The servants were given the day off, and only Mrs. Jamison and the cook remained in the house. Georgiana had just left with the Bingleys. She was to stay with them at Netherfield until Elizabeth and Darcy joined them in two weeks.

There had been a warm send off by Jane who knew full well the pleasures that Elizabeth could expect that night. "Are you nervous, Lizzy?"

"Were you?"

"I was nervous when Charles first came to me, but I trusted him. Everything was perfect. I could not have wished for more."

"And I trust Fitzwilliam."

"Then you will be very happy."

Darcy led Elizabeth through the whole house. Their tour finished in the library.

"How do you like your new home? It is truly yours now, and I must congratulate myself. So far I have kept my promise that we should never be apart, and now we will never spend another night alone."

"You cannot imagine how happy you have made me."

"Was it just last night that we slept in each other's arms on this sofa?"

"Yes, it was. It seems like a lifetime ago. I feel as though I am a new person now. I feel like I am beginning my life."

Darcy interrupted her with a kiss that she gratefully returned. "We are at the beginning of our new life together."

Elizabeth stood next to him, brushed his hair off his forehead and caressed his face. "I am so happy that you are mine. You cannot know the joy you have brought to my life."

Darcy traced her necklace with his finger.

"But I do know it, my beloved. I know it very well."

After sitting through a light dinner that neither of them tasted, Darcy escorted Elizabeth to her bedchamber. Standing in front of the door, Elizabeth embraced him and held herself close against his chest. He returned her embrace, taking pleasure in the closeness of her body.

"Fitzwilliam, I will be changed forever after tonight."

"Are you afraid?"

Of course, how could she not be nervous? He kissed her hair and awaited her answer.

"I trust you."

Releasing herself from his embrace, she opened the door to her room, took one step inside, and then turned to face Darcy with a look of expectation on her face.

"When shall I come to you, Elizabeth?"

"In a half-hour."

"A half-hour it is, then. Is there anything I can do or provide for your present comfort? I am at your service."

"Yes, there is something. Is there a clock in this room? I would like to know when a half-hour has passed."

"I do not recall, but here, take my watch." He lifted his watch out of his pocket and detached the chain from his coat.

"If you give me your watch, I shall never return it," laughed Elizabeth as she opened her hand to receive it.

Just as she was folding her fingers around it, Darcy pulled it away. "Never?"

"Well," smiled Elizabeth, "I will return it on one condition."

Darcy pulled the watch away from her as she tried again to take it.

"No, no, no, Elizabeth. Not until you tell me how to get it back. This is my favorite watch, you know."

"I will return it if you promise to change one part of our wedding vow."

"What? Are you a little heretic and I never knew it?" he said laughing.

"I just want to add a little part, just a little something about…" She paused and eyed the watch. "We must add a part about you honoring and obeying me, as well!"

He laughed. "You drive a hard bargain, Mrs. Darcy."

"Yes, I do, but if your watch is that important to you, of course, you will agree to it!"

"Come here," he said, putting the watch in her hand.

She stepped up next to him and put her arms around his neck.

"Mrs. Darcy," he said, with his lips pressed against her cheek, "I promise to honor and obey you all the days of my life, but I want you to keep the watch."

"You are too good to me, Fitzwilliam."

In a hushed voice, he made a request of her. "Please do not let down your hair tonight." He kissed her lips, and she felt a shiver run down her spine.

"Very well."

Darcy released her, and she stepped back, holding out her hand to him. After he kissed her fingers, she withdrew into the room and shut the door.

A HALF-HOUR, DARCY THOUGHT AS he entered his room. *A half-hour and I will make her mine. How I have longed for this moment! How I suffered when I thought it could never be!*

Darcy stepped out of his clothes and into the black dressing gown he wore the previous night when he encountered Elizabeth in the library. Stepping to the fire, he stirred new life into the fading embers and sat down. Looking into the flames, he inhaled deeply, and by closing his eyes, could imagine Elizabeth standing before him.

The vision began to move, and in an instant, the image of his father appeared behind Elizabeth. He walked slowly up to her and put his hand on her shoulder.

She offered him her cheek, which he gently kissed. With an expression on his face that spoke of pride and admiration, old Mr. Darcy took Elizabeth's hand and offered it to Darcy. Just as he reached out to take her hand from his father, the vision faded, and he fell back against the sofa.

Since his decision to return to Netherfield and regain Elizabeth's love, Darcy had never doubted his intentions or questioned his motives. If she would have him, he was going to marry her. His satisfaction with having done so was now heightened by what was to him the acknowledgement of his father's approval.

Darcy glanced up at the clock on the mantelpiece. There yet remained a quarter-hour. His anticipation grew. Last night he had taken great pleasure in being with Elizabeth and holding her through the night. Soon, he would find great delight in her love and tenderness.

ELIZABETH SAT IN FRONT OF a dressing table and set Darcy's watch down near a brush and comb. The face of the watch was white with gold numerals that marked the hour. When she closed the lid, she noticed that the Darcy crest had been engraved on the cover. This was no ordinary watch, but rather an emblem of the traditions of the Darcy family. By satisfying her desire to keep the watch, he had symbolically given her all that he had, and thus, she became an heiress to wealth, honor and kinship.

She opened the watch again and saw the second hand trace an arc around the numbers. Moments in time blurred into seconds, and seconds grew into minutes before she caught herself dreaming about Darcy and his proposal to her by the stream. Was it really only three days ago? The emotion she felt on his appearance there had been so intense. He had come contritely, blanketed in uncertainty in an attempt to change the past in such a way that he might enjoy a future with her.

She had to confess that there was once a part of her that had difficulty accepting his explanation for abandoning her, but there was no question of her forgiveness. Despite his imperfections, she was fully prepared to give herself to him. The instant he took her in his arms and kissed her, all her pain was overcome by the happiness of being desired by him.

Him, she thought to herself... *Mr. Fitzwilliam Darcy of Pemberley*. Soon that man, her husband, would be coming to her. Coming for her, truly, to claim her as his own.

She looked at the watch. There were ten minutes remaining until he came.

She eyed the door that joined their rooms and wondered what her husband was feeling.

DARCY'S COMPOSURE FAILED HIM, AND he was now pacing the floor near the fire, his mind and eyes never dwelling long on any object but focusing inward on the image he had created in his mind of how Elizabeth would look when he first saw her.

He recalled the first sight he had of her in her room at Netherfield after her fall. She was resting peacefully, her hands at her side outside the blanket and her face surrounded by a pool of curls that tumbled below her shoulders. Her pale skin appeared so white in contrast to the dark color of her hair. He remembered another occasion when he was looking at her while she was asleep. He had been attracted to the fullness of her lips and the hint of a smile that graced them. All he felt for her, everything for which he yearned, he expressed in three words — Please, come back!

She had come back and had brought him the love and acceptance he had sought all his life. Now she was his wife, and the happiness he would derive from his relationship with her would be unbounded. There could be nothing greater.

Darcy looked at the clock. Five more minutes.

THE NIGHTGOWN THAT JANE HAD chosen as her gift for Elizabeth was soft and delicate, and Jane assured her it was very becoming. Elizabeth felt beautiful in it. It was a simple white silk design that was edged with lace. Her feet were bare. She had prepared herself to receive him in the simplicity of her love.

Elizabeth rose when she heard his knock. She glanced at the watch and smiled. It had been exactly a half-hour.

"COME IN, FITZWILLIAM."

Darcy took a deep breath and slowly entered the room. He stepped aside to shut the door, then turned to face Elizabeth and raised his eyes.

"Elizabeth!" A vision of arresting beauty stood before him. She was perfect.

She answered with a smile and a gesture of her hand that invited him to come near her.

"You cannot know, you have no idea…you are so beautiful! Oh, my love, I —"

"Thank you, Fitzwilliam," she interrupted with a shy smile.

He closed the distance between them and took hold of her hand. He opened his mouth to speak again, but she put a finger against his lips and hushed him into silence. "You may tell me how beautiful I am as many times as you wish, but I want you to know how much I adore you, and I am proud, so very proud, to be your wife."

Darcy raised both hands to her face and kissed her. It was a delicate, tender kiss that confirmed the emotions they felt for each other. He broke the kiss just in time to see her open her eyes. Her smile melted his heart. He took her hand, led her to the bed, and sat next to her. They turned to face each other, holding hands and rejoicing in the intimacy of the occasion.

"I never dared hope that this day would come until I received your note."

"I wished with all my heart that you would come back."

"I remember coming upon you by the stream. You had let your hair down, and it was flowing across your back, tossed around by the breeze. Your head was tilted, revealing your lovely throat. I have never seen such an enticing image as you appeared to me at that moment."

"I did not know you were watching me, Fitzwilliam. It is not very gentlemanly to spy, you know!" The teasing look in her eye spoke of the humor she felt as she recalled the incident.

"I wish I could have been there when you let down your hair." He reached up and cupped her cheek, then slid his hand around the nape of her neck to the knot of hair on the top of her head.

"I wish I could have witnessed this," he said as he pulled out a hairpin. A lock of hair fell free. "And this." He pulled out another pin.

She looked up at him with growing desire. Her hair was loosened and she shook it free around her shoulders.

"You are so beautiful." He pulled her close and combed his fingers through her hair. "Since that time by the stream, I have wanted to do this."

She felt a shiver run down her spine as he brushed her hair to one side and slowly trailed kisses down her neck.

"Fitzwilliam..."

Elizabeth's words were lost when his lips claimed hers with fierce intensity. Words could no longer describe their love or express the passionate feelings in their hearts. As Darcy untied the fastenings of her nightgown, and it pooled at her waist, he knew that she was not the only one who would be forever changed that night.

IT WAS A BEAUTIFUL MORNING. The air was fresh and clean and the sun warm and bright, and most importantly, Elizabeth was not alone. "Fitzwilliam," she whispered, "are you awake?"

Darcy's happiness knew no bounds. His dreams had come true. He would be quite content to spend the rest of the day holding her. He had been careful not to move, not wanting to wake her, but when he heard her voice, he gently caressed her hair and shoulders. "Yes. Good morning, my love."

"How long have you been awake?"

"For a little while. I have been lying here thinking of last night."

"I do hope they were agreeable thoughts."

"They were exceedingly pleasant, I assure you."

"It was my pleasure, sir. I have never been happier!"

"My love, you cannot imagine how I feel when you say such things."

But she could imagine, and did, as his hands slid across the silken curves of her body and his lips devoured hers.

Chapter 23

"Elizabeth," Darcy and his bride were sitting in the drawing room later that morning. "I have made a little change in our plans. I hope you do not mind."

Elizabeth was looking at a display of elegant glass figurines over the chimneypiece. "I am sure I shall not. What change did you make?"

"I have instructed everyone in the household and asked all who attended our wedding to keep our marriage a secret. No one is to know. I want you all to myself for as long as possible."

"Does that mean that there will be no callers offering their congratulations and that I shall have you all to myself? Will I not be required to share your time and attention?" She slowly walked towards him.

"No one knows we are here. We will be entirely left alone."

"Then I thank you very much for that change in plan," she said softly, "because having you all to myself is my only wish."

She was close enough for him to reach her. He quickly took her hand and pulled her onto his lap. She threw her arms around his neck with a laugh.

Mrs. Jamison thought that Mr. and Mrs. Darcy might enjoy some tea, and she was just approaching the drawing room when she heard the sound of laughter that forestalled her progress.

With a smile, Mrs. Jamison silently retreated to the kitchen. The Darcys would not require tea that afternoon.

The pleasant weather on the following day was similar to that of the day Darcy received Elizabeth's letter containing her ribbon. He wanted to tell her about that day, and the present moment seemed particularly suited to the occasion.

"Elizabeth, would you like to take a walk in the park?"

"I would like that very much."

Elizabeth slipped her arm through his as they crossed the busy street. They entered the park and turned down a path with which Darcy was quite familiar.

"My love, I came to this park, to this very spot, after I received your letter."

"You came here?"

"Yes. I could hardly contain myself. I came and nearly ran down the walks out of sheer joy. That ribbon had meant too much for me to mistake your meaning. I saw it as an invitation to love you again. The darkness that had weighed on me was suddenly lifted, and I felt free and alive for the first time since…" He hesitated and then paused as painful memories intruded.

"I knew when you wrote your letter to Mr. Bingley that you were writing to me."

"I was, as much as I dared. Bingley's letter taught me to hope."

"I was very nervous about sending the ribbon, but Jane said I needed to let you know how I felt."

"Here it is." Darcy took the ribbon out of his pocket. Elizabeth stopped walking and leaned into him and he put his arm around her. "I carry it with me wherever I go. I lace it through my fingers and let my mind run away with thoughts of you. I fell in love with you while you were still asleep. I have never been able to confide in anyone until I met you. It was such a relief to unburden my heart to you that day. When I am with you, I am filled with feelings of happiness and joy which I have never experienced."

"Thank you for telling me that. I was very much in love with you from almost the first moment I saw you. I recognized your voice and the touch of your hand. I know you must have spent many hours with me while I was asleep."

Darcy took a quick look around them, and determining that they were unobserved, he kissed her. Elizabeth caressed his face as he held her against him. All her feelings of love swelled in her breast as she realized once again how truly she loved him.

After a kiss that seemed all too short, he pulled back from her and with a smile, led her down another walk.

Towards the end of the Darcys' first week of marriage, Mrs. Jamison found Elizabeth sitting alone in the library behind her husband's desk. Mr. Darcy had stepped out, but he was expected back at any moment. "Mrs. Darcy, I am sorry to disturb you, ma'am, but there are two people who wish to call on you."

"They asked to see me?"

"Yes, ma'am. The people who are here to see you are Mr. Tilden and his daughter, Miss Tilden. I do not know how they even knew you were here. Mr. Darcy's instructions were that the servants tell no one, and I am certain we have not."

Mrs. Jamison knew Mr. Darcy and Mr. Tilden had disagreed, and she knew very well that it concerned Miss Tilden.

"Please lead the way, Mrs. Jamison. I will do the best I can."

Mr. Tilden had heard through obscure channels that Mr. Darcy had married. Apparently, his suspicions regarding Darcy were well founded. He had been attached to someone else, and that is why he refused his daughter. "Who was she?" and "Did he regret it?" were questions that he wished to settle for himself. He was offended on his daughter's behalf at Darcy's refusal, and he knew he would find satisfaction in demonstrating to the lady herself the superiority of his daughter. It was convenient that Mr. Darcy was not home.

Elizabeth followed Mrs. Jamison to the drawing room. The Tildens rose at her entrance.

Mr. Tilden walked over to her and bowed. "Mrs. Darcy, thank you for seeing us. It is a pleasure to meet you. We have been eager to become acquainted with Mr. Darcy's wife."

"Thank you, Mr. Tilden, though I was not aware that my marriage was generally known." Elizabeth gave him a sidelong glance. "I apologize for Mr. Darcy's absence. He has been called away on business, but I expect him very shortly."

"Mrs. Darcy, please allow me to introduce you to my daughter, Miss Clara Tilden."

Miss Tilden curtseyed, and Elizabeth invited them both to sit, eyeing Miss Tilden with interest. She was a pretty, young woman.

Elizabeth took a chair opposite the sofa she had offered to the Tildens. From her vantage point, she was able to see the entrance to the room and was expecting her husband to enter momentarily.

Darcy had guarded the fact of their marriage from common knowledge in an effort to give them privacy and had hoped to do so at least for another day or two. Elizabeth felt he would not be pleased to see these visitors. This consideration led her to feel cautious.

"Mrs. Darcy," began Mr. Tilden, "the social world of London knows nothing about you —"

Elizabeth interrupted him with a laugh. "And you are their representative, Mr. Tilden?"

"I…well…I am just curious, that is all — one of many who are. Mr. Darcy and I have been friends for some time now, and that he would marry, but say nothing to me about it, is a little surprising."

"I can understand that you might feel that way, but it is not for me to venture an opinion on my husband's motives."

"Of course not." He was impressed by Elizabeth's discretion and beauty, but he came to humble her, and he would. "My daughter descends from an ancient family and is blessed with a noble fortune. Tell me about your family."

Elizabeth was shocked, but immediately recovered, and chose to give him the answer he must wish to hear.

"I am the daughter of a country gentleman of no importance in the world, having few accomplishments, even fewer connections, and no fortune at all." Elizabeth could not suppress a smile. "I am afraid, Mr. Tilden, that in my marriage, I received all the advantage, and Mr. Darcy, none."

Mr. Tilden seemed taken back.

"Indeed, sir, I am afraid that I bring only one benefit to Mr. Darcy."

"And just what is that?"

"I love him."

"Ah…love… Yes, Mr. Darcy said something to me of that, though I cannot remember exactly what it was. Do you not believe, though, that it takes more than love to make a good marriage? Do you not believe that if a man has an opportunity to make an equal match as to fortune and family, that it is his obligation to take advantage of such an offer?"

Elizabeth looked at Miss Tilden, who was staring down at her hands in her lap, and despite a pause on Elizabeth's part, would not look up. "When it comes to marriage, I do not believe anyone has an obligation until they have exchanged their wedding vows. Each person, man or woman, must decide on his or her priorities. If fortune and connection are important, then by all means, a match under any other conditions ought not to be formed."

It was now obvious that Mr. Tilden had considered Darcy a worthy match for his daughter. How far Darcy had pursued the matter was irrelevant. He had returned to Hertfordshire and married her. She rejoiced in the thought, but spared just enough feeling to have compassion for Miss Tilden. It would be impossible for her not to know her father's intentions, and in all likelihood, she had been encouraged to attach herself to Darcy and must now be suffering some disappointment.

"There had been some talk of my daughter marrying Mr. Darcy, but that was before he fell under your influence."

Elizabeth would not respond to the provocation.

"Have you nothing to say, madam?" asked Mr. Tilden with some frustration.

"No," replied Elizabeth in a quiet but deliberate voice, "I have not."

Mr. Tilden eyed Elizabeth carefully. She was a beautiful woman, but no more so than Clara. She confessed to having no accomplishments, no connections and no fortune. What did she have?

"What were Mr. Darcy's motives in marrying you? Could you possibly explain them?"

Elizabeth did not conceal her contempt when she answered. "Yes, Mr. Tilden, I can explain them in one word. Happiness."

Mr. Tilden shook his head and Elizabeth saw Miss Tilden redden.

Elizabeth rose to indicate an end to the interview. Miss Tilden rose also, but Mr. Tilden remained seated. "Mr. Tilden," she said, concealing the offense she felt at his rudeness, "I am sorry for any disappointment you and your daughter have suffered on hearing that Mr. Darcy has married elsewhere. I am his wife and am under his protection now, and I believe he would not appreciate me allowing myself to continue to be subjected to your questions and demands."

DARCY RETURNED TO ELIZABETH AS quickly as he could. Being away from her at this special time was not pleasant. He was impatient to see her and was filled with anticipation as he entered his house knowing he would spend the rest of the day and night with her. He expected to find her in the library behind his desk. With playful impertinence so entertaining to a lover, he had submitted to her desire of writing and reading there. She told him it gave her a feeling of connection to him during those times when they must be apart, and those feelings were of a kind to be encouraged. With these pleasant thoughts in mind, he was annoyed to learn from Mrs. Jamison that the Tildens were at that moment with his wife in the drawing room.

As Darcy approached the drawing room, he heard Elizabeth speaking. Her voice was firm, and though not loud, it was tinctured with anger.

"…married elsewhere. I am his wife and am under his protection now, and I believe he would not appreciate me allowing myself to continue to be subject to your questions and demands."

Before Mr. Tilden could respond, Darcy entered the room. "Indeed, I would not!"

Elizabeth looked at her husband with a smile. Having acknowledged his protection, it was gratifying to benefit from it. He returned her smile, but as he turned away from her, she saw his countenance change from the warmth he had shown her to one of severity and coldness.

Mr. Tilden rose from his seat when Darcy entered the room. The slight to his wife had not gone unnoticed by him. "Mr. Tilden, you seem to choose particularly inconvenient times to call."

"There is nothing in that. I just wanted to meet your wife; that is all."

"Your desire to meet my wife seems to have descended into an opportunity to insult her. Well, Mr. Tilden, I suppose it will have to be swords or pistols at dawn. I will allow you your choice of weapon."

Elizabeth had never heard of her husband ever being involved in a duel and could not possibly imagine that he would take such offense to Mr. Tilden's remarks. She gave her husband a look of surprise, concern and astonishment. Darcy returned her glance with a wink. She understood and turned away to hide a smile.

Mr. Tilden was shocked into silence.

"My cousin, Colonel Richard Fitzwilliam, has been my tutor in both weapons, and I feel quite confident in prevailing. He will be my second and can be reached in St. James Street. He has just returned to London from a foreign post and is currently on leave from his regiment. Please contact him to make arrangements for a place to meet so that you may voice your ill opinion of my wife, and I can defend her from the insult."

"I...sir..."

"Is there anything else you wish to say before you leave?"

"Mr. Darcy, are you calling me out?"

"Sir, you leave me no option when you enter my home uninvited and insult my wife."

"I cannot fight you, Mr. Darcy," insisted Mr. Tilden. "I have never —"

"Are you afraid, Mr. Tilden? Surely you cannot be. You must be quite confident in your abilities to be so bold as to treat, in the worst possible manner, another man's wife."

"Mr. Darcy, this has gone far enough!"

"Far enough for your honor, but not mine. You have assaulted that which is most precious to me, and I must be allowed satisfaction."

"Please, this is not right. Surely, you cannot be serious. I admit that I was unkind, that I —"

"If you are forming an apology, it should be directed to my wife."

"Yes, of course." Mr. Tilden cleared his throat and turned to face Elizabeth. "Mrs. Darcy, please forgive me for insulting and offending you. It is my pride that has been hurt, which I wanted to heal by humbling yours. I admit I was very wrong, and I am sorry. Please, I beg of you, do not allow my indiscretion to become something even more grievous."

Miss Tilden spoke for the first time. "Mrs. Darcy, I am very sorry for both my father and myself," she said nervously and with a voice barely heard. "His...our...intentions...were wrong."

Mr. Tilden began to speak, but was cut off by his daughter. "Father, please! No more!"

Elizabeth looked at Miss Tilden with a smile. It was obvious that she was just another pawn that her father utilized to gratify his own ambitions.

"I accept your apology, Mr. Tilden," said Elizabeth. She walked up to him and offered her hand. "Good day."

Mr. Tilden took her hand with some confusion. "Thank you, ma'am. Please excuse us."

He bowed to Mr. Darcy.

Darcy did not acknowledge him.

When the door closed on the Tildens, Elizabeth broke out in so much laughter that she was required to sit down. Darcy sat next to her, as amused by her mirth as he was by the encounter with Mr. Tilden.

WHEN ELIZABETH HAD HAD HER laugh, Darcy realized that Mr. Tilden was not the only one who owed her an apology. "I am so sorry. You should not have had to endure that. I will ensure that no one has access to the house when I am not in."

"Thank you, but I am quite well, as you can see." Elizabeth leaned into him and kissed his cheek. "Who is Miss Tilden?"

"Uh...Mr. Tilden's daughter, of course," hemmed Darcy. "An acquaintance, that is all."

"An acquaintance? Come now, Fitzwilliam, who is she?"

Darcy looked to her for some sign of escape, but she would not provide it. He acknowledged his defeat with lowered eyes and began his explanation. "She is a young woman to whom I tried to attach myself."

"And when was that?"

"I met her two years ago at her coming out ball. She is a pleasant, amiable young woman who is well educated and highly accomplished."

"In other words, everything that I am not." Elizabeth was conscious that her strength was in her ability to love Darcy and make him happy. Of all the accomplishments to which she could possibly attain, this was the only one that mattered. She knew it, and so did he.

"Her father spent a fortune on her education, and as luck would have it, she was a good student. Since that ball, I have maintained a casual acquaintance with Miss Tilden and her father. When they entertain large parties, I am generally invited." He was silent for a moment, but her eyes commanded that he continue. "I am very embarrassed by this, Elizabeth."

She took his hand and kissed it. "You must know that all wives are curious about the former love interests of their husbands."

"I assure you that there was never any love involved." Darcy cleared his throat. "After I left Netherfield the first time, Mr. Tilden invited me to a small dinner party. The obvious purpose of this meeting was to provide me an opportunity to begin forming an attachment with Miss Tilden. I saw them several times in like manner. I tried to interest myself with Miss Tilden, but I could not. She was not you. I could never forget you and the love I felt for you and from you. No woman could replace that, and having tasted your affection, no other was satisfying to me.

"I suppose I should have discouraged their attentions to me, but I did not. I was flattered, and I was lonely. One evening after dinner, Mr. Tilden took me aside in his study to talk about Miss Tilden. It was his desire that I marry his daughter. I told him I did not love her. He said that it takes more than love to make a good marriage, and he offered me £35,000 if I would marry her."

"What were her feelings?"

"We were comfortable with each other, but at no time had we discussed anything of a personal nature. It is my opinion that she has no thoughts at present of marriage, though she could be persuaded by her father to do almost anything. I made no promise to her. I have not broken faith with anyone."

"You walked away from an immense fortune, Fitzwilliam."

"My experiences with you and the Tildens taught me that there is nothing other than love that is required to make a good marriage. I wanted happiness, not money. I knew you loved me and I was more confident in that than in any other thing. I loved you, and having acknowledged my desire, which was to marry you, I set everything in motion for an immediate removal back to Hertfordshire. Before I could leave, I received Bingley's letter announcing your engagement."

"That is quite a story, sir," she said as he took her up in his arms, "and I am highly gratified to know that you acted honorably towards Miss Tilden. Let us speak of it no more."

DARCY DID NOT KEEP HIS promise of showing off his bride to his friends and family. They had obliged themselves for every evening during the second week of their marriage, but each day the engagements fell away in favor of privacy and solitude.

Elizabeth was quite comfortable with her new husband and returned his attentions to her as eagerly as he gave them. Never had she known such a period of happiness and contentment. She looked forward to the future. The life they would lead at Pemberley would be filled with pleasure and delight. They would participate in what society the neighborhood had to offer, but mostly they would stay in their quiet family party. Elizabeth looked forward to the days she would spend with Georgiana when Darcy was away.

At the end of the second week, Mr. and Mrs. Darcy entered their traveling carriage and embarked on the road to Hertfordshire. In addition to changing horses, Darcy anticipated one additional stop on their way to Netherfield.

WHEN THE CARRIAGE PULLED UP in front of Longbourn, the door was opened and Darcy stepped down. After a word to his coachman requesting that he remain in front of the house, he silently approached the door. He was nervous, not for his own sake, but because he hoped to effect a reconciliation between Elizabeth and her mother. He felt responsible for their breach. If he had never returned to Hertfordshire, Elizabeth would be married to Mr. Grinly and happy in her mother's affection. As this was not an alternative he wished to consider, his only satisfaction would be in a reunion of mother and daughter. To this end, he knocked on the door.

Mrs. Hill answered. "Oh, Mr. Darcy! Welcome, sir. How may I help you?"

"Good day, Mrs. Hill. Would it be possible for me to see Mrs. Bennet?"

"Do please come in, sir. I will let Mrs. Bennet know that you are here."

Hill took his hat and gloves, ushered him into the drawing room, and seated him there with a promise of returning quickly with Mrs. Bennet.

After she left the room, Darcy rose from his seat and walked to the window. The lawn and grounds of Longbourn were pleasant to view. Looking to the right, he could see their carriage in the paddock and wondered what Elizabeth might be feeling.

"You are very welcome to Longbourn, Mr. Darcy," said Mrs. Bennet as she entered the drawing room.

Darcy turned to her and bowed. "Thank you, Mrs. Bennet."

Mrs. Bennet was confused by his presence. Mr. Darcy had been a rare visitor at Longbourn and she had never seen him outside the company of Mr. Bingley. She was aware that he had not been in Hertfordshire for some time now, and so she was quite surprised when Hill announced that he was in the drawing room waiting for her.

"Please forgive me for calling at such an inconvenient hour, but I have just arrived in Hertfordshire for a visit with the Bingleys, and I wanted to call and learn for myself that you were well."

Mrs. Bennet was pleased with the attention. Moving to a sofa, she sat down and invited him to do the same. "It has been a long time since I have seen you, sir, and it is very kind of you to call."

"May I inquire after the health of you and your daughters?"

"I am quite well, thank you, and so are my daughters, at least, I hope all of them are well."

"What do you mean?"

"You would not be interested…"

"No, no. Please, continue."

"Well, I…I have not seen Elizabeth in quite some time. She has been staying at Netherfield with the Bingleys and has recently accompanied them to London, or so I am told. We had a disagreement, and I have not seen her recently."

"I am sorry to hear that. Is there anything I can do?"

"Did you happen to see her when you were in Town? I know that Mr. Bingley is your close friend."

"Yes. I did meet Miss Bennet on several occasions."

"And how is she?"

"I have never seen her looking better, and she appeared to be so happy. She is a very beautiful woman. You must be proud of her. I am grieved that difficulties have arisen between you."

Mrs. Bennet was silent for a moment "Sir, did you happen to know that she was engaged to be married?"

"I did hear something of that from Bingley. I believe it was to a gentleman from Wiltshire?"

"Yes, but it did not turn out well. He changed his mind and would not have her. He said that he could not make Elizabeth happy, and that it was impossible for him to marry her. He would not be persuaded otherwise. I blamed Elizabeth. She became very upset and left Longbourn to stay with Mrs. Bingley."

"I am very sorry that anything occurred that made either of you unhappy."

"I had such great hopes for her being happily settled, and now they are all ruined."

"Miss Bennet is all loveliness. She will find a man who will love her."

"I hope so. I miss her very much." She hesitated. "I must confess, and I do regret, that I was so very unkind to her. You will see her I am sure, while you are at Netherfield. Would you tell her…well…I…"

"I understand, ma'am. When I see Miss Bennet, I will let her know that you are thinking about her."

"That is kind of you."

"I have not told you my good news, Mrs. Bennet."

"Oh, and what is that?"

"I have recently married. Just two weeks ago."

"You have? Congratulations, sir. I wish you joy! When will I be introduced to your bride?"

"She has accompanied me, but desired to remain in the coach until she knew she would be welcome."

"Welcome, Mr. Darcy? Of course, she is welcome! How could you allow her to remain out of doors when we have been sitting here so comfortably? I insist that you bring her inside. Oh, I am mortified! What will she think of me?" Mrs. Bennet jumped to her feet and hurried from the room. "Come along, Mr. Darcy. It is abominably rude to keep her waiting."

Darcy smiled to himself and followed her from the room.

ELIZABETH FELT UNCERTAIN. DARCY HAD been in the house for what seemed like an eternity, and she had heard and seen nothing.

She had just looked away when suddenly the front door of the house was thrown open, and Mrs. Bennet came rushing across the paddock and up to the carriage. Elizabeth sat back to avoid her sight until the last possible moment.

Mrs. Bennet grasped the handle to the carriage and turned the lock, at the same time pushing aside the coachman who had been waiting to perform that duty.

"Mrs. Darcy," cried Mrs. Bennet as she opened the door, "you are very welcome to Longbourn. Please forgive me for allowing you to —"

Mrs. Bennet saw Elizabeth and was silenced. Darcy came up to the door and reached in for Elizabeth's hand.

"Mrs. Bennet, please allow me to introduce you to my wife, Elizabeth Darcy."

Elizabeth stood in silent suspense, not knowing how her mother would react.

"Elizabeth Darcy!" repeated Mrs. Bennet. "Lizzy, is it true? Did you really marry Mr. Darcy?"

"Yes, Mama."

"Lizzy, my girl! How very clever of you to reject Mr. Grinly when you knew that you could have Mr. Darcy. He is so very rich, you know…"

"Mama!" Elizabeth could have died for shame. "That is not —"

"Mrs. Bennet, I cannot begin to tell you how happy I am being married to your lovely daughter. She has brought so much joy to my life, she —"

"Oh, Lizzy! Jane will be nothing to you, nothing at all…"

"…She is the dearest person to me, and it will be a pleasure for me to be called your son."

"Son? Well, I suppose that is true. Here," she giggled, "let me give you a kiss."

"Thank you, ma'am." Darcy bent down so she could reach his cheek while looking up at Elizabeth with a twinkle of humor in his eyes. She was visibly relieved.

Mrs. Bennet had the ability to bring out unknown aspects, both good and bad, in nearly everyone's personality as they struggled to deal with her coarseness, noise, and silliness. Elizabeth was surprised to witness the easy manner in which her husband directed her mother's thoughts and conversation. The prospect of bringing Darcy to Longbourn seemed a little less daunting, knowing that he understood her mother so well.

"This is quite a surprise," said Mrs. Bennet. "I must say, though, that I should have been present at your wedding. I should have been consulted. Lizzy, whatever did you do for wedding clothes?"

"Please do not be angry, Mama."

"Angry? Well, I suppose I should be, but how could I be angry when you have brought home such a delightful young man."

"He is delightful, Mama, and I am glad that you appreciate his good qualities."

Chapter 24

Jane was pleased to spend so much time with Elizabeth, enjoying her liveliness and high spirits. Her easy manner and the simple joy of living that she projected made Elizabeth lovelier than ever. Jane gave Darcy all the credit for the improvements in her sister. "Oh, Lizzy, it is good to see you so happy."

"I am happy, and I owe so much of it to you. Let me thank you with all my heart for your kindness in reuniting Mr. Darcy and me."

"I do not feel as though I have done much. Indeed, I feel it is quite the opposite, for it was I who encouraged you to accept Mr. Grinly's offer, and that brought you nothing but grief and heartache, and it was I who was resistant to your relationship with Mr. Darcy, but look how well that has turned out."

"I know that all you wanted was my happiness, and I could not and do not fault you for that. And besides, as soon as I convinced you of my love for Mr. Darcy, you did everything in your power to reunite us. Without you, I would not be so happy. We are greatly indebted to you."

"I have something I want to tell you! I want you to be the first to know," said Jane, her excitement building. "Well, maybe the second," she laughed. "I am with child!"

"Jane, that is wonderful news! I am so happy for you. What does Charles think of this?"

"He is so proud. He will make such a good father. Oh, Lizzy, everything I have wished for in my life is coming true. I have such a kind and loving husband, you are so happily settled, and now Charles and I are to have a child. How will I bear such happiness?"

"Does our mother know she is to be a grandmama soon?"

"No, I have not yet told her. I did not want you to hear it from anyone but me, so only Charles knows and Mr. Manning, of course. Charles insisted that he come from London to attend me."

"What a considerate man your husband is! I feel nothing but respect for Mr. Manning. You will have the best of care. And if anybody deserves it, it is you."

Epilogue

Elizabeth was just returning from a solitary walk around the grounds of Netherfield when a footman brought her a letter. Elizabeth took it and thanked the man. It was addressed to "Miss Elizabeth Bennet," and as she was not expecting any correspondence, she was surprised to receive it. She turned the letter over to see from whence it came. Her heart sank. It was from Mr. Grinly.

Elizabeth walked to a secluded bench where she could be assured of privacy while thinking about what it meant to receive a letter from him. He could not possibly know that she was married. Had he changed his mind? Did he still want her? Was there something the matter with Constance?

As she explored these feelings, she knew that regardless of Mr. Grinly's sentiments, marrying Mr. Darcy was the right thing to do. Her heart was all Darcy's and it had been ever since she met him. She had no regrets. She loved Darcy and could love no other. She recalled the time, when she was still engaged to Mr. Grinly, that she had received Darcy's farewell letter and had doubted the wisdom of opening it. How would her life be different had she given it to Mr. Grinly, as she knew she ought to have done? Putting Mr. Grinly's unopened letter in her pocket, she returned to the house nervously to await the return of her husband.

DARCY ENJOYED THE MORNING SHOOTING with Bingley. Since his return to Hertfordshire, there had been no tension at all between the friends. It was a relief to be on such good terms with Bingley once again.

Elizabeth could easily part with Mr. Darcy when she could spend that time with Jane, but now that he had returned, it was a pleasure to have him back by her side. She was a little apprehensive when she considered her errand. More than once, she tried to approach him and tell him about the letter, but with each attempt, her courage failed her.

When they retired to dress for dinner, she followed him into his dressing room to make another attempt. He sensed her uneasiness and asked the reason for it.

"I confess that there is a matter that is weighing on me. I want to discuss it with you, but I do not want you to become angry or unhappy."

"Well, my love, if I promise to do neither, will you confide in me?"

"I will." His calm demeanor was reassuring. "I received a letter today, but I am uncertain of its contents."

"You did not open it?"

"No, I did not."

"Pray, why would you not?"

"Because I do not know if it is appropriate for me to have received it and I want your opinion as to what I should do, whether I should read it or return it unopened."

"And why would it not be right for you to have this letter?"

"Because, sir, it is from Mr. Grinly."

There was a moment of silence between them as Darcy considered the matter. His name had not been mentioned between them since their wedding.

"Here it is." She offered the letter to her husband. "Would you care to read it?"

Darcy looked at the letter, but did not take it from her.

"Elizabeth, thank you for your faith in me. Thank you for trusting me, but you see, I also trust you. The letter is addressed to you, and I think you should read it. If it contains anything you want to tell me, I would be happy to hear it, but if it is of a personal nature, I do not wish to intrude on your privacy."

"In that case, will you read it with me?"

"Certainly."

They sat next to each other on a sofa near the fireplace and Elizabeth opened the letter.

Sappingford

Miss Bennet,

Please forgive the liberty I am taking in writing to you, but as I feel confident in your regard and friendship for me, I wanted to share with you certain recent events in my life.

First of all, Constance is very well and sends her love. She does not cease to speak of you, and I thank you again and again for the good influence you were in her life.

I want to thank you for the opportunity you gave me to love once more. I learned a great deal from your kindness and affection. I have recently become engaged to a lovely woman named Susannah Cook. We have known each other for many years, as she is a former schoolmistress at a school that Constance attended. She has recently returned home to care for her elderly mother. She is the joy of my life, and I love her ever so dearly. We will be married within the month. I am very pleased with the kindness and gentleness with which Susannah treats Constance. Constance has confided in me that she will love Susannah as much as she does you and approves very much of our marriage.

I wanted you to know how things stood with me. I hope that you are well. I am certain that Constance would enjoy hearing from you.

Yours, &c.
Thomas Grinly

Darcy was the first to comment. "That is wonderful news about Mr. Grinly. I am delighted for him."

"I am so happy for him and for Constance. They both deserve to be happy, and knowing that they are gives me great pleasure."

"You were very close to Constance, were you not?"

"Yes, I love her dearly. I am going to take the first opportunity to write to Mr. Grinly and wish him joy and announce our marriage. I am so pleased that he wrote." Elizabeth was silent for a moment, and then she took Darcy's hand in both of hers.

"I love you very much, sir." She held his hand against her heart.

"I love you, too, Elizabeth. Thank you for sharing your letter with me."

THE DAY ARRIVED THAT WAS to take Elizabeth, Georgiana, and Darcy to Pemberley. The pain of separation that Jane and Elizabeth felt was more than made up for by the anticipation of a reunion in a few months' time. Elizabeth and Darcy would soon return to Netherfield to stand as godparents to the Bingleys' child.

The trip was accomplished without alarm or inconvenience. Elizabeth was enchanted by her new home and spent hours wandering through its halls. Of particular interest to her was the portrait gallery, where she regularly visited the paintings of Darcy's parents. Just as Georgiana had predicted, Elizabeth discovered their mother to be a beautiful woman.

Darcy promised her that soon her own likeness would adorn the wall of the gallery, and she fancied what it would look like hanging there next to his parents. Darcy's likeness already occupied a place on the wall, and hers would proudly join his.

EVERY DAY FOR ELIZABETH WAS new and exciting and the happiness that she felt did not wane. Every moment she spent with her husband brought a new sense of belonging. She recalled the way she felt with him when they used to talk while she was recovering at Netherfield. The intimacy of those moments was such a joy to her, yet it paled in comparison to the love and closeness she now felt.

Like Jane, she felt that her life was complete. She, too, gloried in the happiness of a beloved sister and rejoiced in her own situation. Surrounded by Darcy's love and Georgiana's affection, her own happiness knew no bounds. The beauty of the estate and park of Pemberley added to her pleasures as she explored the turning of every path that wound its way through Pemberley Woods.

DARCY SAW HIS OWN IMAGE in the face of his child, a son, born within a year of his marriage. Elizabeth quickly recovered and rejoiced in the happiness that her son and husband brought into her life.

Mrs. Bennet, now a grandmother for the second time, divided her time between the homes of her two grandchildren. Her nurturing instincts flourished as she assisted in the care of the infants. Her noise and silliness decreased, and she was a welcome visitor at both Netherfield and Pemberley.

Mary Bennet accepted Elizabeth's invitation to reside at Pemberley, and she and Elizabeth grew as close in love and sisterly affection with each other and with Georgiana as any of them could wish.

The presence of love had long ago overwhelmed past feelings of sorrow for Elizabeth and Darcy, and everyday it grew stronger and deeper.

Twice a year, the Darcy family visited the Bingleys, and on every occasion, Elizabeth and Darcy walked out in the woods alone to rediscover each other by the *rocks in the stream*.

THE END

Lightning Source UK Ltd.
Milton Keynes UK

176868UK00001B/291/P